The Rise of Lykos

The Life of Lykos, Volume 1

William Savage

Published by William Savage, 2018.

This is a work of fiction. Similarities to real people, places, or events are entirely coincidental.

THE RISE OF LYKOS

First edition. May 27, 2018.

Copyright © 2018 William Savage.

Written by William Savage.

For Falka,

you know why.

Chapter One

"Help me!" Lykos cried out as the stones shifted around him. "Get me out of here!" Yet he could hear the startled shouts of his fellow slaves fade as they rushed away from the point of the cave-in. A spectrum of colors surrounded him, the sharp edges of crystals moving dangerously close to his struggling body. As the rocks settled the crystals moved one last time, piercing his flesh.

Pain can be described in many forms and he was well versed in many of them. Broken bones from falling rocks, bruises and cuts from fists and whips. The constant companionship of starvation and having to fight for the bitter reality of survival, was a daily struggle every slave knew well. Yet he would trade anything in the world for those lesser pains than feel the sensation of his body being burned from the inside out. If this was what magic felt like to mages, they must be demons to survive.

"Help!" His desperate plea for aid went unheeded as he heard the last of the slaves scramble away, their fear driving them from the area. His body began to convulse, forcing him into contact with more of the crystals surrounding him, the sharp pain of shards paling to the intense fire setting his body aflame. The sound of footsteps approached and he briefly felt hope.

"Can we get him out?" a cold voice echoed down from above and the hope died. It was one of the guards who watched over the slaves as they worked. There was a brief pause as his companion examined the cave-in.

"No. Vinr Freya will have to do with the others, this one's too far beneath the stone for us to reach him. We'll tell the other slaves that he died from touching the crystals, his screams will make them think it's the truth."

"Agreed. Enjoy your tomb slave." Cruel laughter echoed unpleasantly in Lykos' ears as they walked away but he could pay their words no mind. He was too concerned with howling in pain as his bones felt like they were breaking one by one, his blood boiling beneath his skin. No one was going to save him from this torment.

He could not say how long he lay there, pinned by razor sharp crystals burning and breaking his body into nothing. Time lost its meaning as his screams of pain faded into whimpers, his throat too hoarse to continue. His twitching limbs no longer thrashed but twinged as each new jolt of pain racked his form every few moments. Each new cut bringing a renewed jolt of pain that was unlike any he had experienced before. Every inhale fed fuel to the flames in his chest and burned more fiercely than any fire.

"I am going to die," he whispered to himself in one of the few moments he could catch his breathe, "I am going to die."

The words did not bring any peace or panic to his mind as he whispered them softly. Instead he felt the flames of his chest hardening in a peculiar manner as the words echoed in the small space.

"I am going to die," he said the words slightly firmer, feeling how the flames in his chest reacted to the statement. The hardening sensation grew and he realized it was not the burning touch of magic as it destroyed his body, no it was something that living in the slave mines had repeatedly hammered into him over the long harsh years: defiance.

For he refused to die. He had clung to life, enduring the suffering in the mines with a will power that refused to yield to each inhumane punishment. Defeat was not something he accepted easily, was not something he would ever willingly accept. The crystals wanted to take his life, his hard earned will to live that had endured dozens of cruel guards and Tainted attacks for years?

Never. He felt for that rock hard defiance sitting in his chest and grasped at it desperately. It slipped through his mind as if it were made of ice but he had felt it once and now knew what to look for. Fighting through the pain he grasped that small globe of defiance and felt it harden within his grasp. Without knowing how he used it to push back against the burning magic. It fought back, fire trying to melt the ice, but he could feel its strength and found it wanting. The burning pain of magic rampaging through his body subsided as it came under his control but he was not done. Lykos extended his will upon the magic, squeezing it violently in retribution and he screamed in mind and body at being trapped, at being attacked, at being left for dead....

And felt his world view shift. One moment he was trapped within the earth, magic crystals burning and attacking him from all sides, and the next he fell through the air to land on cold snow underneath moonlight. He lay there stunned, more from the sight of the stars than the cold, his ruthless grip upon the magic relaxing as the snow melted from his body heat. The cool night air pierced his torn clothes, revealing wounds that were no longer losing blood. But Lykos only had eyes for the stars.

He could never remember such a sight. Once, several years ago, he managed to work in the loading bay moving crates around. The heavy metal door had been opened slightly, blinding him and the other slaves. But for one glorious moment he saw the sky and the image had stayed with him ever since. And now he was under it.

So enraptured was he by the stars he did not notice a guard bearing a torch approaching until he stood over him, blocking his view of the night sky. The guard frowned at him.

"What are you doing out here slave? How did you escape?" He drew his sword and brandished it at Lykos' face. "Tell me how!"

Lykos threw up his arms to protect his face and it had an unintended consequence. The magic within him reacted without his will influencing it and rushed from his body. It struck the guard in the chest with a wave of solid air, throwing him back to lay motionless in the snow. The sharp snap of bones breaking echoed in the cold night air and he knew instantly that the man was dead. He slowly crawled over, his eyes wide at what his magic had just done.

It was not the first time he had seen a dead man nor was it the first time someone's life had ended by his actions. Such was life in the mines and using his magic to do the deed did not cause him any distress. However killing or harming a guard often heralded a painful punishment followed by a slow death and he almost expected a patrol to walk by and spot his foul deed. Yet no shouts of alarm were raised, no outraged cries or sounds of steel being drawn, he was alone. He was free.

Lykos laughed. He stood unsteadily to his feet and laughed joyously to the heavens. He paid no mind to the bitter chill as it bit into his limbs, the drying blood adorning his rags. But he did notice when the magic within him reacted and caused several nearby snow drifts to explode spectacularly. He crouched low, sharp eyes focused intently on his surroundings, waiting to see if the person responsible for the exploding snow drifts would reveal themselves but none did. After several tense moments he realized he was responsible.

Magic! His magic! He had magic and it was responsible for the exploding snow, the dead guard, his freedom. The magic from the crystals may had left him but it had left behind its power and now it was his. Pilfering the dead man's cloak he gazed once more at the moon shining in the sky. He knew that whatever may come his way, at least he would be free. That he would die free.

Chapter Two

It took Lykos several cold hours to escape the desolate tundra but he eventually found civilization in the form of several low stone buildings built on the edge of a large body of water. He would have missed the buildings entirely were it not for the massive wooden and cloth structures floating above them, bobbing softly in the winds. He approached the buildings cautiously, well aware that their occupants might not take kindly to his presence despite his theft of the guard's clothes. Not all humans were allies in the mines, why would things be any different on the surface?

He needn't have worried. The few men and women present moved with purpose between the buildings, determined to get out of the cold as quickly as possible. They all seemed to congregate at one building in particular and it was towards that one that he made his way to. Passing through the thickly furred doorway Lykos almost dove back outside to avoid the sweltering heat. Within the center of the room roared a great fire and its oppressive heat was hotter than anything he had ever experienced before, save magic.

"If your goal is to let all of the warmth out you're succeeding," a man sitting at a table next to the doorway said. He was glaring at Lykos out of the corner of his eye, not taking his full attention off of the parchments that were before him. "Although if you do it much longer you'll draw the attention of everyone in this bar."

"Bar?" Lykos asked. As his eyes adjusted he saw half a dozen more tables scattered throughout the room, each full of occupants who drank and talked quietly. In the short time he had stood in the doorway several interested individuals had begun to stare at him, drawing unneeded attention. He quickly stepped away from the doorway allowing the furs to move back in place. The air grew noticeably warmer and the few curious onlookers returned to their drinks.

"Much better," the man said as he moved one of his parchments to the side. Seeing Lykos still standing there he pointed at a rickety wooden chair on the other side of his table. "Well sit down boy!"

Lykos obeyed quickly, both relieved and terrified. How should he act? Would the man be able to tell he was an escaped slave? Would he call the guards to punish him and send him back to the mines? Or would he enact justice himself, breaking Lykos' limbs before killing him slowly? So focused was he on the possibilities he missed the most obvious one: nothing happened.

The man sat quietly in his seat, examining odd symbols and lines on his parchments, and the other bar patrons paying no heed to anything beyond their drinks. Lykos sat quietly and felt relief wash through him at being an unknown. He curiously examined the man whose table he shared.

"Where are we?" Lykos asked. The man's pale eyes were sharp as they darted back and forth over his parchments and the instant he finished speaking they darted up to pierce Lykos' own. A strange sense of vertigo overcame him momentarily but it passed when the man answered.

"An outpost on the most southwestern spur of the northern kingdom of Svellheim," he replied before returning to his papers. Lykos stared at him in confusion.

"Where?" he asked.

The man sighed. "We are in an outpost," he spoke slowly and deliberately, as if Lykos were hard of hearing.

"Yes but-"

"In Svellheim."

"So you said but-"

"A kingdom on the northern tip of the continent of Kardia."

"None of that means anything to me."

Lykos and the unknown man stared at each other in frustration, neither man understanding the other. He tried to maintain eye contact the best he could but felt as if he were staring into a bright flame, flames that were searing into his mind. It was far worse than the cold hatred within a Tainted's eyes and felt so wrong to experience.

"Could you show me on a map?" Lykos finally asked. The man's eyes narrowed and Lykos found himself blinking spots from his eyes before the odd effect vanished.

"I am an architect not a cartographer!" he objected harshly, gesturing at his many parchments. "These are the most carefully laid out plans and creations and you are asking for a map? Never have I met one so ill prepared as you!"

Lykos glanced around but none of the bar patrons seemed interested in their little table. Turning back to the Architect he was startled to see him standing. "Try not to get eaten by a Tainted," he ordered harshly before stomping away, exiting the bar. Lykos sat there blinking in confusion at the hasty departure when the furs were pushed aside again and a large group of men and women entered the bar.

"Drink up lads, we make way soon!" a thin man with an authoritative air shouted. He glanced around the bar and frowned in displeasure at the lack of room available. He then saw Lykos with an empty table and spoke directly to him, "Oi, lad. Are you waiting for anyone?"

Lykos was startled at being addressed but shook his head no. "No I was just-"

"Fantastic!" The man clapped his hand on Lykos' shoulder jarring him. "Bring the mead over here to join our new friend lads!" Cheers were heard, coin was exchanged, and several casks of mead were dragged over. "Now what's your story friend?"

Lykos opened and closed his mouth several times, trying to come to terms with the sudden company of a dozen men and women clustered around one small table to no avail. "I'm a," he panicked realizing he hadn't the faintest clue to say, "traveler." he finished trying to buy some time.

"Oh and what have you been traveling for? Riches? Women? Men? Sorry lad but you're not my type." Their crowd laughed at the man's joke. "Drink up!"

"Freedom," Lykos replied honestly. The rowdy men and women calmed down and the man gave him a long look as if he had never seen someone like him before. He nodded solemnly.

"Freedom," he repeated. "Now that's a concept not seen in any of the three kingdoms, especially not Svellheim. Why do you seek freedom lad?"

Lykos stared at the dark wood table, tracing the dents, burns, and nicks in the surface with his eyes. Slowly, so quietly that their small crowd had to lean in to listen, he answered, "Is it not the truest cause to fight for? If placed with your back to a wall would you not fight all the more fervently to keep it? Go to any length to preserve it? To be free of the trappings society places on us, to be free to choose, to be free. I will always choose to be free...."

He trailed off when he realized how foolish he had been. Escaping from slavery then claiming to seek freedom? Even a dim guard could see through his words and would not hesitate to clap him in irons. Yet all he heard around him were murmurs of agreement as several hands slapped him solidly on the back.

"Aye. You're a smart one lad. What's your name?"

"Lykos."

"Well met Lykos. I am Captain Cael of House Falknor and this band of misfits is my crew. We man the airship Logwind. If there is anything I understand it's freedom."

"What do you mean, captain?" Lykos asked, tacking the honorific on at the end belatedly.

"House Falknor once was a member of Svellheim's ruling elite until my father took the helm. For far too long we helped transport slaves between the kingdoms, earning quite a bit of gold from our routes as each kingdom paid us. My uncle uprooted the family after meeting Lord Talal from Mycenae.

"You see that was another man who believed people should be free of the trappings of society, to choose, much like you yourself said. He believed it so much that he led a rebellion in Mycenae for it. It's a shame that he failed, he left behind a pregnant wife. Rumor has it she lost the child but no one knows for sure."

He stared in contemplation at Lykos for an uncomfortable minute. "And Mycenae?" Lykos prodded. Captain Cael nodded as if confirming something to himself.

"Slavery still exists but Leon caused enough of a fuss that it's far less than the other kingdoms. Chances are every third person you meet are a slave though," Captain Cael explained before shaking himself. "I dislike dark thoughts before starting a journey, it only brings peril. Lykos! Where be your next heading?"

It took Lykos a moment to grasp his meaning. "I think I'll head to Mycenae but I'll have to find a cartographer." He frowned as he remembered the odd Architect.

"A cartographer? Whatever for?" Captain Cael asked in surprise.

"I don't know the way to Mycenae, I need a map."

Captain Cael laughed. "You think you can walk there? Between the Tainted and the mountains I don't know which would kill you first. Maybe if you had an army with you...." he trailed off chuckling.

Lykos frowned. "Then how else do you get there?"

"You take an airship! Or you could travel by boat I suppose but those are often attacked by Tainted Leviathans." Captain Cael shuddered. "You'll never catch me on the seas, those beasts are infamous for their ability to decimate convoys."

Lykos examined Captain Cael's crew, their merriment through intoxication climbing. "Are you taking on any more crew Captain Cael?"

It took little convincing on his part to get Captain Cael to accept him as a member of his crew and he found himself climbing a rope ladder onto the floating Logwind. The cold air was sharp but one of the other crew members graciously spared Lykos a thicker shirt and pants to help keep him warm. Combined with his stolen boots and cloak, he was quite possibly warm for the first time in his life.

"Move lively lads the good winds are dying!" Captain Cael ordered from the helm. "Lykos! You'll be shadowing Hogthar! You do what he tells you, you hear?"

"Aye captain!" Lykos answered with a grin on his face. This was new, exciting, and he was having a terribly grand time. "Who is Hogthar?"

"I am," a bearded man answered near the port railing, pulling on ropes leading up to the sails. "Grab some rope boy."

He obeyed, grasping the coarse hemp rope with his hands and pulling with the grizzled airman. In short order the sails unfurled and immediately caught wind, pulling the ship beneath them with a jolt. Lykos staggered and grasped the rail to steady himself.

Hogthar laughed. "You'll get used to it boy! Still a damn bit easier to sail on air than on water but beware when you're back on dry land! You'll most likely keel over with dizzies. Now let me show you how to tie knots."

And Lykos learned. How to tie knots and raise sail. How to prepare food and cook in the galley. Every night he would join the other crewmen in tracking their course with the stars and from this they taught him the basics of navigation. Through the month long journey he helped land, sail, and maintain the Logwind and he was surprised to find himself displeased they would soon arrive in Mycenae. Flight was freedom and it was sights like the one before him that he would burn into his mind forever.

"Have you ever seen the ocean boy?" Hogthar asked him as they kept watch for Tainted. It was a constant chore all members of the crew participated in but they had remarkable luck, the few beasts spotted had not attacked them on this journey.

"No I've spent most of my life in a dark hole breaking rocks with my bare hands." Lykos had reluctantly told the crew of his former station in life after a slip of the tongue. Rather than throw him overboard they had been understandably sympathetic, sharing some of their own sad tales. However Lykos often caught Captain Cael giving him long glances, examining his features as if he could see someone else within them. It was unsettling and Lykos made a point of avoiding the captain as much as possible on the small airship.

He also never told the crew about his unique escape method nor his possession of magic. At first he kept silent because he was kept far too busy to experiment with it, the endless chores to maintain the Logwind providing little spare time. However as time went on he realized none of the crew used any magic and thus could not help him cultivate his ability. So it was with great reluctance that he kept his magic a secret.

Though their journey had begun in the frigid north they now flew over large swathes of forests, hills, and plains. Lykos had never seen such sights before and eagerly drank them in. Here and there were small villages, using natural formations for protection from the elements and the Tainted Hordes. It was at those villages that they stopped to resupply and transport goods. The people were cautious but grateful and after spending a few hours at each one, they'd move on. And now they were on the last part of their journey before the reached Mycenae.

During much of their journey a mountain range had been on the horizon, getting larger with each passing day. They had angled towards the closest edge and began to follow it, maintaining a careful distance so as to not entice any roosting Tainted into attacking. But it was the sight to their starboard that drew his attention, an endless expanse of water glistening in the setting sun. It was beautiful.

"Get some rest boy. Now that we've reached the mountains we should be in Mycenae by dawn tomorrow." Hogthar ordered as he stepped away from the railing.

"So soon?" Lykos asked.

"Aye. There are no villages this close to Mycenae so no need for us to stop. Especially near these mountains, too many Tainted have made nests near here so they can attack the kingdom more easily."

"Why haven't they cleared them out?"

"There are more Tainted in this land than stars in the sky boy. For every one that we kill two more will take its place. They're a plague on us, always have and always will." Hogthar walked off to the crew's quarters and after giving the shining water a longing glance Lykos followed. He needed his rest before his watch tonight.

It was many hours later that he was shaken awake by Petty, a redheaded spitfire who enjoyed singing the songs of her family while she worked. "Your time to go on watch," she whispered. Lykos groaned but rolled out of the hammock, Petty stealing his spot and the warmth that remained. While far warmer than the frigid north, the air this high up held a sharp bite that could be unforgiving. Lykos wrapped his ragged cloak tightly around himself and climbed to the upper deck to begin his rounds.

Nodding respectfully to Captain Cael who manned the helm, Lykos walked around the deck double checking that all the ropes were secure. Finding them acceptable, he walked to the front of the ship and gazed out into the darkness, watching the mountains pass slowly beside them. A small light shown around the curve of one such monolith and as they rounded it Lykos gasped at the sight before him.

Between the end of the mountain range and the great ocean, lay a sea of lights shining bright in a sea of darkness. It swept from the dark forests beneath them all the way up the side of the mountains and Lykos could see the tallest lights rivaled their own lofty height. It was beautiful....

A Tainted Piercer screamed in his face, knocking him to the floor.

"Tainted!" he shouted as loud as he could. "Tainted off the bow!" Behind him he could hear Captain Cael ringing the bell and began to bellow orders, rousing the slumbering crew. But Lykos did not have the time for to focus on that for the Piercer had followed him onto the Logwind.

He looked upon its grotesque form with disgust and fear. Each of its feathers was oily, barely covering its needle like form and not disguising its skeletal shape. Its beak, that which earned it the name Piercer, matched the length of its body and was sharp enough to pierce wood. But worst were the dozen eyes clustered around the base of its beak burning hatefully at Lykos. It attacked.

He rolled out of the way. The Piercer's beak penetrated deep into the wood and stuck it in place. It struggled frantically to free itself but it was not quick enough, a sword swipe severed its head from its body. Lykos looked up with grateful eyes to see Captain Cael standing over him with a bloody sword.

"Up you get lad," Captain Cael ordered, pulling him to his feet, "we need to find the rest of its flock."

"Flock captain?" Lykos asked as more of the crew swarmed the deck, lighting lanterns to give more light to the defenders.

"Aye Piercers are never alone." As if confirming his words dozens of sharp cries sounded from all around them, shredding the peaceful night. And what followed was chaos.

Dozens of dark forms descended on the Logwind, darting all over the deck like deadly shadows. The crew cried out in shock and anger and defended their ship, striking back with sword and arrow. Lykos joined in, shoving his dagger at any Piercer that drew close but it was difficult. The beasts were quick and he desperately wished he had a bow of his own to use. Then he remembered his magic.

Trying to feel for it while dodging the sharp beak of a Piercer was no easy task but Lykos tried. All around him he could see wounded crew members, friends he had made, being picked apart by the swarming monsters. Even Captain Cael was in bad shape, leaning heavily against his ship for support as he bled from multiple wounds, the swing of his sword erratic. And still the monsters kept on coming.

Lykos burned with hatred at these fell beasts. Never before had he hated something as much as he did now and the magic within him burned with that rage. He glared hatefully at the Tainted and roared his anger, causing his magic to finally react by creating a fireball in his palm. The heat burned his skin and he threw it with a shout at the nearest Piercer where it hit and exploded.

A great blast of heat and fire spread out, knocking him to the deck. The other Tainted fled into the night screeching warnings to one another but the Logwind was still in danger. Between his fireball and the Tainted's attack it was rapidly losing altitude. He grasped a wooden railing with desperate hands and closed his eyes as the forest rushed to meet them.

The crash was jarring. One moment he was half-falling through air, only attached to the airship by the strength of his desperate limbs and then the next he flew through the air still clutching the now detached wooden railing. He hit something hard and bounced, the wooden railing flying from his shocked hands, and crashed into a bush. He blacked out.

When he came to he was half-blind from smoke and fire. Coughing, he felt each pain in his body carefully to determine if anything was broken. To his surprise he was fine, a collection of cuts and bruises from his impromptu flight were his only injuries. Staggering to his feet he looked around to see a burning forest surrounding the crashed Logwind many paces away. A nearby groan alerted him of another survivor.

Moving through burning bushes and broken trees he came across Captain Cael dragging himself across the ground. The man's legs were obviously broken and the beak of a Piercer stabbed through his chest. Yet the man still moved and Lykos rushed forward eager to help save his captain.

"Captain!" he called out, grasping the man's shoulders frantically. Captain Cael sagged in his hands and it was all he could do to turn the man over. "Captain, what do we do?"

"You have magic," Captain Cael gasped insensate as Lykos examined the beak piercing the man's chest. Judging by the blackened blood Lykos knew he could not save the man who had saved his life. "You have magic."

"Aye, I touched a crystal in the mines. It was so painful I thought I was dying," he hurriedly confirmed. The mortally wounded captain shook his head slowly.

"Only noble blood may touch those crystals and live. You need to find House Talal," Captain Cael gasped, blood bubbling from his lips. "They'll.... Help.... Family." Captain Cael shuddered before falling still. Lykos lowered his head out of respect but whipped it back up as faint growling could be heard. More Tainted were swarming the downed airship and it was with a heavy heart he knew he had to leave the dead captain behind to be burned with his ship.

Chapter Three

Lykos rushed away from the downed Logwind surrounded by rustling bushes and the grunts of Tainted on all sides. He hurried through the thick brush cursing at the realization that his knife had been lost in the crash. With no weapon on hand and no time to craft one he knew reaching the kingdom of Mycenae was his only chance of survival. And so he ran.

Fortunately the site of the crash had been on top of a hill. On his descent he had seen the wall of lights that signified Mycenae and made all possible haste towards it. He was not concerned with losing his direction, so long as he kept the mountains to his left he knew he would arrive at the kingdom eventually. So long as the Tainted did not get to him first.

Even now he could hear them keeping pace, the beasts grunting with exertion. Branches and leaves slapped him in the face during his mad dash through the woods and he knew he needed to lose them somehow. A nearby river gave him an idea and without pausing he abruptly changed his direction towards the running water. With a mighty leap, he dove in.

He had learned how to swim in the mines by necessity. Some of the caves were in danger of being flooded from underground rivers or lakes at any moment and the slaves were at the mercy of their chilly waters. As if that weren't reason enough, the guards liked to "clean" the slaves by forcing them into those flooded caves. Needless to say any slave that didn't learn soon drowned.

The water, while cold in the night, was not as freezing as the north and Lykos found it quite easy to push through the current by grasping the rocks along the river bottom. When his lungs failed him, he carefully broke the surface of the water and hid behind a partly submerged tree, his eyes wary for his pursuers. Then the Tainted broke the treeline.

They were brutes with thick, stocky bodies, dissimilar to their Piercer brethren. Their mottled gray hides stretched over muscled frames but it was the powerful legs and curious head that drew ones attention. A series of horns grew out from all angles of the beasts face, curved and wicked sharp, to surround a gaping maw with exposed teeth. As Lykos watched one of the beasts huffed and charged into the river, impacting an exposed rock near to where he had jumped into the water. The rock audibly cracked and snapped down the middle and the beast rose from the water unharmed. For several long moments the beasts examined the water, sniffing along the banks. Several of them looked up stream at the rushing water near Lykos before turning down stream and following the current. The rest followed.

He let out a sigh of relief. The beasts were far smarter than their blood lust suggested, he could see how they had been thinking about which way he had moved. It was only chance that they chose to pursue the easier course. Carefully exiting the water he resumed his trek towards Mycenae at a much more sedate pace.

As he walked he considered Captain Cael's dying words. The captain seemed to believe that only those of noble blood could safely handle the magic crystals with bare hands. And why point him towards House Talal, why not point Lykos towards Captain Cael's own house, House Falknor? But it was one word that confused him most of all.

Family. As far as he knew he had no family, the only life he had known was that of a slave in the mines. When he was younger he followed the older slaves, carrying stones wrapped in canvas until he grew stronger, then breaking rocks with the other adults. He only knew his name because that was what the other slaves called him when the guards were out of sight, one of the freedoms they still retained. Did Captain Cael mean to tell Lykos that he had family?

Lykos wrestled with his thoughts as he walked, always pausing when he heard a Tainted move through the brush nearby, careful to not draw their attention. As dawn began to shine over the mountains he broke the treeline and found himself looking at an equally surprised group of humans digging a large ditch. Several armored guards with black squares on their arms were staring at him in surprise.

"Where did you come from?" one of the men digging in the ditch called out, catching the attention of everyone nearby. Lykos slowly walked forward, showing his empty hands to the guards.

"Our airship crashed in the forest during the night," he explained as he gestured behind him. A small column of smoke spiraled upwards in the distance. "I'm the only survivor."

One of the guards stepped forward with his hand on his sword. "That's an impressive claim stranger. How do we know you're telling the truth?"

A second worker spoke up. "Look at the state of his clothes. Between the burns and the slashes it's obvious he's honest."

"Still I'll be damned by the Goddesses if we just let every vagabond into our kingdom," the first guard replied never taking his eyes off Lykos.

"Bully to your absent Gods Picario, they've never done anything for you! Leave that young man alone," another worker said and the rest of his fellows followed suit with similar calls. The guard named Picario ground his teeth.

"Fine but none of my men will escort him back to Mycenae rock-eater," Picario replied. He spat at Lykos' feet before standing aside to let him pass. Lykos moved closer to the ditch while one of the men climbed out of it. He waved off the angry guard.

"Go pray to thin air Picario, I'll take him back. If your men have done their job there shouldn't be any Tainted left in this part of the woods," he said before gesturing with a hand to Lykos to follow. "I'm Garrick and don't mind the Citadel guard, they're a bunch of superstitious idiots," he whispered the last bit to Lykos as they walked past a pair of glaring guards.

"Lykos. What Goddesses were you talking about?" he asked, unfamiliar with the religions of Mycenae. Garrick looked confused but understanding quickly dawned in his eyes.

"You must have been raised in Svellheim. Only they still insist on calling the Goddesses that funny word, Valkyries. Mycenae and Istani relabeled them to explain their absent presence in recent years," Garrick explained as they walked a well beaten dirt path. On either side of them were the stumps of trees long since felled and various groups of men and women moving through the remaining forest with various burdens.

"So there's more than one? And what's everyone here doing?" he asked not confirming Garrick's observation. He had heard stories of the Valkyries or Goddesses or whatever. They had never answered his prayers in the mines thus he would pay no mind to anyone proclaiming their message.

"Supposedly there are dozens of Goddesses but depending on who you ask they all have different names and faces. Balderdash if you ask me. As for our work here, we're clearing out this part of the forest to expand Mycenae with a new quarter. They may mock us "rock-eaters" but when it comes to moving earth and stone they always come to us first," Garrick finished proudly.

" And what did he mean by rock-eaters?"

"Ah yes, you're not of this kingdom. Most of the noble houses have some sort of nickname referring to their interests. We rock-eaters serve House Vrachos, we've mined most of the stone that makes up this kingdom. There are swamp dwellers, grave robbers, purse pinchers, and so on. Every noble house has had some sort of nickname from the common folk."

"Including House Talal?"

Garrick paused in their walk and gave him a dark look. "Those arrogant rebels have many unflattering nicknames, thank the Goddesses or the Tainted that there's only one of their wretched number left and she is not even blood. A pox on all of them."

"I meant no offense," Lykos offered quickly, surprised at the man's vitriol. Garrick nodded in acceptance.

"You're a foreigner, you wouldn't know. Because of House Talal's actions years ago the slaves of Mycenae have been one step away from open rebellion. House Talal lies in ruins and still the slaves have hope!" Garrick all but shouted, pointing towards one of the peaks overlooking the kingdom. Lykos noted the location and wondered if that's where the last Talal was. The men and women working under the careful eyes of the guards took on a new meaning and his eyes spotted chains and collars binding them together. He took note that they had arrived at a tall gate where hand pulled wagons and crowds made their way in and out.

"The Gates of Mycenae! Every quarter has them, just keep an eye out for the beasts carved above them. This is where I part with you Lykos, I have to return to overseeing my men. If you're looking for work you're more than welcome to join us, we can always use another oversee for the slaves."

Lykos burned in anger but let none of it color his voice as he responded, "I'll keep that in mind." Garrick gave him a nod before turning away. Expelling a huff of air Lykos took his first step into Mycenae.

Chapter Four

The kingdom of Mycenae was remarkably different from anything Lykos had ever seen before. The walls on the edge of the kingdom rose higher than the tallest arc of the Logwind's balloon, with towers and holes for archers to fire from covering the surface. He idly wondered what terrible Tainted force necessitated the need for such monumental construction.

Exiting the dark tunnel into the morning light, he found himself in awe at the sight before him. A smooth stone street lined with flowers and trees cut away into the distance, full of wagons being pulled by slaves carrying finely dressed men and women to various destinations. The buildings were adorned in water spouts and vines and beautiful women in loose clothing lounged in the windows of many of them. Wooden stalls were here and there, selling their wares of food, metal, and cloth. The workmanship of everything was like nothing Lykos has ever seen before so used was he to cold caves, rough walls, and coarse fabric.

Walking through the bustling crowd he looked again for the peak Garrick had pointed out. Spying it beyond the corner of what Lykos understood to be a bakery he began his trek, all the while looking around with wide eyes at a civilization the likes he had never seen.

The kingdom of Mycenae was massive as he came to find out. The quarters as Garrick called them, were kingdoms unto themselves with large sprawling buildings, farms, and homes. Natural rivers flowed through the land with man made canals connecting them. A series of structures he learned to be called levies helped the endless streams of barges with cargo or passengers sail on the waters that flowed uphill. And surrounding each quarter were thick stone walls, each taller than the airships that he saw floating through the sky above.

Each quarter was as different as its people. In the first one he walked through he was surrounded by dozens of private homes and quite rivers, populated by wealthy men and women. The next had far more warehouses and an impressive air dock built up the mountain's side. The third Lykos entered contained many fields of stone, with names and faces carved into them. He was shocked to discover that thousands, tens of thousands, of dead lay in those fields, the more wealthy and known having greater tombs. Quickly leaving that one he found himself looking into deep pits, seeing dozens of homes and buildings carved out of the caverns and fading into the darkness below.

Yet he climbed higher into Mycenae, ever closer to the peak Garrick pointed to. Upon entering a new quarter he was struck by how rundown the streets and buildings were, missing stones and timber. The people moved quickly under the harsh gaze of soldiers bearing yellow ribbons on their arms, who would stop the occasional passerby and question them. Occasionally one would beat a random person and riffle through their belongings as they lay bleeding on the stones. It reminded Lykos strongly of the mines and how the overseers treated him and his fellow slaves.

However nothing could be done for them. Lykos knew his own station in life was tenuous at best and that he could easily become a slave again if he was not careful. He needed to tread carefully while he searched for the remnant of House Talal. He was so focused on his task that he almost tripped over a blind man laying in the street.

"Sorry," he apologized. The man's brow furrowed and Lykos was treated to the unpleasant sight of empty eye sockets. "Do you know where I could find House Talal?"

"House Talal?" the man sneered hatefully. "I lost my eyes for House Talal! Fought in that bastards war and what did it get me? Blindness! He should have stayed in his snooty manor like the rest of those nobles and left us common folk alone."

"Perhaps he was trying to help the common folk?" Lykos countered. The blind man snorted.

"More likely the fool was trying to help himself. Didn't matter in the end, left his wife all alone in that manor on the hill, a prisoner in her own home."

"Thanks for the information," Lykos walked away and the blind man began to laugh quietly.

"He thanked me. Maybe he's a fool too...."

There was only one area that could be considered a hill in this quarter but its rocky sides were too steep to climb. Walking around the base he saw a large group of soldiers standing guard around a stone wall. Beyond it he could see a stately manor that had fallen into disrepair and he reasoned that this was the Talal home. But he could not see a way past them and had the feeling that asking for entry would end badly. So finding another entrance would be necessary.

Retreating into the quarter Lykos was surprised by the setting sun on the horizon. Walking to a nearby ledge he gazed in awe at the sight before him. Towers and walls rose like trees below, bisected by shining lines of water that crossed the kingdom. Dozens of airship were still sailing through the air looking quite amusing to his eyes, their bloated shapes moving awkwardly in the air currents. He leaned against the stone railing and enjoyed the view.

Something caught his attention out of the corner of his eye. The barest edge of the Talal manor could be seen with a worn terrace overlooking the cliffs, much like the one he stood upon now. And along the rocks, leading away from where he stood, were a series of broken rocks perfect for climbing. Having climbed upon hundreds of similar shelves in the mines Lykos knew that they could hold his weight however it was what was below that gave him pause.

For he was standing above a truly colossal drop. Looking down he could see murky green swirls of a swamp far below him, the ships bobbing on the water looking like toys. Panic flooded his body, the recent airship crash fresh in his mind. He was in no rush to re-experience a similar fall, especially since he was lucky to survive the first, but he needed aid. Aid that Captain Cael told him House Talal could provide.

So screwing up his courage Lykos climbed over the stone railing and grasped the first handhold. The stone held his weight firmly under his pull and with a sigh of reluctance the rest of his body swung free of its perch. Carefully, much more so than any other time in his life, he began to climb.

I could have just gone to House Falknor, he thought to himself. Although telling them that one of their number died in a crash that he partially caused would end poorly in his opinion. One of the things he always envied were the bonds blood families shared: fighting, dying, and killing for one another. He wondered what it would be like having people to trust. Or would he even be able to?

One of the rocks broke free of its perch as soon as he put weight on it. Flailing wildly, he managed to grab another handhold before gravity could drag him to his death. Grasping it desperately he breathed heavily as the sensation of falling continued. Slowly his racing heart quieted and his breathing evened out. Knowing he could not turn back now he continued his climb even more cautiously.

Finally, after what felt like an eternity, Lykos once more griped the smooth stone of carved masonry. Eagerly he grasped it, pulling himself over the edge to collapse heavily on the mossy cobblestone to catch his breathe. Before him lay the grounds, years absent of basic maintenance had led to its overgrown and decrepit state. A large fountain with broken figures posing sat off to one side, overgrown with vines and moss. A walking path circled the garden but was missing stones and pitted with large holes from damage. The many flower beds were overgrown with weeds and the malevolent eyes of Tainted Gnawers glared out from them. His breathing calmed, he stood and looked behind him, past the worn stone of the balcony and paused.

The whole Kingdom of Mycenae was alight in a sea of lights in the dark night. It hugged along the mountain range in a beautiful slope that descended all the way to the ocean below. A twisted pain in his stomach reminded him that not even a day ago he had seen a similar sight from the Logwind before the crash. He shook himself of his morbid thoughts and turned back to the task at hand.

The manor showed similar signs of damage to the quarter and grounds, caused by the elements and human hands. He approached and began to carefully push on the windows and doors, trying to see if any were accessible, but it was futile as they all appeared to be bolted shut. He was careful not to move to the side of the building lest the soldiers at the gate see or hear him and raise the alarm.

Instead he examined the second floor of the manor and saw one of the windows was ajar. Below it were a series of broken stones and exposed wooden beams that would make acceptable handholds. Climbing up the stone and wood wall he paused underneath the window. Glancing over the edge into the dark interior of the house he neither saw nor heard any movement. Carefully he slid over the edge and into the dark house.

The dark shapes of furniture covered in dusty white cloths could barely be seen in the moonlight. Peeking under them he saw well made furniture which surprised him as they did not match the destroyed state of the rest of the building. Curious to see if anything else had been left behind Lykos began to go through them.

The nightstands on either side of the bed were empty, as was underneath the bed itself. He had more success with the desk, finding a ring, several gold trinkets, and a bag of coins. He placed the ring on his finger and admired the simple design for a moment before placing the rest of his spoils in a pouch on his hip. The only furniture left was an exquisitely carved wardrobe standing tall in the corner.

The wardrobe opened on squeaky hinges at his touch causing him to flinch at the suddenly loud noise in the quiet night. He listened quietly to see if any shouts of alarm were raised but none came forth. Turning his attention back to the wardrobe he saw several objects of interest but only one grabbed his attention. On the center shelf sat an eagle carved out of the same magical crystal he had harvested in the mines, glowing with a soft blue light. Lykos thought back to Captain Cael and his dying words: only noble blood could touch those crystals and live.

He slowly reached out and touched the softly glowing eagle. It felt cool to his touch. No it felt warm. He marveled at the temperature fluctuating within the crystal before a jolt of energy shot through his body shocking him. Crying out, Lykos fell backwards hitting his head on a thick wooden table. Darkness descended as the sound of footsteps approached.

Chapter Five

L ykos awoke suddenly and painfully, his head ringing with some unholy noise. Clutching his head, he felt the fading pain of a rather large lump on the back of his head, the obvious culprit of his incapacitated state. A soft hand brushed his hair and he flinched, suddenly aware that there was someone sitting near him. Reluctantly his eyes opened to reveal the brightly lit room he had entered during the night, its dusty glory illuminated in the morning light. The light was obscured by a feminine form.

"Oh you're awake! Rest my child and do not strain yourself, all will be well in time. I am so happy to finally meet you and on such a joyous occasion!" The revealed woman reached out with a bony hand to stroke Lykos' face. He shied away from her hand but winced at the last fading twinge of his head injury. He tensed realizing the potentially dangerous situation he found himself in and tried to focus his thoughts to listen to her words.

"What is your name child?" she asked. Her eyes shown with curiosity as they stared intently at him.

"Lykos. What happened?" He examined the woman's elegant but threadbare clothes but could see no hidden weapons. Still she could be a mage and so he watched her hands and eyes cautiously.

"Lykos," she tested out his name before continuing pleased, "it is a good name, a strong name. As for what happened to you, you touched the awakening stone! It gifted you magic! I knew you would come back home one day." Lykos examined the woman's

28

graying brown hair and the matching eyes as he considered her words.

Awakening stone? He had been "gifted" magic in the slave mines far north of here. He had been surrounded on all sides, pinned between massive crystals, and their power had seared into his flesh. It wasn't awakened by that unpleasant jolt. Yet this woman talked of magic as if it were common and Captain Cael's dying words sprang to mind. Had he been trying to tell Lykos he had living family? Was this woman his family?

"Who are you?" he finally asked.

"I am your mother, Shawna of House Talal, formerly of House Agroti," she explained with a smile, " and I am so happy you're finally home. The man with the pale eyes told me you would return to me one day so long as I waited patiently. He was right."

Lykos was still uncertain. "My mother died years ago. My father as well."

Shawna smiled sadly at him while shaking her head. "Your father, Leon, died with the rest of House Talal several years ago, attempting to help this kingdom. You were taken from me after he failed, just after your birth, and I was only given bones picked clean by Tainted in return. However I knew they weren't yours and I was right," she finished excitedly. Lykos shifted uncomfortably.

"But how do you know I'm your child?" he asked incredulously as he attempted to sit up. She leaned forward and offered her hand which he reluctantly took. As she aided him in sitting up she also turned her hand so the ring he placed on his finger shown. The simple ring with a blue gem shown faintly on his finger.

She carefully grasped the ring, being careful not to touch the gem, and pulled it off his left hand. She reached over for his right hand and slid it back on. "You wear the ring on the right hand dear, so that others may see it when you grasp hands," she explained gently. She gestured to the still glowing crystal figure in the wardrobe. "The gem is a sliver of the carved eagle, the mark of House Talal. Only someone of Talal blood may safely touch the crystal on the ring or the statue. Anyone else will be punished harshly before they are killed."

Lykos frowned, still not convinced that he was who this woman thought he was. He jerked in surprise when she grabbed his left hand and placed it on his right. Feeling the cool crystal shard under his hand he felt a familiar jolt of energy and jerked. Shawna laughed joyously at his displeased expression.

"The magic within the ring should feel energizing, it's letting you know that it recognizes you as one of Talal blood. Crystals such as these can provide a brief boost of energy in times of need but until then they sleep."

The confusion he felt knew no bounds. The woman before he talked of magic, family, rings and none of it made any sense to him. The softly glowing crystal in the wardrobe did not appear to be asleep, no it looked alive, like the thousands of its kin in the mines. He slowly stood and tried to stretch his body to relieve his soreness to no avail. Carefully walking to the still open wardrobe and he closed it, no longer desiring to see the glowing crystal anymore.

Turning to face the woman who claimed to be his mother he examined her once more. He could not honestly say that Shawna was not his mother as he never knew either of his parents, there was no memory of either caring for him in the mines and that was all he could recall. He looked down upon the petite woman and wondered if it was the truth. No answer revealed itself in his mind.

As if reading his thoughts Shawna pulled her robes around herself tighter and asked him where he had been these long years. With a sigh Lykos decided to tell the strange woman part of the truth for if she truly is his family then he would prefer to be honest. It was an unsettling feeling in his gut as he began to speak.

"I've been living in Svellheim my entire life. A few weeks ago I met an airship captain and traded work for passage on his ship. We crashed in the forest two nights ago and I was chased by Tainted all the way to the kingdom's gate," he summarized. He was more concerned with the odd tenseness in his limbs. He flexed his hands, feeling the muscles moving easily but realizing there was something else that he could feel. After a moment of thought he deduced it to be his magic, stirring almost contently under his flesh after being touched by another form of magic. Shawna grasped his fingers and held them tightly in her own distracting his thoughts.

"Oh my dear son, such sorrows you must have felt." Lykos did not have the heart to tell Shawna he faced far worse than whatever she was imagining in the mines. She took him by the arm and led him slowly from the room. He belatedly realized that he must have been unconscious for most of the night if the sun was now shining. "But now you're home and everything will be well again. Welcome to Hearthome Lykos."

The manor showed signs of obvious neglect as he was led down stairs. The mythical eagle laid in the stonework below was scratched and missing entire pieces making the bird appear wounded. Holes and burn damage covered the wood walls yet little smashed furniture remained and Lykos concluded that the woman who claimed to be his mother most likely took care of it. But that did raise the question as to why she was still here.

"My family would not take me back for fear of enticing enemies," she answered his question easily enough but he could detect her frustration and betrayal. "I am a Talal in name only yet my own blood has forsaken me."

"Why would they leave you alive though? Mother?" He awkwardly and belatedly added realizing his question could be considered rude. Shawna appeared not to mind and squeezed his arms warmly.

"House Talal's enemies wanted a reminder for the other houses of what might happen if they stepped out of line. I was never that prominent in house politics nor a great combatant. I am lesser still as my magic was never as good as others in my family." Here she flicked a hand at a half-melted candle and only brought forth a spark that sizzled out. "Still, they wanted a warning and thus my unfortunate circumstances."

The spark impressed Lykos as it was the first sign of a mage outside of the mines that he had seen. He turned to the candles himself and flicked his hand as Shawna had but was disappointed a single spark did not even appear. She laughed at his crestfallen expression.

"Do not worry I will find you a suitable tutor. Although if you take after your father as I expect you have you will find many things within your grasp. Moving earth, summoning water, bringing down lightning," she sighed wistfully as she directed Lykos into a moderately clean kitchen and sat him down at the worn table. She opened and shut the cabinets looking for food but clucked her tongue when she could not find any. She vanished through a door off to the side that led to what appeared to be a cellar. After several minutes of her moving furiously within the dark room, she returned into the kitchen wringing her hands.

"We have no food," she said morosely, looking to Lykos as if she were moments away from tears. "I'm a horrible mother, I cannot even feed my own child."

Lykos seized the opportunity with two hands, indeed he leaped to his feet and grasped Shawna's hands gently, halting her tears. "Allow me to go the market then. I'll be back in just a little while with enough food for the both of us."

Shawna wiped away her tears and stroked his cheek. "Such a caring young man looking out for his mother. Here take these coins. In the meantime I'll send a courier to my cousin to determine if he is willing to tutor you. Something tells me you'll like one another."

He took the proffered gold and bid her goodbye. Walking through the kitchen and to the front door she accompanied him and waved him out the entryway her brilliant smile never leaving her face. He gave the well meaning woman a weak smile in return and turned to walk down the worn path to the gate.

Chapter Six

Two soldiers were sitting in the shade dozing when he approached the overgrown gates of Hearthome. His time with the Logwind's crew had allowed him to develop a sense of humor and so it was with a smirk he decided to have a little fun with the two drunkards.

"By the Valkyrie's might what the blazes do you think you're doing?" he roared as he kicked the rusty gate, rattling its entire length and causing a terrible racket. The two men shot to their feet and looked in entirely wrong directions.

"Uh, my lord?" asked the fat one.

"I don't see no one," the thin one whispered. Lykos looked at the two incredulously before clearing his throat. The thin one looked to his left but the fat one turned about and his eyes widened at seeing Lykos there.

"Who the forsaken are you! Why are you waking up us respectable folk? We work hard you know!" he shouted in Lykos' face, whose nose wrinkled at the rank odor wafting off his breathe. Clearly the spirits he drank last night were far too strong.

"Could you open the gate please? I seem to have lost my key," Lykos smiled at the two men who looked at him with dumbfounded expressions, only now realizing he was on the opposite side of the gate they were supposed to be guarding. The thin soldier reached into his pouch and pulled out a key which he fitted into the gate, pulling forcefully against rusted hinges.

"Thank you," Lykos resisted the urge to laugh as the thin man smiled, pleased with his implied good deed, while the fat one fumed. He stepped through the gate but quickly stepped back as the fat soldier's rusted sword was waved in his direction. "You might want to be careful with that, it's a dangerous weapon."

"Where are you going?" the fat soldier demanded angrily as the thin soldier scrambled for his sword. Lykos smiled pleasantly at the pair before answering.

"Why I'm going to the market of course!" His grin could not be any wider as the two soldiers stared at him befuddled. The thin one indeed looked so confused that Lykos wondered if his face would be permanently stuck in such an odd manner. The fat, now frustrated, one rallied back.

"But why are you trespassing! No one but a Talal is supposed to be on these grounds!" His face turned a marvelous shade of purple Lykos had never before seen. He took a moment to examine the pulsating mass before replying.

"And you've done an excellent job of it," he replied. He could feel his face straining from smiling so much. Were it not for Captain Cael and his crew broadening his horizons on their journey he doubted he would have been capable of even this much.

"But who are you?" the fat one roared.

"Yeah who are you?" the thin one demanded. That the thin one managed to speak too impressed Lykos so much he gave the man a surprised nod.

"Well if you're only supposed to allow members of House Talal here and you just opened the gate for me, what does that make me?" Lykos briefly wondered if he should use simpler words when dealing with the two men.

"A trespasser!" shouted the fat soldier viciously.

"A burglar!" answered the thin one excitedly.

Lykos rubbed his forehead staving off a brief headache as he looked at the two men in concern for two different reasons. He pointed to the ring on his finger. "I'm a Talal," he said despondently.

Their jaws were agape in shock and confusion. They turned to stare at each other before turning back to Lykos.

"That isn't possible," said the thin one.

"Why is this happening?" the fat one lamented as he leaned against the stone wall.

"All of House Talal is dead!" the thin one cried.

"Why did it have to be on my watch?" the fat one moaned.

"Well except the old bat but she's insane!"

"We're going to be sent to patrol the forest. We're dead!" The fat one collapsed onto the ground and the thin one soon joined him bemoaning their fortunes. Lykos stared at the two soldiers before nodding to himself. He decided he had much better things to do and walked away.

Sidestepping a cart pulled by a farmer he considered his options. The first was he could go to the market and return to the woman who believed herself to be his mother. Whether she was or not was a non-issue, returning promised shelter, food, and tutoring that he would otherwise never receive. On the other hand the woman was most likely insane despite her kind and caring appearance and he might be better off simply running as far away as possible as fast as possible and chancing living on the streets.

Shawna was kind and generous, if a bit unbalanced. She could just as easily do as she claimed as she was to slit his throat while he slumbered. However she could provide him a new path towards life that he never have had anyways. Even if he were not her child, could he pretend for a moment of safety?

Lykos pondered his dilemma as he wandered the streets of Pyrgos, the quarter he found himself in, looking at the citizens going about their business. He looked upon their down trodden expressions, their feeble attempts to survive in the harsh environment of the kingdom, this world. He nearly stumbled in his walk as his eyes fell upon two such common folk.

A young woman stood offering her body for coin in a darkened alley off the street. Those passing by ignored her plight as a hand reached out from the shadows, revealing a small boy. The woman tearfully stroked the child's face before kissing him on the brow and redoubling her efforts to sell her body. Lykos turned away in disgust knowing he had his answer. As he turned in the direction of the market he knew it was not out of concern for a possible family member that made his decision, it was the thought of starving and being forced to live at the "kindness" of others once more that chose his path.

"You just have to be a greedy idiot don't you?" he muttered rhetorically to himself. "Can't just go stealing from stalls or rubbish bins, you have to go for the feast! Now you have to pretend to be some woman's son."

Entering the crowded market he began to browse the merchant stalls. A green flag hung on many of them proudly and these stalls were crowded with citizens eager for quality wares, praising House Emporo. He walked to one of the unmarked, less crowded stalls and attempted to look at their products but an extraordinarily large man with an impressive girth blocked his way. He attempted to move past him but found the obese man blocking his path each time, seemingly without notice. With a huff he tapped the man on his shoulder.

The man's face was squashed, as if he had had an unfortunate accident with a boulder and he sneered at Lykos. "What do you want boy?" he asked. His voice was surprisingly feminine but Lykos shook off his surprise and responded.

"I want to browse the wares and you're in the way," he said. Despite the man's impressive size he feared little retribution, the large man was not even visibly armed meaning he was most likely not a threat. A small scuffle broke out next to them and he ignored it, determined not to lose a contest of wills with this man.

The staring and scuffle both grew in intensity until Lykos found himself staggering to his left. The argument next to them had devolved into blows and one participant had been launched into him sending them both flying. The pair crashed into another man and all three were sent harshly into the dirty stones beneath their feet.

"Who dare knock me down!" the man beneath Lykos shouted drawing the attention of the entire marketplace. Lykos felt the brawler on top of him leap off and run away before the man even finished his question and soon felt a cool pit of dread form in his belly as two rough pairs of hands grabbed him and hauled him to his feet.

The two pairs of hands belonged to two equally rough looking brutes who glared menacingly down at him. He returned his attention to the man who had spoken, whose finely crafted clothes had been dirtied in their fall. He rose to his feet and glared at Lykos who quickly became aware of the suddenly quiet marketplace. He fingers brushed the dagger at his side to reassure himself before answering the question.

"That would be that man," Lykos gestured in a random direction, unable to see the men who caused the pile up in question. "Yes I saw him do it and these two men are my witnesses."

His brazen lie seemed to confuse the three men who looked at one another questioningly. He tried to edge away in the confusion but found himself boxed in between the two giants on either side of him and a stall to his back.

"You lie!" the third, smaller man shouted as he pulled out a sword. The two guards grasped Lykos' arms with bruising strength. "I'll show you what happens to those who insult House Kolos!"

Before the man could move forward Lykos used the leverage provided by the two men to leap up and kick him solidly in the face. He fell backwards with a cry as Lykos forcefully removed himself from the grip of the two brutes. He rolled backwards over the stall, scattering the wares laid there, and drew his dagger in time to slash at one of the men. The man fell back with a cry as the crowd began to cheer and jeer in equal measure, shouting encouragement and insults at all involved.

Lykos went after the man he slashed and viciously brought his weapon down again and again, until the second man pulled him off his companion. Losing his knife Lykos pulled free of his captor's grip and stumbled away. The first man arose despite the kick to the face and attacked Lykos with his fists. Despite the relative quickness and ferocity of his initial surprise attack, Lykos found himself being forced to the ground as his body took the beating.

He curled up and tried to protect his head as the beating intensified as the second man joined in. He could feel his trembling muscles scream in torment and the oddly tense feeling of magic over them aching almost painfully. Without quite knowing how Lykos flexed the tense feeling and the painful punishment ceased at the sound of a high wind.

Warily looking around he was surprised to see the two men on the ground a dozen yards from him, groaning in pain. Lykos looked at them in surprise and awe realizing he just used magic. Elated at the use of magic he searched for his discarded knife. Plunging his hands into the filth around him, he almost stabbed himself on its sharp edge. Grabbing it he stood up only to duck as the now bloodied man he had kicked in the face swung his sword at his neck.

"Give me your name so that I Viktor, Heir of House Kolos, may kill you and all will know of your foolishness!" he demanded angrily. The now named Viktor spat great globes of blood as he swung wildly at Lykos. Lykos for his part did not try to block the heavier weapon with his knife, correctly assuming it'd be ineffective. Instead he reached once more for the tense feeling underneath his skin, the feeling of *magic*, and flicked his fingers at the raging man. He was elated that a small fireball the size of his fist raced out but disheartened when it died out before it went even half the distance between them. He then smelled burning flesh and realized his hand had been burned.

"I don't recognize you from the Citadel rogue mage, who trained you?" Viktor demanded.

"Trained?" Lykos repeated confused. The man's eyes widened in shock before he let loose a great roar of laughter.

"You haven't been trained! What kind of mage goes off half-cocked into battle?" Viktor continued to laugh into Lykos' reddening face and so did the watching crowd.

"Lykos of House Talal and I do not need training to defeat the likes of you!"

The whole marketplace turned deathly quiet as they all stared at him. The laughing Viktor laughed no more, indeed he looked enraged as he stared at his hand where the ring marked his claim.

"That's impossible," he whispered and the crowd began to murmur at the shocking news. "Your entire house was eradicated except for an insane old woman. This cannot be the truth!"

"Well the ring and the creepy eagle statue say otherwise," Lykos answered but found himself dodging as Viktor once more swung at him. He experienced the disappointing realization that Viktor's skill with a sword, even enraged, far outstripped his own combat ability. It was time to escape.

"Would. You. Stop. Moving. Scum!" Each word was accompanied by a swing of the sword and Lykos began to tire from all of the dodging he was being forced to do. His eyes then widened in surprise as Viktor thrust his sword into the ground and a sharp spear of earth thrust up from below. "I'll show you how to truly use magic!"

Fireballs, spears of earth, and gusts of wind chased Lykos around the market as he frantically dodged. Every attempt to use magic failed as his concentration was interrupted by a timely attack from Viktor. Cuts, bruises, and burns began to accumulate as he slowed, his endurance fading and Lykos found himself collapsing in a dark corner of the market.

"Now to end you," Viktor snarled as he lunged forth with his sword. The world slowed down to Lykos and he found himself thinking back on his life. Beaten and tortured in the mines, escaping to the Kingdom of Mycenae on an airship he helped crash, breaking into the Talal manor and meeting Shawna. A determined calm fell over him as Viktor moved in closer. He was not ready to die just yet and with one last flex of will he opened himself to his magic and swung his dagger.

The result was not what he expected. A dark vortex opened up beneath him and gravity did the rest. With a rush of air he found himself flying through the air, tumbling head over heels before he collided with a pile of rubbish. He groaned and closed his eyes waiting for the world to stop spinning itself.

"Well that was entertaining Lykos of House Talal," a soft voice spoke as equilibrium was restored. He opened his eyes and pushed the rubbish off of him as the fat man from the market stared down at him over his impressive girth. "On your feet boy, I have questions and you will provide answers."

He warily rose and eyed the man who examined him with a strange intensity. "What do you want?" he asked the man.

"That remains to be determined," his soft voice and demeanor set Lykos on edge as he continued, "was that the first time you have used magic consciously?"

The question puzzled him but he answered affirmatively. For several long moments the man hummed in thought as he stared at Lykos. "I'm going to go now," Lykos said turning away but the man grabbed him with a large meaty hand. The strength in the hand was puzzling as it did not match the meaty fingers wrapped his arms. Indeed it felt as if a smaller hand was gripping his arms in the exact place. "Is there something wrong with your hand?"

The man quirked an eyebrow and nodded impressed before answering, "well that is fascinating, new to magic and already feeling through illusions."

"Illusions?" Lykos asked confused but found himself staring into empty sky. The obese man had disappeared and in his place was a wizened old woman in torn leathers and furs clutching a cane. "You're a woman!"

"Observant too," she remarked dryly, her soft voice suiting her new appearance much more suitably. "Who is your instructor boy?"

"I don't have one."

"Very well then boy lead on!" she ordered. The diminutive woman prodded him with her cane.

"Lead on? Why should I lead you anywhere, who are you anyways?" he exclaimed as she began to hit him harder and harder with the cane.

"Because I will train you boy! Now enough dawdling, take me to your home!" she ordered once more. She pushed him harder with her cane and he found himself walking down the stone street with an old woman hobbling behind him.

"Who are you?" he asked as they passed many citizens amused by his plight.

"I am Illusionist Maeve, former Sorceress of Kremos Keep! Now move faster boy I'm not getting any younger!"

And thus Lykos found himself leading a crazy woman to meet his crazy mother. *Life had certainly gotten interesting,* he thought.

Chapter Seven

As he found himself herded back to his new home with a violent old woman at his heels he enjoyed the brief delusion that this was all a vivid hallucination and he was back in the mines dying. The repeated flinches of pain as Illusionist Maeve hit a fresh bruise or cut soundly defeated that argument however and firmly anchored this painful experience as real. As they approached the gates leading to his new home, he was relieved to find that the thin and fat soldiers had vanished leaving the rusted gate unoccupied. With a sigh he held the gate open for the old woman who finally halted in her abuse.

Entering the dusty manor once more he admired the eagle laid into the tile before glancing around wondering where Shawna was in the manor. Hearing the sound of conversation through the door on the left, he walked across the stone floor and entered, Illusionist Maeve following his steps with a click as her cane hit the floor. Inside he found a dusty parlor occupied by Shawna who was talking to an unknown man.

"Lykos!" Shawna greeted rising to hug him. He bore it gingerly as she pressed upon his bruises. "Oh my, what happened to you? And who is this?" she asked, glancing at Illusionist Maeve.

"Illusionist Maeve," the unknown man spat, glaring hatefully at the old woman. Illusionist Maeve smirked playfully at the unknown man and winked. Shawna turned back to Lykos.

"This is my cousin Adelram, he's agreed to train you in how to handle weapons," she paused as Maeve snorted and Adelram's glare deepened into a scowl, "although for magic we'll have to look elsewhere...."

"Ha! I will train the boy and he will be greater for it," Illusionist Maeve declared as she hobbled over to a chair and sat down under Shawna's disproving stare. "He shows great promise and it shouldn't be wasted at the Citadel."

"So you say witch," Adelram growled as he gripped the sword by his side. Lykos respect for the dark haired man went up a notch; brazenly insulting a mage was not the action of a man who desired to live for long.

"Oh Adelram you should let go of the past before it ends badly for you. Again." Adelram's glare did not lessen at her words yet his hand dropped from his sword in defeat.

"Adelram?" Shawna asked. He took several deep breathes while Maeve quietly chuckled in her chair. He then turned to his cousin and spoke:

"Before I retired, Sorceress Maeve," the title was said mockingly, "had become infamous for her merciless cruelty in dealing with prisoners. I was placed in a legion under her command and she took a great deal of pleasure in enforcing discipline among the troops. It was exceedingly unpleasant," he finished with a shudder and Lykos pondered if he too felt the old woman's cane assaulting him during his service.

"Oh tosh, men used to be made of sterner stuff wouldn't you agree Dowager Talal? I heard of Leon's death, he ripped through a solid chunk of the Citadel guard before perishing," Illusionist Maeve nodded respectfully towards Shawna before continuing, "but I was unaware that your son survived. I thought Kopanos had him killed," she trailed off, staring at Lykos who shifted uncomfortably.

Shawna sighed deeply before smiling sadly at him. "The Goddesses' smiled upon us and brought my boy home. It is a shame that they could not return my husband but we have been blessed and we should be thankful. Although I am curious as to why you wish to train him?"

All turned to stare at Maeve as she fiddled with her cane, examining the fine, if worn, craftsmanship. "I lost my post at Kremos Keep, not through honorable combat but from politics," she spat the word hatefully. "Officially my brethren in House Miles felt that younger blood was needed to represent our family in the defense of Mycenae and so forced my retirement. Unofficially they wished to gain favor with House Kolos and gave my post to one of their useless bastards! An insult! I have a few years left in me and I will not see my legacy ruined by my foolish family." Maeve turned towards Lykos and he unconsciously straightened.

"That boy achieved a partial portal relocation on his first true day as a mage. With training he will become magnificent but with how the Citadel coddles its trainees he would never reach his full potential there. So Goddesses willing, I will train him to become as powerful as the sorcerers of old!"

Adelram snorted from his seat. "Elegant words witch but we shall see if he has potential. Boy!" Lykos face snapped towards the armed man. "Are you ready to begin your training?"

He opened his mouth to respond but was interrupted by someone forcing open the front door. Puzzled, the quartet moved to the entrance hall and found the thin and fat soldiers escorting a dirty man in fine robes. Garish yellow ribbons were tied to the sleeves of all three men but the new man was practically covered in the things.

"So it's true then, the heir of House Talal lives." The dirty man sneered at Lykos and moved into his personal space. His rancid breathe made Lykos' eyes water. "I am Elias, Lord of House Stultus boy and don't you go getting any funny ideas about following in your fathers footsteps! House Stultus controls this quarter now." Elias puffed out his chest proudly as the two dim soldiers nodded their heads in agreement.

"Lord Stultus it's a," Shawna paused distastefully, "pleasure to have you in our home."

Lykos stepped away from the foul smelling Elias and gave Shawna a look of respect at her subtle insult. Illusionist Maeve took the moment to mutter under her breathe on how they'd never get the filth out. Suppressing a laugh he turned to Elias and put on his most insincere smile.

"Lord Stultus," he sketched a mocking bow, "I've walked through Pyrgos this morning and I found it to be in such a deplorable state! How could this decline occur?" The implication was plain to hear in his tone but seemed to go right over the trio's head as Elias began to rant.

"It's all that blasted Leon's fault!" Spittle flew from Elias lips. "If he had just minded his own business this quarter wouldn't be the laughing stock of the kingdom. Instead we're looked down on by everyone, the people are lazy and worthless, and we've lost all our power and prestige!" He ranted on for several more minutes but Lykos paid him no heed, instead he spent it pondering his words.

The quarter was suffering it was true but Lykos did not believe it was from a decades old action. No the sickness that plagued Pyrgos was ongoing, being reinforced each day by the soldiers under the command of one Elias of House Stultus. He felt his lips curl in a sneer of disgust at the pathetically raving man who was now cursing the entire Talal bloodline. Possible relations or not, he was not going to take such insults laying down.

With a flick of his wrist his dagger was in his hand and at Elias' throat cutting his rant off. His eyes widened drastically and the thin and fat soldiers were slow to react as Illusionist Maeve tripped them with a subtle wave of air magic. The dirty man's breathe came out in rancid waves and Lykos wrinkled his nose in distaste.

"Insult me at your leisure but do not expect me to not respond in kind, *lord*." The word was spoken menacing, a subtle reminder that in this moment matters of nobility were secondary to the blade and the one who wielded it. And Lykos wielded it.

"You'll pay for this insult," Elias whispered, sweat pouring down his face as he looked at Lykos with fearful eyes. "I'll see your family hung!"

Lykos paused to consider the threat before responding, "I doubt that, would you care to guess why?"

"Why?" the question was almost mocking were it not the tremble of fear in his voice.

"For if it were truly in your power you wouldn't have talked with us these past few minutes, with two incompetent men to protect you. You would have brought all of your men to bring House Talal to extinction. For whatever reason you aren't allowed to kill us. But there is nothing to stop me from ending you."

No one spoke or moved as they stared at Lykos holding the Lord of Stultus at knife point. With a dismissive gesture Lykos removed his knife from his throat who began to breathe heavily and back away. The thin and fat soldiers regained their footing and dutifully helped their lord out the door.

"You'll pay for this insult, Talal brat! I'll get my revenge!" The thick wooden door cut off the angry shouts of retribution and Lykos turned towards the other three. Adelram and Maeve almost looked impressed with him while Shawna looked at him fretfully.

"So about that training?" Lykos asked determinedly.

"You are your father's son." Shawna claimed while shaking her head sadly. Adelram and Illusionist Maeve snorted in amusement.

Chapter Eight

L ykos followed Adelram out into the overgrown garden and aimed to mimic his dangerous swagger. Indeed every step the older man took promised to bring his remarkable strength and power down upon any who drew his ire. He was startled out of his attempt when the target of his observation barked out an order.

"I'm sorry what did you say?" he asked as they stopped by the broken fountain. Adelram's hard stare said that he was unimpressed with the question.

"I said don't try to mimic me. You are young and still growing into your powers and body, allow yourself to find your own niche rather than forcing yourself into one that has already been claimed." Lykos nodded and paid attention as he continued speaking. "You will address me as Instructor Adelram or sir as benefiting my rank, is that understood?"

Lykos nodded but realized Adelram was awaiting vocal confirmation of his understanding of the order. "I understand sir."

Adelram nodded approvingly. "Illusionist Maeve is the witches proper title as she is no longer allowed to claim the Sorceress rank. She will not be as forgiving as I if you do not use her correct title," he warned as he turned away examining the grounds. "House Talal's enemies will see your return as a challenge to their authority and will seek to eliminate you, my cousin, and myself. I will not die because you were incapable of defeating a Citadel guard."

Lykos bristled in anger for a moment before allowing it to burn out. If their positions were reversed he would be of the same mind, not wanting his safety or continued living to be reliant on the ability of an unknown quantity. "I understand Instructor."

He threw himself out of the way as Adelram suddenly whirled around and struck at him. Undeterred, Adelram punched again and again, forcing him to scramble wildly to avoid the blows. Tripping over a piece of broken masonry Lykos found himself flying through the air to land in a heap on the broken fountain. With nary a blink of the eye Adelram was upon him, striking him repeatedly as he struggled to free himself. In an act of desperation Lykos grabbed his dagger and stabbed Adelram in the arm.

Suddenly the attacks halted and he looked up to see Adelram examining his bleeding wound. It was slowly healing before his eyes and the older man nodded approvingly before turning his attention to Lykos. "Poor start but towards the end there you showed potential. I think with a little work you might actually put up a decent fight. Why are you still laying down boy, on your feet."

"What is wrong with you?" Lykos demanded as he scooted backwards. Between fighting Viktor earlier and this pummeling he was feeling quite exhausted. Adelram looked disapprovingly at him.

"Mind your tongue. We do not have the luxury of spending years to teach and drill you repeatedly. Instead experience must be your teacher and it is never kind. It is better for you to learn the pain of failure here than out there with a guard's sword chopping off your head or some Tainted beast digging into your guts." Lykos shook with anger before gingerly standing and holding his knife before him. Adelram nodded approvingly.

What followed was an exercise in pain as Adelram pummeled and threw him around like a sack of flour. As Lykos forced himself to stand after each fall he found his will power tested and he had to remind himself why he hadn't simply run when he had the chance. So with gritted teeth he bore each ache and pain for as long as he could before his strength left him. As he lay gasping for breathe Adelram leaned over him and spoke.

"And now you'll learn your first true bit of magic, that which any competent mage will master. How to use your magic to re-vitalize and energize you." He knelt beside Lykos and closed his eyes, brow furrowed in concentration. "I want you to reach for your magic, feel it resting underneath your skin. Do you feel it resisting you, constantly pushing and twisting within you? You must force it down, allow it to seep into your muscles and blood. It will know what to do."

Lykos focused on the tense feeling of magic within his body. As he flexed it mentally he could feel it strain against him but he persevered, forcing it to go down. It resisted his actions weakly but obeyed and he gasped as his bruises began to fade and his cuts began to heal. It was slow, far slower than Adelram's earlier healing of his knife wound yet it healed faster than any other injury he had ever experienced. He opened his eyes and grinned at Adelram who returned it before offering him a hand up.

Taking it Lykos pulled himself to his feet and asked, "are there any other things that you could use magic for in a fight sir?"

Adelram nodded pleased. "Of a sorts. Magic allows you to grow stronger and faster than other humans and if applied properly can be used to enhance you even further. However most members of the Citadel guard, and the noble houses, don't train their magic further than that, preferring to focus on more practical matters than studying over dusty books in a library or months in the yard. I myself never had the patience to study magic in depth so you are fortunate to study under Illusionist Maeve."

"You almost sound respectful sir," Lykos could not help remark, grinning as they walked back into the manor. Adelram snorted and gave him a dark look.

"You best watch your tongue boy, you'll be learning from the witch soon enough," Adelram paused in thought as they crossed the threshold. "As unpleasant as it was to be under her command she is an exceptional practitioner of the arcane arts. Far better than any teacher you'd receive at the Citadel in any case. Whether you'll learn anything from her or go insane is another issue entirely."

They could find no trace of Shawna or Illusionist Maeve in the parlor but could hear quiet talking through the far door. Entering it they found themselves in a large library whose shelves were almost empty, the few books that remained were damaged beyond use. Walking among the wooden dividers was Shawna and Illusionist Maeve, the former chatting happily at the latter who was scowling is displeasure at her surroundings. The two groups converged near the door.

"You're covered in blood dear." Shawna wiped fitfully at Lykos blood stained clothes. He shrugged then smirked at Adelram.

"Most of it belongs to Adelram." His playful smirk quickly vanished as Adelram smacked the back of his head. Shawna tutted at both of them before looking at Lykos clothes once more.

"I think I have some of your fathers things still. They'll be large on you but should fit well enough," she murmured thoughtfully. "That way you won't have to walk around in rags."

Lykos allowed himself to feel a small amount of guilty pleasure at the thought of a mother taking care of him. The woman fretted with his clothes once more before smiling up at him. "We've been exploring," she said proudly.

"Don't you live here?" he asked in amusement while Illusionist Maeve began to mutter under her breathe. Shawna was momentarily confused before brightening.

"Oh yes I do but Illusionist Maeve was looking for something and I decided to accompany her." Shawna glanced around the near empty library. "What happened to all of the books?"

"They were stolen cousin," Adelram replied with the air of a man who had to answer this question many times before.

Shawna frowned. "I see. That wasn't very nice." She began to hum and sway back and forth to a tune only she could hear.

"She's been like this the entire time you've been beating each other to a pulp. It's making finding the Talal ritual chamber quite vexing," Illusionist Maeve explained and she frowned at the other woman. "I don't think spending all of these years alone was kind to her health."

Lykos agreed wholeheartedly, remembering how convinced this woman is of him being her missing child. Wisely choosing to hold his tongue on voicing that thought he instead questioned Illusionist Maeve. "The Talal ritual chamber?"

"Aye. Most of the noble houses have one as it was where they did their private rites to the Goddesses or trained youth away from the peons at the Citadel. So long as the Talal ritual chamber is as untouched as the rest of the manor it will suffice for your instruction in magic." He nodded before ducking his head as Adelram took another swing at it. Turning to glare at the older man he realized his mistake and turned back to Maeve.

"Illusionist Maeve are there any ways of finding such a chamber?" Lykos asked as respectfully as he could and was pleased to hear Adelram grunt in approval. Illusionist Maeve too was pleased as she answered positively.

"Indeed there are but they're far too advanced for you at the moment. Magics used upon the human body are the most dangerous as one false step may leave you crippled for life. Or worse." Lykos swallowed painfully considering Illusionist Maeve's words before nodding in understanding.

"Our best hope was Dowager Talal over there as she should know it but her mind is scattered in the past. I had hoped to find a journal or grimoire within the library that would hold the location but no such luck. Instead I will have to spend days walking the grounds casting magic in the hope of stumbling upon it." Illusionist Maeve's tone left no mystery as to what she thought of that idea.

Lykos considered their options and felt impatience clogging his mind, his desire to learn magic overpowering everything else. As his eyes wandered the library they fell upon his mother singing softly to herself by the window. With a grimace he knew what he had to do and walked towards the swaying woman.

"Mother?" he asked softly, cringing at the way her face brightened with joy. "Mother, we're looking for the Talal ritual chamber, do you know where it is?"

Shawna shook her head sadly and stroked his arm fondly. "I do not but fret not. There should be journals or a map with the layout of the grounds up in the master's study." She gestured towards the second floor of the library, whose access was reached by an iron spiral staircase behind some shelves. The quartet quickly made their way up to the second floor but confusion and frustration reigned when there was naught but a few almost empty shelves to see.

"So where is the master's study mother?" Lykos asked as they examined the lack of doorway. She smiled at their confusion.

"It is hidden behind one of these shelves, although I cannot remember which. Too many painful memories...." she trailed off with a thousand yard stare. Lykos awkwardly patted her arm before turning his attention to the shelves with Adelram and Maeve. After several moments Illusionist Maeve cried out with success and pointed towards a small indent in the wood in the shape of an eagles head.

"Your ring boy, put it in the indent!" Illusionist Maeve ordered him as they gathered around. Lykos restrained himself from rolling his eyes and instead carefully put his hand up against the wood, the cut stone of the ring fitting perfectly into the indent. With a soft click the entire shelf slid backwards half an inch before the screech of rusted joints met their ears. "Adelram, you and the boy push it open," she ordered when neither man moved.

The two men moved towards the wooden shelf and carefully pushed as hard as they dared, taking care not to damage the aged wood. With a few great heaves the doorway was exposed and they could enter the dark room.

Illusionist Maeve waved a hand and old torches and candles lit up along the walls revealing a long room running the length of the manor. There were two large tables in the center of the room, one covered in maps and charts and the other covered in an odd collection of instruments and gear. Many smaller tables and shelves lined the edges of the room and were covered in dusty books and diaries of the Talal family through time. Each of these tomes were covered in worn covers marked with the passing years and changing owners. This was the legacy of House Talal.

They spread out through the room carefully examining each of the artifacts. The gear was barely adequate, broken and rusted as it had not been cared for in years but various instruments were of interest if Illusionist Maeve's reaction was telling.

"These are early attempts at storing magic!" she cried out excitedly while holding up several small glass balls. Within each one an interesting assortment of metallic wires and burnt out crystals filled in a chaotic manner. "They all failed of course but they showed us it was possible to put our magic into another object beyond mere enchantments! Why with more research we could learn so much."

Adelram rolled his eyes before explaining to Lykos and Shawna. "A few decades ago a trader from Istani raved about traveling to a distant land where great mechanical beasts roamed, containing the souls and magics of the deceased. After a decade of effort and research the Citadel washed its hand of it and declared it to be a fool's tale. Similar tales pop up every few years but all attempts have ended exploding like a Tainted Charger."

Lykos chuckled as the old woman cradled the devices as a mother would her child but his attention was drawn towards the table of maps. There were highly detailed sketches of Mycenae and each quarter and he realized by the seal on the bottom that they had been taken from the Citadel. One of the smaller maps was a rather well done hand drawn map of Hearthome, signed with the name Leon. Shawna was stroking the signature lovingly.

"Your father was always so clever," she whispered as he joined her. "He was always learning or creating or training, never stopping for food or rest at times. It's what drew me to him, he saw that there was always something greater that we had to aspire to, that we could not submit to an mediocre life. It's why he rebelled."

Lykos noticed that her eyes were no longer aware of her surroundings as they were lost in some forgotten memory. He took the fragile woman by the arm and led her to a nearby armchair that released a small cloud of dust when he pressed her onto it.

"He walked the streets of this kingdom and was sickened by what he saw. While no where near as bad as Svellheim, slavery was still prevalent here. And while the Acolytes serving the Goddesses do not hold as much power as they do in Istani, they still enacted terrible crimes in their name. So he gathered his allies, our friends and family, and began to wage a war against the corruption that plagued this kingdom.

"At first it seemed to go so well. He fought bravely on the streets with sword and magic, never fearing in combating a wrong. He took down dangerous Tainted plaguing the lands outside the walls. He battled with word and wit with the other lords and ladies, never giving into their demands while pushing forwards with his own. It seemed like he had such a great chance of success that the future looked brighter for a moment. But you can't push forever without something pushing back.

"There were many in this kingdom who benefited from the pain and misery of their fellow man and Leon made an enemy of them all. They rallied behind Kopanos of House Kolos, a sorcerer of great strength and weak morals. The kingdom almost devolved into total war when Leon sued for peace, he had no desire to tear apart all of the work he had done. He meet with Kopanos in the Citadel, with only a small number of soldiers with him as they were under the rules of parlay," Shawna spat vehemently and Lykos almost jumped at the vitriol in her voice. Adelram and Maeve had joined him without his notice and were listening attentively.

"Their food and drink were poisoned and they were succumbing quickly. Leon used his magic in an attempt to purge himself but only succeed in buying himself a few moments of time. He was gasping on his knees as they took the lives of his men and he struggled to even stand. However taking the lives of his men in front of him caused him such rage that he attacked with all of the magic he possessed. When the light vanished he had taken Kopanos' left eye and left many dead.

"I was there. Leon wanted me with him to prove that he could be reasonable, that he was determined to start a family. He wanted his pregnant wife to be a symbol he told me, that in all of this darkness they could still find hope. I saw his eyes fade as they slit his throat. I raged against my captors but there was little I could do. And in the horror of all horrors I went into labor in the fortress of our enemy.

"Those hours of labor were long and painful. As my body prepared to bring new life into the world Kopanos ordered his army to kill hundreds, thousands of others. With each hour that passed another soldier would walk in reporting the deaths of our allies, our friends, that had fallen. Each soldier might as well struck me a blow for the terrible grief I felt. Finally as the night neared dawn my beautiful baby boy was born.

"I looked at you through weary eyes and saw my husbands hope be taken away from me by his hated enemy. He took you from the room and I could hear the ferocious sounds of Tainted and your screams as you were led closer and closer. And then there was a terrible tearing of flesh as your screams were cut off. I raged and cried and screamed against my captors but I could not go to you and sometime later Kolos returned with a bloody bundle.

"He tossed a bag of bloody bones at me! I could feel my world shattering as I beheld the remains. He talked then at great length but I never answered or listened to what he said. All I could do was stare at the horrible image in my arms. Finally he ordered his guards to take me back to Hearthome.

"I was dimly aware of the horrible crimes going on in the city, of the raping, pillaging, and violence. I could hear the cries for aid go unanswered and the stone ran red with the blood of innocents. After that long, torturous march we arrived here and I was dragged inside. The servants who didn't run were swiftly killed and their bodies thrown over the terrace into the Marsh below. Much of the gold and silver was taken, along with the books, but the majority of the furniture was left behind. The men then surrounded me and I prepared myself to be raped and killed in my home but it never happened.

"The men told me that soldiers would be positioned at the gate and that should I require food I was to ask them. Then they left. I wondered why Kopanos ordered them to leave me untouched and as I sat trembling with exhaustion in the hall I realized why. The bones that I had been staring did not belong to my child as I thought for they were too strong and firm to be a newborns. As I stared at their shape I realized that my son was still alive and that *he* had him. My life was to be a punishment, to never know my son.

"I struggled to my feet despite my exhaustion and made my way to the gate. The two soldiers standing guard though would not allow me to pass and dragged me back into the manor. I kicked and raged but they bore my attacks and left me alone in the dark with a bag bones belonging to a child not my own. As I cried in helplessness I fell asleep.

"That night though, as the kingdom delved into chaos and violence around me I dreamed a most peculiar dream. A man with sharp pale eyes appeared before me and encouraged me to hold on for my son would one day return to me. He told me to place the Talal awakening stone in that bedroom and that everything would go as planned. I waited for so long I feared I would die before I saw my son but then the most miraculous thing happened, my son came home."

Shawna's eyes shown brightly as she stared up at Lykos and he felt his own eyes grow blurry. Wiping them he looked down at Shawna, no his mother, and felt a warm feeling grow inside of him. He didn't know how or why he had been in that slave mine but he was with his family once more and that's all that mattered to him. He smiled at his mother and she smiled back and their little family reunion was perfect.

"I found the ritual chamber!" Illusionist Maeve's excited voice sliced through the tender moment like a knife through rotten rope and mother and son stared at the ancient woman in disbelief. "Oh that was a family moment wasn't it?"

Adelram's harsh coughing did little to conceal his laughter.

Chapter Nine

Lykos followed Illusionist Maeve as the little old woman crept through Hearthome with her cane clicking every other step. Adelram had elected to stay with Shawna, to keep her company and to go through Leon's things, searching for useful items or information. Lykos allowed himself to feel a happy glow at the thought of having living family. Even the gruff Adelram gave him a warm feeling of belonging.

As they walked through the kitchen and entered the pantry he admired the architecture of his family's home. The arches adorned with cobwebs no longer looked depressing, indeed he could spy a hidden nobility concealed in their stone recesses. As he stood among empty shelves and barrels he smiled to himself.

"Stop standing around grinning like a loon boy, help me find the entrance! It should be somewhere by these casks." Illusionist Maeve's voice pulled him out of his introspection and he noticed the old woman standing by the wall of casks, each almost as big as he. Looking over the shorter woman's head he looked at the map in her hands and examined the wall. Reaching out he grabbed the handle on the spigot and pulled it down but was disappointed when a secret passage did not open.

"I expected something to happen," he said, releasing the handle. Illusionist Maeve rolled her eyes and grabbed it herself. Turning the handle instead of pulling it down resulted with a click and a small crawl space opening between the two casks. He followed the elderly woman into the dark space.

With a flick of Illusionist Maeve's wrists the torches were set ablaze illuminating the large room. Lykos looked around impressed at the carvings and dusty weapons along the walls and said as much, "this is an impressive room."

If he had to describe the look Illusionist Maeve gave him at that exact moment he wouldn't be able to explain just which was worse. The fact that with a single look she was questioning every minuscule scrap of intelligence he possessed or that she was wondering if killing him was worth the hassle of hiding the body. It was an unsettling expression to witness much less have directed at himself.

"This is merely an ante chamber, a distraction to prevent any outsiders from looking further. You can tell because while seemingly advanced, most of these rune etchings are meaningless dribble with no real meaning. The true ritual chamber entrance is hidden here somewhere. Now start looking boy," Illusionist Maeve ordered menacingly.

Lykos meekly followed her order and began to examine the walls of the room. Now that he was closer to the runes he realized they were indeed a dull history of House Talal and he found his eyes wandering. As he followed the lines along the walls he saw many indents in the stone, as if someone had taken a small hammer and beaten a small rock into the stone. With a flash of realization he realized all of the indents matched his ring.

"I think I figured it out! These indents all over the walls, they match the one that opened Leon's study!" Illusionist Maeve nodded in approval and agreement but her next word brought his pleased mood crashing down.

"Then which indent opens the door?" Her knowing smirk deflated him further. "If you can't figure it out we could always wait until you try each and every single one."

"You already know which one! Just tell me and we can begin with my training!" he pleaded, trying to convince her. She merely shook her head and smirked at him.

He grumbled under his breathe and turned once more to stare at the walls. He began to pace them, growing more and more frustrated as the answer continued to elude him. He stopped at random points, placing his ring in the indents to no avail. With each failure his anger grew and he angrily raised his fist to strike at the wall before him.

"Stop you fool!" Lykos found a strong force gripping his hand and pulled against it angrily with no success. Turning around he saw Illusionist Maeve with her hand outstretched, obviously using magic to arrest his movement. "You have much to learn if you cannot even ask for aid!"

"You refused to help me instructor," he angrily replied.

"No I refused to give you the answer. If you but asked me to provide teaching you would find it readily available," she replied sternly before releasing him from her magic. He slowly lowered his arm and felt the anger bleed out from his body to be replaced by shame.

"Instructor Maeve will you guide me?" Never had Lykos spoken that phrase, never had he asked another for aid in such a manner. Not after learning so many hard lessons in this cruel world. The Logwind's crew had freely offered their knowledge, as basic as it was, but this was on a whole other level. Magic after all separated the ruling elite from the common folk.

"Why don't you try this spot?" Illusionist Maeve's feet moved to the side revealing an indent with two lines crossing through it. Pushing aside his annoyance at her for concealing the spot, he pressed his ring to the floor and was pleased to hear the clicking of metal and grinding of stone. The section of floor he knelt upon jerked and lowered slightly, becoming the first of many steps leading down into darkness.

"Get up off the floor apprentice we have things to do!" Illusionist Maeve's cackling did not put him at ease as he followed her down into the darkness. With one hand tracing the rough stone walls to his left, the light from the false chamber slowly vanished as they followed the curving tunnel downwards. Up ahead he heard the labored breathes of Illusionist Maeve as she stepped in a puddle and likewise found himself stepping in it a moment later. The moist air coming into his nose confirmed that where ever they were going it was wet.

Finally, after several long moments, he saw light up ahead. With eager footsteps he caught up to the revealed figure of Illusionist Maeve as they entered a large underground cavern to the sound of rushing water. In front of them was a vast space with several waterfalls pouring from the ceiling meeting in a great pool down below. Natural walls and carved pillars separated the space into several smaller caves. In each of those caves was a platform rising up from the swirling water below but with no obvious way to access any of them. The center platform itself was covered in smoother carvings, worn down after years of use with a small stone bridge leading to it. A series of holes in the ceiling let in sunlight, illuminating the cave and the plant life growing on the walls. Lykos was awed.

"Is this the Talal ritual chamber?" he asked, stepping over a small stream and onto the center platform. He walked along the edge, staring into the swirling water below but found himself pulled away by Illusionist Maeve who was giving him a hard look.

"Mind the edge boy, I don't know where that water exits. It'd be unpleasant to have to explain to Dowager Talal how her son disappeared into the depths of the earth," she warned sternly. "This is indeed the Talal ritual chamber, it has a strong connection to each of the elements and you can see where your ancestors carved their history onto these stones." She tapped the stones beneath their feet with her cane.

"You mean these carvings actually are our history? My history? What about the ones in the false chamber?" He knelt to examine the stones beneath him but could make no sense of the archaic writing. There was a reference of a great exodus from a dark force that sounded vaguely familiar but he could make no heads nor tails of the next part concerning someone called The Great Meddler.

"They're probably the common history. Something that if an outsider managed to read they would believe it was the full truth of the Talal family and wouldn't search further. I'm more interested in the chamber itself, these lesser platforms are curious," she trailed off as she examined the closest one, some lengths away. Lykos glanced at them but could see no easy way to access them.

"How are you supposed to reach them?" he asked looking for handholds on the walls. They were slick with water and moss and completely inaccessible.

"Unless I am mistaken I believe you are supposed to use earth magic to create a bridge to each of them. A test of skill, endurance, and faith as it were."

"Faith?"

"Aye faith. For you must walk upon your creation and trust that it will not drop you into the water below." She gestured towards the swirling waters and he felt apprehension about training in such a dangerous room.

"How do you ensure you don't have an accidental swim? It seems like it would be folly to have such a design."

"This chamber tests those who seek to use it, as it should. Magic is a dangerous force, always vying to seduce you while waiting for the best moment to destroy you. If you don't keep a rigid handle on yourself, if you do not employ self-control, you will quickly find yourself a corpse or worse."

"This chamber," Illusionist Maeve gestured grandly, "is a masterpiece and in my hands I will use it to turn you into a sorcerer without peer. And then I will use you to enact my revenge."

"Your revenge?" Lykos grew alarmed at the passion in her voice.

"Yes against my traitorous family and the fools they bow to. Stop worrying boy my enemies are your enemies, Kopanos of Kolos has done many wrongs to many people. If you opened your eyes you'll see the suffering goes much further than just yourself."

"I have seen the suffering with my own eyes! I've lived it! I am not deaf to the cries of beggars and swindlers upon the kingdoms streets but what can I do? I am one man!" he protested.

"You will be vengeance. Your father died for a cause that did not have a chance, he fought because he thought his sacrifice would bring peace. Instead of becoming a martyr upon his death he was branded a traitor! And your family with him! Do not fool yourself for one moment that his enemies will not strike at you because you are young, do not delude yourself to think that you are safe! They are plotting terrible deeds and you must be willing to meet them head on."

He stared at Illusionist Maeve while the endless streams of water passed them by. He thought of his decision to stay, to pretend to be Shawna's son, to the moment where he thought he might actually be her child. As much as he wished to run away, to hide in some forgotten part of this kingdom he knew it would not matter. One way or another he would be found and regardless of his personal feelings and he would not be allowed to be an observer in the coming conflict.

"Where shall we begin Illusionist Maeve?" he asked in reluctant defeat.

The aged woman smiled a cruel smile and answered, "here." And his world dissolved into darkness.

Chapter Ten

He crouched immediately, his hands spread out to feel the ground beneath his feet to reassure himself it was still there. Feeling the worn edges of runes beneath his hands he felt reassured until his body began to numb. All too swiftly he could not feel the stone or the flecks of water from the waterfalls on his skin. He was lost in a prison he could not see or feel.

"Lykos," Illusionist Maeve's voice seemed to echo around him as she dragged out his name. He tried to move his arms to find her but couldn't tell if they were moving or not. He snarled in displeasure and was horrified to find his hearing disappear slowly as well. "Lykos. If you haven't figured it out yet I'm using illusions to hide your senses from you. You must find me in order to complete this exercise. Try to be mindful of the edge."

He once again snarled at the infernal witch but no sound reached his ears. Unable to see, feel, or hear Illusionist Maeve's task felt impossible and he nearly began to rampage around in anger but his fear of falling into the water below halted him. Instead he tried to determine how he could find the wretched old woman without endangering himself. As he stood the smell of fresh water and air left his nose and he nearly panicked thinking his breathe had stopped. Fortunately air still came through his mouth but he did not know how long that would last.

It has to do with magic, he thought. He could still feel the tense muscle like feeling of his magic under his skin, despite the illusions.

With his senses blocked as they were it was as if his magic was thrown in sharp relief, with nothing to distract him from its full power. With a start he realized he could see the magic beneath his flesh with his own eyes, a dark blue and purple coiling and shifting like a snake upon the sand. Lykos gleefully felt it stretch and flex and let its never ending movements and strength consume his attention.

He felt a sharp slap across his face suddenly and the sudden feeling of touch snapped his concentration. He tried to feel the floor again but was met with the numbing feeling once more. "Do not waste time, we have many things to do. Now break my illusion." Illusionist Maeve's voice returned suddenly with the sound of rushing water and vanished just as fast.

His excitement at seeing magic became determined concentration as he focused once more upon it. Rather than gazing into its form he glanced beyond it. He could see his arms and legs take shape slowly through a black haze, illuminated by this light within him. The stone beneath him was dark but the runes the Talal family carved onto them glowed brightly, each one blazed as a star beneath him. He looked beyond the stone as he stood up, trusting his magic to guide him, but gasped at the sight before him.

The previously dark space was alive with colors, moving and shifting like his magic. Slow moving browns shifted underneath his feet and through the walls, endless cascades of blues poured past him in never ending of streams of light. And in the air all around them danced carefree whites, with no pattern to their madness. As he stared in awe at their majesty a series of reds sprung into being from a still dark corner of the platform, and launched themselves at the walls. There they blossomed into a ferocious blaze of rising power.

However Lykos turned his attention back to that still dark corner of the platform and focused more and more upon it. Slowly, unwillingly, the darkness yielded to his sight and he beheld Illusion-ist Maeve's magic. It was a regal purple with streaks of cruel black through it, moving methodically, like a Tainted in the hunt. And then he suddenly found his sight restored.

The magic of the world vanished and he was left blinking spots from his vision. Reeling at the loss of so much beauty he cried out and fell to his knees. Illusionist Maeve moved over to him and of-fered her hand.

"That was magic in its most primal form. It is full of deep mysteries that are dangerous to those who explore its depths but the rewards are promising to the few who are cautious and wise. Congratulations Lykos, few have ever grasped their magic and seen through my illusions so quickly under my tutelage. You might ac-tually aspire to something."

It took him several long moments to find his voice as he stared up at her. "How?" he managed to finally say, grasping her hand to pull himself up.

"Most find the material world too distracting to ever see magic. That is why despite it being unlocked in so many of the noble hous-es few train it past physical combat." There was no mistaking the scorn in her tone. "They do not even scratch the surface of our gift, they play with parlor tricks and think it makes them better. A sin-gle trained mage is worth an army."

"An army?" Lykos repeated in astonishment.

"An army. Paired with a creative mind and an iron will there are very few limits as to what can be achieved with magic. It is why mages usually die from poison or treachery, a fight between two ac-complished sorcerers can create a desolation."

Lykos reeled from this information but felt a hunger grow in-side of him. He vowed he would become one of the most danger-ous mages in the land, no the world! Never again would he have to fear where his next meal came from or a beating from some low life guard. He would become a force to be reckoned with. Illusionist Maeve must have seen the naked hunger in his eyes for she gave him a dark smile.

"Ah yes, keep that desire apprentice. Feed that burning flame inside of you and constantly seek to understand the magic of the world. However you must pay heed. Without control the magic may run away from your grasp and consume you. You would become a mindless beast whose only desire would be destruction." Her warning caused him to shudder at the idea of magic consuming him. It sounded similar to a Tainted beast but chained within his body. Voicing this thought Illusionist Maeve laughed.

"Aye it is like those beasts that hunt mankind but we will train you. You will learn the control necessary to do magnificent things. Now prepare yourself!"

She again took his senses from him and ordered him to find her with magic. She would often move behind him, hindering his progress with distractions or suddenly overwhelming his senses with images of mutilated corpses or piercing screams. He persevered no matter how much her illusions caused him to tremble but they began to wear on him. Finally it became too much and he collapsed to the floor holding his head as pain and exhaustion fell upon him.

"Adequate," she told him in a flat voice. "However I hope you last longer in the future. Time is of the essence but for now calm yourself now with deep breathes."

Lykos did as he was told and slowed his troubled breathe. His magic, seemed almost lethargic to his touch and concerned he questioned Illusionist Maeve about it.

"It is not surprising, it has been used almost constantly this day and it has had little time to rest. It is like a muscle. As you use it, it grows more powerful but it takes time. Unlike a muscle you do not have to worry about it breaking or leaving you, so revel in its use.

Now that it is free it will only fail you when you attempt something beyond your strength."

They made their way back up into Hearthome and in the silence he contemplated his magic. It moved sluggishly within his body, no longer mending his cuts and bruises and he thought back to Adelram's injuries and his rapid recovery.

"Earlier today I wounded Adelram and his injuries recovered seemingly instantly. However mine are still unhealed. Is it because he uses his magic more instructor?" Lykos asked.

Illusionist Maeve shook her head. "Both yes and no. Adelram's magic matches his actions, he cares little for the grander displays of magic as he knows they're beyond his mind and so he focus solely on the magics that can be worked upon the body. Healing, strengthening, agility, all are great boons to a soldier of his caliber.

"However he is weaker because of it. While his magic may focus solely upon his body it grows slower for it. You'll find in the coming months that your strength will match and even exceed his as we force your magic to its limits everyday. Another aspect you must be aware that as you do certain acts more and more often, the magic within you gets used to doing them. It will strive to find more efficient ways to do things, leaving you a greater pool of magic while doing so with less.

"So while Adelram's magic within his body is working at an inhuman level of efficiency it is still working with a smaller pool of magic. In even a few months your magic will match or exceed his own even if achieving his mastery over body magics will take you decades."

Lykos pondered her words but pushed for further clarification. "What do you mean some magics are beyond him instructor? My mother said something similar and I'm not sure what either of you mean by it."

"Some practitioners are partial to illusions, like myself," Illusionist Maeve said while creating the image of a snarling Tainted Charger in front of them. The great beast roared and charged at them but vanished before contact. "While others can create life like golems or elemental storms. You, I believe will be exceptionally gifted in the creation of portals especially after your earlier display but time will tell. However just because you are partial to some magics does not mean you cannot master others. Preconceived ideas and beliefs hinder the learning process, as do hearsay and traditions. But every sorcerer and sorceresses in our history have all had one thing in common, do you care to guess what that is?"

"They learned it all instructor."

"The learned everything they could," she corrected. "Knowledge has been gained and lost repeatedly throughout our history which is why your families library is so important. The missing grimoires of your forefathers contained secrets to techniques lost to the ages, that granted them an edge over their enemies. Enchantments imprinted upon objects, abilities of past masters, magic is infinitely variable and powerful because it can be used in so many different ways. Hence the need to record it."

"Do other families have grimoires as well?" Lykos asked as they entered kitchen. Hearing low voices from the next room over they entered a large and spacious dining room adorned with dust and cobwebs. Adelram and Shawna sat at the stout wooden table talking quietly and both rose when the pair entered the room. His mother smiled at him and he tentatively returned it before turning his hungry eyes to the simple fare on the table.

"They most certainly do and if you see the opportunity to steal one you should take it," Illusionist Maeve ordered and Lykos nodded as the four of them sat at the table.

"What should he steal?" Shawna asked sharply, glaring at Illusionist Maeve as the elderly woman tore into a hunk of bread.

"The grimoires that have been taken from this manor and the ones belonging to those who posses them," Illusionist Maeve answered simply as Lykos hungrily dug into the simple meal. It was most likely his imagination but he could almost feel energy returning to his body with each bite.

"He will not become a thief!" she declared fiercely. Three snorts answered her. She ignored the collective response and continued. "I will not have him put himself in danger to retrieve a few dusty books!"

"Foolish woman! You may be more blind to magic than your cousin but I would have expected a lady of a noble house to know the value of a grimoire!"

"Value or not I will not risk my son to this harebrained scheme!"

"I think you should reconsider cousin," Adelram's voice cut through Shawna and Maeve's argument like a knife. Lykos' eyes rapidly darted from one person to another as he consumed the forgotten meal. Illusionist Maeve look satisfied that Adelram agreed with her and sat back smugly to gnaw on her bread.

"What did you say?" Shawna's voice and eyes were sharply focused on Adelram and for the first time Lykos could see a woman who would stand tall and strong at the head of a house.

"I think you should reconsider," Adelram spoke softly but Shawna's eyes widened in betrayal.

"Do you wish my son to be taken from me once more? To have him crippled before he can grow old? I will not have it no I will not!"

"Enough!" Adelram roared, silencing the dining room. Lykos and Maeve paused in their eating and stared at him who only had a eyes for a shocked Shawna. "We cannot coddle the boy Shawna, not now, not ever. We must make him strong lest he be torn apart by our enemies and every advantage will help. If he sees an opportunity to learn the secrets of our enemies he should take it or he'll die like Leon did!"

Shawna deflated as Adelram finished and wilted in her chair. She trembled slightly before composing herself, straightening once more and giving a slight nod of deference to Adelram. "Very well."

All four returned to their meal quietly and for several moments all that could be heard was the clink of a goblet or knife. However as Lykos stared at his mother she did not return to her slightly crazed self, not fully. There was now a bar of iron straightening her posture and he looked at her in admiration. She turned towards him.

"Why are you slouching? And where are your table manners young man! Use a knife and fork and chew with your mouth shut!"

May the Valkyries have mercy on my soul, he groaned in thought.

Chapter Eleven

The inevitable march of time passes regardless of the wishes of mortals. Lykos found the coming weeks to be endless days of training with his three mentors, always learning some new technique or skill that would prove invaluable in the future.

Each morning Adelram would wake him in some cruel and unusual manner. Sometimes he would throw a knife at his sleeping form. Other times he would flip the bed, sending him to the floor painfully. One time he threw a bag of Tainted Gnawers at Lykos who awakened to feel their sharp teeth biting into his flesh. However Lykos was quickly learning how to adapt to Adelram's wake up calls and began to react instinctively to the varied assaults.

Regardless of his success or not he would find himself out in the garden training under the rising sun. Each day Adelram would pick a weapon they would spar with and Lykos would have to find where his instructor had hidden his, all while the fiend attacked him. He would often find it too late as being attacked would hinder anyone's concentration yet his skill in searching and defending himself unarmed grew each day. However Adelram soon noticed a peculiar fact about him that he had hoped none of the three adults would comment on.

"Your pain tolerance is impressive for someone of your youth. Explain," Adelram ordered during a brief lull in their combat. Lykos was leaning heavily on his sword as his many cuts and bruises slowly healed. He grimaced as the cool morning air fogged his breathe.

"I worked on an airship. Not all of the ports we landed in were friendly," Lykos said hoping to mislead Adelram.

"Bullshit." No such luck.

Lykos scowled as he stared at the ground in front of him. "The mines of Svellheim were not easy," he eventually muttered. He was surprised when he felt a heavy hand land on his shoulder and for it to squeeze him gently. He looked up to see Adelram frowning at him.

"Have no shame in your past, least of all for actions not of your own. Instead use the lessons of yesterday to teach you today so that you might succeed tomorrow. Besides you should feel proud." Adelram grinned at his questioning look. "Many experienced soldiers have no where near your level of pain tolerance and often quit before they've reached their limits. You keep rising up to my torments, something they rarely did."

Lykos felt a brief flash of pride and smiled at Adelram before flailing his arms wildly. While he had been distracted Adelram had tripped him, throwing him on his back. He knocked away Adelram's descending sword and lunged forward in a tackle, dragging the laughing man to the ground to rub his face in the dirt.

Adelram would occasionally give him an errand to run after their training sessions. Usually running to some merchant or bar to get Adelram's spirits. A few times to hunt a Tainted that bothered a local merchant or farmer. However he had to be quick for with each turn of the hourglass Adelram would add one hourglass to their duels when he returned. Lykos was given no chance to rest and found the activities grueling if rewarding.

Once the morning had passed he would teach Lykos how to combat certain foes over a light lunch, showing him how to find the weak points in Tainted armor or human chain mail. While his body rested his mind was tested but Adelram's teachings were still far less brutal than Illusionist Maeve's who claimed his afternoons.

Retreating to the Talal ritual chamber Lykos would be deadened to his senses to train him to more easily feel his magic. His magic more readily responded to his calls as time passed and soon he found it simple to bring it forth with the "minor" distractions Illusionist Maeve played upon him. However as his ability grew so too did the details of her illusions and all too often he found them indistinguishable from reality. Terrible Tainted, horrific mutilations upon man, being suffocated by water, drinking fire, the illusions she played upon his mind were not kind.

Illusionist Maeve slowly began to teach Lykos how to manipulate the elements, teasing existing magic into doing his will. It was not uncommon for fire to singe his skin and clothes, sparks to shock him without warning, or sudden downpours to soak him. It was difficult work that often backfired spectacularly on him but he learned from his mistakes and looked forward to the lessons each day.

"These are the building blocks of all magic," Illusionist Maeve told him one day after the stone he was working with shattered, sending out shards that cut his skin. "Magic is connected in a beautiful web that holds itself up against the forces of the world. If you master the basic strands holding up that web you can begin to branch off of them, learning new methods and techniques as you create your own masterpiece."

He slowly began to understand her teachings. How water quenched fire who fed off of air. Of how lightning was halted by earth but quickened by water. Air combined with water in a magnificent storm or dried out the earth cracking its form. Each aspect both strengthened and weakened the others, equal in all regards. It was beautiful watching their chaotic forms interact.

However each element translated well into combat as well. Earth was defensive, providing sturdy walls to take cover behind or traps to snare. Air empowered or hindered movement, allowing you to speed up yourself or slow down your foes. Water was life, allowing for healing or poisoning, working in balance with one another. Fire was offensive, burning friend and foe alike. However Lykos did not quite understand lightning, although he believed it related to illusions.

"What is lightning Instructor Maeve?" he asked her one day as she instructed him in bringing up earthen walls. His attempts were laughable, thin structures that the old woman took a fiendish delight in smashing with magically thrown rocks. The old sorceresses paused mid throw, allowing the rocks she was holding up with her magic to clatter to the floor.

"Why do you ask?" she replied and Lykos explained his thoughts and understanding of magic to her. She nodded with approval.

"You are mostly correct but do not think you cannot use water for defense or earth for speed. Is the ocean not unassailable? Is a landslide not quick? They are only limited by your mind and ability even if they do translate remarkably well to certain aspects. As to your question, lightning is often considered the pure embodiment of thought."

"Of thought?" Lykos asked in confusion. Lightning didn't seem very thoughtful.

"Aye thought. You have not yet observed natural lightning with your magic have you?" Lykos nodded in confirmation as she continued. "It is a beautiful crystallization of energy that rips through the world, almost simple in its power. However this particular pattern of energy is not solely beheld only in nature, nay if you peer deep into someones eyes you can see an endless storm of magic in their minds. From the poorest peasant to the highest noble everyone is the same."

"If you could control lightning could you control someone's thoughts or actions instructor?" Lykos asked slightly fearful that such an action had been done to him. Illusionist Maeve gave him a small smirk but replied in the negative.

"Many have tried and failed to control the thoughts and actions of others. The closest you can ever get is the field of illusions and even then you are manipulating their senses. A sufficiently trained mind can overcome the illusions of magic, flesh, or words."

"Flesh or words?"

"There is more than one way to combat a foe. You could use magic, blade, or arrows. Or you could seduce them or someone else who in turn turns against your target. You could sway public opinion with the correct words and even start a war if you but only tried. Logic and reasoning are two critical aspects of your training, do not discount them simply because one piece of information negates them."

His lessons in magic continued under Illusionist Maeve's care and as she believed he would he grasped the concept of portals much more easily than any of the others. She had him train until exhaustion, at first only a few minutes were possible but as his strength grew, hours were spent in that chamber each day. His mastery over portals grew slowly, their fragile states easily broken by outside influence and the few times they remained stable, his exit strategy left something to be desired for.

"Foolish boy!" Illusionist Maeve spat as she picked herself off the ground, having thrown herself to safety as he flew through the air. As for Lykos, he was holding his head where he had bashed it into the hard stone beneath their feet. "You must be aware of your surroundings before you enter and after you exit the portals, lest you find yourself impaling yourself upon a sword!"

"I tried instructor but it's disorientating," Lykos replied as he stood up. "I'm not used to the shift in perception when I enter and exit them."

"That's why you practice foolish boy! Again! Perhaps this time we'll be fortunate and you'll land in the water!" Lykos groaned but had long since learned the futility of arguing. He continued his lessons under her tutelage regardless of personal injury attained.

Shawna had taken to teaching him all about the Talal family and the other noble houses of Mycenae. He learned how House Talal was one of the original settlers of the kingdom and helped designed the plans for each expansion, each quarter. Many of those blue prints were archived in Leon's study and showed the true scope and scale of their construction, the alleys, sewers, and aqueducts that crossed the kingdom. He was pleased to discover that his family had the foresight to place many secret passages through each wall and into and out of the kingdom for safety.

His mother also taught him how to manage House Talal's finances but things were truly in a sorry state. With no true businesses under their name, no protection money being paid, and their vast estate pillaged by the other houses, it was no wonder for the decrepit state of Hearthome. Lykos talked with Shawna, Maeve, and Adelram as to possible solutions but was told to wait until he was stronger. He complied.

These lessons were also accompanied by a crash course in politics and etiquette to his immense displeasure. Living in the mines had ill prepared him for the rigors of a dinner party, of paying tribute to the host before taking part of the meal. Adelram and Maeve would often play the part of dinner guests and took great pleasure in taking offense at every slip up he made. Still these meals were often paired with stories of noteworthy individuals and historical events and he found himself enjoying them regardless.

Not all was well of course. As the spring air gave way to summer heat he became aware of the precarious position they were. While there were no longer Stultus soldiers posted at the entrance of Hearthome they patrolled the rest of Pyrgos, lording their might over the common folk. He knew they had to do something to help others but what?

And how?

Chapter Twelve

"Who rules the kingdom?" Adelram asked one evening. Lykos, Adelram, and Shawna were quietly conversing in the parlor, enjoying a private family moment that Lykos was quickly learning to long for. He considered the question carefully before answering.

"We have no singular ruler. The noble houses control territories, usually entire quarters, and provide security for the whole kingdom against the Tainted," he answered. Adelram nodded in approval.

"And who controls the Citadel?"

Lykos frowned in thought. "No one?" he answered tentatively.

"No. House Kolos controls the Citadel and with it this kingdom."

Lykos was confused. "Why would that matter? I thought the noble houses ran this kingdom?"

"They do but the Citadel has always had an important role in Mycenae. It's where this kingdom was founded for one, where we spread out once we established ourselves on these mountains. It has the strongest and thickest defenses that have only been reinforced throughout the centuries we have lived here but it is important for two simple facts: it's where the Citadel guards are trained and where the wealthiest houses reside."

"The old bastard is right," Illusionist Maeve suddenly spoke, the illusion of an empty chair fading into her wizened form knitting calmly besides Shawna. Lykos and Adelram nearly leaped to their feet with swords drawn before calming down. "The Citadel guard is the closest thing to a unified army Mycenae has, the forces of every house must yield to their superiority lest sanctions be placed against them. However it's their force of mages that truly establish their power.

"While many noble houses train their heirs privately, bastards are unsurprisingly common among the nobility. Rather than contaminate their heirs with the influence of common blood they send the bastards off to the Citadel to be trained. The instructors at the Citadel use crude, inefficient methods to train masses of mages, by their standards you'd be nearly ready to graduate. Still, even a dozen poorly trained mages could wreck a large amount of damage, imagine what hundreds could do?"

Illusionist Maeve paused in her speech to undo a row of knots in her knitting. Adelram continued where she left off. "There is also the matter of wealth. No army can breach the Citadel's walls and no Tainted beast can reach its streets. So the wealthy and powerful merchants and nobles maintain their homes and businesses there, a status symbol if you will. However the constantly replenishing army of mages combined with an unending flow of gold into the Citadel means that whoever controls that territory effectively rule the kingdom."

"Who is House Kolos, who would be more than happy to kill me simply for being Leon's son," Lykos stated in understanding. It was a disquieting thought. Time passed in companionable silence as each person reflected on their reality, only Illusionist Maeve's knitting needles making any sound. Lykos pondered the challenge they faced, an enemy with almost limitless resources and none of their own to combat them with. They needed an army which needed to be fed, armed, and housed and to do that they needed....

"Gold. We need gold."

His simple declaration was meet with no challenge from Shawna, Adelram or Maeve. Indeed the latter two only looked on approvingly that he understood their current situation.

"We need gold," he repeated," but I don't know how we go about gaining it."

Adelram leaned back in his chair and evenly stared at Lykos. "How did you find gold to eat before you came here?"

Lykos grimaced but answered regardless of his less than honorable actions. "I stole food when I needed to in Svellheim, sometimes even fighting and killing others for it. While traveling here I worked for my meals. I have never needed gold until I arrived here." He did not try to justify his actions, knowing that the words would be empty.

Shawna frowned disapprovingly but Adelram and Maeve nodded in easy acceptance to him. "Fools always talk about doing what is right and what is easy but the wise know that it is only between two evils we pick. Some of us just have the foresight to see the results of those choices," Illusionist Maeve said as she reached for more yarn. Adelram nodded beside her.

"Necessary evils are a term often bandied about by those in command, often as an excuse. There is no avoiding the fact that sometimes you will have to do truly heinous acts but so long as they are not your first choice you will not need to fear the danger of succumbing to the seductive power of oppressing others," Adelram explained. Shawna harrumphed beside her cousin.

"We should petition friendly houses for aid and build strong ties with them, not talk about such dark things," she said firmly. Her eyes narrowed at Adelram and Maeve. "Do not corrupt my son."

"Your son already knows that darkness walks these streets and has gotten his hands dirty before. If anything your talks of politics will ruin more of his innocence than a little bloodshed would," Illusionist Maeve muttered angrily as she undid a poorly stitched row. Shawna rounded on the older woman to retaliate but Lykos spoke up.

"I agree with mother." Silence filled the room at his words. He turned towards Adelram and nodded. "It's like you said, it shouldn't be our first option. We'll go to the other houses and petition for aid and if-"

"-when," Maeve interrupted.

"-if that fails we will we pursue more drastic measures," Lykos finished looking at his three mentors. They shared long looks with one another before Adelram nodded to Shawna who turned her gaze upon Illusionist Maeve. Their staring contest lasted several long moments and Lykos began to fidget when Illusionist Maeve rolled her eyes and spoke.

"Fine but it will be without me. Even with my illusions there would be a riot from the arrogant pricks if I showed up." Lykos broke out in a grin as she turned back to her knitting. It rapidly faded at Adelram's next words.

"As will it be without me."

"What! But why?" Lykos asked. It was Shawna who answered.

"Since he helped me with training you. Until you've proven yourself successful no one from any house will have anything to do with him. It's politics," Shawna explained while gripping Adelram's arm tightly with bright thankful eyes. Adelram stared evenly at Lykos who felt a profound appreciation for the older man.

"Thank you sir, I didn't know," Lykos found himself saying and he knew it wasn't enough to fully convey the level of gratitude he felt. Adelram nodded before excusing himself from the room.

Shawna allowed his abrupt exit without issue by turning her full focus onto her son. "There is a ball at the Stultus estate by the north gate two days from now. I'll find you some of your father's things, you'll look dashing," she said fondly before also leaving the room.

Illusionist Maeve clucked her tongue to gain his attention and he turned towards her. "You're an idiot."

Considering she told him he was an idiot at least half a dozen times a day, he wasn't too surprised but still confused as to what drew her ire this time. "What do you mean instructor?" he asked respectfully, hoping she would be less cryptic.

"Coddling your mother will make our endgame that much more difficult and decreases the chances of you surviving with all of your limbs attached substantially."

Lykos was offended. "What?"

"Don't you what me boy, you're only making your own life more difficult." Illusionist Maeve set aside her knitting and glared at him. "Your mother is thinking under the impression the houses are like they were before Leon and his ruffians waged their little war. They aren't. They've learned from his mistakes and are now a more brutal and cutthroat type of predator which she has never have dealt with before. However you have, haven't you?"

Lykos shifted uncomfortably and avoided her eyes as she continued. "Your mother has no idea what it takes to survive on the streets of this kingdom let alone how to survive in one of the northern slave mines. Adelram does which is why he even agreed to train you after meeting you, he knows you will be ruthless, oh stop that!"

Illusionist Maeve's order caused him to freeze in his uncomfortable shifting by tone alone, no magic needed.

"I know you're faking shyness. You spend enough of your life creating illusions and you can see right through anyone. You're uncomfortable, your manner, your reasons to being here are all an act, a successful one I might add but I will not have you thinking I am a simpleton boy!"

Lykos slowly relaxed his body and slowly raised his eyes to meet Illusionist Maeve's. "What do you know?"

Illusionist Maeve huffed but responded. "I know you are telling the truth about the mines and how you came to this kingdom, all of the marks are there but I am not sure you are Shawna's son. Some bastard of Leon's probably but her flesh and blood? Unlikely. I've met Leon and while there are some similarities there, you do not share enough traits with her to be easily related."

Lykos took in a long, slow breathe before leaping forward with his knife drawn. Illusionist Maeve merely flicked her hand and sent him sprawling back into his seat. With another claw like hand she held him down as her knitting needles rose in the air in front of her, slowly continuing her knitting, while she turned her attention onto the now magically restrained Lykos.

"Good attempt but I expect better from those trying to assassinate me. Now calm down, if I wanted to kill you you would find yourself turned inside out. The reason why I even bring this up is to let you know that I don't care."

"You don't care?" he asked in disbelief. "You literally hold my life in your hands and you tell me you don't care?"

"I don't care," Illusionist Maeve stated firmly, her hands reaching out to take her floating knitting needles and the invisible bindings vanished from Lykos. "The enemy of my enemy is my friend and we all share a common enemy thus such a minor lie is inconsequential to me."

Lykos pondered her words and while he agreed they were sound he had a feeling Shawna and Adelram wouldn't be as understanding. "Does Adelram know? Does Shawna?"

"Adelram reasonably finds your sudden appearance suspicious however he is remarkably loyal to Shawna and thus will be a non-issue so long as you keep her fooled. As for Shawna she fully believes you are her son and wants to protect you. Do you see why that is a problem?" Illusionist Maeve's sharp tone cut through the tension like a knife.

He thought on her question only for a moment before answering. "Our enemies won't be hindered by a mother's protection instructor."

Illusionist Maeve nodded satisfied. "We cannot hide behind any defense, we cannot meet their strength head on, so what must we do?"

A memory from the mines surfaced, a guard being pulled into the darkness by desperate hands. "We strike from the shadows," he said quietly. Illusionist Maeve smiled.

"Congratulations apprentice you're learning. We must reveal their mistresses, rob their libraries, empty their coffers, and burn their places of business down. We must make their loyal friends distrust them, show the common folk that we are the ones to follow, and above all walk the careful edge of obscurity so that our enemies do not strike us down before we are prepared to strike at them. Which brings us to this ball.

"Dance, talk, enjoy the party while Shawna attempts fruitless negotiations with the other noble houses. They already know our plight and only want to watch us come crawling, begging to them. Instead I want you to ignore them. Let their curiosity pull them towards you, draw them in like a spider to her web and spin a gentle cocoon around them, entrapping them. Do you see what you must do apprentice?" Illusionist Maeve whispered, leaning in like a conspirator.

Lykos nodded firmly several times before shaking his head. "No what?"

Illusionist Maeve rolled her eyes. "Go through their libraries, rob their coffers, and slice any Stultus throat you can without drawing attention to yourself. Idiot boy...." Illusionist Maeve muttered as she returned to her knitting.

Chapter Thirteen

The Stultus estate was a gaudy affair whose excessive ornamentation adorning the walls, soldiers, and party guests bordered on obscene. Intoxicated men and women leaned out of windows and off of balconies, spilling their drink and other liquids on their fellow guests below as they bellowed out vulgar comments and jaunty tunes. The masquerade theme seemed to have given leave to all sense as many party goers were showing an unnecessary and frankly revolting amount of skin as they reveled in the carnal delights of the evening. These were not men and women ashamed of showing off their flabby and unflattering forms.

As Lykos strode carefully through the trash strewn garden he was glad he and Illusionist Maeve had convinced Shawna to stay at home, citing that he must learn to spread his own wings. In actuality there was a very real chance that he would set off a panic with his mere presence and he had no desire to guard his mother in the event of a riot.

Adorned in Leon's old robes and a handmade gray wolf mask Lykos thought he cut quite the dashing figure. The puddles of vomit on the other hand were not quite as charming and he did his best to avoid them. But it wasn't the foul footing he was concerned with, it was his confrontation with Illusionist Maeve and his own lingering uncertainties.

He would not be the first child to not look like either of his parents yet he agreed with Illusionist Maeve, it seemed too coincidental. Perhaps he was only a distant cousin to the Talal bloodline at best or worse, perhaps he was no one at all. He could not decide which he preferred to be truth.

Glancing at the Stultus estate he compared it to Hearthome in his mind and found the simplistic structures of his home much more comfortable to be near. Shawna had told him how the Stultus estate had actually belonged to the Talal family, used to host balls and festivals for the common folk while they lived up near the cliffs. While he recognized the wisdom of that decision, he wished they had chosen someplace closer to the ground. He had not gotten over his near death sneaking into Hearthome all those months ago.

The Stultus estate was loud, not just in noise but stature. Everything screamed superiority, that visitors were mere peasants beneath their feet. The grand pillars towering everywhere seemed to loom over the guests below making the rooms feel so much taller than they actually were. Opulent tapestries and paintings were accompanied by fountains and statues, each more garish and vulgar than the last.

Rail thin servants carried platters of mead and exquisite dishes, their thin limbs trembling from the exertion. The guests took a fiendish delight in belittling them as they partook of their savory smelling cargo. Lykos spied several of the servants bound with iron chain to the walls and floor, some of the near by guests poking at them mockingly, and he realized the awful truth. That these men and women were not servants but slaves and he was reminded harshly of his own past. He forced the burning anger that flared in his chest down lest it show on his face. He had too much to lose tonight if he lost his temper now.

So he ignored the proffered food and drink two nervous slaves offered and began to look deeper into his surroundings. His observations were quickly interrupted however as he bumped into a man with a black wolf mask. The two men stared at one another for a long moment and their obvious standoff was beginning to draw attention.

"Well one of us is going to have to go home and change," Lykos remarked dryly and the surrounding crowd laughed appreciatively. The man in the black wolf mask sneered before turning and walking away and Lykos smirked to himself at the minor victory. The victorious feeling rapidly faded as he turned his attention to the ball.

The lords and ladies of Mycenae were joyously celebrating this evening, partaking in food, drink, and pleasurable company. Few bare faces walked through the crowds and by their expensive clothes Lykos realized that these were the heads of the various noble houses, too prideful to hide their faces. Mindful of his mothers request to ask for aid, he screwed up his courage and approached the nearest one.

"Lykos of House Talal, how do you do?" Lykos attempted his most winning smile while holding out his hand to clasp the barefaced man's own. The man turned from his conversation with a young man in a viper mask, the scales ever shifting in the torch light, and sneered at him.

"One would expect better manners from a noble house such as Talal but I suppose they had so few choices at a proper heir they took whatever trash fit." Lykos raised a brow at the scorn in his voice but blazed on regardless.

"I would have thought a member of a noble house to compose themselves better than to sling insults at any person they meet," Lykos snidely replied. The young man in the viper mask snorted with laughter but quickly quelled his mirth at the older man's glare.

"Indeed." The man gave Lykos a considering look before sneering at the offered hand. Lykos dropped it. "I am Lord Sofos and this is my heir Grimm. How do you do Lykos?" Lord Sofos seemed to take a perverse pleasure in the lack of title.

"How do you do Lord Sofos? Grimm." Lykos nodded at the masked heir who nodded reluctantly back. He took no issue with the lack of title in Lord Sofos' reply. Despite being the head of a noble house and owning his home, he did not rule a territory and thus was beneath his "betters". However he didn't intend to allow that fact to stay true for much longer.

"Pardon my rude greeting but I and my fellow heads simply find it fascinating that you've survived all of these years. Where have you been?" Lord Sofos asked. Lykos felt slimy just being in his presence and began to regret meeting with this man first.

"Oh here and there for my own safety you understand," Lykos started to explain the story he, Maeve, and Shawna had concocted to Adelram's amusement. The old soldier firmly believed that such a story would prove unneeded. "Out of the kingdom to protect my mother-"

"You ran away?" Grimm interrupted. "So the Talal are cowards."

Lykos grew angry. "The decision to leave this kingdom was not my own. That you blame a child for the mistakes of the adults entrusted with its care speaks poorly of your maturity and intelligence."

Grimm huffed in rage. "You wretched scum my house has served this kingdom for generations!"

"Grimm!" Lord Sofos barked sharply drawing the attention of everyone nearby. The party guests quieted as they stared hungrily at the trio, eager for new gossip. The vexed lord drew in a deep breathe before speaking quietly to Lykos. "I'd thank you kindly not to corrupt my son but your family is well known for its preference to running amok and causing chaos."

Lykos raised his eyebrow at the vehemence in Lord Sofos' voice and opened his mouth to rebuke him but was interrupted once more.

"You Talal," Lord Sofos spat, "why can't you ever mind your own business and stick to the status quo? Come Grimm!" He pushed through the watching crowd without another word. Grimm gave Lykos a foul look before following his father away.

Lykos stared at the retreating pair in quiet anger before shrugging. When he returned home he would ask his family what they knew of House Sofos but until then he would banish them from his mind. He had more important tasks at hand.

He attempted to approach a few more of the bare faced party guests but found the crowds blocking him each time. After the third time he realized they were most likely their guards or lackeys and were acting on orders to keep him away lest he create another scene like he had with Lord Sofos. Angrily shaking his head he decided to go through with his and Maeve's plan of robbing the Stultus estate and killing any member they could so that the evening would not be a total waste.

Walking through the many halls and rooms he saw depraved guests enact deplorable things upon the helpless slaves. He fingered the concealed knife in his coat as he watched two women abuse a young boy carrying a tray of roasted vegetables, his anger growing. As he stepped forward to order them to stop he found a dainty hand resting upon his arm.

"Oh my, is that a dagger in your pocket or are you just happy to see me?" a sultry voice whispered into his ear as a feminine body rested against his own. He turned in rage, surprise, and shock towards the speaker and was further surprised when the woman grabbed him by his cloak and dragged him into a dark corner. The slave ran from the room and the two drunk women followed cackling in glee leaving Lykos alone with the woman.

"You have nothing to fear from me," Lykos suddenly found himself slammed against the wall with his own dagger held to his throat, "unless it's me you're here to kill."

He looked into bright blue eyes framed by ebony curls and tried to see past the Piercer mask upon her brow. Despite her slim figure, she pinned him with remarkable strength and he was surprised to feel a short sword brush up against his leg through her dress. Knowing he had to play this safely lest he die a bloody death he tried to charm her.

"Do you threaten everyone you meet or am I simply special?" He tried a roguish smile but the masked woman only snorted as she twisted the knife slowly into his neck. The warm trickle of blood angered him and through a magnificent series of twists he somehow managed to reverse their positions, holding his now bloody knife to her delicate throat. "Perhaps introductions are in order?"

A small half-smile formed underneath the Piercer's fierce visage and Lykos was briefly distracted by it. The woman capitalized on his mistake and freed herself, drawing a sword from the folds of her dress in one swift motion. The two stared each other down, their weapons poised and ready to strike.

"Lykos of House Talal," he said suddenly causing her to twitch in his direction. "Might I know your name fierce lady?"

She gave a joyous laugh and sheathed her weapon and gestured for him to do the same. "Falka of House Falknor and I am both relieved and displeased we are not enemies. You promise to be," she licked her lips, "entertaining."

He raised an eyebrow but said nothing as he too sheathed his weapon.

"So why are you here Lykos of Talal? Have you come to introduce yourself to the ruling elite?" she asked mockingly as she glanced around the room. A shiny bit of metal attracted her attention to his left. She brushed uncomfortably close to him as she approached it and stared curiously at the object, a small celestial globe, in appreciation.

"Oh just thought I'd stop by and see what all the fuss was about. Of dancing lords and vicious ladies. Or was that the other way around?" Falka snorted.

"You've obviously never been to one of these balls before. The lords think they dance but they merely prance and the ladies? Those harlots aspire to be dangerous, the preening fools."

Lykos raised an appreciative eyebrow at her as she began to fiddle with the globe. "So there is no one worth conversing with at these events then? A pity."

Falka laughed as she twisted her hand, opening the globe to reveal a small cache of gold hidden inside. She happily pocketed them and twisted the globe back into its closed position. "Perhaps you've already met the most interesting person here and you're ignoring her?"

"I think a member of a noble house stealing from another is interesting," he remarked, gesturing to her pilfered prize. Falka smiled and began to walk away from him.

"Perhaps she merely recognizes a fellow thief?" she stated boldly before dashing through the open door. Lykos looked after her in surprise before shaking his head in mirth. His hand fell to caress his dagger but grasped nothing but air. Falka had stolen his knife!

He rushed into the hallway to see Falka disappear around a corner up ahead. Following her, he dodged around the party guests clogging the decorated halls, pursuing the female in flight. He managed to catch up to her outside of the kitchen, the slaves obediently bustling to and fro carrying empty trays or delicious treats. "You have something that belongs to me," Lykos demanded angrily of her.

Falka smiled with such innocence that he was thrown for a loop before rallying and grasping her arm, directing her away from the kitchen and its curious onlookers. She allowed him to before responding to his accusation.

"Why would you think little old me was capable of such an unladylike task?" She batted her eyes at him demurely but he remained firm in his glare. With a sigh she gave up her spoils, returning his dagger to him. "I just wanted to show my interest, I guess you're not fun."

Thrown for a loop Lykos immediately and vocally disagreed, "I am plenty fun!"

"Fantastic! Then you won't mind if I accompany you for the remainder of the evening! We can split the loot eighty-twenty to me." She smiled beautifully and he found himself at a loss of words.

"I do too mind! And seventy-thirty to me!" Lykos objected.

"Why would a young man object to a young woman's companionship? Oh you're one of them aren't you? Sixty-forty." Falka insinuated leaning in close and patting him on the arm in a falsely concerned manner. His jaw dropped out of surprise at the sheer lunacy of the woman.

"I am not!" he exclaimed shaking her arm off and checking his pockets to make sure she hadn't made off with his dagger once more.

"It's perfectly fine Lykos, I accept you for who you are you don't need to hide from me. But I'll help you keep your secret for a price." She continued to smile into his outraged face for several long moments before laughing merrily.

"Oh you cheeky wench. Fifty-fifty is my final offer," Lykos muttered realizing he had been had.

Falka's joyous peals of laughter echoed through the hall once more.

Chapter Fourteen

"Is my presence truly that disagreeable? People are beginning to stare," Falka of Falknor asked Lykos as his gaze roamed the crowds. She had been following him grumpily for several minutes now and he was being a poor companion. "When I offered to accompany you I thought we would be doing something fun such as fighting guards or robbing the Stultus. Instead we're back with the bores."

Lykos gave her a sharp look and she quickly stopped whining. "I'm looking for the Stultus family so I can kill them and take back control of this quarter. Stealing from the people that I intend to kill and attain their holdings feels counter-productive in the long run."

He continued walking but Falka remained where she stood, her eyes wide in surprise. Shaking her head she rushed forwards and took his arm. "Well House Stultus doesn't have an alliance with House Falknor so that doesn't bother me in the slightest but are sure your actions are wise? You'll make a lot of powerful enemies."

Lykos snorted. "I already have powerful enemies, I need resources to combat them. Besides this removes a weakness."

"A weakness?" Falka asked with doubt coloring her tone. He decided to explain himself.

"So long as House Stulus controls Pyrgos my enemies will have a willing ally to spy, harass, and attack me at their leisure." He spun in one final turn to take in the full ballroom before sighing at the lack of his target. "There is also the matter of revenge. House Stultus was a minor player in my families fall but they eagerly took over under House Kolos reign. Under their direction they plundered my family's home, robbed and abused our people, and are loathsome creatures of vulgar vices. I will not stand for such acts and thus House Talal will not stand for such atrocities anymore."

Lykos trailed off and Falka looked at him with surprise and respect at his passion but the moment was quickly interrupted by a voice beside them.

"Harassing my guests, insulting me in my own home? It's no wonder that House Talal has fallen so low in recent years." Lykos tensed and turned angrily to face the speaker. Standing before him were four men dressed in magnificent robes that bore food and drink stains. The speaker, Elias, was glaring at Lykos with his beady eyes while fingering a sword at his waist. Lykos narrowed his eyes seeing the Talal crest upon the hilt.

"Lord Stultus. I've been looking forward to meeting you again ever since I learned how you sold out your own allies." Many of the party guests seemed content to watch the two men insult each other but the members of House Stultus rustled angrily at his words.

Lord Stultus merely chuckled. "My house acted more intelligently than many in the days of old. Why some even started a foolish rebellion that caused them to fall from grace. They were stamped down to a senile old woman and her ill begotten spawn."

It was Lykos' turn to redden in rage beneath his wolf mask but one of the men accompanying Lord Stultus spoke up before he could reply. However it wasn't to him but to his companion Falka.

"Good evening beautiful. I'm Brutus, heir of House Stultus." The blonde haired man bowed in a charming way that was blessedly lost upon Falka who looked upon him with disinterest.

"Greeting Heir Stultus," she reluctantly replied. Brutus was not dissuaded by her standoffish response.

"Now now beautiful. I can promise you a very enjoyable evening. I'm famed for my technique." The two silent men so far chuckled appreciatively and even Lord Stultus smiled darkly at his heir's words. Lykos' rage was growing by the second but Falka's turned icy.

"I've heard of your lauded abilities Heir Stultus." The smile that grew upon Brutus' face was rapidly crushed by her next words. "Why I've heard more than a few Emporo merchants whisper of the bounty placed upon your manhood by their slighted lady. Something about deflowering her favorite nieces?"

Lykos admired the pale color Brutus turned while his father darkened to a rich plum shade. Falka curtsied to Lord Stultus before walking away, the crowd parting around her as they gossiped about this latest development.

"Well you chased away the only enjoyable part of this entire farce tonight so if you'll excuse me I must be off," Lykos jovially said as he sketched a mocking bow to Lord Stultus. The man stomped away angrily and the two silent men followed. Brutus sneered at Lykos.

"The wench will be mine and you'll be nothing! Not now, not ever!" The angry young man declared before following his family away leaving Lykos alone. He gave the departing man a hard look before he turned to follow Falka across the ballroom. Catching up to her by a pillar the pair shared a polite nod and the curious crowd soon lost interest.

"Did you see where they went?" Lykos asked Falka quietly as she stared deliberately at a window in stony silence. There was no need to clarify who "they" were.

"Yes, they exited the hall opposite of the entrance and went left." He offered his arm and she took it mechanically as they casually cut through the crowd of masked individuals. To any outside observer they looked similar to the other young couples dancing in the room and no one paid them any mind as they exited into an empty hallway. Lykos took a deep breathe and blinked slowly, his magic infusing his sight and allowing him to see beyond the normal world.

The color of the magics at the Stultus estate were both stronger and more muted than the magic at Hearthome. The four elements weren't in balance here, fire and earth overwhelmed and muddled air and water. Lykos glanced back at the party in the ballroom and had to quickly turn away at the headache inducing kaleidoscope of colors that undulated painfully behind them. However most importantly there were no figures hidden by illusions within the hall.

"Having second thoughts?" Falka asked him teasingly. "It's not unheard of for men to have performance anxiety."

"No, merely checking to make sure we haven't been followed. You're not the most discreet person in the kingdom," Lykos countered as he completed his observation, noting that save for a few soldiers and slaves the halls nearby were empty of witnesses. He nodded to her pleased she was no longer silent and withdrawn. "Shall we my lady?"

Falka rolled her eyes but took his arm again with a smirk and the two walked down through the hall. The slaves paid them no heed as their duties consumed their attention but Lykos paid close attention to them. They were beaten, all of them, and many walked with limps, a symptom of more violent injuries or an all together worse act imparted upon them. He felt his rage climb as he looked upon their broken forms and knew his actions tonight were righteous, despite their bloody intentions. He steeled his heart for the kills to come and walked through the door leading to the family's private wing.

Immediately he pulled Falka to the side and hid in a shadowy alcove as patrolling soldiers kept the area secure. Against such a large number he did not like their odds, especially as he knew so little of her skills. He leaned over to whisper in her ear.

"I count a dozen soldiers leading further into the wing." He tried to gauge her response to his words. She appeared unimpressed.

"So are we going to kill them?" she asked slowly, as if trying to tell a child the correct answer by phrasing it as a question. He scowled.

"I dislike our odds so I'm going to sneak above them and draw a few off through that door over there." He gestured towards a balcony above them. It ran the length of the room to the far side and it was fortunately empty of soldiers.

Falka stared at him without blinking before shrugging. "Fine, let's go."

He stopped her motion with a raised arm. "It would be safer for you to stay here while I clear out the soldiers. I can move quicker without having to protect you."

His explanation did not please her and her visage became decidedly cold. However he was determined to stand firm in his decision and held her gaze. Falka glanced at the patrolling soldiers with a calculating eye then turned towards him with a smirk.

"Very well, I will await your return in this room. You best not keep a lady waiting," she ordered imperiously, her smirk never fading. Lykos gave her a long glance but nodded, accepting her concession easily.

Deciding to conserve his magical strength by not utilizing a portal, he turned and rapidly climbed the ornate wall to the balcony. Sticking to the shadows he walked along the length of the room before entering a second, smaller hall that only had three men within. While the men in the outer hall were mere common soldiers, these three were obviously their leaders and were enjoying wine and mead while quietly conversing.

As Lykos sneaked along the balcony overlooking them he spied a spear leaning against the wall beneath him near an empty suit of armor slumped on a bench. With a wicked smile he positioned himself above two of the men and leaped down with his knife drawn.

He landed heavily upon the two of the men who cried out in alarm. Swinging his knife down on one of their necks, it sprayed a fountain of blood in the air as he stumbled to his feet. He quickly stabbed the other man in the gut but found the knife wrenched from his hand by the man's violent struggles. He rolled backwards to dodge the third man's wild swing of a sword and his hand found the spear against the wall. With a smirk he brought it forward.

Rather, he attempted to bring the spear forward but found it solidly resisting his efforts. He turned and saw that the suit of armor was not as empty as it had first appeared to be. Indeed it encased a rather large man who stubbornly gripped the weapon that Lykos was trying to claim.

"Excuse me sir do you mind?" Lykos quipped, tugging at the spear in both of their grasps. With a roar the man leaped to his feet and threw him away with a mighty heave. Bereft of a weapon he eyed the two men before trying to explain this was all a misunderstanding.

"Die scum!" Lykos shouted as he threw a fireball at the pair. The unarmored man cried out in pain and shock but the armored titan shrugged off the blaze and moved forward menacingly. Lykos threw another fireball to slow him down as he glanced around for a weapon to use. Spying his dagger in one of the corpses, he threw one final fireball before lunging across the room. His attack was barely noticed as the armored titan stabbed at him with his spear, roaring in rage.

As his hands closed around the dagger and wrenched it free of the corpse with a sickening squelch, Lykos briefly pondered the absence of any reinforcements from the other soldiers. They were making a not insignificant amount of racket and someone should have investigated by now. With a sharp gasp his attention was brought back to the armored titan who had just stabbed him in the arm.

He gritted his teeth and brought his dagger down upon the wooden shaft of the spear, shattering it and jarring his arm. The two men reeled backwards, one in surprise and the other pain as his wound was jarred. However the pain gave Lykos rage and the rage gave him focus. Thrusting forth his hand he created a jet of fire that poured out in a blaze of destruction. Armored or not the titan could not ignore the sheer destruction of the blaze as he was cooked within his armor and rapidly joined the other three men, dead upon the floor.

Lykos cut off the magic and panted as a wave of exhaustion hit him. He admired his handiwork for a moment, pleased with how far he had grown, as killing even one soldier would have been beyond him a few months ago. He smiled a macabre grin but scowled as he looked at the spear head still jutting out of his arm. Knowing he had to remove it so his magic could heal his body he wrapped a hand firmly around the exposed wood and pulled.

Although he was no stranger to pain he could not prevent the groan escaping his lips as the metal and wood impaled through his arm was pulled out. He dropped it to the floor and admired the wound. Before his eyes the wound healed slowly and after just a few minutes the only evidence that remained of the wound was a tender red circle on both sides of his arm. He sighed in relief as the pain faded from his mind before glancing towards the door where the entry hall was.

Someone should have heard that racket by now yet there was no one checking in on the men he had just killed. An unpleasant feeling arose in his gut and he made his way to the doorway. Carefully pushing the carved wood open slightly he gazed into the entry hall to see what the soldiers were doing.

Nothing. Or rather no one. There was no one in the entry hall that was packed just minutes ago. With unease growing in his belly Lykos slipped through the door and strode towards Falka's hiding spot. Rounding a pillar his jaw dropped at the sight before him.

Falka of Falknor was sitting upon a throne of corpses in her little alcove. The soldiers who had just been patrolling a few moments ago were impaled with their own swords and spears and were arranged in a rather artfully done chair that the young woman sat elegantly on with a large smile.

"Welcome back dear," she said coyly. He could only gawk at her.

"I thought I told you not to leave your spot," he finally managed to say. She snorted in amusement.

"I didn't leave my spot, they all came to me. I was a good girl." With how Falka purred that last comment he sincerely doubted that. He shook his head and opened his mouth to argue otherwise but she beat him to it.

"And you would do well to remember that I am a woman of the noble house of Falknor in the Kingdom of Mycenae. I am no midwife to wait at home, no peasant to cower in the shadows. We stand equal to the men of this kingdom in combat."

Lykos looked at Falka with respect, mentally comparing her to Illusionist Maeve. The same fiery passion dwelled in the elderly woman and he was reminded of a simple fact she stated repeatedly:

"No matter who you are, how old you are, or your station in this kingdom we all share a common enemy. Since the dawn of man the Tainted have shadowed our steps and they care not for anything save your death. In such a world all must be willing to wield a blade and to end a life."

She would then rant about how lazy and squeamish the common folk were which was when Lykos would tune out his instructor. Returning to the present he nodded to Falka.

"I will endeavor to remember such from now on," he vowed. She looked at him haughtily before accepting his words with a regal nod. She rose from her bloody throne and idly brushed her hands along her dress to smooth the edges.

"So what took you?" she asked with interest as they began to walk towards the chamber he had just exited from. As he glanced at her impressive throne of corpses he realized that she had killed far more men than he had. Panicking he turned to see Falka enter the room and raced after her. Entering the room just after her he had to slid to a halt lest he run into her.

Two of the corpses were still quietly smoldering and the furniture in the room was wrecked from the fight. He tried to bravado his way through.

"As you can see I was interrupting a party. The participants were most inhospitable."

Falka's laugh briefly raised his spirits before he realized she was pointing and laughing at him. He scowled at her and pushed past her to check the doors around the room.

"Poor Lykos, he had to face four big strong men. I'm so glad he left me behind for my own safety." She fainted mockingly against the wall as he pointedly confirmed that the most of the rooms were just bedrooms or storage. The last however led to a dusty study that prickled something in his senses. He ignored the quietly giggling woman behind him and entered the room, his body tense in anticipation.

A tinkle of metal behind him caused him to jump, whirling about with his dagger in hand. Falka merely grinned at him as she patted down the dead soldiers, taking their coin for herself. "Jumpy are we?"

"Falka get over here," Lykos ordered as his rapidly beating heart calmed. Her amusement subsiding, she followed him into the study and joined him in his search of the study that was for all appearances empty.

"Did our dear hosts leave us to entertain ourselves?" she asked as she began to pilfer the valuables from the room. Lykos frowned as she pocketed a handful of coins. Despite the large amount of soldiers in this section of the estate, there were still no members of House Stultus. He embraced his magic once more to examine the room in greater detail.

The wash of colors appeared again and he once more looked for areas concealed by magic. Yet no illusions glistened like spidery strands, just the steady traces of earth, air and fire. A hand touching his face started him from his observation and the magic faded from his eyes.

"That's the second time your eyes have shone like that. You have magic don't you?" Falka asked him with wide, eager eyes. He raised an eyebrow in confusion.

"Of course I do, don't you? I thought all members of the noble houses unlocked their magic?" Lykos asked as he moved closer to exam a bookshelf. It was remarkably clear of dust unlike the other pieces of furniture in the room.

"They're supposed to yes but someone stole the Falknor awakening stone," she lamented sorrowfully as he knelt to check the lower shelves. "I've spent my entire life training with weapons but without the magic of the stone to awaken mine I will never reach my full potential. There are only a scant few Falknor who don't have access to their magic and I am one of them," she finished bitterly.

Lykos paused in his examinations of the shelf. "I'm sorry. I could not even begin to imagine what that must be like for you. You have no idea where the stone might be?"

Falka shrugged. "Rumors and hearsay. I had wondered if House Stultus had knowledge or even possessed our awakening stone but I haven't seen a hint of anything."

Lykos felt for the young woman, he truly did. Which is why his next action, while impulsive, was heartfelt and honest.

"I will help you find your families awakening stone Falka. I promise." He looked up at Falka who brushed at wet eyes underneath her mask. She smiled at him.

"I swear if you ever tell anyone I cried no one will ever find your body." He rolled his eyes and turned back to the shelf. "I take it this shelf is somehow important?"

"Yes. This entire room is dusty except for this one shelf. Neither of those facts makes sense however since this is supposed to be the lord's study. So why this shelf?"

"Well it's obviously a secret passage of some sort." She eyed the shelf and wall critically. "So why are you on the ground when the way to open it is up here?"

"....What?"

"To open the door? To the secret passage? It's right here." She pointed at an utterly blank section of the stone wall next to the bookshelf. Lykos rose to his feet and stared at it but could see no discernible markings on it.

"How can you tell?" he asked. She rolled her eyes and pushed a stone on it. With a click the bookshelf swung open on oiled hinges.

"Because magic isn't everything." Falka winked at Lykos as she entered the hidden passage. With an impressed stare he followed her into the dark.

"No seriously, how did you tell? The stone looks completely identical to the others." Lykos created a small flare in his hand to illuminate their way as they walked down stone steps underneath the Stultus estate.

"Nothing is ever completely identical, least of all in deception. They'll mimic it as closely as they can but there will always be a tell. You'd be surprised by how many secret passageways and tunnels exist in Mycenae." Her coy answer did not fully satisfy him but he had to halt his questioning as voices were heard echoing ahead. Snuffing out his flare he and Falka crept carefully towards the voices.

"Slice the bitch again!" Four men laughed as a woman sobbed uncontrollably. A brief pause was heard before a woman screamed loudly. Lykos could spy a light just ahead and followed Falka to the corner to peek around.

The room before them was roughly cut from stone yet smoothed over the years by the elements. Along the closest wall were many papers and documents tossed carelessly onto shelves and stone tables. The far wall was cut away to reveal a passing river raging by, overlooking the kingdom of Mycenae sleeping through a quiet night.

Said silence was shattered when a young woman in the center of the room screamed as Brutus cut along the length of her stomach. The woman was held up by the two brutish men following Lord Stultus at the party and said lord was savoring a glass of wine as he watched his heir work.

"Be careful not to cut too deep or too shallow Brutus. You want to make it last for as long as you can while not giving her the relief of death," Lord Stultus commented idly as his heir nodded.

"Yes father." The younger man bent over the trembling woman and cut her again to release her screams once more into the night air. Falka and Lykos raged from their spot and she made to move forward but he held her back. She glared up at him but he moved close to her ear to whisper:

"If we charge in they'll just slit her throat. I'll move up to that ledge right there," he pointed to a dark ledge above the four men and their crying victim, "and come down hard upon them. When I'm in position you can distract them and we will kill them."

Falka nodded but was confused by part of his instructions. "How will you get up to the ledge? It's in the middle of the room."

He grinned. "Like this." And with a sweep of his hand the dark stone of the wall gave way to a dark vortex of swirling energy. Pleased the portal remained stable he winked at Falka's shocked expression before stepping through. Suddenly finding himself on the rock ledge, he carefully grasped the rock to steady himself. Glancing back to where he once was, he waved at Falka who was gaping in surprise at his sudden relocation. A feral smile spread across her lips underneath the Piercer mask and he felt a matching one on his own lips. He nodded to her, signaling his preparedness and both turned their attention to the four men torturing the poor woman.

"Oh boys?" Falka's sing-song tone echoed through the room as she stepped around the corner. "Is this a party anyone may invite themselves to?"

The gathered men turned to face her. Brutus gave her a demented smile as she stepped forward and he matched her pace for pace until they were standing within arms reach of one another. He licked his lips as he looked down at her.

"I knew you'd come back to me, you're one of those girls who likes a bit of danger." He reached out to caress her cheek with the bloody knife. Falka only smiled. "Something you would like to share pet?"

With a whirl of motion Falka drew her sword and swung it up between Brutus' legs, the sharp metal cutting through bones, muscles, and organs with ease before coming to a halt against his ribs. The blade in his hands fell to the ground as she pulled her sword, bringing him closer to her so she could whisper coldly.

"I'm glad we could share this moment."

Lykos saw little of her movements after that as the three other men roared in rage and rushed forwards. Leaping from his ledge he tackled them, throwing them all to the ground. Pulling out his knife he stabbed into the confused pile of limbs beneath him and was rewarded with startled cries. The four men leaped to their feet and Lykos enjoyed the sight of the deep stab wounds on their bodies, blood gushing everywhere.

"Andron! Alec! Kill the brat and capture the whore! I'll use her to make a new heir!" Lord Stultus ordered his brothers as Falka joined Lykos, sword in hand. Andron glared at Lykos while Alec gave Falka a blood thirsty smile. With a roar the four met in combat.

Lykos found Andron a fierce foe, whose longer and stronger reach made getting close all but impossible so long as he only wielded his knife. With no other weapons available however Lykos was forced to rely on his magic to even the odds. The large man was forced into a defensive position as he threw fireballs at him, scorching his decorative robes. However underneath those robes was a gleaming set of armor.

"Am I the only one who came dressed for a party?" Lykos shouted to no one in particular as he suddenly found Alec swinging at his head, aiming to protect Andron who had stopped to tear off his burning clothes.

"Yes!" Falka replied as she jumped over the cowering form of the woman on the floor and delivered a devastating blow to Alec whose distraction with Lykos proved costly. The man slumped to the floor bleeding heavily from his neck. Andron roared and tackled Falka off to the side where they continued to fight.

Lykos turned to Lord Stultus who drew his sword and pointed it at the young man. His eyes narrowed as he brandished his knife pointedly. "That sword belongs to my family."

"Come and take it brat," Lord Stultus challenged. He swung the sword viciously at Lykos who was forced to roll on the ground to avoid its wicked bite. "Your family should have died out long ago!"

Lykos raged and drew once more upon his magic to throw a fireball. However he was shocked when Lord Stultus waved his arm to form a wall of mist that dispersed the flames. The fog then turned to ice which was sent with another wave to bite into his flesh. He gritted his teeth in pain but pressed forward and struck Lord Stultus solidly with a punch to the jaw.

The lord staggered backwards in surprise and Lykos gave him no time to recover. He kicked the sword out of his hand and struck forward with his fist driving Lord Stultus closer to the raging river. With a savage cry he sank his knife deep into his chest and the obese man's eyes widened in shock.

"My family will rise again," Lykos declared. He pushed the man into the roaring river, his body disappearing into the dark water.

Lykos watched the river for a moment but the sound of Falka's pained cry snapped his focus to her. Turning around he was dismayed to see a bloody Andron standing over the disarmed woman, his sword posed to strike. Lykos lunged forward as the blade fell but knew he would not reach her in time. Pulling on his exhausted magic he threw forth every remaining shred of it he possessed, and the resulting flare blinded everyone in the room.

He collapsed to his knees as his vision slowly returned. Falka was alive, blinking away the magic induced blindness, but alive. However Andron remained on his feet. With a snarl the angry man turned towards Lykos and staggered towards him, the wounds Falka having inflicted upon him mortal. Rage clouded his eyes and the knowledge that he was dying did little to slow his arm as he raised his sword to strike down Lykos. As the blade fell Lykos raised his own arm in defiance.

Time slowed as pain, comparable to the night when his magic was awoken, sliced into his arm. The more his arm resisted that forceful downwards motion the worst it became and then with a terrible lurch the pressure pushed past any remaining resistance. Andron fell to the side as the wounds Falka inflicted upon him finally took their toll. And next to the dead man lay Lykos' hand.

Darkness rushed in and Lykos fell into its embrace willingly as the pain raged from his amputated limb through his body.

Chapter Fifteen

Lykos jerked awake with a gasp, a phantom pain wracking in his left arm causing him to flinch. He recognized his bedroom ceiling and briefly wondered how he managed to get home. Then he remembered what happened.

With trembling fingers he reached over and felt his left arm, tracing down from the elbow. He reached the raised edge of bandages and with his eyes fixed pointedly upon the ceiling, he traced along the edge. Slowly he pushed along the bandages to where a terrible stump must now be....

Only for a sharp pain to shoot through his wrist. He whipped his head down and was shocked to see his left hand attached to his arm, wrapped tightly in bandages. He tried to wiggle his fingers and was rewarded with more blinding pain. He collapsed gasping on the bed as a voice laughed besides him. Turning he saw Shawna smiling down at him.

"Good you're awake. Illusionist Maeve said you'd be up today but you know how I worry." She patted his good arm. "There's a pretty young lady down stairs calling herself Falka of Falknor. She brought you and another young woman home last night. Gave me a fright showing up with you missing a hand and that tortured girl. However Illusionist Maeve took care of all of you."

Lykos slowly forced himself off the bed and Shawna helpfully steadied him when he began to sway. "Falka is here?" he asked as he lurched towards the door. Shawna fretted by his side.

"Yes she refused to leave until she knew you were fine. I think she'll be happy to see you on your feet." She helped him down the stairs and out the back door to reveal the other inhabitants of the house chatting on the terrace overlooking the kingdom. Lykos was pleased to see a woman who could only be Falka sitting next to the unknown woman they rescued. The two young women were talking amiably with Illusionist Maeve and Adelram while enjoying the setting sun.

"Ah the young fool lives," Illusionist Maeve called out. Adelram restricted himself to smirking yet Falka laughed appreciatively at her joke. "Come over here boy so I can examine your stupidity."

Lykos gritted his teeth but obediently moved to her side and held out his injured arm for her inspection. Illusionist Maeve roughly grabbed it and began to unwind the bandages. "So what have you learned from this latest lesson?"

"Wear arm guards?" he answered with snark but winced as Illusionist Maeve prodded his wrist in a particularly unkind manner. "That does hurt you know."

"Good to know, it means you'll regain the full use of your hand. If it were numb your hand would be little more than ornamentation at this point." Illusionist Maeve continued her examination of his hand. "Judging from how uncomfortable you are you should make a full recovery. So long as someone doesn't chop it off again."

Lykos gritted his teeth. "If I'm going to be fine why have you not released my hand instructor?" he asked as Illusionist Maeve continued to manhandle his arm.

"You're too tall for me to smack your fool head while I'm sitting boy."

With an angry growl he pulled back his hand to the laughter of their observers. Even Shawna was smiling at the old witch! He held up his arm in the weak sunlight to examine it.

A thick red scar slashed along his arm diagonally, looping around the entire limb like a morbid bracelet. Touching it with his hand was peculiar, the skin on either side of the scar had feeling yet the raised flesh did not.

"When I touch the skin around the scar I can feel my finger but on the scar itself there's nothing. Is that normal?" Lykos asked the group at large. It was Adelram who answered.

"The human body does not like to be cut up surprisingly. You may eventually regain feeling in the scar but do not count on it. Be happy you may even use your hand after having it removed. Look at my leg." He stuck his left leg out and rolled up the bottom of his pants. All along the leg were scars like the one on Lykos, vicious red marks standing out on the pale skin and hard muscles. Rolling his pants leg down he continued.

"I have just as many on my other leg, a lasting reminder from each battle that almost but never quiet killed me. You'll gain more of your own if you get into enough scuffles."

"But why doesn't your magic just heal the scars? You both have it unlocked," Falka questioned from her seat, her silent companion watching them all with wide eyes.

"Just because magic allows them to reattach their limbs does not mean it does not exact its price from them. As it is Adelram has no feeling in his lower legs and if Lykos isn't careful he'll turn out the same." Illusionist Maeve explained to her. Lykos considered her words before whirling towards Adelram outraged.

"No wonder you never get tired on our runs, your legs never feel pain!" The group laughed at Lykos' expense but this drew his attention back to the unknown woman they had rescued. He turned towards her and bowed his head.

"I apologize miss for how long it took to rescue you from the Stultus. My name is Lykos." The young woman's eyes widened and she hurried to stand and curtsy. Lykos belatedly noticed she had been cleaned and fresh white bandages peeked above the hem of her dress.

"I am Ana Del Rosa my lord. I thank you for saving me and beg your forgiveness for my lapse in manners." Disproving frowns marred Shawna and Falka's faces and Lykos correctly understood their reasoning.

"No need to beg my forgiveness, indeed I should be offering my own. You should not be standing after your ordeal." He motioned for the confused woman to return to her seat and she slowly obliged. "Could you tell me how you came to be in the clutches of the Stultus?"

Ana Del Rosa looked at him carefully, as if he were a predator laying a cunning trap to snare her. She reluctantly began to speak. "I worked at a flesh palace by the northern gate. Yesterday morning the Stultus approached the matron for "entertainment" for their party and they procured my services. They took me and one of the new girls to that room and had their way with her before they...."

She trailed off in broken sobs. No further words were needed for any of the listeners, knowing that the unknown woman had most likely been used and murdered. Falka comforted the young women while the others waited in patient silence for her to collect herself. Lykos turned towards the horizon, watching a convoy of airships taking off in the distance, wondering which of the other kingdoms it was going to. She spoke once more.

"They came back. Dressed in their resplendent robes but they were oh so angry." Lykos felt his neck prickle with shame at the cause of that anger. "They touched me and cut me and bruised me and it was horrible and then you two were suddenly there. You saved me from them."

Lykos kept his gaze focused on the airships as they caught a breeze and were blown away. "What happens now?" he asked the group at large.

Shawna excused herself to fetch tea and Ana Del Rosa followed to assist her. Adelram spoke. "Now we make sure you're rested for the Succession Trial."

"Succession Trial?" Lykos asked unfamiliar with the term.

"Aye, ritualistic combat to determine who inherits the Stultus territory as their established line has been killed. The rest of the kingdom doesn't know yet but in the next few days word will get out and the Succession Trial will be announced."

"So I can't just claim their territory and assets for us?"

"You could but it'd just be admitting you killed them. Easier to just win it honestly at this point so no one acts aggressively towards us." Adelram looked between Falka and Lykos. "Will House Falknor make a claim?"

"Unlikely. House Falknor is content with their current holdings and the other houses leave us alone. Wise considering our fleet of airships," Falka answered. Lykos thought of the nice big empty Stultus Estate.

"Any chance we could just sneak in and steal everything?" he asked. Illusionist Maeve cackled from her seat.

"If you wish to wage war against the entire kingdom boy be my guest however the other houses will make short work of you. That was your little friends first thought too." Indeed Falka was blushing and he flashed her a quick smirk but soon frowned.

"So we'll have to wait for me to heal. How long will we have once they discover House Stultus extinction?"

"At worst a week, at best a month. Either will be sufficient for your arm to heal yet the latter would give you the better chance of success."

"So how is the Succession Trial done?" Lykos asked Adelram who frowned.

"All eligible and able-bodied combatants of Mycenae will gather at the Citadel and duel each other for the Stultus holdings. It was originally done to prevent one house from annihilating the others and controlling the kingdom through murder but the Trial itself has never been bloodless. Indeed while the duels are often done to submission or surrender many bloodthirsty individuals use it as a means to eliminate their enemies."

Falka spoke up. "The last one to be held was when my family won the former Pylkaes holdings a few years ago. A series of smaller tournaments have sprung up since then among the common folk but that's just for entertainment."

Adelram sneered. "Yes the criminal elements enjoy using them to make a quick bit of gold and to establish a pecking order among themselves. I'm surprised you've never heard about it, they're popular in other kingdoms as well."

Lykos shrugged. "Despite my willingness to learn I don't fight for fighting's sake. Everything I do is to survive." He eyed Falka who looked entirely too interested in the criminal tournaments and vowed to discuss it with her later. Shawna and Ana Del Rosa returned with tea.

"So what happens after I win?" Lykos asked as Shawna and Ana Del Rosa set down their burdens. Everyone sat themselves comfortably and began to partake of the light snack. It was Adelram who answered him.

"The former Stultus men will have to swear allegiance to you if they wish to remain living and working in Pyrgos. Some of the soldiers will inevitably jump ship however for the most part we'll be looking at a sizable force to begin securing our holdings with. As for the quarter, we won't gain total control overnight but the other noble houses will know House Talal is serious business and here to stay. We'll have to establish dominance fast otherwise they'll never respect you."

Illusionist Maeve laughed around her biscuit. "Let me at them apprentice, I will teach them the meaning of fear!"

Lykos shared a look with Adelram and Shawna, conveying silently he had no desire to inflict that upon anyone. He was relieved that they both seemed to agree. He turned towards Illusionist Maeve and bowed his head. "We shall see instructor."

The group quietly enjoyed a few moments of silence, each absorbed in their own thoughts before Ana Del Rosa spoke up in a meek tone. "Am I to remain a prisoner here my lord?"

The group turned to Lykos and he blanched when he realized that as the head of House Talal the others would defer to his decision. Swallowing his uncertainty, he hoped his next decision was wise. "Do you wish to return to the flesh palace?"

Ana Del Rosa shook her head but her next words contradicted her desires. "I do not wish to but I fear I must."

Lykos and the others frowned and it was Falka who expressed their confusion. "You never have to return to that wretched place if you don't desire to." She reached out to grasp Ana Del Rosa's hand.

The tearful young woman griped Falka's hand gratefully but shook her head. "I must for I cannot abandon my family." Cold anger began to burn in Lykos' chest as he contemplated her words.

"Who has your family?" Ana Del Rosa flinched at his harsh tone but answered.

"I don't know but I do know where they're being held prisoner. There is a warehouse in Ploio that has my family along with many others. The guards threaten to hurt them if they aren't paid. It's why I started working as a flesh maiden, to earn the money to keep them safe," she answered desperately.

"Feel like going on a rescue mission?" Falka asked Lykos. He raised his eyebrow and looked pointedly at his still healing arm but her face remained firm. He sighed but nodded.

"Fine." Ana Del Rosa's whole face light up with joy but Shawna interrupted

"Absolutely not! You're not to go out until your arm is fully healed young man!" she ordered Lykos. The slight woman puffed up in rage to issue several more ultimatums but Falka quickly cut in.

"I was thinking in several days actually. We can't do anything until we find the warehouse anyways. While I do that, Lykos can stay here and rest." Falka's smile wouldn't melt snow yet Lykos couldn't help but feel betrayed. The mothering Shawna would do until he was healed would be unbearable.

"Well that's alright then." Shawna returned to her tea satisfied while Ana Del Rosa lit up with joy.

"Oh thank you! Thank you! Thank you!" Ana Del Rosa clasped her hands in front of her in joy. Falka smiled at the woman and then rose from her seat. Gesturing for Ana to join her, she bowed to Shawna and Illusionist Maeve.

"I thank you for welcoming me into your home Dowager Talal but it is time I return to my own. Illusionist Maeve, the men of Kremos Keep still whisper your name with fear, I shall pass on your well wishes to them." She turned towards Lykos and smirked. "Perhaps you'll kill more than I next time Lykos."

Lykos' jaw dropped in offense as Falka took the bowing Ana Del Rosa's arm and led her away from the laughing group. He glared at the chuckling Adelram and Maeve but felt utterly betrayed by Shawna's quiet laughter.

"Mother!"

His outraged shout caused all three of his mentors to burst out into laughter as the evening sun set.

"I thought you said I'd have at least a week to recover before the Succession Trial?"

"Aye, well I wasn't expecting for the dead Lord Stultus to wash up on a beach in Latom."

Lykos was sparring with Adelram in the garden, his left arm stiff but usable. Today's lessen involved random debris strewn about the garden making their footing treacherous. Adelram seemed determined to provide ever more difficult challenges yet Lykos was met with the peculiar sensation as this training sensation continued.

Adelram was slowing down.

He still struck with his great speed and strength yet as Lykos met each sword strike with his own he found the blows weren't as difficult to evade. Indeed as Adelram lunged forward to stab at him, he leaned to the side and almost casually flicked his sword out. Adelram's sword was flung through the air and landed in a nearby rosebush. With another flick he held his sword to Adelram's throat.

"Yield," he ordered. Lykos could not stop the surprise from coloring his tone but remained firm with his sword, having fallen for too many of Adelram's tricks over the past few months to not remain vigilant.

"I yield," Adelram said simply, peering at him with calculating eyes. "Could you retrieve my sword Lykos?"

Lykos looked at him in surprise at the easy acceptance but concentrated on the sword in the rosebush. Pushing on his magic he wrapped it around the hilt and pulled it towards him. As it flew through the air he heard a step behind him and instinctively threw himself to the side. A knife flew through the air where he had just been, followed by the sword he had just summoned. He turned to look haughtily at Adelram to find the old man grinning at him.

"Well done Lykos. Were we at the Citadel you would have just graduated into the army. You would pick a discipline to study but I have little else to teach you now." Adelram held out his arm and Lykos clasped it happily, feeling proud of his accomplishment.

"Does that mean we'll no longer train together?" he asked.

"Aye, you still have much to learn but I have taught you all I know of combat and leadership. Time will tell how much of it you learned but I have high hopes, you have excelled under my tutelage." Lykos rolled his eyes at Adelram's self-compliment but he was concerned.

"How will I learn more then? I doubt that anyone would be willing to share their knowledge with me, even if I win the Succession Trial." Adelram nodded at his astute observation.

"Aye they'd treat you like a dangerous Tainted beast in their midst. No you'll have to learn by doing something that will make Shawna skin me alive. You'll have to pick a fight." Lykos raised an interested eyebrow.

"You want me to go pick a fight?" he asked to clarify. Adelram nodded.

"More than one. I want you to find the most degenerate criminals and low lives and pick a fight with all of them." Lykos considered the odd order but nodded. Who better to teach him dirty tricks than those who use them regularly? It would keep his skills sharp at least.

"I'm rather surprised you're recommending this. I would have thought your sense of honor would be against it." Lykos questioned as the two men cleaned up the mess they made. Adelram huffed.

"The she-witch and your new friend cornered me yesterday, insisting I tell you. They seem to think you pay my words respect." Lykos paused and put a look of confusion on his face.

"Where would they get a foolish idea like that?" He tried to keep a straight face but it cracked at Adelram's face turning red.

"Get out of here runt before I throw you into the Marsh!" Adelram roared, throwing a plank of wood at him. Laughing, Lykos raced into the house to find Illusionist Maeve for their magic practice. He admired the cleaned wooden halls that seemed to feel alive as walked through them. When he had first broken in months ago the large manor had felt like a tomb but now it felt like a home.

Finding Illusionist Maeve in the library he hurriedly hid behind a bookshelf. Pulling the magic around him he cast an illusion to blend him into the books and shelves around him as best he could. He carefully sneaked closer to the sitting illusionist and reached out a hand to touch her shoulder only to find his hand touching nothing.

Illusionist Maeve disappeared from her position and Lykos heard her walking stick swing through the air behind him. He attempted to duck but found himself moving into the path of the hard wood and it impacted his head quite solidly. With a groan he pulled backwards as his magically created camouflage faded.

"Unacceptable. You forgot to make sure the designs kept shifting with your movement, nothing in nature is static! And the colors were all wrong, air does not have substance. You still have much to learn apprentice," Illusionist Maeve said as she moved to the seat her illusion had sat in. "Is your morning session of banging metal over already?"

Lykos rubbed his sore head but nodded. "Yes. Adelram also told me an interesting request you and Falka made. Wanting me to beat up criminals? Seems rather tame and noble for you instructor."

Illusionist Maeve scowled and flicked her hand. A phantom hand smacked the back of his head but as it lacked the bite of her walking stick he was able to ignore it with ease.

"Despite his skill Adelram lacks foresight. We will need a lot of soldiers and quickly. There are very few ways to do so and none of them are cheap. So we will instead cheat and make the most of what we have. And what we have currently is you," Illusionist Maeve paused as she considered her next words carefully.

"It's a shame that the Falknor awakening stone was lost, that girl," Lykos knew Illusionist Maeve to be speaking of Falka, "has a remarkable mind and she's content to aid us. Do not screw it up by attempting to bed her," Illusionist Maeve warned him with a dangerous look.

Lykos burned red in embarrassment. "She is a remarkable warrior but I agree. Attempting to court her would be disastrous in any case, she's far too...." he trailed off.

"Far too out going for you. Especially after your life in the mines," she finished for him and he was forced to agree with the elderly woman. "Still, her companionship will be good for you, it will help you both grow."

Lykos silently nodded but decided to return their conversation back to the original topic. "I take it going out into the street and picking a fight with random people would end poorly?" he asked. Illusionist Maeve snorted.

"It would. Wait for the lass to find the flesh maiden's family, she'll lead you to the best place to fight. Try not to die apprentice, I've rather enjoyed living here and I would hate to have to go back to stealing from fat merchants."

Lykos rolled his eyes and thought back to this morning's training with Adelram. The ease with how he disarmed the more experienced man bothered him for even with his training he did not expect that he would have the strength to overcome him. Illusionist Maeve noticed his furrowed brow.

"Don't strain yourself boy speak what's on your mind!" she ordered. He rolled his eyes but dutifully reported what had occurred in this mornings training session. Illusionist Maeve turned a feral smile on him. "Finally."

"Finally what?" he asked, not liking the look on her face as she stood up.

"Finally we can accelerate your training! There are so many things to teach you now that you've begun to unconsciously channel magic into your body!" The wizened old woman gestured him to his feet. Bemused he followed her through the manor to the Talal ritual chamber.

"What do you mean instructor?" Lykos asked curiously.

"Bringing magic to your eyes boy! Did you not wonder why I had you learn to do that first? At the Citadel they teach those brats to channel magic into their limbs first, to strengthen and quicken them, so why did I teach you to see magic through your eyes?"

Lykos thought back to that first lesson, so long ago and tried to see past his excitement of seeing magic. After a moment it came to him. "Control."

Illusionist Maeve nodded approvingly. "Because of my illusions I could teach you the hardest part of learning magic, the art of feeling it, seeing it, knowing it. Most have no where near your skill with detecting magic and for good reason! Bringing magic into such delicate organs such as your ears or eyes can cause you to become permanently blind or deaf!"

Lykos looked at her in shock and anger. "You mean you could have crippled me?" he shouted upset.

A flurry of ghostly hands swatted at his head as she used her magic to punish him. Trying to protect his head from her magic distracted him from the danger of her walking stick, swung viciously into his knees, driving him to the ground.

"A fool would have crippled you. I have a mastery over illusions! I have practiced my craft for longer than you have been alive, than your parents have been alive! I knew what warning signs to watch for, so you would do well to treat me with the respect of my station!"

Lykos remained kneeling, trembling with shame and rage. He bowed his head and stated firmly, "I apologize for the insult Sorceress Maeve, I did not mean offense."

Illusionist Maeve grumbled yet waved for him to rise and follow her once more. He did so and she continued to speak.

"You have spent these past few months learning massive amounts of control so you do not destroy yourself or others while learning the more dangerous forms of magic. The Citadel is so sturdily built not just to keep out attacking forces but to make sure young mages do not level the kingdom.

"Your duel with Adelram this morning has revealed your magic has recognized your body as its vessel and it will always feed a small stream of magic into it, to protect it, heal it, improve it. You will find it a great boon and I will teach you how to increase the magic safely so your magic does not consume your body."

Lykos paused in shock. "My magic can consume my body?" he asked horrified.

"Aye, if you do not get your magic and body used to one another your magic will attempt to attack and consume it. Fear not, it rarely happens. Often the growth of your magic remains steady with the growth of your body, meaning that so long as you live the two will grow in sync."

"And why didn't you tell me this earlier? Before I started throwing fireballs around?" he asked, cross with her for withholding this information.

"It was found telling new mages that their magic could consume them often caused them to lose control and cause it to happen. So to limit the number of explosive fatalities it was agreed that the truth would be kept hidden until they were ready. However time fades truth and truth fades into myth. Only a few ever told their apprentices believing that such knowledge was too dangerous to possess and now few are even aware of the dangers."

Lykos nodded but still found the knowledge upsetting. "Do we know why magic consumes us?"

Illusionist Maeve gave a mirthless laugh. "No. All we know is that without control it consumes the mage from the inside out, causing them to go insane and lash out. The control needed to not die painfully is barely taught in the Citadel. If you had not been instructed by me your tutelage would already be completed under their system. Their combat instructors," she sneered, "would teach you how to use magic like a hammer, only refining their chosen heirs abilities while the rest suffered. A waste of magic!"

She suddenly leaped forwards and grabbed his arm with bruising strength. He attempted to break her grip but to his shock could not, the old woman's strength greater than even Adelram's. She pulled his face down to her own and whispered with deadly intent.

"My body may be frail but I have honed my magic for decades. It strengthens me beyond you now but so long as you keep training and practicing your control you will surpass me. But never lose sight of the simple fact that this gift may just as easily destroy you as it will empower you. So always treat it with the respect it deserves apprentice."

Her crushing grip relaxed and allowed him to pull his arm free. He nodded warily to his teacher as pins and needles flooded his arm, the blood pumping painfully with each heartbeat. However his eyes shone eagerly as he looked into Illusionist Maeve's own.

"Teach me."

Chapter Sixteen

"Boy! Are you down here?" Adelram's roar surprised Lykos causing his concentration to lapse. The magic in his limbs failed him and with a squawk of surprise he found his grip of a single finger on the wall no longer supporting his weight. He landed on the stone floor harshly and Illusionist Maeve cackled in glee at his failure.

"Down here!" he called out, rubbing his sore backside. As he rose to his feet Adelram strode angrily into the Talal ritual chamber and punched him square in the jaw.

"Of all the stupid bloody fool things to do!" Each word was punctuated with a punch thrown at Lykos but the young man was not going to take such an assault laying down. Kicking out with his legs he sent his foe to the floor. After several frantic minutes of grappling he managed to pin Adelram to the ground.

"Hello cousin, has something happened?" Lykos asked calmly, stretching his jaw carefully to make sure it wasn't broken.

"Get off me you peon!" Adelram struggled fruitlessly against him, unable to use his greater size and strength to his advantage.

"Are you going to punch me again?"

Adelram glared at him but his struggles were for naught. For one long moment Lykos kept him pinned but finally Adelram huffed in defeat.

"No."

Lykos released him and rose to his feet. After a moment of consideration he held out a hand to the downed man. He grasped Lykos' arm and began to pull himself upwards, only to find himself slamming into the ground as Lykos slammed his fist into his face. Illusionist Maeve cackled at the brutality.

"One good deed deserves another cousin. Now would you care to tell me why you're so vexed?" Lykos ignored the glare Adelram sent him with seasoned practice. Extending his arm once more Adelram warily took it but Lykos felt no need to strike him again. Fair is fair after all.

"Word in the quarter is that House Talal murdered House Stultus. Someone saw you at the ball and connected you to their deaths." Adelram spat out a glob of blood with a mildly impressed look. "Do you have any idea who?"

Lykos furrowed his brow in thought. "No I wore the mask the entire evening. The only people to see my face were Falka and Ana Del Rosa."

"Then how the hell were you discovered?" Adelram asked.

"Did you go through with your mother's plan to build relations between houses?" Illusionist Maeve interjected from the side. Lykos frowned.

"Well yes but after being denied by the first house I gave it up."

"Which house boy?" the wizened old woman demanded.

"House Sofos?" Both Adelram and Maeve groaned and Lykos looked between them in confusion. "Why would that matter, I was masked?"

"May the Goddesses damn that bastard," Adelram muttered as he paced angrily. Illusionist Maeve was just as displeased but turned towards Lykos to explain.

"Lord Sofos, or Arachnis as he was born, was allies with your father Leon during his rebellion. However when Leon went to go negotiate in the Citadel Arachnis was the one who began to slaughter and kill Leon's army. Everything was seemingly fine but his wife was caught in a crossfire between Talal and Kolos forces and died. To this day he hates two houses, care to guess which two?"

"Talal and Kolos." The obvious answer made Lykos groan as well.

"It would have been better for everyone if that bastard did us all a favor and died," Adelram spat. Lykos and Illusionist Maeve ignored him.

"So will their be any repercussions for my involvement in the extinction of House Stultus?" Lykos asked. Illusionist Maeve smirked at Adelram who rolled his eyes.

"Besides pointing a great big target at all of us?" he asked rhetorically. "The entire blasted kingdom of Mycenae will be watching us! Goodbye having time to build up our strength. And the Succession Trial tomorrow? Every single person will be aiming their blades at your back!" Adelram raged against their misfortune.

"So what can we do?" Lykos asked. Adelram sighed.

"Hope that the training you've received so far is enough for you to survive. Because if it isn't we're all dead. We need the Stultus resources to buy us time, until we can stand firm on our own strength. So try not to die tomorrow."

It was a somber mood that evening during supper as their small rag tag group considered their options. Even Illusionist Maeve found their change of fortunes vexing, her normally caustic attitude subdued. Thankfully the somber atmosphere was broken with a welcome interruption.

"Lykos! Want to go free a bunch of slaves? Whoa! Who died?" Falka of Falknor and Ana Del Rosa rushed excitedly through the dining room door.

"Probably us tomorrow," he answered without enthusiasm.

"How about maybe you tonight?" she asked with a grin. Shawna shot her a sharp look that was ignored.

"What did you have in mind?" Lykos asked rising from the table, his half-eaten meal forgotten.

"You need rest for the Succession Trial tomorrow," Adelram warned.

"I have too much energy to sleep. It will be good to do something useful instead of laying awake in bed all night." No one else protested as he followed Falka and Ana Del Rosa out of the Talal grounds.

"We found where Ana's family was being kept. It's an Emporo warehouse in Ploio, heavily guarded of course. We need your help in killing the guards so we can get in and out easily," she explained as they walked down the dark streets of Pyrgos. The night was young and tavern patrons, flesh workers, and more nefarious personalities shared the cobblestones with them.

"Sounds fun and distracting. Do you have an escape plan already prepared?"

"I do indeed so don't worry your pretty little head over it." Lykos rolled his eyes but decided to trust her.

"How have you been Ana?" he asked the silent young woman who almost blended into the masses around them. She perked up.

"Much better. I don't mind flesh work but all of this sneaking around is so much fun! Is it always this enjoyable for you?" she asked him excitedly. He gave a small chuckle.

"Well if you're caught everyone tries to kill you but for the most part it's not bad. Just the other day I had someone hold a knife to my throat and promise to gut and rob my corpse."

"I didn't threaten to rob your corpse," Falka muttered in a childish manner.

"No but we both know you would have," Lykos replied dryly. The trio laughed and paused at a portion of the wall signifying the boundary of Pyrgos. To their left were many rundown buildings that looked ready to fall over and to their right were several large warehouses. Lykos looked around curiously before turning to Falka. "Don't we need to go down to reach Ploio?"

Falka smirked and he felt a brief shiver of fear down his spine. "We do."

"Then shouldn't we be heading towards the gate?" He gestured opposite of the way they had walked. Her smirk grew into a full blown grin and even Ana Del Rosa seemed to find something amusing about their conversation.

"Behold! The Descent of Tartarus!" Falka bowed and gestured in a grand fashion to the dilapidated building behind her. Lykos looked at the run down building with a blank stare before turning back to her.

"Okay." The word was dragged out slowly, unwillingly from his lips. "I'll bite. What is the Descent of Tartarus?"

Falka and Ana shared a grin as they advanced on him. Each taking an arm they began to drag him into the building.

"It is the most-"

"Fiendish-"

"Devilish-"

"Dangerous-"

"Exhilarating-"

"Thing I have ever done!" Ana Del Rosa finished with a shout. Lykos gave her an indulging smile before turning to Falka. She gave him a lazy grin.

"The aqueduct that provides the lower quarters with fresh water has an entrance underneath this building. If you're not afraid to get a little wet it's an excellent way to descend to the lower quarters without all of that tedious walking."

He looked around at the old building's interior with renewed interest at her words. If what she said was true then this building was extremely valuable. He looked around and was impressed with the quality of furniture and fixtures on display, if a bit dirty. He couldn't understand why it was abandoned.

"Oh it's supposedly haunted," Falka replied to his inquiry. "It was once one of the high end flesh palaces in the kingdom, famed for its exceptional workers but one night disaster struck. A young lord felt slighted by one of the flesh maidens and tried to force himself upon her. When she refused, he persisted, and in retaliation she castrated and killed him. The lord's family grew enraged and attacked the brothel, slaying all of the workers and patrons. The flesh maiden in question was hung off the chandelier there. Ever since then horrifying moans could be heard every night."

Lykos looked around at the chandelier and could indeed see the ends of a rope hanging from one of the hooks, the dangling end cut. As he opened his mouth to speak a garbled moan sounded from behind him. Turning, he scowled at Falka.

"Ha ha. You scared me," he deadpanned.

"That wasn't me though!" she denied. Lykos turned to glare accusingly at Ana only for all three of them to freeze as another moan echoed through the broken building. The trio turned and looked up at the ceiling in surprise.

"Huh," Lykos said simply. He rushed to the stairs, drawings his sword with a quick motion. Falka followed his steps closely, also drawing her sword as a delighted smile crossed her face. Ana Del Rosa called after them.

"Wait! What are you two doing?" she asked. She followed them up as she was unwilling to be alone in the creepy building.

"I've never fought a ghost before!" Lykos whispered excitedly. Falka nodded in agreement beside him as they crept up the stairs to the next floor. The furnishings were just as decorative here, covered in dirt and cobwebs of passing years. A few Tainted Gnawers scurried along the floor, ignoring the humans intruding on their nests. The moans continued, echoing from down the hall and Falka and

Lykos crept excitedly towards them. An odd noise could be heard accompanying the moans now.

"I really think we should just go," Ana Del Rosa tried to convince them to no avail, as the sounds began to sound familiar to her.

"Nonsense!" Falka laid a hand on the doorknob and turned towards Lykos. "Ready to slay a ghost?"

"Ready," he replied with a feral grin on his face. This night was already more promising than laying in bed at home dreading tomorrow.

Falka threw open the door and Lykos and she charged in with their swords raised high, war cries shouting from their lips. A moment later their shouts of wars turned to screams of terror and they bolted back through the door and towards the stairs. Ana Del Rosa looked into the room and glimpsed two naked, sweating bodies interrupted mid-coitus, staring with surprise at the interruption.

"Uh, excuse us," she apologized. Ana Del Rosa raced down after her companions as the fatter of the two figures on the bed cursed while the thinner one blinked in shock.

"What was that all about?" the thin soldier who once guarded Hearthome asked his fat companion as they lay in bed.

Downstairs Falka was frantically pulling at an old door while Lykos heaved out an open window. Ana Del Rosa calmly joined the pair and looked at them in confusion. "Haven't you ever seen two men make love before?"

Falka joined Lykos at the window.

A short time later, after their heaves had subsided and Ana Del Rosa had stopped laughing at the pair, Lykos assisted Falka in opening the old door. He summoned a ball of fire to illuminate the room to reveal a basement cluttered with cushions, bunks, and a kitchen. It was to the kitchen the trio went.

In the corner was a smooth stone slab secured snugly yet Falka pried it loose with a length of iron. Leaning over the hole Lykos could see an ever flowing current of water rush by. He turned to Falka.

"How many times have you done this?" he asked as his thoughts strayed to his time in the cold mines of Svellheim and the dangers of dark watery graves.

"Enough to know it's safe," she replied cheerfully.

"That strangely doesn't fill me with confidence," he replied as Falka made a gesture to Ana Del Rosa. He found himself flailing through the air as the young woman pushed him into the hole. With a sudden splash he found himself carried away by a strong current.

Breaching the surface Lykos heard two more splashes echoing behind him, signifying his companions joining him in the aqueduct. As nerve wracking as the experience was, he found the steady descent of water pleasing to float down, having more than enough room that he did not have to worry about bumping unnecessarily into the walls.

"Here's the fun part!" Falka cried from behind him, her voice echoing.

"I thought we already did the fun part?" Lykos asked. He cried out as he found out what she meant, the water around him suddenly vanished as he found himself airborne. Flailing through the air he was surprised once more when he landed in a large body of water, the surface indistinguishable from the pitch black darkness of the reservoir. Struggling to the surface, he narrowly avoided Falka and Ana Del Rosa landing on top of him as they joined him in the pool. The trio breached the surface.

"That was not fun," Lykos muttered unconvincingly as the two women laughed joyfully. Falka led the way to a nearby ledge and they climbed up, laying gasping on the cool stone. She slapped his arm lightly.

"Hush you. It is simply the most marvelous way to get around the kingdom. Those aqueducts are everywhere and they're much cleaner to go through than the sewers."

Lykos was forced to agree. With the numerous underground lakes in the mountain range around them the citizens of Mycenae use of water was to their advantage. With aqueducts, canals, and levies crisscrossing the rivers of the kingdom, water transport was just as comfortable as travel by airship but far cheaper. However if one wanted privacy, the catacombs and sewers were far more secluded.

When their breathe returned the trio stood and walked down one of the tunnels leading away. Lykos once more summoned fire to provide light and he peered inquisitively at the carved walls along their path. "What are these markings?"

Falka waved her hand dismissively. "Some of these walls talk about our early history but reading them is beyond pointless. Generations of miscreant youths," she grinned as she gestured at their group, "have added their own additions over time. Only a few of the original carvings remain. A shame really."

Lykos agreed as he read a portion of one wall depicting how the people of Latom carved great furrows into the earth for Mycenae's stone. That they choose to build their buildings and homes in those holes instead of on top led to the large height difference between them and the quarter of Pyrgos. However he was displeased to find the rest of the passage erased by the crude marking of Anglo the Hung.

Ahead of them a torrent of water cascaded and Falka led them off to one side of its unending stream. Squeezing through a small tunnel Lykos found himself standing on a ledge overlooking the merchant quarter of Ploio. Looking up he saw the towering cliff face give way to the smooth stone walls of the kingdom. He quenched the conjured flame and the darkness of night once more consumed them.

"Expedient. You say there are other short cuts like this one?" he asked. They began to make their way down an almost invisible path.

"Aye, all over the kingdom. I've only heard of them this past year and found a scant few." Falka shot a coy look over her shoulder. "I wonder how many you can find."

Lykos rolled his eyes but firmly decided to find every single one of them, even if only just to rub it in her face. The use of his father's maps would prove invaluable in this unspoken contest. The trio descended from the ledge quickly and found themselves moving along the dark streets towards the river front.

"How many guards?" Lykos asked after several minutes of walking.

"Two days ago it was ten, yesterday it was fourteen, and this morning it was twelve. Let us hope a few more didn't stop by the bakers while we were gone," Falka replied as she gestured for them to join her in climbing a nearby building.

Lykos and Falka had no issue, used to climbing buildings and the like throughout their lives but Ana Del Rosa found herself struggling to clamber the sturdy structures. Finally they took pity on her and helped her climb up as time was of the essence. The trio laid along the edge of the roof looking out over the docks.

Before them lay a long line of wooden warehouses, built along the waterfront in an orderly fashion. A few boats still sailed up and down the river but their attention was unimportant as the sailors would not halt their deliveries for anything short of Armageddon. The true issue at hand were the two dozen guards patrolling around the buildings.

"Well this will be enjoyable," Lykos muttered as he examined them. A brief pulse of magic to his eyes allowed him to see if any of the guards possessed magic and thankfully the answer was none as it would have made their task impossible. As it were he did not like the odds of a frontal assault. Stealth on the other hand was much more promising.

"Oh Goddesses, what will we do? There's so many! We'll never get my family out of there!" Ana Del Rosa began to wail and Falka wrapped the shorter woman in a hug. Lykos frowned at the noise and was relieved no one noticed them. He examined the patrolling men and saw a pattern.

"It's not all bad Ana, I can see a pattern in their movements. Falka and I can go down there, eliminate the men quietly, then we can get your family out. See look over there at those men by the docks, they're-" Lykos found himself cut off by a soft moan beside him. Turning, his eyes widened in surprise and anger at the sight of Falka and Ana Del Rosa kissing passionately on the rooftop beside him.

"Falka!" Lykos hissed to no avail as the young women ignored him. "Falka!" He tried once more, poking her insistently as several of the guards broke off their patrol to vanish inside a warehouse. She merely waved a hand at him dismissively, never halting in kissing Ana. Annoyed at the dismissal he rolled his eyes and turned back to the patrolling men.

"Fine I'll just do it all myself," he muttered as he crawled off the roof, leaving the two women to their activities. Frustrated with himself and them, he found himself quite brutally strangling the first guard and tossing him into the deep river. Exhaling deeply to calm himself he moved onto the next guard determined to complete this mission by himself. There were lives to be saved.

He moved patiently and efficiently through the patrolling men, killing and hiding their bodies lest they be discovered and raise an alarm. The fact that none of the men had noticed their compatriots disappearances spoke ill of their discipline and Lykos vowed to never allow anyone under his command to be this lax.

Finally all that remained were two men standing guard around a burning brazier for warmth near the warehouse door. Chancing a portal creation Lykos was pleased when it stabilized and he quickly went through it, his sword swinging. The first guard was not even aware of his death with how smoothly it occurred but the second guard saw him appear seemingly out of thin air, a terrifying bloody specter killing his friend with ease. He opened his mouth to scream and Lykos lunged forth, burying the blade in his mouth. He fell to the ground as he choked on his blood.

Removing his weapon, Lykos calmly flicked the blood from it. He turned to the dark warehouse door and moved closer to listen through the wood. The sounds of crying men and women could be heard and the few wails of children tugged at his conscience. Enraged, he swiftly entered and hid behind a nearby crate to survey the large space although his eyes popped open with disbelief at the sheer number of prisoners contained therein. The poor lighting could not conceal the dozens of caged men, women, and children along the walls nor could anything disguise the smell of unwashed bodies in an enclosed space. And in the center of the room stood the guards around several bloody prisoners.

They were all clothed, for what little comfort that might provide as the guards beat them without mercy. "This batch is worthless!" one of them mocked in a rough voice as he kicked a young boy's side. The child did not move and Lykos almost snarled at the sight of broken bones sticking out of his sides. "There's no fight in any of them! I doubt we'll get our gold's worth out of any of them."

The men laughed and jeered in equal measure at the cowering slaves underneath their feet. Lykos' anger burned coldly within him and he almost rose to his feet to slay them when one of the other guards spoke up.

"They're not for fighting anyways. Lord Kolos wants them for his men for *practice*." The guards laughed once more at their fellow's inflection and Lykos knew without a doubt that he would not allow these men to live. Realizing the distance between them would give the guards too much time to prepare he thought of a cunning plan. Sheathing his sword he stood and walked boldly towards them with a smile.

"Gentlemen! It's a fine evening, is it not?" he asked in a loud voice, catching the attention of everyone in the warehouse. Silence hung heavily in the air as the slaves stared at him in fear and the guards with confusion.

"Who the hell are you?" one of the guards asked. All of the men had a black rectangle sewn on their clothes, signifying their allegiance to the Citadel guard and thus House Kolos. Their hands went to their weapons as Lykos stepped closer.

"Why Lord Kolos sent me! I am Lord Talal and I am here to move this shipment." Lykos gestured towards the slaves in the room who whimpered in response. Some of the guards nodded and relaxed their grips on their weapons, grinning at who they thought to be a kindred soul. *Their mistake*, Lykos thought darkly as he moved ever closer.

"He's been extremely pleased with your work and you shall all be richly rewarded!" This statement relaxed the other men's hands from their weapons and they looked incredibly satisfied with themselves. Lykos moved closer yet.

"Will he let us pick?" the first man asked with a greedy expression, gesturing to the terrified slaves all around them. Lykos smile deepened even more as he neared them.

"No he has something of a much greater value to bestow upon you!" Lykos replied as he gestured grandiosely to the building around them.

"Lord Kolos will give us this warehouse?" the same man asked and his fellow guards began to talk of what they would do with their shares. Lykos gave them a slow shake of his head as he stopped next to them, the six of them arrayed around him in a circle. Understanding dawned in the man's eyes.

"He will recognize us?" The other five men stopped talking as they looked upon him with eager eyes. Lykos realized these men were probably bastards of House Kolos.

"He will recognize you indeed," he said with a smirk. The men cheered and Lykos blurred. Throwing two knives out they impaled the throats of the guards on either side of him, men whose jubilation was cut short by cold steel. He reached forward and grabbed a man's sword from his waist and drew it with one hand as he drew his own with the other. He slashed, once, twice, three times at the man's chest and he went down with a cry. The slaves under their feet cried out as blood poured over them.

Lykos turned around and the last three men had recovered enough to draw their weapons for what little good it did them. For while they fought with fear against him, he fought with hate, his memories of spending years as a slave in the mines fresh in his mind as he met them in bloody combat. Two of the guards fell in bloody chunks, such was the ferocity of his strikes. The last guard stumbled backwards, trying to flee him in terror, but Lykos refused to stop. Lunging forwards he impaled the man with both blades and took him brutally down.

The sudden violence was over in a flash and the only sounds in the room were the slaves crying softly underfoot. The dozens of slaves in cages watched Lykos in fear and curiosity as he ignored them. He instead choose to stab each man he killed once in the heart to ensure they were indeed dead and took the time to retrieve his knives. Finally the last man lay before him, the one he had slashed with his own sword, gasping for breathe.

"Why has father killed us?" Blood bubbled at his lips and Lykos knew he was not long for the world. "We did everything he asked."

Lykos knelt next to the man and stabbed him with a knife. With a shuddering gasp the man died and he withdrew from the corpse. "Your father killed mine." The words rang hollow in his ears as he turned to face the caged men and women. For a long moment all was silent.

"Slave!" Lykos roared, startling many of those entrapped. "That is what they call you. Slave. That is the only name they allow you to have. But you all have names don't you? You whisper them to yourselves at night, while the guards tighten your chains. You scream them in your mind when they beat at you with whips! You have been enslaved against your own will, subjugated by your fellow man and they think they can take away everything that makes you human!

"I too have been where you are, kneeling at the feet of unworthy masters and I too desired the freedom you all seek, to shout my name to the sky above! However I know the truth, it wasn't just freedom I wanted. It was revenge. I wanted to slaughter my oppressors, inflict the wounds they inflicted upon me a hundred times over! I wanted them to know true suffering! I wanted them to know the helplessness I had been forced to endure for years!

"When I was freed I was denied my revenge. I was denied that sweet fruit. But all of you have been enslaved by House Kolos and House Kolos is my enemy! If you join me I will deliver you to your revenge and I will help you take it!"

The slaves banged on their cages with their chains, shouts and cries tore from their lips as they listened to his words. Many began to shout their names, determined to no longer be addressed as *slave,* determined to be someone. With a satisfied nod Lykos called forth two brilliant balls of flames to the amazement of the slaves and threw them at the locks of the cages. They burned through the metal locks slowly but with desperate heaves the slaves pushed themselves free. Lykos stood tall and proud in the center of the room as they encircled him.

"My name is Lykos," he told the men and women near him, their expressions set in determination. "Who among you will stand with me? Name yourself!"

The answering roar of names shook the warehouse walls. Lykos looked upon those dirty, determined faces and knew that this is how he would fix this broken kingdom. With the slaves, the down-trodden, the outcasts. He would gather the scraps of Mycenae and forge a new kingdom out of the ashes.

And his family would be safe. He would be safe.

Chapter Seventeen

"Well look who finally joined us," Lykos snarked as he was joined by an unabashed Falka and anxious Ana Del Rosa. Falka merely smirked at him as Ana searched the large crowd of men and women for her family. Lykos gestured for a nearby man to direct the former slaves to break into the nearby warehouses and steal their goods.

"You seem to have things handled." Falka smiled at his unamused expression. He gave her a dark look before walking to a nearby crate to examine its contents. Upon seeing it full of swords, he gestured to two nearby men to take it.

"We'll talk about this later. Right now I hope you have a plan to move all of these people out of the quarter before they're captured again. Several concerned citizens have already been spotted watching us," he told her firmly.

"Oh ye of little faith. I got us here and I can get us out again. Send a fireball as high as you can into the sky," she ordered. Lykos eyed her but did as he was told. The nearby freed slaves gasped in shock as the fireball flew high up into the sky and exploded with a soft boom. He turned back to Falka.

"Now that I've announced to everyone in the quarter that we're here, what's the next suicidal move?" he asked. Falka merely smiled and pointed into the dark night. One moment there was nothing near them and the next a large airship was landing with a splash in the dark waters of the river. He gave her an unimpressed look.

"This is a horrible idea."

"Relax, once we get high enough in the sky no one will be able to see the airship, thus we can safely land anywhere in the kingdom. Although we should be landing at Hearthome. You have plenty of room to house all of these people and I don't feel like explaining to my father why we're suddenly caring for dozens of people." Lykos' annoyance at Falka's presumptive nature grew stronger with each passing moment.

Deciding to discuss it later, and he truly did have the room for all of these people, he ordered the former slaves to load their stolen goods and persons onto the airship. As the mass of people approached the massive vessel long planks and ropes were thrown overboard to aid in the transfer. Within moments, the docks were empty and Lykos found himself boarding the airship last, making sure no one was left behind. The ropes and planks were withdrawn and the airship began the laborious task of rising.

It was not a moment too soon as a squad of Citadel guards rushed onto the docks shooting arrows at the airship. The former slaves cried out in alarm but Lykos watched as the men and women manning the ship stepped up to the rails and returned fire with bows of their own. Against their superior numbers and height advantage, the guards retreated.

"Take that black hearts! To your station men!" one of the men shouted and the rest of the crew scurried about the airship. Lykos approached him and spied Falka by his side. "Ah Lord Talal, welcome aboard the Falling Star!"

"Thank you captain," Lykos bowed his head in respect. The man shot a smirk at Falka.

"You didn't tell him did you?" the man asked Falka rhetorically. "I'm Captain Avarc of Falknor. Falka's my youngest sister."

Peering between the two Lykos could see the similarities. With long, thin limbs and dark hair the two could almost pass as twins. He nodded and shook the other man's hand.

"You have my sympathies," Lykos ignored Falka's pout with ease, "and thank you for your passage this evening Captain Avarc. Will we have any issues with uninvited passengers?" Captain Avarc smiled appreciatively at his wit.

"No the only thing we'll have to worry about are-"

"Tainted off the starboard side!" a panicked cry called out. Lykos and Captain Avarc rushed to the railing and could see the dark shapes of Tainted Razorbacks swarming the airship in a black cloud. They blended almost perfectly into the dark night and it was only the sound of their metallic wing beats that alerted the Falling Star's crew.

"To stations! Repel the Tainted!" Captain Avarc's crew worked efficiently, arming the ballista lining the ships deck. "Take us above the cloud layer!"

The airship lurched and began to rapidly rise once more. Lykos was glad the night was as dark as it was so that the height they had reached was not discernible. Between the first airship voyage which had ended in a crash and climbing into Hearthome, he was still not overly fond of heights.

"Tainted off the port side!" another voice cried out. Captain Avarc cursed before calling out to Lykos.

"Lord Talal! Could you assist in evicting our uninvited guests?" Captain Avarc threw a bolt of lightning that streaked through the night illuminating a sizable horde swarming the Falling Star. Several Tainted were struck and screamed violent death cries as they fell.

"Of course captain!" Lykos rushed to the opposite side of the ship and conjured up a fireball. One of Captain Avarc's crew cried out in alarm.

"Not fire my lord! You'll ignite the gas!" The deckhand pointed to the inflated balloon above them. "Bring lightning down upon them and they'll flee soon enough!"

Lykos nodded abashed and quenched the flame in his hands. Breathing in deep he thrust out his hand and was pleased when a lightning bolt left, dashing through the air. While not as large or widespread as Captain Avarc's, his was still able to strike several Razorbacks. The beasts fell out of the sky, spiraling down to the kingdom below. Despite their numerical advantage the Razorbacks were comparatively weak due to their small size.

"Take cover!" a voice shouted and Lykos dove behind a ballista with two other men. A series of bone shards embedded in the wood around them and one of the men cried out as he was pinned to the deck.

"Help him, I'll take care of the Tainted," Lykos ordered standing up from his cover. Sending out several more bolts of lightning he could see the culprit, an enormous Tainted Razorback hovered in the air next to them. Narrowing his eyes, he traded several volleys with the beast, taking cover when it launched bone spikes from its back.

Lykos felt his strength waning as the battle dragged on. No matter his attack the Tainted beast shrugged it off and he despaired that he would be unable to kill it. Fortunately aid came in the form of Captain Avarc.

"Thank you for your assistance Lord Talal, allow me to return the favor!" Captain Avarc focused his magic in a ball between his hands and Lykos could see the energy desperate to escape. The strength grew and grew before finally the older man deemed it enough. Thrusting forward with both hands the electric energy lanced forward and burned into the wretched beast. With a pained croak, its wings stilled and slowly gravity claimed its corpse.

With its death the other Tainted retreated, allowing peace to return to the night. While none of the crew had died, many had been wounded including many of the freed slaves who had been huddling on the deck. The crew members began basic repairs and first aid as Lykos turned towards Captain Avarc.

"Are voyages always this exciting on board the Falling Star?"

The captain's laugh echoed through the cool night as they flew towards Hearthome.

Shawna was pleased to have so many guests. Illusionist Maeve was not.

"How do you know there aren't any spies among them boy! You could be inviting the enemy right into your home!"

"I sincerely doubt any potential spies locked themselves in cages instructor. However on the off chance that I am wrong, you're more than welcome to tell me I told you so before they stab me in the back." His reply was not appreciated and Illusionist Maeve spent several minutes whacking him with her wooden walking stick.

The group was gathered on the terrace overlooking Mycenae after he had awoken them in the middle of the night with a ship full of ecstatic former slaves. Captain Avarc laughed with Adelram as they watched Lykos be attacked by the elderly woman, the spectacle a welcome respite to the night's dangerous activities. The two had been acquaintances some years back and enjoyed the opportunity to catch up as Captain Avarc's men unloaded his airship of supplies and freed slaves. Shawna was settling them in the servants lodge built into the mountain and Falka was approaching their group with several of the former slaves.

"Well I think tonight was a success! Lykos please meet Ana's family. This is her father Kavar, her mother Castalia, and her sister Elanor." Falka gestured to each member as she named them. All three of them had worn, tired expressions due to the excitement of the evening but their eyes shown brightly as they gratefully thanked him for freeing them. He waved away their bowing.

"A friend of mine said she needed some help and I was more than willing to lend a hand. I'm pleased this evening has ended so well."

"Don't be so modest Lykos you performed admirably tonight," Falka drawled as she stroked Ana Del Rosa's arm. He gave her a hard stare.

"Indeed. Could we talk privately for a moment Falka?" He gestured towards the house. She nodded agreeably and the pair left behind the group and approached the house.

"So what was it that you wanted to talk to me about?" she asked. He waited until they were around the corner and out of sight of the freed slaves and before turning to the shorter woman.

"What the hell was that tonight?" he demanded angrily. Falka looked at him in surprise.

"What do you mean?" she tried asking.

"Inviting me along to help you on a rescue mission that will anger another house at my expense and abandoning me to suck face with another woman." Lykos forced himself to keep his voice calm but it was a trying experience.

"You had it well in hand!" she protested.

"That's not the point Falka! The point is you dragged me along to help you and did nothing! I am not some mercenary to use for your own purposes! I'm stealing the *property*," he spat the word hatefully, "of another house and if they identify me they'll descend on us like a plague! I'm not going to die because you were in a mood!"

Silence descended between them as they considered their actions and words, mindful that the true victory tonight were the dozens of freed men and women. As the silence grew longer both shot the other a shy glance out of the corner of their eyes and sighed. They both opened their mouth to speak.

"I'm sorry-"

"No I am-"

"No I've been an utter fool."

"Well that makes two of us."

Falka and Lykos shared a smile.

"Are we friends again?"

"As far as I'm concerned we never stopped." The pair shared a warm smile at his words. They began to walk back to their families quietly in companionable peace.

"So you and Ana huh?"

The dark night was once more illuminated with the laughter of their families as Falka chased Lykos through the garden. Despite the trials and blood to come the small group of allies had high spirits, self-assured in their own ability and covert actions. But in the dark Citadel, malevolent eyes watched their meeting with hatred. And it plotted.

Chapter Eighteen

The towers of the Citadel rose high against the mountains surrounding Mycenae, its walls smoothed over years by erosion yet they still stood thick and tall, a defiant testament of their strength. Guards manned the walls, for despite the distance to the wilds to the north and west Tainted would never be allowed to breach their boundary, let alone reach them. It was within these walls that the Citadel guard were trained and housed, dispensing justice throughout Mycenae and acting as its army against other kingdoms. It was the pride of the kingdom.

Lykos loathed it.

It was a constant reminder to him that his life in Mycenae would not be easy, bloodless, for he was now the possible son of a man he had never met and whose actions nearly destroyed the kingdom two decades before. Each guard with that small black square on their arms was an enemy he would eventually face and conquer, otherwise he would killed or worse, captured. Lykos shuddered with the thoughts of being whipped, dunked under freezing falls, and tortured once more.

"Having second thoughts boy?" Adelram asked gruffly from beside him. With them were Shawna and Illusionist Maeve, who were both looking up at the Citadel with a variety of emotions. Behind the two women were two of the former slaves, tall and strong men who volunteered to guard the two women during the day. Lykos had supplied them with spears and shields and was pleased that they held them firmly, without fear. Their presence was largely a smokescreen, if it came to a fight Illusionist Maeve would be more than capable of destroying their attackers. Still, appearances mattered.

"No," Lykos stated firmly before following the influx of common folk into the Citadel. Like the rest of the kingdom the quarter had been rebuilt over time with sturdier materials as they became available. As such, the stone streets and buildings were old, strong, and oppressive as they loomed down upon them. The Citadel Keep blended in seamlessly with the walls and quarter, to refer to any part was to refer to all of it.

The citizens of this quarter were the elite, the wealthiest or most powerful individuals in the kingdom. Many noble houses resided within these buildings, content to not fight over territory but to consolidate their own power, and it was from this quarter that the rest of Mycenae was controlled through wealth and brute might. Lykos wanted to raze it to the ground and force the ignorant lords and ladies to live the harsh life of a laborer.

Following the crowd they approached a large basin in the mountain, where gatherings and rainfall had formed a large depression over thousands of years. Stone steps led down to a circular patch of dirt and it was towards this arena that everyone was moving. After all, no one wanted to miss the Succession Trial.

"Do you understand how the events will proceed today?" Adelram asked Lykos as they made their way down the steps. Shawna and Illusionist Maeve parted from them with quiet words, their guards following them like shadows. Lykos gave his mother a smile and was pleased she returned it briefly before the crowds separated them.

"The Commander of the Citadel will open the ceremony. After his speech he will call for challengers from the population to prove their worth. The only ones allowed to challenge will be those who sit on the bottom row of the arena, anyone else will be turned away. The combatants will battle until there are no more challengers remaining," he obediently summarized.

"Good, now I suggest conserving your strength, you should stand after the competition has thinned itself out a little." Adelram began to advise before Lykos cut him off.

"No." They reached the bottom steps and began to move towards the far side of the arena, where seating was still available. There were many challengers waiting already and they eyed their competition and Lykos warily. However some of them looked at him with hate in their eyes and he knew that they would desire his death.

Fortunately he was prepared to meet them.

"What do you mean no?" Adelram demanded. Lykos calmly sat down on the lowest stone bench with the other challengers.

"I will be the first to stand in the Succession Trial and the last to walk away," he informed his cousin succinctly.

"Are you mad boy!" Adelram stared at Lykos in horror as the young man ignored him in favor of checking the straps on his vambraces. "That would allow every single one of these morons to attack you right from the get go! No one has ever lasted the entire time of the arena, the sheer number of foes you'll have to face will exhaust you alone!"

Satisfied that his forearms would not be getting severed in the coming conflict Lykos checked his boots next. "Which will make it all the more impressive when I destroy them. I must strike down so many today that it will give our enemies pause. They must fear the retribution I can bring down upon them or else they will strike at us before we can gather an army, before we can fight back. We need time and this is how we'll get it."

Lykos could see the wisdom in his words infuriate his cousin but he understood it was not directed at him. Their position was precarious and if he did not tread carefully they would all die before they could truly begin.

"Do you disagree?" Lykos asked sitting up straight. He held the older man's eyes steadily, not allowing any of the uncertainty or fear clawing within him out. To break now would spell their deaths. Adelram finally nodded.

"Your father would be proud of you," Adelram said softly. Lykos smiled at the thought.

"Did you know him well?" he asked as Adelram climbed around him on the stone bench, sitting on the next level up as he was not vying for the right to the Stultus Holdings.

"Not as well as Shawna but I knew him well enough. He fought with a ferocity unlike any I had ever seen. I once heard tale of how he slew forty men pillaging his quarter."

"There are a lot more than forty men here."

"Aye there is." Adelram's voice was grim and they both lapsed into silence, dark thoughts plaguing their minds.

The arena steadily filled and more challengers sat upon the lowest stone bench. However as the seats filled up Lykos became aware of a disturbing fact. For no matter how crowded the bench across from him became no one sat near him. Indeed many of the challengers crowded next to one another and shared whispers as they all stared at him.

"It appears the rumor that I ended House Stultus has been spreading. I think that even if I tried to play it safe everyone in this arena would be after me regardless."

"Well of course, you're just a pathetic upstart," a voice behind him sneered. Turning his head he saw Viktor of House Kolos stepping across the stone benches with a retinue of guards. They pushed Adelram to the side as Viktor took the seat next to Lykos. "There's the small matter of someone placing a nice bounty on your head this morning as well. I think it was a hundred pieces of gold for your death."

Viktor and his guards shared a dark laugh that left no illusion as to who put up the bounty. Lykos however would not let the slight be.

"A hundred gold pieces? I feel honored, that could buy your house!" Lykos drawled. Viktor sneered at him.

"Laugh all you want worm, I look forward to slitting your throat today." Viktor was interrupted by another voice.

"Is this spot taken?" Grimm stood before them, gesturing towards the spot next to Lykos.

"Sure, might as well make it a party." Lykos gestured to the stone beside him. "Come to kill me as well?"

"Oh I'll be getting my pound of flesh from you no doubt, before Viktor gets to you at any rate. He's a messy eater." Grimm sat down as Viktor scowled. "Careful Vicky, your face might get stuck that way."

"You will pay me the respect I am due Grimm! I am the heir of Kopanos!" Viktor demanded.

"Kopanos is bald?" Grimm asked. Lykos decided a moment of levity before death was needed.

"Of course not, you heard Vicky, he has a single hair." Viktor shook with rage as Grimm and Lykos laughed.

"If you fight as well as you jest I might have a challenge today," Grimm casually remarked.

"If you fight as well as you jest I might as well leave," Lykos replied.

"Even if you ran away I would still have to fight you. I would merely have to hunt you down as well," his grim reply caused Lykos to look at him with interest.

"Oh? And for what slight has captured my pursuers interest? I haven't slept with your sister have I?"

"You don't even know? Surely you are a cruel jester," Grimm said with interest. Lykos shook his head.

"To my knowledge we first met at the Stultus Ball Heir Sofos." Lykos could feel Adelram stiffen behind him and belatedly remembered the reason why. Grimm for his part looked surprised.

"My mother died due to your father's rebellion. As he is dead I will take my revenge out on his son," Grimm's voice was steel as he explained. Lykos nodded and wondered just how many enemies he inherited from Leon.

"My apologies," Lykos said honestly but the words came out strained. Grimm gave him a hard look before nodding once with a tightened jaw.

"Heir Kolos your father said you were not to participate," an authoritative voice ordered. Looking over Lykos saw a man their age with close cut hair staring down at the enraged heir beside him. Something struck him as familiar within the features of his face but he knew not where he knew the man from.

"I don't care what father wants Alithis, I'm teaching this cur some respect!" Viktor protested.

"And I don't care what you want. Lord Kolos ordered me to break your legs if you so much as stand from this step." The newly named Alithis sat next to Viktor but Lykos could feel his eyes on him as well. So he couldn't help but speak up.

"Are you here to try your luck too Alithis?"

The cold eyes seemed to freeze over and both men tensed, preparing themselves for violence. After a moment Alithis relaxed and Lykos reluctantly followed suit.

"I am patient in my hunt," Alithis said simply and purposely turned his head away.

"Looks like the bastard saves you from my blade Lykos," Viktor muttered angrily. Lykos sensed Grimm turn to him once more.

"But not from mine." Lykos eyed him before staring into the center of the arena.

"Oh joy," he sighed. This day promised to be fun.

It was only a few more minutes of waiting before everyone was settled in the arena. Try as Lykos might he could not find his mother Shawna or Illusionist Maeve in the crowds and instead settled for the quiet support of Adelram at his back. Finally the moment arrived and he watched as the Commander of the Citadel entered the arena.

The crowds hushed themselves as he descended the steps and by the time he reached the bottom it was dead silent. Lykos felt his heart pumping faster and faster as the anticipation as to what would come dominated his mind, captivated his spirit. The Commander of the Citadel walked to the center of the arena and spoke:

"Brothers! Sisters! Citizens of Mycenae, the greatest kingdom in the world! We have gathered here today for the most terrible of events! The noble house of Stultus has been rendered extinct and all that remains of its once proud ranks are the bastards here to make a claim today.

"Long ago when this Citadel was first constructed it was meant to be protection from our ancient foe the Tainted! However as time went on and the enemy outside our walls grew weaker and yielded to our might petty jealousy and feuds erupted from within our own ranks! Family turned against family, friends against friends. They were dark days in our kingdom and it was by the Goddesses wisdom we forged a lasting peace!

"The Succession Trial is a remnant from that era! It was a contest to allow only the most worthy warriors to stand among the elite and guide our kingdom! Here any man or woman, be they noble, common, or bastard, is allowed to put forth a claim! Any bastard who wins here today will be recognized as a true member of their house. Any common man may stand equal to a noble and any noble who prevails here shall expand their families holdings greatly!

"The time is at hand for our victor to emerge! Only those sitting upon the bottom row may enter the arena floor, only they may attempt the challenge. To prevail you must defeat your opponents until death or submission. Now who among you will rise to the challenge of the Succession Trial?"

The crowd went frantic with noise and energy as the Commander of the Citadel wound up their excitement. Lykos himself could feel his blood pumping with energy, his muscles tensing, magic begging to be released. With one last deep breathe he stood and all eyes in the arena snapped towards him. With bold steps he walked towards his destiny.

Chapter Nineteen

Lykos could not hear the roaring crowd as they cheered and mocked him in equal measure. He could not see the Commander of the Citadel back away from the center of the arena as he approached it. And he could not know that at that moment in the stands, his mother Shawna prayed to the Goddesses, their absent gods, for his protection.

He did know that every single warrior on the bottom row was focused on him, eyeing his worth. He halted in the center of the arena and bared his neck in defiance, turning their judgment back onto them. With a smooth motion Lykos drew his sword.

Immediately half a dozen challengers stood up and raced towards him. If Lykos had the time to learn their stories he would discover that they were some of the Stultus' many unrecognized children, hoping to kill the man who slayed their fathers. However he was more than equal to these men and women and had little trouble holding his ground. Pushing them back with a blast of magic to give himself some space, he thrust out an arm sending a bolt of lightning to chain from one bastard to the next. After several sizzling moments of pain and torture for them, they collapsed to the ground trembling.

Lykos and the other warriors looked at the fallen foes, with apathetic and evaluating eyes respectively. His swift and brutal response had convinced a small number of challengers to remain seated lest they meet the same fate. However one woman rose to the challenge.

The woman was from House Vrachos, the stone workers who built Mycenae, and she possessed no meager skill with earth magic. Forgoing her blade she brought forth several rocks from the earth and launched them at Lykos. Attempting to dodge was futile as she merely summoned them back to her for reuse. He knew he had to finish the woman quickly or she'd turn him into a bloody pulp.

So he sent forth a bolt of lightning at the Vrachos woman who raised an earthen shield. The bolt danced harmlessly against the earthen surface but he quickly changed tactics, leaping up on top of the wall. From his height he quickly rained down several fireballs on the surprised woman who belatedly collapsed the wall, sending him tumbling. A cloud of dust covered the immediate area and Lykos used the cover it provided to move closer and hold the woman at sword point.

A breeze of strong wind swept the dust from the battlefield revealing Lykos and his captive. The woman nodded to him in respect. "I yield Lord Talal," she stated in a raspy voice. She glanced behind him before bowing herself out. "I wish you the Goddesses' strength in dealing with your next foe."

Forgoing an answer he turned around and saw the man responsible for the gust of wind with four other men brandishing their weapons before him. Brandishing his own weapon Lykos stepped forwards and the men matched his steps, the crowd furiously shouting their anticipation of the oncoming melee.

Dodging the first wide slash Lykos nearly found himself skewered by a surprise thrust. Fortunately the men were ill prepared to work together despite attacking him all at once and he was saved from a painful injury by his opponents getting in each others way. However their fifth member was not idly standing by.

A sailor whose magic helped steer his ship in harsh storms and dead winds was observing their fight with sharp eyes. While the four men distracted Lykos with their bodies and steel he began to summon a tempest storm within the arena. The crowd shrieked in awe and surprise at the storm being summoned, its mighty winds swirling dust around the combatants. Heavy rain drops began to fall from the air and each fell like a stone upon Lykos, weighing him down.

The other combatants forgotten, Lykos sent forth a bolt of lightning, hoping it would strike the sailor. It did strike but he was disappointed to see no significant damage occur, the man must have been wearing leather under his great coat. He knew he would have to get closer and rely on his sword.

It was an infuriatingly difficult prospect however. Every step forward was blasted by the wind and slowed by an endless torment of water. Lightning struck dangerously close and Lykos could feel dread rise as his strength waned. Yet fortune struck him with an idea and he stopped his advance.

Instead he pushed his hands down onto the muddy ground and pushed magic into the earth like the woman from House Vrachos. Four earthen walls raised around him and closed above, encasing him in a tomb of his own design. Inside he felt the walls shake and shudder from the ferocity of the storm being created but smiled as it beat harmlessly around him. Such a magnificent piece of magic as that storm was taxing to create, maintain, and control and he knew the other man would have to desist in his attack soon.

Indeed it was less than a minute later, long enough for Lykos to regain his breathe, that he could feel fewer shakes to his earthen fortifications and he chanced taking them down. The walls crumbled into the surrounding mud and he struggled to peer through the fog all about him. A few drizzles of rain were all that remained from the mighty torrents that had previously besieged him and he was satisfied that he endured the storm.

Walking towards where he remembered the sailor standing he found the man kneeling, exhausted. As he approached the man looked up in surprise that he looked perfectly fine, if a bit wet. Lykos respectfully offered the man a hand up and he gratefully took it.

"I yield," the man shouted and Lykos could hear the crowd excitedly talk as the fog dispersed. "I posses no skill with a blade so there's no need to beat me up over it."

Lykos nodded and the man departed the arena floor leaving him alone in a circle of destruction, bodies both dead and unconscious littering the muddy ground. With a feral smile Lykos roared towards the crowd.

"Is there no one else to challenge me! Have the best of this kingdom already proven their worth?" The crowd joyfully booed, wishing for more bloody fighting and Lykos heard a sword being drawn from behind him.

"Let us test your worth Lord Talal." Grimm stood from his seat with his sword in hand. Viktor glared from his spot beside him, Alithis' firm hand on the furious heir preventing him from rising. Lykos nodded to his challenger.

"Show me yours," he challenged.

The two men met in combat and it was ferocious. Steel clashed with steel as they danced around the arena floor, their footing hindered by the muddy ground and fallen foes. Lykos was pleased to find such a worthy opponent who forced him to rely on instinct, not form, as they traded blows. Grimm was likewise impressed with his skill but was determined to get his vengeance for his fallen mother and fought all the more brutally. The two men traded blows to the delight of the crowd, awed at the dance of steel and death before them.

However the other challengers on the lowest stone bench were eager for their own prestige. First one, then two, then a dozen more rose from their seats and charged the field. Several enterprising combatants struck at those beside them but many of them sought Grimm and Lykos, to capitalize on the distraction their duel created.

Grimm and Lykos locked swords and were trying to overpower each other when this wave of enemies fell upon them. Snarling at the interruption the two men disengaged and turned so they were back to back. In their minds none of the other fighters present would get the privilege of defeating such a worthy foe and thus for a time, their duel was put on hold.

Lykos grabbed a nearby foe to stop a young women's spear thrust from impaling him. The man screamed as his flesh was pierced and Lykos dropped him to the floor. Behind him he could hear Grimm roar as an arrow pierced his arm. "Switch!" Lykos shouted and with a smooth slide the two men switched foes.

Throwing a fireball to consume a hail of arrows sent by a trio of figures Lykos smoothly blocked a slash from a scarred mercenary. Sending another ball of fire at the archers he was pleased to hear their screams as they were viciously burned. The mercenary fell back under his retaliatory strikes and fled the dirt circle to the crowd's insults. His elated face fell as he turned towards his next opponent.

A beast of a man from House Agroti stood before him, his body heavily armored and a great war hammer in his grasp. The large man swung it as easily as Lykos swung his sword and the muddy ground shook and rippled with his steps. He was not looking forward to facing the titan.

"Grimm do you want to switch?" Lykos called behind him as the giant lumbered forth with a stupid grin on his face.

"Having trouble back there Lykos?" Grimm mocked.

"I just wanted to see if you desired to prove your worth to the kingdom." His sly attempt to convince Grimm to switch caused him to turn around to see the issue at hand. His eyes widened and with a quick thrust he slashed Lykos' arm.

"What the hell was that for?" he demanded as his arm throbbed. He was tempted to drive his sword into Grimm's gut as repayment.

"I told you I wanted my pound of flesh, it's no fun taking it from a corpse," Grimm replied as he turned back to his opponents. "Good luck Lykos, you'll need it!"

Lykos scowled as he turned back to the much closer giant. "First I'll defeat you, then I'm going to educate Grimm on why he's a prick. I expect instructing him to be time consuming task so let's get this over with."

The giant man looked at him in confusion. The man's birth name was long forgotten, now he was only known as Plower by his friends for when he was growing up he could push a plow all by himself. Growing up under the care of House Agroti he served as their champion in disputes, fighting in their name. Usually his size and strength alone scared off foes but the little man in front of him was not fleeing like many of the others.

"I'll crush you!" Plower roared as he swung his war hammer down. The muddy ground shook as it heavily impacted it. Pulling against the earth's suction Plower was disappointed that the little man hadn't been crushed by his swing.

Wiping the mud from his eyes Lykos looked at Plower who stood several paces away. "That was not nice," he tried to tell him sternly but was forced to duck as the giant man pulled his weapon free finally. With another, more accurate swing, Lykos was forced to dodge.

Scrambling through the mud he wondered how he was going to defeat Plower whose strength far outstripped his own. Sheathing his sword he called upon his magic for aid and threw fireballs, earth, and water at the massive man hoping to slow him down. The large man merely shrugged off the attacks and Lykos almost became desperate until a memory from a few days ago rose in his mind.

Adelram had asked him to describe how he had fought against the men at the Stultus ball and Lykos spoke of the encounters. When he reached the part of burning the man in the metal armor Illusionist Maeve smacked his head violently with her walking stick.

"You think like a soldier boy!" Illusionist Maeve had spat accusingly. He remembered her bearing a striking similarity to a Tainted Viper but had been too distracted by pain to voice that thought. It probably saved his life in retrospect.

"Well aren't I one?" he asked. His question had been met by another violent blow.

"We've been training you to survive not stand guard on the wall and you seem determined to stick your fool nose into every single disaster you can find! If you don't use common sense you won't live out the year!" A series of blows continued to rain on him and he was careful not to use his injured arm to block them. That didn't stop them from hurting the rest of him however.

"Then please tell me what I'm doing wrong instructor!" Lykos cried out hoping his respect would abate her attack. He was fortunate that the blows stopped.

"Fire can melt metal yes but rarely will you have the time or energy to do it efficiently. So use lightning boy! It will travel along the metal like it does water and the effects are devastating. Just pray your foe does not wear leather for then your attack will be for naught."

Looking at the towering figure of Plower Lykos hoped that Illusionist Maeve was correct or this duel would end quickly in a bad way. Throwing out a hand he sent a sharp bolt of lightning through the air, creating a sharp smell of ozone. It struck the towering figure of Plower who roared in displeasure and charged.

Dodging out of the way he threw another bolt of lightning and then one more. Both struck true and brought Plower to his knees. Stepping up to the man, whose great height merely made them eye level, he readied himself in case he needed to strike again.

"....I tired," Plower said. His eyes rolled into the back of his head and he fell sideways to the now charred arena floor. The earth shook as Lykos stood over his fallen foe. Exhausted as he was, he almost didn't hear the swing of smooth metal through air behind him.

Raising his bracer he blocked a blade aimed for his neck and turned around. There before him was a bloodied Grimm whose own opponents lay defeated on the ground behind him. He looked at the defeated form of Plower with interest.

"Well that was shocking," Grimm deadpanned as if he hadn't tried to behead Lykos a moment earlier. With narrowed eyes Lykos grabbed his sword and held it up at the ready.

"Are you ready to yield?" he asked as they circled one another.

"No but I am prepared to accept your surrender," Grimm replied. The two men leaped forwards and met once more in combat to the delight of the cheering crowd.

Despite Lykos rationing of his strength throughout the Succession Trial he was close to exhaustion as he traded blows. His magic was spent and he doubted he could light so much as a candle at the moment yet he knew he could not yield. With his death all of those slaves would be recaptured, Adelram would be an outcast and his mother....

Grimm flicked his wrist and sent Lykos' sword spinning up into the air. He did not feel despair or anger or regret as his weapon flew, merely a burning determination that he would not allow Shawna to suffer for his actions. Grimm slashed with his sword and Lykos blocked the strike with his bracer, the leather slowing the weapon enough that it would not kill or maim him although it bit deeply into his arm. But the bracer did its purpose and prevented his arm from being removed from his body. Again.

Lunging forward with his free hand Lykos struck Grimm on the jaw, lifting the man clean off his feet to collapse on the muddy ground. The action ripped Grimm's sword out of his arm, the pain nearly unbearable but he pushed through it. He stepped forward and could see the shining edge of his sword spinning downwards out of the corner of his eye, with a quick snatch of his uninjured wrist the weapon was firmly within his grip and pointed at Grimm's throat.

The crowd went silent in awe before erupting once more into cheers and shouts. Both men breathed heavily as they looked at one another and the victor was clear. Grimm nodded to Lykos.

"Looks like House Talal doesn't end today." Lykos quirked an eyebrow causing Grimm to sigh theatrically. "I yield."

Satisfied Lykos lifted his blade from Grimm's throat and sheathed it. After a moment of consideration he offered his uninjured arm to the downed man. Grimm eyed the offered hand warily but nonetheless took it and Lykos heaved him to his feet. The two men eyed each other distrustfully, unsure if the other would attack.

"Watch your back Lord Talal. Don't make your father's mistakes," Grimm warned. Lykos' jaw clenched.

"Don't make your father's either," Lykos shot back. With a nod Grimm left the arena floor leaving him alone dripping blood, water, and sweat.

He strode once more to the center of the arena and the crowd roared approvingly. He saw a sea of faces and bodies, undulating like a single organism but the crowd saw a lord taking his place.

They saw honor in victory, brutality against enemies, they saw someone worthy of their respect.

"Talal! Talal! Talal!" The crowd began to chant as Lykos looked at the remaining challengers on the stone bench. With their numbers drastically reduced the few remaining challengers nodded in respect towards Lykos, unwilling to face him. Viktor was actively trying to stand but Alithis had restrained the enraged youth with a bone white grip. It was a pity in his opinion, even though he was exhausted, his left arm in agony, and magic depleted he would have liked to scar Viktor without repercussion.

"Are there no other challengers?" the Commander of the Citadel asked, his voice carrying above the chanting crowd. He eyed the furious Viktor for a moment yet Alithis' presence remained unyielding. Since no one stood he continued to speak. "Then I proclaim the winner Lord Talal!"

The crowd went wild and stomped their feet upon the stone seats, shaking the ground and creating the most glorious noise. The day was over, Lykos had won and his family was safe.

With a proud cry Lykos raised his bloody fist to the sky.

Chapter Twenty

"Why didn't you let me fight father?" Viktor demanded. He was with his father in their private chambers within the Citadel Keep. They were far behind its walls, with an entire army and slew of fortifications protecting them that had held against the Tainted and forces of man for centuries. They were in the most private of all locations, guaranteed that their conversation could not be overheard or seen by anyone.

A loud smack cracked through the air as Lord Kolos backhanded his son. Viktor reared back in shock that his father actually struck him. Pain and anger bloomed across his face as his father stared down at him with disgust.

Lord Kolos was a tall man with strong features, even if they were marred by missing an eye. He had survived many harsh winters, wars, and battles with Tainted and he was the most powerful figure in the kingdom of Mycenae. He did not tolerate disrespect, least of all from his disappointing son and heir.

"Speak to me in that tone again and I will gut you where you stand," Lord Kolos reprimanded him harshly. He was tempted to kill the aggravating brat anyways and recognize one of his bastards as his true heir but the majority of them were just as worthless. It would be years before the younger ones showed any promise so for now, Lord Kolos would keep his current heir. But accidents happen.

A short knock on the door interrupted the father and son and Lord Kolos moved behind his desk. "Enter!" he ordered as he began to peruse through the papers that lay there.

Alithis and the Commander of the Citadel entered and stood before him at attention, with rigid arms and stance. The one-eyed lord waved for the two men to relax.

"What news do you have for me?" Lord Kolos questioned the commander before turning towards Alithis. "Serve drinks."

"My lord. Lord Talal has ordered the former Stultus men at arms to retire to their barracks pending a review tomorrow morning. He was favoring his left arm yet to my knowledge no one other than Heir Sofos is aware of the injury," he dutifully reported to his master while Alithis offered him a goblet of mead. He gratefully accepted and drank the cold liquid.

Once upon a time the Commander of the Citadel would have only answered to a single man, the Warmaster of the Citadel who was chosen by vote among the noble houses. However the machinations of man were insidious things. During Leon's Rebellion Lord Kolos seized the opportunity to kill the Warmaster enabling him to forcefully seize control of the Citadel for himself. But that wasn't enough for him.

Each quarter was ruled as a miniature kingdom, the noble house or houses controlling them were responsible for their defense and prosperity. Each would then in turn pay tribute to the Citadel to maintain the kingdom's security. Hypothetically if one controlled the Citadel, as House Kolos did, then the influx of wealth and recruits would mean that all power would rest firmly with them. Realistically this was also true but power is a drug: once you have a taste for it you pursue it endlessly. And after Leon's actions Lord Kolos began to pursue it most eagerly.

During the rebellion Leon had almost stamped out the slave trade but it sprung back up almost over night as wealthy lords and ladies used the common folk for their own ends. The population of bastards grew as many took advantage of new state of affairs, taking favors and privileges where they pleased among the common folk. Lord Kolos was chief among them, using the recent actions of Leon to firmly establish the slave population of Mycenae. Slave labor now provided for a not insignificant portion of Mycenae's infrastructure with the last notable holdouts being House Agroti's farmers, who were too poor to own slaves, and House Falknor who required skilled crews to man their airships. And all the while House Kolos steadily grabbed for more wealth, more power, only now their eyes were turning to the other noble houses.

"And what information do you have for me Alithis?" Lord Kolos asked the quiet man.

The man named Alithis was a mystery to many of the noble houses of Mycenae. It was rumored that he was a bastard of Lord Kolos, whose exceptional skills and abilities were valued by Lord Kolos. Others claimed he was the offspring of the Goddesses, birthed during a ritual and through great sorcery but most decried that as lunacy. Many attempts to find out more information always ended in failure as House Kolos was tight lipped and Alithis was prone to ending conversations with the violent deaths of would be interrogators.

"I have discovered a spy and a traitor in the Citadel my lord," Alithis stated calmly. Lord Kolos looked up from his paperwork and eyed the young man as the Commander of the Citadel froze in terror.

"Preposterous I would have known if we were infiltrated!" he protested once his emotions settled. Viktor was quick to side with him.

"You see enemies everywhere," Viktor told Alithis scornfully. However despite the protests of the two men Alithis only looked at Lord Kolos. The one-eyed lord returned the gaze evenly.

"Explain," Lord Kolos ordered tersely.

"During my observation of the members of a certain noble house of interest I noticed they frequented the same flesh palace near the Lowland. That is not uncommon as the depravities of the various individuals involved are well known, what is interesting is that once within the flesh palace they would be spotted just a short time later in the Nero entering a bar."

"Congratulations you've discovered that people drink and have sex," Viktor mocked. He clapped his hands slowly in a mock congratulatory manner. Meanwhile the Commander of the Citadel began to lightly sweat.

"Continue." Lord Kolos shot Viktor a look that immediately silenced him.

"Within this bar the members of that certain noble house would enter the basement and access a hidden passage in the back. In this room was a shadowed figure who would proceed to give those noble house members a scroll with information. This week the information was concerning shipments of supplies entering the Citadel. Previous weeks detailed troop movements, reports of day to day activities upon various House Kolos individuals, and a few other interesting tidbits. In return this shadowed figure would receive a large sack of coin."

The Commander of the Citadel face burned red as his vision became blurry and dizzy. Only Viktor paid his heavy breathing any mind as Lord Kolos was giving his full attention to Alithis' report.

"Did you discover the identity of this man?" Lord Kolos inquired.

"I have," Alithis confirmed.

"Who might this traitor be?"

"It's the man standing right next to me." Alithis and Lord Kolos both turned dispassionate eyes towards the gasping commander, who felt as if a mountain weighed down upon his chest. The tankard of mead in his hands fell to the stone beneath his feet and with terror he realized he had been poisoned.

"Preposterous my lord I only serve you," he struggled to say. He gasped painfully as he coughed up blood. Viktor looked on with disgusted interest as the man began to cry blood.

"Alithis?" Lord Kolos quirked an eyebrow.

"I have loyalists from your house going through his stash in the Nero. He kept detailed records in case he would need to blackmail House Emporo for protection at a later date. I have the payments and copies of the information in a chest in your study Lord Kolos. House Emporo has been heavily involved and as such they're being kept in the dark to our actions."

The Commander of the Citadel died a gruesome, honorless death in the study of the man he betrayed. Alithis nudged the body with his foot and was satisfied that he was dead.

"What the hell was that?" Viktor demanded looking between his father and the man many considered to be his half-brother.

"That was Alithis being useful instead of a whining brat," Lord Kolos snapped as he glared at his son. "He found and eliminated a foe to House Kolos while you whined about not getting to die in the Succession Trial."

"I could have killed that Talal bastard!" Viktor protested. He recoiled as Alithis actually growled at him.

"You would die." Alithis took an angry step towards the Kolos heir, ignoring the cooling corpse at his feet. "He tore through the Stultus bastards without pausing and you still think that you're his equal? Grow up."

"I think I could kill one bastard," Viktor threatened placing his hand on his sword. Less than a heartbeat later he found himself on his back with a knife being pressed to his throat.

"Enough. Alithis let him stand up. Viktor do not take offense to the fact that your strengths do not lay on the field of battle. I raised you to lead, not be led," Lord Kolos spoke, returning to his papers.

They parted slowly and Alithis was even slower in putting his blade away. However the two were interrupted in their non-verbal pissing contest by Lord Kolos speaking once more.

"How about a test. Viktor, what should be done with the body?"

Viktor gave his father a dark smile. "It should be dropped off somewhere inconvenient. Perhaps somewhere to implicate House Talal." Viktor ignored Alithis glare beside him.

Lord Kolos nodded approvingly. "Excellent plan but I have a much better target in mind. Alithis."

The young man's anger washed away in approval as Lord Kolos explained his plan to weaken all of his enemies at once. And it all started with House Emporo.

"I'll be home late tonight sweetie," Lord Emporo told his wife Eliza as he put on his coat. "We're still finalizing the fees for the canals."

Lady Emporo smiled at her dimwitted husband as he used the same lie he's always used before going to a flesh palace. "Of course Charles, I know how frustrating those talks can be." Kissing the disgusting man on the cheek Eliza waved farewell as she shut the door, pleased that this would be the last time she would see him alive.

If Eliza had less restraint she might have killed her husband before now. As tempting as it was, being married kept most potential suitors away and allowed her to maintain House Emporo's holdings without interference. As the blood borne Emporo leader, it was she who held control of the house instead of the absentminded man who only ever thought with his prick. However the time to end their relations was at hand and she gleefully took it.

"Finally I thought he would never leave." Eliza turned to see her delicious companion Delilah standing behind her, her glorious body encased in tight leather. "Shall we begin my lady?

"We shall my love." The two exchanged a tender kiss before Delilah backhanded Eliza. Grasping the shorter woman by her hair she shoved Lady Emporo to her knees.

"You will address me as mistress or you will face harsh punishment!" Delilah ordered as she attached a lead around Eliza's neck.

"Yes mistress!" Eliza cried as she was tugged forward. Delilah led Eliza to the basement on her knees where she proceeded to strap her victim to a table. Using a knife she delicately cut away Eliza's Tainted silk garments leaving the woman's bare body exposed to the cool air. Eliza moaned as Delilah's hands stroked her body but whined when they left.

"My my, so needy today. My plaything needs to learn her place," Delilah spoke to herself as she grabbed her whip. Pulling a lever Eliza was pulled from the table and hung suspended in the air by metal chains. The noblewoman gasped in pain at the sensation. Delilah began to stroke Eliza with her whip causing her to quickly become aroused.

"I wonder what naughty thing you've done today," Delilah whispered into her ear. This was a game the two women had played many times when they'd seen the success of one of their plots. They relished it almost as much as the actual acts.

"Oh so many things mistress! I've been a very naughty girl." Eliza practically purred as Delilah continued to stroke her with the whip.

"Tell me what you've done pet and I will decide if you've earned a reward or a punishment." Both women knew that the result would be exactly the same but could not help anticipate the delightful sensations to come.

"I've plotted to murder my husband!" Eliza moaned as Delilah caressed her buttocks before gasping as the woman smacked it.

"You forgot to call me mistress pet." Delilah warned as she stepped back, flicking her whip several times.

"I beg your forgiveness mistress!"

Delilah hummed. "So you plotted your husband's murder. How?" She flicked her whip gently to lick at Eliza's bare back. Eliza closed her eyes to enjoy the sensations as satisfaction bloomed inside of her.

"I found which flesh palace he partakes in instead of pleasing his wife." Eliza gasped as Delilah whipped her back viciously, the pain searing before fading as her magic healed her wound.

"No one pleases my pet but me," she stated firmly. "Continue."

"Yes mistress." Eliza took a breathe before continuing. "I arranged for one of the flesh maidens to be given a special lipstick to wear tonight. I paid her to seduce my husband and to ensure that they lock lips. But I know a secret mistress," she stated proudly. The whip lashed out to give her a mild caress, harsh but not enough to draw blood.

"What's the secret pet?" Delilah asked.

"The special lipstick needs a secret ingredient mistress, one I gave my husband with dinner in his wine. When he locks lips with that Agroti whore the wine on his breathe will turn to acid." Eliza moaned with delight as Delilah struck her twice in succession.

"But what of the flesh maiden pet?"

Eliza smirked as Delilah moved to stand in front of her. "The acid will burn her face off too."

The evening between the two woman passed all too quickly for their liking and after their passionate lovemaking they lay together on Eliza's bed in the masters bedroom. Their bodies were bruised and bloodied but their wounds were being healed by their innate magic. Eliza stretched next to her lover.

"That was excellent my dear."

"I will do anything for my lady." Delilah's smile was marred by Eliza's blood yet the woman was enraptured by the sight before her. "I take it your husband should be dead by now?"

Eliza smiled in satisfaction. "If he's not he'll find no relief here."

The two women shared a laugh before Delilah asked, "why an Agroti flesh maiden?"

"So I can accuse them of impropriety and start to move against their house of course. It's not polite to simply declare war," Eliza stated matter of factually.

"Not going to follow Lord Talal's example?" Delilah asked, referring to the young man's assassination of House Stultus before absorbing their resources. Both women had heard of his performance at the Succession Trial but had been unimpressed. He was an usurper to the natural order in their eyes.

"Let the young fool run about and make noise. I will settle for a quiet conquering of this kingdom and will take pleasure in him serving at my feet with the rest." Eliza laid upon her soft bed with her lover as elsewhere her husband's cooling corpse caused a riot. Her mind drifted to the future and her plans for her kingdom.

The other noble houses would either kneel at her feet or be buried underneath, it mattered not to her which.

Elsewhere in the kingdom a father stood over his son while a healer tended to his injuries.

"I'm disappointed in you Grimm." Lord Sofos looked down upon his son as the healer tried to expedite his healing. In his final bout with Lord Talal the other man had broken several of Grimm's ribs thus necessitating the need for a healer to guide his magic.

"Yeah, well you could be in the arena next time," Grimm replied under his breathe as the healer stood and walked away, her task done.

"What was that?" Lord Sofos asked his son sharply. Grimm sighed.

"Nothing father. The day was not a complete loss, I drew first blood from him." Lord Sofos sneered at his son.

"You claim a honorless attack as vengeance? Perhaps your mother died of shame." Grimm felt anger at his fathers words and forced himself into a sitting position.

"Perhaps she died to leave you!" As soon as the words left his mouth Grimm regretted them as his fathers temper had not been the most stable of late. Indeed as quick as a Tainted Viper Lord Sofos lashed out and violently smacked him.

"You know well that House Talal is to blame for your mothers death! Do not push your inadequacies upon me!" Lord Sofos roared before stomping out of the room. With a huff Grimm collapsed back on the bed.

He did not mean to speak out against his father in such a manner but he found it trying. Ever since the Stultus Ball Arachnis had been increasingly volatile, pushing him harder and harder to "prepare" him for taking over the family. However Grimm could not help but get the feeling that his father was reacting poorly to the emergence of a Talal heir.

Grimm scowled. Lykos of Talal was an aggravating annoyance that was as contradictory as he was curious. The man had appeared seemingly from no where and had remained out of public eye until the Stultus Ball. Since that night it seems as if you couldn't go anywhere in the kingdom without hearing his name, even more so since he won the Succession Trial.

Yet the man walked like a common man. No he walked like a street urchin, with his eyes constantly scanning the area for something. Members of the noble houses walked with an air of superiority, assured that their skill in magic and wealth made them greater than the common folk of Mycenae. Yet Lykos' skill with blade and magic surpassed many of the Citadel instructors who had taught Grimm in his youth and he walked as if he feared an attack at any moment. It was odd.

Grimm's thoughts kept him awake as his body healed and the night passed. Growing hungry he descended the stairs of his home and joined his family at their dining table for breakfast.

"I apologize for my words last night father, I was out of line," Grimm apologized to his father who sat stiffly at the head of the table. His uncles, aunts, and cousins eyed the pair curiously but none questioned the duo. Lord Sofos gave him a small nod but choose not to speak, focusing instead on his meal.

"So what did you think of Lord Talal?" Grimm's uncle Fernuclus, known to his family as Ferny, asked when the silence grew longer than sociably acceptable.

"He is a skilled foe," he replied honestly. His family laughed.

"He beat you!" One of his younger cousins pointed a food smeared hand at him and Grimm wrinkled his nose in disgust.

"Everyone gets lucky once," he tried to defend himself.

"No excuse," Lord Sofos muttered and the table's mood turned somber at his dark look.

Losing his appetite Grimm stood and excused himself. As he walked to the door his father called out to him.

"Later you will help your aunt with running her flesh palaces. It's time you learn more about that aspect of the family business."

Grimm nodded obediently. "Of course father."

Grimm retired to his room and stared angrily at the wall. Like all young men and women in the kingdom he had been to the flesh palaces before and sampled their services. While many of the flesh maidens and flesh lads were there for good honest work, House Sofos employed almost exclusively slaves to increase their profits. How those men and women were treated was ghastly and it made him sick.

His thoughts turned to his mother who had also been disgusted by the practice of slavery. As Lady Sofos the flesh palaces under her control had been manned by free citizens earning an honest wage. At least that's what her journals had claimed.

Years ago he had visited his families businesses and seen the poor conditions the slaves were kept in. Filth and disease were everywhere and the poor souls who had died in those conditions were disposed of like trash outside the kingdoms walls for the Tainted to feast on, they didn't warrant an honest burial in the kingdom's catacombs.

His mother died, a bystander in Leon's Rebellion, and his father had been harsh to Grimm all his life for it. Sometimes he wondered if this is what life was supposed to be like, a miserable kingdom, violent rule, and harsh families. Yet as he looked as the sorry state of the kingdom he knew it wasn't Leon's Rebellion that broke it.

It was the ones who were left.

Chapter Twenty-One

The morning after the Succession Trial had dawned and Lykos and Adelram had traveled to the barracks where the new Talal soldiers were stationed. It was a large, squat building that had several rundown training grounds surrounding it. The men and women stationed there were as just as unkempt as the building they lived in, unwashed and ragged, and smelling most foul.

As Lykos looked upon the men and women as they slowly formed ranks and stood at attention he could not help but feel disgust. These so called soldiers filled him with disappointment as it was unlikely they could effectively perform any tasks of significant importance, let alone fight for him. As he glared into their ranks he knew what most of them had been used for. The dilapidated state of Pyrgos, the beaten common folk, it was obvious that these men and women were just a step above criminals. Without a doubt almost all of them took protection money or outright stole from the very people they were supposed to be protecting. He would put a stop to that.

His thoughts were interrupted by Commander Alec, a Stultus bastard standing next to Adelram. Unlike the rest of his half-siblings Alec had managed to seize a small amount of power within the quarter by maintaining the Stultus forces. Now he, and they, answered to Lykos.

"The men for your inspection, my lord." The title was said with barely restrained hatred as Commander Alec glared at Lykos. He had most likely watched him kill several of his half-siblings the previous day and was understandably upset about that.

Lykos paid him no mind as he began to walk in front of the assembled soldiers, examining them critically as he casually stretched his once again healing arm. "How many are there?"

"Just over one hundred my lord. A large portion of the men left your service prior to the Succession Trial." Lykos ignored the gleeful tone in Commander Alec's voice and knew the spiteful man took his silence to mean he was displeased.

In truth he was but he buried it deep. The oaths and honor of those men were in question but considering those that remained were just as dishonorable he did not think the missing men minded.

"You're their only commander?" Lykos asked. Commander Alec shook his head.

"There's a centurion somewhere in there but he's probably sleeping off his drink." This time Lykos did scowl.

"Is that why discipline is so lacking?" Lykos asked Adelram, ignoring Commander Alec who reddened in anger. Adelram sneered at the assembled soldiers.

"Aye, too much leeway with these men and not enough of the whip." Adelram's face was carved in stone as he looked on with narrowed eyes. Commander Alec rounded on the older man.

"Do not speak so disrespectfully of my lord's men." Lykos raised an amused eyebrow at Adelram as Commander Alec tried to deflect blame from himself. "They protect his holdings and people!"

"Yes my people," Lykos spoke up causing Commander Alec to turn and plaster a fake smile on his face. "Tell me Alec why do my people look so beaten?"

Commander Alec appeared confused. Glancing between Lykos and the lax soldiers he answered honestly. "Well the men beat them of course."

"The men beat them," Lykos repeated in a monotone voice.

"Of course my lord! Otherwise they get violent and try to subvert your will!" Commander Alec explained, pleased that he understood.

"Tell me Alec, do any of my soldiers take liberties with the common folk? Do you?"

"Of course my lord. The Lord's Stultus established a fine practice among the common folk providing whatever we desired, whenever we desired. Why I myself had this pretty little red girl this morning-"

Whatever Commander Alec had been about to say was violently cut off as Lykos drew a knife and stabbed it into his throat. He fell to his knees, choking on blood as Lykos turned to the assembled men and women who had begun to move towards them with alarm and weapons drawn.

"Stop," Lykos ordered firmly, his magic boiling beneath his skin like a pot of water. It lent power to his voice in the form of oppressive air, halting the advancing soldiers. They turned fearful and shocked eyes towards him as Commander Alec expired at his feet. Lykos stepped towards them and a few of the more intelligent ones tried to flee to no avail, tripping over their comrades.

"You are now soldiers of House Talal. You are not common thugs who take advantage of the very people beneath your shield! You are meant to stand tall and firm, protecting them from the evils of this world! You are not supposed to be one of those evils! Each and every one of you has a debt to these people, a debt you must now pay. They do not live to serve you. You live to serve them. No more taking liberties, no more brutalizing innocents, no more! If any of you think you can do as you please after this warning think again. Adelram has agreed to become the new commander of the Talal forces and thus you all answer to him. Commander Adelram, would you kindly educate our men as to what happens should they attempt to circumvent these rules?"

Lykos had sprung this moment on Adelram without preparation or prior notice but he felt it was the correct decision. By Adelram's own admission there was little else he could be taught about physical combat and he would learn more by fighting new foes. As a gift of appreciation Lykos would give him a role that would allow Adelram to stand proudly in public once more. Being commander of House Talal's forces was a prestigious position, regardless of how far the house had fallen in recent years. It would also allow him to place someone he trusted and knew to be competent in a position of power which was always a boon.

Adelram for his part was only briefly expressed surprise before he quickly hid it behind professionalism. Stepping before the paralyzed soldiers he glared down his nose at them before gruffly speaking.

"Lord Talal is too kind to you worms! The lot of you should be strung up by your toes and whipped a hair near death for your crimes and shame! However Lord Talal is a kinder man than I and has instead decided that each and every single one of you has a chance to redeem themselves! Aye you'll get to earn the right to serve your lord! Because if you fail him you will be harshly punished. Public lashings for any infractions and woe be unto any of you thinking of committing treason! Form up!"

Lykos watched as Adelram put the soldiers through their paces. He knew in the coming days almost all of them would have to be disciplined to some degree but for right now Adelram could keep them in line. However he needed more soldiers, more trustworthy commanders, and he *needed* mages. He would question the older man later about recruitment, once he had gotten settled into his new post.

Bidding farewell to Adelram, he left the barracks and made his way through the streets of Pyrgos. Many of the common folk gave him tentative smiles and partial bows as he walked which pleased him. The fear and suffering they experienced when they had lived under the Stultus rule would soon be gone he vowed. It was time for this quarter to be brought back to its former glory.

Entering Hearthome he was intrigued to see Falka and Ana Del Rosa directing the former slaves now servants at restoring the ruined grounds. He stopped next to the pair and briefly examined an odd patch of rock and wood next to them that looked perfectly normal before nodding respectfully towards the servants.

"Thank you for your assistance Falka, Ana, although I can't help but wonder what the pair of you want." Ana blushed in embarrassment while Falka smiled innocently at him.

"How would you like to have some fun Lykos?" she asked him stroking his arm almost seductively. Lykos quirked an eyebrow at her boldness.

"Somehow I don't think that statement means what your body or tone is implying," he replied dryly. It was a shame since while Falka was a beautiful woman Lykos had grown rather fond of Ana and had no desire to see them part.

Falka laughed and nodded. "What happened to the boy hiding his face at the ball, worried about little old me?"

"He had his hand chopped off," he replied darkly, rubbing the scarred flesh through his bracer. Fresh bandages wrapped around the scar from his recent duel with Grimm but still the wounds hurt. Falka looked at him in delight.

"And he grew a sense of humor. An improvement I say." Ana laughed appreciatively at her jest.

"Falka? You spoke of having some fun?" he asked attempting to bring her back to focus. She nodded.

"Through some careful snooping I've discovered more warehouses full of slaves in quarters throughout the kingdom. All of them guarded of course but they're perfect to sow a little chaos among the noble houses, depriving them of their cheap labor. My brother has agreed to help facilitate their escape so long as you can clear out the guards."

"Good." Lykos glanced at the many busy workers restoring his home. "I need more soldiers otherwise our enemies will sweep us aside like a wave. Freeing more slaves will give us much needed reinforcements although finding centurions and commanders to lead them will be a chore. Any ideas?"

Both Falka and Ana shook their heads but a voice called out from behind them. "Perhaps I could provide some assistance Lord Talal?"

Walking down the path was the sailor from the Succession Trial with a devious smile on his face. The man was still wearing his weather worn clothing and not a weapon could be spied upon him. Remembering the man used magic almost exclusively Lykos looked at him with his magic.

An endless torrent of blue and yellow swirled within the man, with a dark cloud of black resting on top. Lykos determined by the brilliant shade of light that the man was fully rested and was impressed with the amount of magic at his disposal. The more he looked the more he could see how different shades of blue formed waves while the yellow sparked like lightning all about. He allowed the magic to fade as he answered him.

"How can a stranger help me?" Lykos was satisfied that he could defeat the man should he prove hostile. Although from the look Falka was giving the sailor he wondered if she would kill him first.

"My apologies Lord Talal my name is Bartholomew, I served as an Emporo sailor until recently." The man held out an arm and Lykos grasped it, pleased to find no hidden dagger up the man's sleeve.

"Well met Bartholomew."

"Call me Bart my lord, no need to speak that mouthful," Bart requested.

"Bart then. How would a sailor provide service to me?" Lykos asked as he gestured for the man to join them. Falka and Ana excused themselves leaving the two men alone.

"Until recently I served on a cargo ship between Istani and Mycenae, hauling goods that both kingdoms sought. However my captain took on a load of slaves on our last trip." Bart hung his head in shame. "I listened to the cries of men and women and children for weeks and I did not aid them. It's not right what we did. Once a day we'd throw down food and drink but that was the only comfort my captain would allow us to provide.

"We arrived here and unloaded our human cargo in one of the warehouses off the river. A few days passed and I was drinking away my pay in shame when a red flare went up in the sky. Rushing with my fellow sailors to the warehouses we found dozens of slaves, more than we had stored there, scurrying all over the docks. They were loading cargo onto a ship docked in the water and overseeing them was a figure cloaked by darkness. The night hid your features well but the moon has always been my ally and illuminated the scene for me perfectly.

"As the other sailors retreated to fetch the guards I hid myself and watched as you saved those slaves. I saw nobility, purpose, a fierce protection for those who had suffered. I said to myself that is a man worthy of service! Imagine my surprise when I faced you in the Succession Trial but I hoped I gave you a good run. I haven't had to use that much magic in years."

Lykos said nothing for several long moments, quietly contemplating Bart and his story. There had indeed been several dark figures who had walked in upon their escape and several of them had stayed while the others fled. He privately admitted that one of those dark figures could have been the man who stood before him now.

"So what will you do now?" he finally asked.

"Why I offer my services! And after overhearing your troubles I believe I can offer a solution as well. I know several individuals who are in similar positions as myself and would be happy for work," Bart offered excitedly.

"Similar positions? Have many sailors jumped ship?" Lykos inquired.

"In a manner of speaking. A lot of my," Bart paused with a considering look, "friends, have had difficulties with the law. If we were to lend a hand they'd be grateful for the opportunity to raise a little chaos."

"And they are all as skilled in magic as you?" Lykos pondered if this was good fortune or a trap.

"Oh most of them my lord! They all have some skill in leading men in battle as well. A true boon for your work here," Bart eagerly replied. Lykos kept his face cool as he nodded.

"Very well. I'll meet with your friends and see if any that are willing to lend aid are suitable for our purposes here." He found himself not liking Bart's answering chuckle.

"You'll most likely have to prove yourself to this lot, they don't take kindly to young lords wet behind the ears. But it shouldn't be an issue for you, you weathered my storms well enough!" Bart joked clapping him on the shoulder. Lykos for his part was unimpressed and Bart coughed awkwardly. "Meet me by the Grand Temple in Naos this afternoon, we should be able to find one of the more levelheaded ones near there."

Lykos nodded and Bart jovially left the Talal estate. He waited until the man was out of sight before turning towards the odd pattern of wood and stone that he had spied earlier next to Falka.

"Do you think it's a trap instructor?"

Illusionist Maeve faded into view and nodded approvingly at him. "Well done my apprentice for both spotting me and recognizing that this might be a trap. To answer your question I'm not sure."

He nodded, annoyed but not surprised that the possibility wasn't ruled out. "It simply seems too good to be true."

Illusionist Maeve shrugged her bony shoulders. "Sometimes life throws you a sword and sometimes you catch it before it impales you. Keep your wits about you and you should be fine."

Lykos nodded in understanding and agreement. "I don't think I've ever been to the Grand Temple in Naos, what can you tell me of it?"

"A bunch of opportunistic harlots." She spat on the ground between them and he was impressed with the amount of ire in her voice. "They call themselves the Acolytes and claim to be pacifistic healers doing the will of the Goddesses yet most of them wouldn't piss on you if you were on fire. The lesser temples throughout the kingdom are almost as bad, charging an arm and a leg for minor services."

"Do they serve House Kolos?" Lykos asked and she shook her head.

"If they did it would make life so much more difficult. Even before Leon's Rebellion the healers," Illusionist Maeve spat the title, "often doubled as assassins. In recent years they're just as likely to heal you of your injuries as they are to kill you for a reward. Fortunately no one has put a high enough price on your head for it to be an issue. Yet."

"Healers and assassins? That seems as if it would be an odd combination." He gripped his swords hilt as if one would spring out of hiding nearby to kill him.

"You would think so but both professions use many of the same tools. Knives, poisons, elixirs. It's not surprising that they would start taking bounties for coin," Illusionist Maeve explained.

"So I'm about to follow a possible spy, to recruit one of his "friends", who is located near the center of a den of healers and assassins while all of our enemies have our recent successes fresh in their minds."

"Aye."

Lykos briefly marveled at how his life had changed since escaping the mines. It sure became a lot more complicated.

Chapter Twenty-Two

"So where are the assassins?" Lykos knew asking Falka to come along as back up was a good idea yet he forgot how playful she could be. Still he wasn't going to walk into a potential trap alone and she was the only one he could call on for aid, much to the fiendish woman's delight.

"Hopefully all of them are asleep," he replied as they walked the streets of Naos. As one of the older quarters in the kingdom, the buildings on either side of them were sturdily built from stone and were adorned with magnificent carvings of Mycenae's history. He wished he had the time to examine them in detail but that was not possible at the moment. They had assassins to dodge and criminals to recruit.

"It's midday!" Falka protested and Lykos was vividly reminded of a child protesting her bedtime.

"They could be napping," he argued. Finally they rounded a stone corner and saw the Grand Temple before them. It was actually a series of buildings adorned with statues of winged women posed dramatically along the walls, connected by elevated walkways. The grounds around them were littered with fountains whose waters danced merrily in the strong sunlight. And at every entrance stood a pair of armored guards.

"What an ugly building." Lykos turned to look at Falka in surprise. "Where are the murals of bloody sacrifices, the carvings of armies meeting in deadly combat? If I wanted to look at exemplary examples of the female form I'd go seduce Ana Del Rosa." Lykos smirked at her pout but was interrupted before he could speak.

"You keep such interesting company Lord Talal," Bart the sailor stated as he walked up to the pair. "My name is Bartholomew my lady but you may call me-"

"Don't care, where's the bloodshed?" Falka asked as she ignored his greeting, choosing instead to leer at one of the statues. Lykos looked at a perplexed Bart and smirked.

"Don't mind Falka she's been mortally offended," he offered by way of explanation. Unfortunately for Bart it did not ease his confusion.

"Right. Well let me show you to my friend and then we can begin!" Bart walked to a nearby building gesturing for them to follow. Grasping Falka's arm, Lykos pulled the young woman away from her inspection of the statue's breasts and followed the sailor inside.

Before them lay a scene of debauchery and sin that even the devil would blink at. Lykos found himself stuck in the entryway in shock as piles of naked flesh undulated around him. The smell of sex and sweat in the air burned his nose and the scented candles did little to aid in disguising the musky smell. Falka eyed the participants critically, as a teacher would her students.

"This way to my friend Lord Talal!" Bart gestured from across the room to them before disappearing through a door. Carefully stepping his way across the wet and sticky floor the pair followed the sailor deeper into what Lykos quickly determined to be a flesh palace.

"Amateurs," Falka whispered to him as they stepped around the many participants. He rolled his eyes and tried not to breathe the air too deeply as the smell worsened. Rotting food now filled their noses as they entered another room full of gluttons, ecstasy on their faces as they shoved obscene amounts of food into their mouths.

Bart led the pair through several more rooms each more depraved and curious than the last. A series of exquisite beds, with soft sheets and full of down feathers beckoned to them in one while in the next several slaves were tied to the walls and were beaten by cackling men and women. The next room was curious for it was full of richly dressed nobles, bowing and talking to one another, preening in front of mirrors. As they walked through the room they saw the nobles were really stealing from each others pockets in an endless circle, like some perverse dance. At the head of the room was a massive throne and the nearby nobles fought over who was allowed to sit upon it. Walking past the struggle they entered a door hidden behind the throne.

This room was richly decorated with tapestries and paintings and each of them bore the likeness of a single man, distorted across multiple mediums. A low table with several men and women sitting at it were eating off of exquisite plates and bowls, each carved with the same face. At the head of the table sat the man himself.

His face had been portrayed with fierce lines yet in reality it was cruel. A sadistic smirk and heavy brow glared at Lykos from across the room and his body was fat and heavy from his consumption of food. He smiled and waved his meaty hand and the conversation halted in the room. A significant look to the door behind them caused two burly men to shut and lock it before joining four others in surrounding the trio.

"Bart, my oldest friend, I am so pleased to see you have delivered!" the man cried out in a reedy voice. Falka and Lykos shared dark looks before turning to the slimy man beside them.

"Please my lord you promised." Bart's voice was no longer pleasant, it had changed to a desperate pleading tone as he stepped forward. Two of the guards barred his way.

"I did promise but did you explain to our guests just what you've done Bartholomew?" the man asked grasping the wine glass in front of him. The other men and women at the table were quiet, keeping their eyes down as their host drank. Lykos realized with dread that they had manacles around their ankles chaining them to each other and the floor.

Bart turned to Lykos and Falka. "I beg your forgiveness my lord but they have my family! I had to do whatever he asked!" His statement caused the men and women at the table to rustle their legs but they said nothing.

"Is that why you entered the Succession Trial?" Lykos asked trying to understand how this man had set this all up.

"That would be my doing, allow me to introduce myself. I am Drakken and I require your assistance my dear Lord Talal. I used the Succession Trial as a little test so to speak." The man named Drakken sketched a small bow from his seat but Lykos was ill inclined to return it.

"Oh bravo, you're so smart and cunning," The sarcasm dripped heavily from Falka's tongue, "it's a shame this will never work."

"Oh and why is that?" Drakken asked with interest as his eyes traced her lithe form.

"Well we are going to kill you." In a quick motion Falka drove her elbow into the closest guards side while drawing her sword. Lykos too matched her motions and together the pair quickly slayed the guards nearest to them. With bloodied blades the pair turned towards Drakken only to find the final two guards holding a sweating Bart at knife point.

"Release the man and his family," Lykos ordered, wondering if he was strong enough to rip the men's weapons from their grip with air magic. It was a tricky bit of sorcery at the best of times and two strong grips were not helpful in such an endeavor.

"I'm going to have to decline. Put down your weapons or I slaughter him, his family, these slaves, and your families. I might have calmed down by then to not do anything truly drastic," Drakken replied calmly returning to his meal.

"We can take them," Falka whispered to him out of the corner of her mouth. Personally he agreed but Drakken seemed entirely too calm concerning the situation he was in. Either the man was bluffing or he had another card to play.

"I think we've gotten off track. How about we return to the reason why you had us brought here?" Lykos tried to ask the man in a civil tongue but it was difficult to restrain his blood lust.

"Well I find myself in a conundrum you see. The Grand Temple houses an assassin who has been contracted to kill me. I of course find this disagreeable but all of the men I send after her die quite painfully. I'd go myself but well, you know...." Drakken trailed off as he smirked at them.

"Because you're a bloody coward?" Falka finished angrily.

"Because allowing the assassin to get that close could just as easily backfire on you," Lykos answered neutrally. Drakken beamed at the young lord. Lykos briefly wondered how he thought hiding in a flesh palace practically right next to the temple was a good idea.

"Quite so my friend! I hope you can see where I'm going with this." Falka swore darkly and turned pleading eyes to Lykos.

"Please let me kill him?" she whined. He ignored her plea despite agreeing with her intent. Drakken was not a man he wished to help however he wasn't about to condemn a bunch of innocent lives for his own morals. With a twisted feeling in his gut he sheathed his sword and motioned Falka to do the same.

"You want us to kill the assassin for you," Lykos answered finally.

"Yes! Well no. I want you," Drakkens emphasis made his skin crawl, "to kill the assassin. Your companion stays here with me to make sure you don't do anything stupid."

"And if I refuse?" Lykos asked out of curiosity. Drakken merely snapped his fingers and a dozen more guards rushed into the room from behind the tapestries and paintings pointing their weapons at the duo with deadly intent. Bart whimpered as one of his captors pressed the knife into his flesh.

Lykos nodded and turned towards Falka. "Keep your blades ready. If they try anything funny do that thing you showed at that place that one time."

Falka smiled. "The one you told me to never do again because it was unspeakably cruel?"

"That's the one." Lykos turned to the confused Drakken who wasn't sure if he had just threatened him or not. "Who's the assassin you need dead?"

A short few moments later Lykos exited the den of depravity and emerged in the shadow of the setting sun. Breathing deeply of the fresh air he moved towards the closest entrance of the Grand Temple with a measured pace.

The last little bit of confusion he had thrown out to Falka before leaving was merely a bluff to buy his friend some time. The guards would wonder what she could do and thus allow him more time to figure out a way out of this mess. For despite fighting more than a dozen warriors in the Succession Trial he didn't have to worry about bystanders, in this case the slaves and Bart, being injured or killed. Even with Falka's aid he would be hard pressed to successfully protect them all while killing their foes.

So while his movement and face were calm and free of emotion, internally he raged at the injustice of it all and vowed to find someway to prevail. Perhaps he could discover who had placed a contract on Drakken with the assassin named Helen and he could join forces with them?

Approaching the entrance he was barred entry by one of the two helmeted guards garbed in resplendent robes and armor. Their weapons were shiny and sharp and were gripped in experienced hands as they blocked his path.

"I have business with an assassin within," he tried to explain.

"No more contracts may be placed today. Return tomorrow before sunset," one of the guards ordered, their voice distorted by the helms they wore.

"It is of a most time sensitive nature," Lykos tried again.

"No exceptions," the other guard growled. Lykos was tempted to reveal his identity or even draw his blade but instead turned his back and walked away. "Arrogant bastard," one of the guards muttered.

Lykos ignored the pair as he retreated around a corner. Seeing no one around he focused, drawing on his magic to create a portal. It flickered in and out of creation unsure of its own purpose but his will firmed. With a snap the portal stabilized and he stepped through.

Blood was to be spilled tonight and it would be by his blade.

Chapter Twenty-Three

Stepping into existence behind the two rude guards Lykos resisted the temptation to attack them, knowing that he served a higher purpose here tonight. So turning away he began to move through dark corridors in search of his prey. As he walked his thoughts turned to the successful creation of his portal. It had flickered for a moment before stabilizing but that it had formed so quickly pleased him. His growing power and control was slowly narrowing the gap between him and his foes but it would not due to celebrate yet. After all, he still had many powerful enemies.

The Acolytes had many smaller temples throughout the kingdom. Most of them would provide medical services for a price and he had unknowingly used their services while training with Adelram when Illusionist Maeve was too spiteful to heal him. However some of the temples he avoided simply because of the rumors of unwanted interlopers disappearing without a trace. It would appear that had been a wise decision.

None were so infamous as the Grand Temple located in Naos. Lykos could understand why as he walked its dark halls, carvings and paintings depicting terrifying images of women laying waste to armies all about. Peering at the words underneath one he attempted to decipher the archaic script. An exodus to flee from Tainted creatures was readable yet he could not tell if it was historical or prophetic. As he read of the bloodshed he hoped it was the former.

Resuming his search he peered into the various halls and rooms, staying out of sight of the occupants contained within. He hadn't the foggiest idea how to find Helen and didn't think asking any acolytes in residence would end well.

"So I heard you tried to court that crazy bitch?" Lykos dove behind cover as a pair of voices echoed through the hall behind him. Quieting his breathing he watched as a pair of men walked into view, their arms bearing the mark of the Goddesses proudly. The multi-colored harpy was rather impressive and intimidating to his eyes but it loudly proclaimed their allegiance. An oddity for part-time assassins he thought.

"I tell you friend, I'll woo her yet," one of the men spoke to his companion. The other man snorted.

"And I tell you you're insane. That witch castrated the last fool who made a pass at her."

"Helen is a sweet soul wrapped in a bitter past, I'll warm her frozen heart just you watch." The first man protested as the pair passed Lykos' hiding spot.

"Look if you want to gamble with your life that's your business but I'm staying the hell away from the dungeons. I don't know why we still put up with her...." his voice faded as the pair disappeared around the corner. Lykos smiled at his fortune and made way to the stairs he had passed earlier.

He stepped carefully down the stone steps that led him down into the earth. Several doorways broke the monotonous descent but a swift investigation revealed store rooms or guarded passages into the sewers and catacombs beneath Mycenae. Making a note of their locations in case he needed to make a quick escape he continued down the stairs.

Finally his journey came to an end and he found himself before a great iron door. Frowning in thought, knowing that he could not open it lest he alert the occupants of his presence, Lykos knew he would have to use a portal. It would not be impossible, creating a portal into a locked room was entirely within his powers but it required more magic to safely guide oneself. Closing his eyes he concentrated and raised his hand. With a quick slash the portal opened and a surprising amount of his magic went into its creation. Knowing it would only tire him the longer he kept it open, he walked through and stood deathly still as his portal faded into nothing.

For instead of dark and grimy walls, blazing torches lined clean stone, illuminating the room more than enough to see its contents. Inhuman instruments of torture lined the walls and racks, wagons, and other depraved tools of insanity filled the floor. Cages lined the walls and floor and Lykos spied several corpses decomposing within. However it was the center of the room that captivated his attention.

An altar stood tall, proud, and cruel with fire licking at its edges. Carved into the marble surface were faces in pain, reaching out with desperate hands. And sitting upon a throne of broken bodies was carved a winged figure of feminine beauty holding forth claws wreathed in fire. In those claws rested the still bleeding corpse of a man. As the mans blood dripped into the flames below, the statue's eyes burned brighter and Lykos felt a tremor go down his spine. It was as if the statue could see him with those eyes.

So shocking was the altar that he almost missed the two figures who stood at its base. A man and a woman staring at each other with an intensity unlike two lovers, no this was the stare of foes. And as he examined the pair he knew immediately that the man was merely humoring the woman's presence and he wondered if the man was a fool.

For the woman was as deadly as she was beautiful. Knives and potion vials gleamed in the firelight, silver edges polished brightly. Her hands stood ready to use those tools at a moments notice against the man before her yet he showed no fear or caution. Lykos was unsettled to see the man to be amused. He stood without a care in the world in his peculiar clothes and his inhuman stare. So focused on his examination of the dangerous pair Lykos almost missed their conversation.

"You would do well to pay respect interloper," the woman warned the man. "I am blessed by the Valkyrie's themselves! I am their champion!"

The man twitched his hand and the woman gasped in pain despite no blow landing. "Stay your tongue child. You are but a pebble to a mountain. Do not speak to your betters in such a disrespectful manner and do not delude yourself to believe your are more than you're not."

The woman bristled angrily at the words. "Heathen! You will burn for your insult regardless of your stature!"

The man rolled his eyes unconcernedly. "Enough. Prepare yourself Helen for your guest's arrival is nigh. You know what you must do." The man's tone was mild but the warning was clear. Lykos watched with wide eyes as the dangerous woman bowed her head in acceptance.

"The Valkyrie's will be done," the assassin named Helen intoned. Lykos realized with a start that it was the same man from the outpost in Svellheim. The Architect nodded firmly before walking towards the door Lykos now realized he stood next to. Before he could react the man grasped the door handle pulling it open all the way, leaving Lykos awkwardly standing there beside him. However the man paid barely any attention to him and walked away after giving him a cursory glance. Perplexed he turned his attention back to Helen who knelt at the altar in prayer.

"I plead for thy guidance Valkyrie for I am lost without your light. Your champion I may be but without your direction I know not what to do. The Interloper's guidance is a poor shadow of your own and his orders border on heretical. Send me a sign Valkyrie so that I might do your will."

As Lykos listened to Helen's prayers he considered her plea. Her armor and weapons suggested a high level of skill yet she seemed to pray to an unseen deity for guidance? Why not enact her own will upon the world around her? Perhaps something restrained her? Whoever she was she was from Svellheim as it was a custom of northerners to call the deities Valkyries, a custom he was partial to as well.

As Lykos examined the room looking for clues to the mysteries in front of him Helen continued her prayer for guidance. He regretfully decided that he must kill the young women and return with her body back to Drakken, to fulfill the man's "quest". He drew his sword and prepared himself to do the deed when it happened.

The altar, quietly burning without creating smoke, changed colors. An impossible collection of shades of blue danced in the flames, swirling along the stone surface of the statue. A soft gasp escaping Helen's mouth alerted Lykos that she too saw the blue storm around the altar, could feel the magic in the air as it whipped at their hair and clothes.

"Valkyries! Your servant is here! Allow me to do thy bidding!" Helen cried, her hands held high adulation. However the statue remained unresponsive to her pleas and the swirls of blue concentrated upon statue's empty eyes.

Lykos was aware of a pull of magic as he stepped further into the room, the two blue pools of magical energy staring directly at him. It examined him as he it and with a sharp intake of breathe he could feel it caressing his magic. The touch was soft and rough, gentle and hard, as every facet of him was laid bare to the presence's eyes. However he grew tense despite its relaxing influence and pushed back with his own magic.

The presence was as surprised as he was that his push moved past the magic touching him. His own magic followed the being's magic for what seemed a great distance yet passed by in an instant. He nearly wept for the beautiful form that formed in his mind for it was one of the Valkyries and her brilliance was blinding. However that joy turned to rage when he felt chains binding the Valkyrie, restricting that glorious being from her full power. Lykos and the Valkyrie stared into each other for an eternity and he knew he was before a legend, a myth, a god!

A tendril of thought approached Lykos from the being before him. No words could be spoken, no sounds to be heard but colors, impressions, and feelings passed. *Save her*, the Valkyrie asked, *save me. Find me, free me!* The last was almost screamed at him for all the intensity of pain and rage that was felt. With a snap Lykos found himself kneeling on the ground before the altar.

"She touched you!" an awed voice from beside him spoke. Dazed he turned his head to see Helen beside him. "She brought you here!"

Lykos had a hundred questions rushing through his mind but the one the was voiced was, "was that a...?"

Helen seemed to understand. "A Valkyrie! You have been blessed by the gods! Are you their prophet?"

Lykos felt himself stand on a knives edge, a harrowing drop on either side as possibilities lay before him. Should he tell Helen the truth, that he was here to kill her? Or lie, claim to be the Valkyrie's prophet? The weight of his sword grip in his hand was heavy as he looked into her desperate eyes.

"I was sent here to kill you," Lykos whispered. Helen's eyes widened drastically in shock.

"But I've been a faithful servant to the Valkyries!" she protested. Lykos shook his head.

"The Valkyries didn't send me to end you," he started to explain yet the words fell silent in his mouth. He looked upon that confused face and felt her despair. "I am just a man."

"But the altar, a Valkyrie channeled power through it! I have longed for years to see such a sight yet it was only with your presence that they took note! You must have been sent by them, you must!" Helen was fervent in her belief and Lykos felt pity.

"My friend was taken from me," he explained. "A man named Drakken took my friend from me and told me that if I didn't kill you she would suffer. That my family would suffer," he snarled and began to pace.

"I have killed before and I will kill again but never have I taken blood from someone who has not wronged me. Never! Yet this pathetic excuse for a man dare to command me!" Lykos could not help his run away emotions and lashed out with his magic. The chains rattled, the tables shook, and the flames on the altar tinged purple as his magic raged throughout the dungeon.

A sharp prick stabbed his neck and he swore. The towering rage left him in a moment, feeling exhaustion hitting him like an avalanche. Turning he saw Helen returning an empty syringe to her robes. Warily he eyed her.

"What did you just do to me?" Lykos words slurred to his ears as he collapsed. Helen's eyes held a vindictive edge as she gazed down upon him.

"You are not the Valkyrie's prophet nor are you here to aid me. Thus you shall die while I plot to end Drakken's life. This must be the Valkyrie's will!" Lykos rage grew as he listened to the assassin's words. His magic sluggishly responded in purging the poison from his veins and with a faint terror he realized this was how his father had died. Betrayed by his own body.

He felt himself grow weak as Helen rationalized that he had been sent there for her to kill. Pleased she settled in to watch his expiration patiently. His gaze fell upon the burning altar, the stone face of the Valkyrie looked neutrally down upon him as the flames licked its surface. As his strength failed him, he extended a weak limb of magic to the angelic figure.

The flames changed color once more, blue fire and magic swirling. However this time the magic was angry and it lashed out. Helen fell to her knees as the Valkyrie's magic struck at her angrily. The assassin wailed in pain as she joined Lykos on the floor and he could not help but entertain the thought that at least she would die with him.

"My lady please! Tell me what I must do!" she cried as the Valkyrie tortured her, pushing and pulling and twisting her body and magic. The presence of the Valkyrie filled the room and Lykos could feel it focus on him. "Him? He will die in moments from the poison."

Helen's cry seared through the air as the Valkyrie's magic flexed painfully upon her. Then as suddenly as it struck it pulled back to the statue, caressing its surface as the two humans gasped on the floor.

"You want me to heal him? But he was sent here to kill me!" Helen gasped. The Valkyrie's magic swelled angrily and Helen quickly threw up her arms in a futile attempt of protection. "I'll do it!"

The magic settled once more as she dragged herself over to him. A quick jab of her hand with another syringe sent a jolt of energy through his limbs and relief spread. His raspy breathes faded along with the magic from the Valkyrie's altar and silence descended upon the dungeon.

With a quick lunge Lykos tackled Helen and pinned her to the ground. An angry snarl took over his face as he held a knife to her throat and glared angrily down upon her. "That was rude," he stated firmly. Helen sulked beneath his blade.

"You did just say you were here for that craven coward Drakken to kill me," she argued as he pushed down with his knife. He internally conceded her that point but the fact of the matter was he had never felt so vulnerable and weak since his magic had been awakened. It was unpleasant and he vowed to never be put in that position again. Or if he was to kill those responsible.

"Will you try to kill me again?" he asked.

Helen glanced up at the quietly burning altar before returning her gaze to Lykos. "No," the assassin stated sullenly. After a moment of consideration he judged her words to be honest and stood up. Offering his hand as a peace offering, Helen grasped it and was pulled to her feet.

"So now what?"

Chapter Twenty-Four

"This won't work," Helen muttered as Lykos wrapped chains around her wrists.

"Not with that attitude it won't," he replied as he clamped the lock shut. He held out the key for her. She rolled her eyes as she swiftly hid it in her hand.

"Not with any attitude, you're trying to pull a fast one on Drakken. Do you even know why there was a kill contract ordered on him?" she asked as they left the dark alley that had hidden them from prying eyes. Not that there were many as night had fallen upon the kingdom of Mycenae and the pubs and flesh palaces were full.

"He kicked someone's puppy?" he tried as he grabbed her arm and made of a show of dragging her along. The assassin rolled her eyes once more.

"He set loose a trio of Tainted Chargers as a distraction so he could raid an Emporo vault." Impressed, Lykos almost reevaluated his opinion of killing the man before remembering he was currently holding Falka and several other men and women hostage.

"Do you think he would tell us how he pulled that off? I thought those vaults were practically unbreakable."

"I do not intend to engage him in small talk before I put my sword through his heart."

He sighed but was not surprised. In the short time he had shared with Helen he had discovered an almost burning hatred for

Drakken that bordered upon obsessive. Perhaps the young women knew someone who had been killed or injured by the criminal's actions? Further questions would have to wait as the pair had reached Drakken's building.

Knocking on the wooden door, a slit opened up revealing suspicious eyes. "What's the password?"

"What password?" Lykos asked outraged.

"The password to get in!" The eyes narrowed in anger.

"There wasn't a password last time!" he tried to argue.

"There's always been a password!" the eyes countered.

"Valkyries grant me strength," Helen muttered.

"Drakken sent me out to get her!" Lykos tried. The eyes considered the pair.

"I'll be right back." The wooden slit slid shut leaving them alone on the street. The duo stared at the worn wood in front of them in silence, determined not to comment of the ridiculous of the situation. Lykos opened his mouth but Helen beat him to the punch.

"Unless the words that are about to come out of your mouth are "Helen we can slaughter our way to Drakken and impale him on the doorkeepers spine" I don't want to hear it." Lykos' mouth snapped shut with a click and silence returned. After several more moments in the chilly night air the door slit once more slid open.

"I'm only supposed to open for some Lykos git!" The suspicious eyes returned once more to glare at them. Lykos rolled his eyes in frustration.

"I am that Lykos git, I mean I am Lykos! Now open up!" He fought down the rising rage that the doorkeeper's ridiculousness was causing.

"I don't know. You seem sort of shifty! How do I know you are who you say you are?"

"Oh for crying out loud, just kill me now!" Helen wailed. Lykos shushed her.

"Tell you what, why don't you take us back to Drakken and ask if we are who we say we are. If we aren't then you can kill us!"

"No funny business?" the eyes asked suspiciously.

"No funny business," Lykos growled out, silently vowing that there would be a great deal of bloody business and that this man would be the first to experience it.

There was a small moment of silence before the sound of a metal bolt sliding. There in the door way stood a midget on a stool glaring at the pair while piles of flesh undulated in the background sickeningly.

"Alright, come with me. And no funny business or I'll gut you with my knife!" The doorkeeper held a small knife, no longer than Lykos' little finger, in a threatening manner.

"Agreed," Lykos commented dryly. He pulled on Helen's arms and whispered to her as the entered the brothel, "time to go kill the fat bastard."

"Fat bastard? Drakken is anything but," Helen replied. Lykos turned questioning eyes towards her but was interrupted by the doorkeeper who was impatiently waiting for them. A pair of enthusiastic flesh maidens writhed next to the oblivious man, a remarkable fact due to his short stature.

"I don't have all night! Hurry along." They had no further time to talk as they were hurried through the rooms. Still, their hurried pace did not stop Lykos from feeling disgust at the extravagance displayed and loathing at the treatment of the slaves. After Drakken was dead he would see about freeing these tortured souls.

Finally they entered Drakken's lair whose occupants had changed since he had left. Drakken, Bart, and a now gagged Falka all remained however the hostages chained to his table had been replaced by several more burly guards, towering above them all. Their thick muscles, heavy armor, and sharp blades promised violence.

Lykos looked forward to it.

The trio stopped before Drakken who looked upon Helen with a greedy smile. Lykos nodded to a relieved Falka who was sandwiched between two burly guards while a third hovered behind Bart whose gaze was firmly fixed downwards. Drakken spoke.

"Helen before me at last." Drakken nodded in satisfaction to the perplexed assassin. "However I thought I told you to kill her?" That had been directed at Lykos who shrugged.

"I thought you'd like to kill her yourself. Now I would like my friends back." Lykos gestured to Falka and Bart.

"You're not Drakken!" Helen snarled from beside him. Lykos furrowed his brow as Falka began to struggle against her gag.

"Don't be absurd, of course I am!" Drakken puffed out his chest and Falka struggled more.

"No you're not! Drakken is a skinny bastard of a slaver who sold my sister and killed my father! I would know his face anywhere and you are not he!" Lykos finely attuned senses screamed that dangers surrounded them and looking around he agreed. Each of the guards had their hands upon their weapons, glaring at them.

"Enough! Kill her!" Drakken thrust out a meaty hand and two of his guards immediately drew their swords. Advancing on her they raised them to strike and Lykos knew it was time to act.

Reaching down, Lykos grabbed the doorkeeper by the back of his shirt and heaved upwards. Lifting the surprisingly heavy midget off the ground, he threw his improvised distraction at the two advancing guards. The two men panicked and slashed at the airborne midget, slicing him into bloody chunks. Using the distraction to its fullest potential he made his way to Falka who was putting up a valiant effort to claw one of her captor's eyes out while bound.

As Lykos freed his friend, Helen slashed her way violently through the remaining guards. After several frantic moments of bloodshed the only souls living souls were Bart, Drakken, Falka, Helen and Lykos. Helen stood over the trembling figure of Bart with her bloody knife raised when Lykos called out to the assassin.

"Helen that isn't Drakken!"

"Of course it is!" Her attention was distracted just enough by his shout that the trembling form of Bart thrust his hands forward. A powerful wave of magic spread out throwing the four remaining men and women to the floor harshly. By the time they recovered, Bart had already vanished through the broken door.

Helen struggled to her feet and cursed when her prey had vanished. Staggering over to Drakken she punched the slowly recovering man in the face to snap his focus upon her. "Where is he going! Where!"

Drakken merely laughed as Falka and Lykos stepped up to her. "Why did you try to kill Bart?" he demanded angrily. Helen gave a mocking laugh.

"Is that what he told you his name was? That skinny bastard is Drakken and this," Helen punched the fat man sitting before them, "is one of his henchmen playing at being their master."

Several things Helen and Bart, now revealed to be the true Drakken, had said suddenly made sense at the moment. Lykos angrily cursed while Helen once more raised her sword over her captive, and this time he was in no mood to stop her as the blade fell. The breathing of four turned to three as the body double breathed his last.

"Drakken must have planned this entire thing since I defeated him in the Succession Trial." Lykos turned to Falka. "I don't suppose you have any idea where a criminal mastermind hangs out?"

"No, despite all my explorations I've stayed away from those areas of the kingdom. Scions of a noble house are tempting targets for extortion and ransom," she replied. They watched as Helen cleaned her sword. "My thanks to you assassin, for saving me from a fate worse than death."

Helen merely nodded towards her before turning to Lykos. "Valkyrie's blessing or not you have caused me to miss my target. You will aid me in hunting him down and ending his miserable life."

Lykos matched her hard glare with one of his own. "I have my own quest to deal with without adding yours along." As the assassin's hands tightened around the hilt of her sword he continued, "I seek centurions and commanders to train and lead my men. I had hoped Bart would aid me but that is not to happen now. However I have seen your skill and propose this: aid me and mine and I will help you end Drakken."

She thought in silence for a long moment before sighing, her hand falling away from her sword. Lykos relaxed as well and was surprised to even find that he had been tensing for a fight. Clearly his body was becoming accustomed to combat.

"I wish I could help you in your quest but I have no great skill in leadership. While I make a passable healer my main skills lay in assassination and torture but I do not think you have need of those skills just yet," she reluctantly explained. Lykos narrowed his eyes in thought.

"Would some of your fellow acolytes aid me? Especially if you told them of our encounter with the Valkyrie's altar?" Lykos asked.

"What altar? Have you been having fun without me? Naughty acolyte and sexy priestess?" Falka whispered to Lykos who hurriedly waved her off. Helen paid her no mind as she considered his question.

"Some but none who are skilled in what you seek. The Acolytes have been corrupted in recent years. They do not pray, they do not worship anything but coin. The order has become nothing more than a breeding ground of thugs and murderers."

"Will they oppose us?" Lykos asked wondering if he had a new enemy to add to his collection.

"Undoubtedly," Helen replied with a wry smile. "Ignoring the fact that anyone could create a contract on your life, the current head of our order is a woman named Andrea of House Vrachos. She's utilized the Valkyrie's absence to subvert the order to her whims, using them as her own personal army. Most of them have turned towards criminal activities when they aren't killing their mistresses enemies."

"Wonderful an army of criminal assassins," Falka angrily muttered as she kicked a corpse. "And how does this help us get useful commanders for our army?"

Helen opened her mouth before pausing. "Perhaps there might be a way for this to work out for us after all. There are an underground tournaments, much like the Succession Trial, that happen weekly. Many of my fellow acolytes participate for coin and prestige and this would allow you to find more suitable warriors for your army."

Lykos hummed in thought. "I'm sure there is betting on those fights as well. So long as I don't die, it could be a nice source of income as well."

"Indeed." Helen nodded in satisfaction.

"But what do you get out of this Helen? How does this help us find Drakken?" he pressed.

"Because you killing or recruiting his best fighters will weaken his hold on the criminal underworld. Give it enough time and someone will lead us right to Drakken. You just have to survive it." Helen's dark grin was matched by his own while Falka looked between the pair with interest.

"Is there anyone we're not declaring war on? I'm not complaining mind you, I just think we should be clear on this before we wage war against the whole world."

Chapter Twenty-Five

Lykos looked down upon his growing army with pride as they trained in the Talal barracks.

In the past few months he and his allies had hit slave pens throughout the kingdom, absconding with hundreds of men, women, and children during the night. Artisans, carpenters, sailors, soldiers and more were all freed in their rescues. Without fail the freed slaves joined him and began to rebuild and fortify Pyrgos.

Men and women trained day after day with weapons stolen from their captors. Unskilled hands practiced with a relentless determination, keen to never be victim to anyone ever again. They served House Talal with loyalty but their admiration for Lykos was fanatical. And joining them were the empowered people of Pyrgos, no longer forced to obey the whims of the corrupt. They welcomed each other with open arms.

It was a heady feeling knowing he had an army of soldiers at his command yet Lykos was fortunate to have friends and family to keep him level headed. Adelram offered sound advice and began to pose scenarios for him to solve involving various amounts of soldiers and Tainted. The mental exercise was taxing but rewarding and he slowly learned how to command his forces effectively.

It fell to Falka and Illusionist Maeve to keep him humble. For all his growing skill with magic he was still very much the elderly sorceresses lesser and she reminded him of that fact regularly. But he found the gaps in his knowledge closing day by day and he knew it was only a matter of time before she taught him all that she knew. He just needed to survive her hellish training.

Falka was a breathe of fresh air for the young lord. She always led him on some odd scavenger hunt or to some ancient corner of the kingdom, sharing its history. Old passageways shed new light on the ancient history of Mycenae or at least that's what they told themselves after crawling through a mossy catacomb beneath Kremos Keep. These excursions were often accompanied by the presence of Ana Del Rosa whose quiet shell was finally worn down by the exuberant Falknor woman.

As Lykos looked upon his soldiers training he saw two recruits begin to bicker over some petty issue. The vocal disruption was easily discernible in the orderly lines and alerted their trainers. One of them rapidly converged upon the duo and restored order without incident. The flash of red hair identified them as one of the brothers.

Lykos nodded in satisfaction as the man turned to reveal Giles' ridiculous beard. It was nothing against his brother, Doukas, but the grizzly figure's commanding presence worked well with the recruits. That and Lykos never liked Doukas' mustache anyways. The two men had been recruited during one of underground fight tournaments that Helen had introduced Lykos to, the brothers working well together in tag team battles. Helen and Lykos had faced a difficult challenge in subduing them but had won their respect and service.

Giles returned to the front of the formation and barked out more orders as his brother walked their lines. Lykos allowed his eyes to drift over to the other side of the barracks where a series of low tents had been raised. A gust of wind flapped its walls revealing a field infirmary with several bloody occupants. One of them gestured excitedly towards several figures.

Demos was a former slave who had served House Stultus as their personal healer. She had shown up and prostrated for forgiveness in front of Lykos and his family, begging to be allowed to continue serving them as she had House Stultus.

He had reddened in embarrassment at her exuberance. To the amusement of his family he had pulled the healer to her feet and tried futilely to wave away her ceaseless gratitude. This encounter would color the next two months, as Demos' unending enthusiasm was a welcome relief among the injured recruits if somewhat trying for Lykos personally.

Soft footfalls on stone alerted him of a presence behind him, echoed by several others. Without turning his gaze to face them he spoke up.

"You're all dead."

Silence met his declaration and Lykos smirked. "Glad to see you're smart enough to keep your mouths shut but I know you're there, there, there, and there."

As Lykos pointed to various spots behind him it was answered by a chorus of groans. Turning he looked to see several recruits dressed in light leathers standing in disappointment behind him. He gave them a small smile.

"Where is Irene?" he asked referring to their dark haired instructor. The final trainer Lykos had managed to recruit was a dark skinned woman who was a close friend of Helen's. Despite operating as a healer for the Acolytes, the mysterious bowman spent most her time foraging and hunting Tainted in the wilds outside of the kingdom.

None of the recruits answered him and several of them began to grin. He rolled his eyes.

"Irene, would you kindly vacate the balcony ledge!" he called out to the surprise of the recruits. A moment passed before the lithe figure of Irene joined them on the balcony, clambering over the ledge that he had just been standing over. She gave him a respectful nod before turning to her students.

"Do any of you rogues have any idea how Lord Talal detected us?" she asked her students.

"He heard us."

"He saw us."

"He's bloody paranoid." Lykos almost smiled at the last one but kept his face neutral as Irene looked at her students unimpressed.

"That explains you four but how did he know I was there?" Her dark green cape swished as she leaped from the wooden banister to stand next to him. The four recruits shared uneasy glances.

"He saw you?" a young man tried and his fellows groaned. Irene fixed the foolish young man a dark glare and he immediately wilted in fright.

"Does anyone else have a preposterous idea?" she asked, giving the young man a look the promised immeasurable pain. A moment of uneasy silence passed as the quartet shared worried glances. Taking pity on them Lykos spoke up.

"I might have an idea."

Irene turned towards him and gave him a falsely cheery smile. "Yes Lord Talal?"

"I understood the methods of the predator hunting me." Lykos winked at Irene who ignored it.

"Precisely." Irene turned back towards her students who were watching them attentively. "When stalking your prey do not follow their footsteps. Instead understand their motives and identify where they intend to go before they themselves have even decided. For when they finally arrive, you will be waiting there for them."

"Yes instructor," they chorused, nodding obediently.

"Return to your exercises." Without a word all four of the students retreated from the balcony leaving Lykos and Irene alone. "How do you like your troops Lord Talal?"

"I've told you before you may call me Lykos," he tried with a small smile but Irene remained standoffish. Frowning slightly he answered honestly, "I'm impressed with how their progress has grown. You and the other instructors are due their credit."

She gave him an appreciative nod but then smirked with a teasing glint in her eye. "No more incidents with the guards at your gates?"

He groaned. The incident in question had spread like a fire, causing him to be the butt of his allies jokes on more than one occasion. He had returned to Hearthome from a rescue mission late one night and had been challenged by the guards. As this was what they were supposed to do he had not been bothered at first but the new guard did not recognize him as Lord Talal. Lykos and the guard had gotten into a shouting match so loud it had awoken nearly everyone in the quarter and they all saw his folly first hand. Weeks later he still did not know why he did not just use magic to surpass the guard.

"No I've had no more issues with my gatekeepers," he ground out through his teeth. Irene laughed softly before turning away.

"Then if you'll excuse me Lord Talal, I must oversee the recruits to prevent such a mistake from repeating itself."

He watched Irene vanish over the balcony as easily as she had appeared and once more his thoughts drifted to the mysterious woman. Her nature was more perplexing as one moment she would be passionate, vigorous as she talked about hunting or tracking, explaining in detail her thoughts. However at other times she would retreat into herself as if the whole experience of social interaction was a chore she had no desire to take part of. He found himself observing the beautiful woman as often as circumstance allowed in an attempt to figure her out.

Unfortunately this was not one such time. His repeated attacks on slave holdings these past few months had forced House Emporo to stop bringing in new shipments. He could no longer grow his army with an influx of ready recruits and thus he needed a new plan to boost his numbers. After all while his enemies had armies at their disposal he only had one and it was pitifully small in comparison.

He made his way down the stairs and moved past the training lines of soldiers. Giving a respectful nod to any man or woman who met his eyes, he did not halt his pace as he crossed the training yard. At the end he found Adelram sitting at a low desk, angrily reading several rolls of parchment. Glancing up, the commander of the Talal forces snarled at his lord.

"I don't know whether to praise you for assigning me this post or curse you for the headaches it has caused me."

"Sounds about as fun as our early morning training sessions where you would wake me with fire and ice," Lykos quipped. Adelram chuckled appreciatively

"Aye, those were good times weren't they?" he asked rhetorically. Lykos only quirked an eyebrow unimpressed. "Well they were good for me."

"From what I see the new recruits are fitting in nicely, how are we on supplying them?" Lykos asked him.

"Well since you've been supplying us with your tournament winnings we've got them all armed and clothed but feeding them will be an issue soon enough. We have enough provisions to last us a month, two tops, but if you're thinking what I think you're thinking we're going to need to find more money."

"I think we need more troops."

"Blast it, I knew it. I don't disagree but we need money and food and space to house them all. The Pyrgos is one of the smallest, if not the smallest, quarter in the entire kingdom. If we had enough money we could simply buy all we needed from the other houses."

"They'd sell to a potential enemy?" Lykos asked doubtfully.

"Oh don't get me wrong, they wouldn't trust you to tell the earth from the sky but they'll still sell to you. Everybody loves gold and what it brings."

"Death."

"Aye that too."

Lykos considered their predicament. Even with acquiring the Stultus holdings and renovating the dilapidated properties contained therein, they still lacked the wealth the other houses had. They could always turn towards pillaging other quarters but it would not be able to support them long term and it would sour their slowly recovering reputation within the kingdom.

"So what can we do?" he finally asked. Adelram hummed.

"Well how I see it we have several options. The first is we continue as we have been and hope that this winter is a warm one otherwise we'll starve to death. The second is that we could wage war against another house and pillage their property and goods for our own use. Finally we could enter an alliance with another house and provide protection for goods."

Lykos considered their options. As much as he might hope otherwise this winter would not be gentle or kind, already the air cooled drastically at night. Waging a war was likewise impossible as they simply lacked the troops to mount any respectable offense, let alone having enough to properly man their defenses. Which left the final option.

"I suppose I'll have to make another social call," he stated sullenly. Adelram laughed at his expression.

"Come now it can't be as bad the witches instruction," Adelram joked referring to Illusionist Maeve's sadistic teaching manner. Lykos groaned in frustration.

"It's actually worse. With Maeve I know she doesn't want to actually kill me, just make me strong enough that our enemies can't break me, but these lords and ladies...." Lykos trailed off in thought.

Adelram looked up from his scrolls. "What about them?"

"I have been a complete and utter moron."

"Well you're young and stupid so it's expected."

"Quiet old man. I just realized I have the best access in the world to an ally that I've been completely neglecting," he explained.

"Oh and who might that be?" Adelram asked when it appeared that he was not going to explain himself. Lykos grinned before spinning around to hunt down his prey.

"Why Falka of Falknor of course."

It was surprisingly easy to find Falka, who often disappeared during the daylight hours to sleep. She was having tea with Ana Del Rosa and Shawna on the terrace overlooking the kingdom and the three woman were chatting happily with one another. Shawna smiled as he approached.

"Come to join us dear?" The past few months had been kind to his mother, the slightly crazed look being replaced by motherly concern as the woman healed mentally from years of solitude. The pride in her eyes as she looked at him caused him to swell with emotion and walk taller.

"Not quite mother. I was hoping to borrow Falka for a moment if you don't mind?" he asked with a smile.

"Of course not, now Ana tell me all about these paintings you saw." Shawna's conversation with Ana faded as Lykos and Falka walked to the edge of the terrace. While the height still caused his gut to clench painfully many flights on board the Falknor airships alleviated the vertigo he once suffered.

"Do you think your father would be willing to enter an alliance with House Talal?" he asked without preamble. Falka blinked owlishly at him.

"What?" she asked blankly. He firmed his lips before asking once more but Falka waved him off. "No I heard what you asked but I thought you knew you were already in an alliance with him?"

Now it was time for Lykos to be confused. "What are you talking about?"

She rolled her eyes at him. "Do you really think I could convince my siblings to use their precious airships to mount rescue missions? And at night? My father has been providing you aid this entire time."

"I've never even met the man!" Lykos protested.

"No but you've met me," Falka grinned cheekily while pointing to herself, "and I'm the apple of his eye. When I told him I was interested in helping you he grilled me for all of the information I had on you. During Leon's Rebellion he was too busy trying to establish our family here but now that we're established he's willing to support you."

Lykos was blown away by the man's generosity. However he grew concerned.

"What does he expect in return for his airships?"

Falka waved away his concerns. "What you would have done anyways, protect me and my family. My family is still new in this kingdom and there are those who would seek to take our fleet of airships and use it for their own ends. In your father's war we were too small to be anything other than a liability but now we are powerful enough to fight."

"I suppose I should meet with him soon then, to thank him."

"Not unless you feel the pressing need to speak with him. Like I said, I'm the apple of his eye, he's more than willing to assist a stranger he has never met so long as I asked. You've been invited to our harvest ball next week anyways so you can always speak to him then." Lykos found the statement odd but let it go. Falka wouldn't hide things from him. Unless she thought it would be funny.

Shaking off his paranoia he shifted his gaze to where he knew Kremos Keep to be. "Do you think your father could assist more?" While he was loathe to ask for more aid he knew he needed it.

Falka shook her head without hesitation. "My father is currently too tied down in trades to even grow our fleet let alone posses a surplus. Otherwise I'd have my own airship by now."

"No wonder you're always getting in trouble, you have nothing to tie you down." Lykos smiled even as Falka whacked him halfheartedly. "I guess I'll have to find another house to gain what we need."

"What do you need anyways?" Falka asked as they returned to Ana and Shawna. Collapsing in a seat he briefly admired his restored home before answering.

"Money, food, space," he listed off. "If I had the first the rest would be a non-issue but we have none so we'll be in trouble soon. Who would have thought housing an army to be so difficult."

The group shared a small laugh but then Shawna spoke up, "have you tried asking the other houses?"

He sighed explosively. "Well House Vrachos has offered to carve me a nice tomb should I die, House Miles don't want anything to do with me as apparently they were allies with the Stultus and suspect I had something to do with that. Sofos and Kolos would rather slit my throat than even meet with me so I'm happily avoiding them and the Prodotis keep postponing every meeting. We haven't been invited to any balls and I've been too busy to crash one either."

Shawna frowned at him. "Have you visited my old house?"

"The Agroti? I thought we weren't to having anything to do with them after how they treated you and Adelram."

Shawna's lips pressed tightly together as she stared out at the kingdom. "I cannot say I am pleased with my former houses actions but I would not think you'd ignore a potential ally, especially when we are in dire need. I shall contact my aunt and uncle and arrange a meeting for you tomorrow."

Lykos smiled. "Thank you mother." Shawna tutted.

"Sit up straight, you'll ruin your posture. No son of mine will be looked down upon by my own family."

He reluctantly obliged and sat in his chair properly as Ana and Falka shared a laugh at his expense. "What can I expect from House Agroti?"

"Well it's led by my aunt, who is Leandra, and my uncle, who is Rolan, who preside over conclave of head farmers of House Agroti. They've managed to survive House Kolos' purge of your fathers allies by being vocal dissidents after his death." she paused as the old pain resurfaced on her face. "I'm not sure what they've done since then but before they managed many of the farms in the Lowland and throughout the kingdom."

"They still do," Falka cut in, "no one else wants to do *menial* labor such as farming."

"So House Agroti will have plenty of food and space if I can convince them to side with us?" Lykos asked as he sipped some tea.

"Indeed. The Lowland is rich in fertile land due to being one of the newer quarters, only several hundred years old. However its proximity to the wilds means a greater number of Tainted attack them than in Pyrgos. As a result they've always sought strong allies. Be prepared to be tested dear."

"Shouldn't be too much of an issue for you," Falka smirked over her teacup at him. "You're used to people trying to kill you."

"Thank you Falka for that ringing endorsement."

"It could always be worse," Ana said.

"How could this possibly be worse?" Lykos asked in exasperation.

She opened and closed her mouth several times before finally speaking, "well everyone could hate you?" she tried causing Falka and Lykos to snort in laughter.

"The only people who don't want to kill him are at this table," Falka paused to give him a considering look, "although it is tempting."

"Bad Falka. No killing your friends."

"You never let me have any fun."

"For good reason," Lykos interjected, tired of being the punching bag. "You once set a Citadel guard on fire and poured alcohol on him to put him out."

"The flames eventually died down!" Falka objected.

"Only because Helen poured acid on him!"

Shawna turned towards Ana as Lykos and Falka argued. "Do they always bicker like children?"

Ana Del Rosa nodded. "Unless I kiss Falka I find she rarely is quiet. Even in her sleep. And I think Lykos enjoys riling her up." The two women turned their attention back to the bickering duo to find them staring at Ana. "What?"

"Falka talks in her sleep? What does she say?" Lykos asked with an eager grin on his face. Falka gave up all pretenses of being civilized as she tackled him off of his chair in an act of impudent rage. Ana Del Rosa and Shawna smiled at the amusing sight.

"It's so nice to have a family again," Shawna said happily.

Chapter Twenty-Six

Lykos' slumber was interrupted by the cry of a Tainted Piercer fledgling that had managed to get into his room during the night. Stabbing it with a dagger he kept under his pillow, it died a quick, startling death and collapsed to the floor. Knowing it would be futile to go back to sleep after such a heart racing event, he armed himself with his other weapons and a light set of armor. Wrapping a cloak around himself to ward off the morning chill he descended the stairs to find Falka of Falknor and Giles of Dumas waiting for him in the kitchen, quietly eating fresh bread and vegetables. Belatedly he remembered he had requested the pair to join him on the days excursion, Falka for her experience in house politics and Giles to provide extra support in case things turned south. Both had readily acquiesced.

After their breakfast the trio quickly made their way to one of the many waterways within the kingdom, chartering a barge to take them to the Agroti Homestead in the Lowland. Despite the expediency of nautical travel, the journey took over a hour as the distance between the corners of Mycenae was great. At times Lykos found himself tempted to simply create portals to hasten his journey but knew leaving behind his two allies would end poorly. So because of his inability to bring along a passenger, he relied on his patience.

The morning passed comfortably enough anyways with Falka and Giles for company and Lykos was pleased that the bearded man was so easy going. Their family had followed House Falknor in their exodus from the kingdom of Svellheim in the cold north, believing that their fortunes could be better gained elsewhere. Giles was an honorable man who only wished to increase his families station in life and for that Lykos could respect and work with him.

Arriving in the Lowland marked a stark change from the more developed portions of Mycenae. For one, the few buildings present were built solely with wood, and were curiously built upon stone pillars taller than any man. The vast areas of space left undeveloped were covered in crops and gardens at various stages of growth, even with the colder weather. The ground all around was muddy yet the rivers that crossed the quarter were not near enough to provide irrigation and Lykos could not understand how the Agroti watered their crops.

It was the man who was providing their transportation that answered the curious enigma.

"The land here floods," he said as he gestured with his straw hat. "Every morning and evening the rivers swell with water and flood the ground. This is the lowest point in the whole kingdom and because of that you won't find any sewers or the like underground. They'd flood too."

The man explained how the water level was was the deepest closest to the rivers and furthest near the walls of the quarter and thus the farmers planted accordingly. This one quarter provided food for a large portion of a kingdom whose hunger only grew with each passing year.

Finally they arrived at the largest building in the entire quarter which had been built on several rocky outcroppings. Built with wood like the rest of the structures, it none the less drew the eye with how massive it was. This was the home of House Agroti, Lykos' family from his mother's side.

They were welcomed warmly enough by several guards bearing the Agorti mark, a yellow oval on a green square, and escorted into the large building. It was not ornate in the sickening way that the Stultus estate had been nor was it reassuring like the stone structures of Hearthome. Instead it felt warm and lived in, full of people cooking around fires, relaxing, and talking over cups of mead. Lykos and company enjoyed the friendly atmosphere as they made their way deeper into the building.

Passing under a wooden arch they find themselves at the top of a vase shaped room made out of stone and open to the sky. Stone seats were carved straight out of the ground, ringing the room as it descended down to a small pond that was created with water from the last rain. In the center of that pond stood a small stone platform where speakers could stand. Lykos realized that this stone room must exist in one of the rocky outcroppings they had seen on approach.

Each of the seats was already filled with one of the dozens of members of the Agroti family. As one of the largest noble houses in the kingdom it was not surprising that the numbers present were so numerous. It was Agroti custom to allow any member who owned land to have a say in house politics and a diverse range of ages and genders sat in this room, ready to pass judgment.

Lykos led Falka and Giles down to the stone platform and nodded in respect to the gathered Agroti and eagerly began their petition.

"How the hell am I related to these Tainted loving morons?" Lykos asked Falka and Giles as they watched the bickering Agroti. He had thought the whole process had gone along swimmingly, he had praised their agricultural powers, cited their family ties, and inquired upon their stance of House Talal. That was when things had rapidly gone down hill.

Every member of House Agroti had an equal opportunity to speak, young or old, wise or not, and all seemed determined to shout their opinion as loudly as they could. The shouting had only been made worse by the curved stone walls, echoing the noise around endlessly. It was not unlike standing beneath a waterfall as torrents of water beat down upon ones head. It was thoroughly unpleasant.

"Sometimes you shout," Falka said as if that explained everything. He gave her a dark look while Giles laughed.

"They certainly seem energetic," Giles remarked. "Although I have difficulties associating the calm and collected Dowager Talal with these boisterous individuals."

"Agreed." Lykos stood in stony silence for several more moments as the gathered Agroti argued ever more fervently. "I've had enough of this."

He raised his arm to the ceiling and gathered his magic. Light seemed to darken around his hand as he slowly closed his fist. A small wind began to tug at his clothes and hair and his clenched fist began to shake. After a moment more he opened his hand and a wave of magic exploded out of above his head.

The gathered Agroti were thrown back into their seats as the wave of magic forced them backwards. Dust was thrown into the air as the magic hit the stone walls, harmlessly dissipating upon the curved surface. The trio standing on the stone platform was unaffected as the magic soared over their heads and with that, silence descended upon the room as everyone turned to stare at them.

"Sorry." Lykos smiled at the stony faces. "But as my mother was Agroti that means that I too have the right to speak here do I not?"

"You don't own a farm!" a squat man shouted.

"I overlook the entire Pyrgos. That includes blacksmiths, carpenters, and more than a few farms." The squat man huffed but did not rise up to the bait. Lykos turned back to the greater portion of Agroti.

"I asked you your stance upon House Talal. I was not aware such diverse and strong opinions for the house you were once strong allies to existed but now that I am, I was hoping I could provide a brief history lesson if you would be willing to indulge me." The entire room fell deathly silent as he composed himself to deliver his thoughts.

"My father Leon led a rebellion against corruption in this kingdom many years ago. This was opposed by those who profited from said corruption and all too quickly lines were being drawn in a kingdom where houses had stood as allies for generations against the Tainted. It was a dark time where families were torn apart and trampled underneath. My father fell and with his death the hope for a kingdom where tyranny and slavery were abolished. He was betrayed under false pretenses and that is something I will never forgive or forget."

Lykos paused looking down in solemn silence as the Agroti watched on. He closed his eyes briefly but opened them to reveal two dangerous orbs burning with determination. He began to speak anew with a harder, more dangerous voice.

"And then there is what happened afterwards. Slavery, almost stomped out, bounced back a hundredfold. Noble houses began to abuse their status, taking liberties with the people they had once sworn to protect. And my father's allies, those that swore to stand with him unto death, they fled! They hid their involvement, forsook their fallen friends, and betrayed the very man they swore to protect like cowards!"

"Lies!" the same fat man from before bellowed as he struggled to his feet.

"Sit down," Lykos ordered darkly, using his magic to force the man to his seat. He turned back to the still and terrified Agroti who realized they were in a room with an angry mage who had no qualms with using his power.

"You fled. You hid. You denied your own blood! My mother Shawna, your sister, your daughter, your cousin, your family! She sat alone in her husband's home friendless and without aid for years, her own family would not dare associate with the wife of a man falsely branded traitor! You sit here and dare to debate the worthiness of House Talal when it is you who have no honor!"

Lykos roared with rage and sent his magic out once more, pinning each of the Agroti down. The magic left him in great waves, rapidly exhausting him but he simply did not care. These men and women betrayed their own oaths, betrayed their blood, and he was finding a new emotion roaring in his chest: protectiveness over his family.

"I should kill you all where you sit," he whispered in the silent chamber, his words echoing like death. "I should end House Agroti for its betrayal." He slowly turned, fixing each terrified pair of eyes in his mind. Making his decision he pulled back on his magic, it reluctantly obeying his command and resting underneath his skin like a restless beast.

"I forgive you," Lykos spoke, his words shocking those gathered their today. Even Falka and Giles looked surprised by this turn of events, their hands having strayed to their weapons during his speech. "I forgive you all but I will not forget that my own blood betrayed my family. I am apathetic towards your fate." And with that Lykos stood silently before them, patiently awaiting their response.

A great bout of laughter echoed through the hall and all turned towards the sound. Lord Agroti, Rolan, sat wheezing in his chair as his frail body was wracked with movement. His amusement finally ceased as he gathered his breathe once more.

"You are brave and foolish. You are like your father." Lord Agroti and Lord Talal stared into each others eyes, fierce youth matching cunning age.

"What does House Talal require?" Lord Agroti finally asked while giving a nod of respect to the younger lord. Lykos returned it.

"I require your aid."

It took several more hours and concessions but eventually an agreement was hammered out.

House Agroti would provide food and shelter at discount for House Talal's growing army with the expectation that House Talal would remember this generosity when they succeeded in overthrowing House Kolos. However House Agroti also required a champion to defend them from challenges from the demands of other houses.

"I will not be at your beck and call," Lykos growled out when the demand was brought up. The gathered Agroti panicked.

"Oh no! Not that we wouldn't appreciate your aid but we require someone who can be on hand at all times. We understand that you would be far too busy to travel here every time we met with another noble house," a thin man by the name of Thaddeus claimed. From what Lykos understood he was in charge at Homestead, keeping the books and insuring all the farms kept up production.

"Then you want me to assign someone?" Lykos asked pondering who he could spare to represent the Agroti. They would need to be competent and intimidating enough to fill the role properly which narrowed the list considerably. Thaddeus waved away his concerns.

"We already have a man in mind, we just need you to convince him to aid us."

"Oh, who might this man be?" Lykos asked wondering if he was about to lose someone irreplaceable.

"His name is Plower, our former champion in fact, and I believe you're already familiar with him." The name did ring a bell but Lykos hoped he was wrong.

"Big guy, tried to crush me at the Succession Trial?" he asked halfhearted, a quick prayer to the Valkyries for deliverance in his mind.

"The one and the same." Thaddeus smiled pleased. Lykos almost cringed before crushing the urge.

"Why?" He knew he should have expounded further on that question but a feeling of dread was already forming in his belly. Fortunately Thaddeus and the other Agroti did not take offense.

"We saw how he fared against you in the Succession Trial! We desire having his might protecting the interests of House Agroti once more."

Falka leaned on Lykos' shoulder to whisper in his ear, "looks like you get to make a new friend."

Lykos shook the infuriating woman off. "And you're sure you want him? Not anyone smarter like, a boulder?"

The insult seemed to go right over Thaddeus' head as he shook his head firmly. "No, no it must be him! He will represent our interests nicely."

"Right. I guess I'll go," Lykos sighed, "find him."

The gathered Agroti murmured approvingly and in short order the enter room emptied itself leaving the trio alone with Thaddeus. Moving towards the doorway Lykos questioned him further.

"Do you know where we can find Plower?" The relaxed atmosphere of Homestead soothed his nerves slightly as they walked the simple wooden halls.

"According to my daughter he spends his time in the Marsh, drinking at the Shallow Swamp," Thaddeus grimaced as he answered. Lykos looked at the man in surprise.

"Your daughter? And isn't the entire Marsh a swamp?"

"The Shallow Swamp is a peculiar kind of pub that uses the swamp gas to ferment their alcohol. Apparently it's a local delicacy. As for my daughter...." Thaddeus trailed off.

"Yes?" Falka asked when it appeared that he was unwilling to continue. The man sighed and gestured to a group of teenagers off to the side. One of the girls waved at him and smiled brightly.

"My daughter is infatuated with the man," he finally explained. Lykos halted as he stared at the man aghast.

"I'm recruiting that giant so your daughter can get lucky?" Lykos shouted outraged as Falka and Giles broke down in laughter behind him. Thaddeus looked terribly embarrassed as his daughter began to chatter excitedly at his exclamation.

"That poor girl, he'll crush her!" Giles cried tears of laughter down his crimson beard and had to grab onto the wall to remain upright. Falka joined him at the offended look Thaddeus gave the pair and Lykos knew that he would never live this down.

Chapter Twenty-Seven

Unlike the Lowland the Marsh was always full of water. Because of this it was full of wooden walkways and houseboats, crisscrossing the entire quarter in an ever changing maze as they rocked gently on the waters. It was as if a great fleet decided to make the swamp their home permanently.

"Why was this ever settled?" Falka asked Lykos and Giles as she slapped at an insect that flew too close. The determined mosquito evaded her attempts to her great displeasure.

"Because the Tainted hate it just as much as you do. Their armored hides are too heavy for the ground here and the waters too shallow for anything more than small Tainted Divers. And because everything is built to float flooding isn't that much of a concern for them. Look see how they tether themselves to the trees." Giles gestured to the ropes that connected the many houseboats to the trees all around. As Lykos watched the ropes slackened and tightened as soft currents rocked them, never allowing them to pull close enough to the trees to damage them. Giles confirmed this observation.

"Each of them has just enough slack to drift freely in case of flooding but not too much to allow them to collide with objects. It's what has allowed the dwellers here to survive almost unmolested since the founding of the quarter."

"Still not worth the bloody insects," Falka muttered. Lykos smiled at her discomfort and her glare sharpened upon him in an instant. "Ready to procure your flesh lad Lord Talal?" she asked in a sickeningly sweet voice. He scowled.

"Come on we're almost there." Their destination was a large ship that had been partially grounded on a sandbar causing it to have a slanted deck. On its side was a picture of a tankard with bubbly green alcohol frothing from the top. This was the Shallow Swamp Pub.

The trio crossed the gang plate and stood on the deck of the ship. With the late noon sun edging towards the horizon many deckhands and off duty Citadel guards sat drinking their pay away merrily. Lykos did not spy the large figure of Plower anywhere however.

"Down below we go," he stated leading Falka and Giles over to the stairwell set in the deck. The rambunctious bar patrons parted easily before the three as they made their way below deck. The air was thick and musty with candle light, sweat, and foul alcohol, green gas lazily drifting from many mugs. It was near a porthole on the far side that he spied the morose figure of Plower staring into a cup that could be confused for a small cask.

The trio approached Plower, snagging a few bottles along the way. Sitting down next to the large man he was reminded once more of how massive the man was. Lykos was of a respectable height yet he barely reached the giant man's chest; sitting down did nothing to disguise Plower's bulk.

"What do you want?" Plower murmured in what was presumably supposed to be a threatening manner but the slurred speech caused it to loose the menacing edge. Lykos was reminded of a large wounded animal. Like a tree.

"To know why you look so glum," Lykos stated pouring a cup of some ghastly concoction that oozed green mist. Plower drank it without hesitation and Lykos was disturbed to hear the sound of hissing.

"I'm nothing!" the large man wailed, burying his head in his hands. Falka patted the large man's shoulder in a slightly condescending manner but he seemed not to notice. "Every since that little man beat me I'm nothing."

"What little man?" Falka asked with a cruel smile on her face, eyes upon Lykos but the young lord cut her off.

"You're not nothing, you're the great Plower!" he exclaimed. The nearest drunks to them cheered and raised their tankards in salute before downing their vile contents.

"I'm great?" Plower raised his head to stare at him with bleary eyes. Lykos tried to force a smile on his face.

"Of course! After all who hasn't heard of the great Plower?" He hissed through the side of his mouth to Falka and Giles, "help me out here."

"Of yes! I heard he fought off a dozen men with his bare hands!" Giles lamely declared. Falka rolled her eyes at the two men.

"I heard the great Plower satisfied a dozen woman," she purred as she rested her hands on Plower's arm. He smiled a great, big dopey smile at her and Lykos resisted the urge to gag at the puppy love in his eyes.

"Really?" Plower's voice cracked. "I mean of course! I'm great!"

Lykos slapped Plower on his back. "You see? I told you my friend! Nothing to be upset about."

The slap seemed to bring him back to reality. "But I am a failure!" the large man wailed as he collapsed into his seat. "I couldn't even squish one puny lord."

"I might be tempted to help," Falka muttered glaring at Lykos. Plower had knocked her into the ship's hull roughly when he dropped into his chair.

"Now Plower," Giles began, "from what I understand that was Lord Talal, you should feel honored!"

"Honored?" he asked. Giles nodded sagely.

"Of course. You see Lord Talal often kills his foes, if he didn't kill you it must mean you have some amount of skill that he can respect!"

Lykos jumped on the lifeline Giles offered. "Of course I do, I mean he does!"

Plower focused his eyes on Lykos and squinted. Closing one eye, then the other, then both, he continued to stare at Lykos, shifting his head in small amounts. Just when Lykos began to feel as if the man would not recognize him his hopes were dashed.

"You're that little lord!" Plower shouted. Fortunately the Shallow Swamp was filling up with ever louder patrons as the evening wore on and no attention had been drawn.

"Why yes I am and it was a honor to fight-" Lykos was cut off as Plower roared and picked him up by his leather tunic. With a mighty heave he was thrown clear across the hold and crashed through a wooden table, scattering food and drink everywhere. Groaning he looked up to see Plower charging at him.

"A little help please?" Lykos called out to Falka and Giles. This unfortunately had opposite of the desired effect as the many bar patrons took it as a sign to block the pair off, leaving Plower and Lykos to fight alone. With a roar of delight the patrons watched as Plower picked him up and threw him again.

Lykos had a brief moment to experience what it was like to fly without an airship but then rediscovered what it felt like to be human as he crashed through another rickety table. Groaning he rolled out of the way of Plower, who had charged him once more, causing the giant to smash headlong into a wooden support. The thick wood stood no chance to his charge and splintered, showering the cheering crowd with wood chunks.

"Plower! I'm here to help you!" Lykos tried to reason with the man as he shook his head to dislodge the splinters from his hair. As tempting as it was he could not kill Plower nor did he want to fling an excess of magic at the large man, someone whose resilience had already been experienced first hand during the Succession Trial. The giant charged once more at him and he desperately searched for a blunt weapon. Grabbing a glass bottle from a nearby table, he smashed it into the charging man's face.

It did slow the giant man down slightly but not enough to prevent him from running into Lykos. Both men went down in a tumble of limbs and the crowd cheered and mocked them in delight. Several patrons began to loudly place bets and a flurry of money began to change hands. One of those voices sounded suspiciously like Falka's.

Lykos rolled to his feet and stood over the dazed Plower. He tried reason once more. "Plower the Agroti want-"

The rest of his sentence was cut off as Plower's thick meaty fist swung up and nailed him right in the jaw. Staggering backwards in shock and anger Lykos spat out a glob of blood as Plower rose back to his feet.

"Fine, time for a good old fashioned beat down!" Lykos shouted and the crowd cheered. If Plower didn't want to play nice then he wouldn't either. With a war cry he charged forwards to defeat the giant!

Lykos groaned as the morning light shone on his face. Rolling over he encountered a warm body and greedily snuggled into it, trying to hide from the persistent light. As he pressed his face into the delightful warmth he was surprised by the feeling of many painful bruises covering his face.

"Good morning Lord Talal." Giles cheery voice cut through his mind like a knife. Hissing in pain as loud sounds echoed unpleasantly in his ears Lykos nonetheless rolled over to sit up, determined to get answers. He slowly opened his eyes to see a small room, sparsely furnished, with Giles sitting next to his head on a rickety old chair. The man smiled in amusement at the hungover lord.

"Why the bloody hell does my face hurt?" he croaked out, a disgusting taste filled his mouth as he spoke. "Have I been drinking? Why don't I remember anything but the abyss that consumes all souls?"

"Yes you have been drinking and as for your face." Giles deliberately nodded his head to the warm body behind him. Lykos turned, expecting to find some flesh worker that he had spent a cold night with warming his sheets but turned stark white in horror instead.

The massive form of Plower lay nude under the blanket next to him, glistening with sweat in the early morning light. Lykos felt revulsion curdle inside of him as the blanket shifted slightly revealing the large and hairy back of the giant man.

"AH!" He would deny shrieking like a startled babe at the sight for the rest of his life nor would he admit that he jumped so high in the air that he actually launched himself off the bed to land at Giles' feet.

Sadly neither fact was true.

As the blood drained from his face, he lay clutching his heart as he feared what his blacked out memories might bring. A fresh wave of revulsion wracked his frame and vomit began to form in his throat. But then "Plower" awoke.

"Baby come back to bed," Falka's sultry voice ordered from Plower's form. He looked on in incomprehension as Plower's massive, nude form shimmered to be replaced by a fully clothed Falka lounging in his place, a satisfied smirk upon her face. "Usually people are jumping to get into bed with me, I've never had someone so eager to leave my embrace before."

Lykos stared with wide, unblinking eyes at the pouting woman before slowly turning his head to Giles. His "loyal" commander sat grinning mischievously down upon him.

"I will make your suffering legendary in hell," he stated blankly, the color still not returning to his face.

"Lord Talal?" Giles chuckled nervously.

"You will know torment like no other mortal has ever suffered," Lykos vowed. Giles began to panic.

"Lord Talal, she requested I aid her in this prank I swear!"

"Your misery will become the stuff of nightmares." Lykos' eyes narrowed slightly as life returned to him.

"Lord Talal I swear! It was all her idea!" Giles shouted, leaping from his seat to point at Falka.

"Traitors suffer doubly," she angrily muttered. Lykos finally turned to face her.

"Why have you attempted to assassinate me by trying to scare me to death?" he asked, his eyes still unblinking.

"Have you not blinked this entire time? That can't be good," she tried in an attempt to distract him. It failed miserably.

"I am terrified that the horrible image of Plower's naked flesh will be forever imprinted in my mind if I blink," Lykos blankly replied. "Now why have you tried to kill me?"

She frowned. "You mocked me yesterday."

You could not find a more quiet silence in a graveyard than the one in that room. Lykos and Falka's staring contest was observed by Giles who would later liken it to two forces of nature preparing to meet in combat. A great deal of build up precluding the destruction of reality.

"You tried to kill me," Lykos drew a deep breathe, "because I mocked you?"

"Aye."

"I hate you."

"That's a lie and we both know it."

"I want to drown you in the bog."

"Maybe throw me in but I don't think you'd hold me down."

"I am going to tell Shawna you hate her cooking."

"You wouldn't dare."

"I will."

"Truce?" she asked with an innocent smile. Lykos' icy stare did not lessen in the slightest.

"You will rue this day." He flopped backwards and rested his head against the wooden wall. "What happened last night that caused me to wake up hungover?"

"Well they'll have to call the Shallow Swamp the Sunken Swamp from now on," Giles said blithely. Lykos tried in vain to call upon his magic for aid but it too acted as sluggish as his limbs. Apparently magic did not like alcohol anymore than his brain did.

"I am never drinking again. What do you mean they'll have to call it the Sunken Swamp, it's a blasted boat." Lykos did not like the grin that broke out on Giles face. "What did I do?"

"Well you and Plower had a rather destructive brawl that caused more than a little structural damage to the ship. Nobody noticed until the water began to lap at our feet and by then it was too late to fix."

"Especially when you sucker punched Plower into the aft of the ship. I never knew someone's head could go through solid wood like that and survive!" Falka cut in excitedly.

"That was a sight! That ugly drunk screamed like a little girl when Plower landed on him." Giles and Falka shared a laugh as Lykos swayed to his feet. His weapons and cloak were propped next to the bed and he slowly armed himself.

"And then?" he pressed his eyes shut as nausea washed over him.

"Well we escaped the sinking ship with plenty of knocks and bruises all around. You and Plower though were determined to finish your fight but he wanted to have a drink before you began again. So you two staggered to the nearest pub, the Beached Mermaid, and began to get roaring drunk.

"It seemed to me and Falka that you two replaced your brawl with a drinking game of that awful swamp ale that everyone here seems to be so fond of. Neither one of you won said game as it was interrupted by some of the other bar patrons wanting to get in on it. You and Plower took offense to the interlopers and started another brawl, only now it was you two against everyone else."

"You two actually cut through a sizable portion of them," Falka told the now dressed Lykos, "but you drew the attention of the bar owner, Lilia." Giles nodded.

"Aye this whale of a woman waded through the crowd and began to pull people apart. When she reached the pair of you, you took one look at her and turned to Plower to say "Well one of us has got to take her." Plower agreed and backhanded you into a wall knocking you unconscious. Plower and Lilia then began to, well...."

A series of loud knocking noises and grunts echoed through the room at that moment. The three turned their eyes to the far wall that shook with each knock.

"Where are we?" Lykos asked with terror and disgust in his eyes.

"Let's just say there's a reason why that illusion was so detailed," Giles said with a green tinged face. The trio quickly left the room to reveal that they were still on the Beached Mermaid. Stepping past sleeping drunks and broken furniture, they left behind the stuffy hold for the slightly less pleasing smell of a swamp in the morning.

"How the hell am I supposed to convince Plower to go serve the Agroti as their champion now?" Lykos asked aggravated. Falka snickered beside him.

"Actually you took care of that," she said.

"What do you mean?" he already dreaded to hear the answer.

"The big guy likes you. Well you gave him a good fight, got roaring drunk, and helped him meet Lilia. I think he said something about naming his first born daughter after his favorite lord but in the end he agreed to go fight for the Agroti."

"....What?"

"Well," Falka paused to raise the tension and his anxiety more, "he was drunk and slurring his words quite badly but I think Plower views you like family."

"If it helps, you probably are related to him through the Agroti," Giles said helpfully. Lykos gave the pair a dead stare before turning and walking away.

"Hey where are you going?" Falka called out as she raced to follow him. Giles followed at a much more leisurely pace.

"To go tell the Agroti that Plower's agreed to be their champion. Then to go find a hole and bury myself in it until this hangover passes."

The three walked in silence for a moment before Falka turned to Giles. "Do you think we should tell him about the three marriage proposals he accepted?"

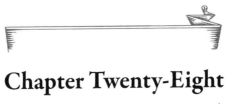

Chapter Twenty-Eight

Fortunately for him Falka was only joking about the three marriage proposals. It had only been one and he had been sober enough to politely refuse and the young woman in question had been reasonable enough to only punch him. That helped explain the bruised face.

It was at a crossroads in Ploio that Lykos realized he could send his two companions in his stead to the Agroti. Pleased he would not have to travel to the Lowland hungover he turned towards his two companions with a spiteful smile. With no small amount of fiendish delight, he ordered them to go inform the Agroti that Plower agreed to be their champion and that he was currently recovering in the Beached Mermaid Pub in the Marsh. Falka was ambivalent about being used as a messenger yet Giles was concerned about sending his lord off alone. Waving away his worries, Lykos bid the duo farewell and that he would see them both later.

As he walked the streets of Ploio he took in the sights. All around him happy common folk walked, guards patrolled, and peace was prevalent. However he knew it was a lie. The man across the street tugged on a chain, dragging a slave along. The shopkeeper behind him had just yelled at a shop hand, berating the young woman viciously. Here and there beggars peeked out, their skeletal hands desperate for aid yet ignored by those passing by. These so called civilized people ignored those who suffered right in front of their eyes and it was revolting.

Lykos wished he could stop next to each one, to alleviate their suffering. *I have been in your place,* he cried in his mind, *I have known your pain.* Yet he knew that if he stopped to help each one he would be swarmed by their desperation. They would tear apart the one person who showed them kindness because in this ruthless world that was what must be done to survive.

So he, like the many others on that cobblestone street, strode past the suffering. Each step left a bitter taste in his mouth. *Soon,* he promised, *soon I will free you from your chains. I will give you the means to live as honest men and women and you will be free.* But he knew he had to start small.

Pyrgos was under his complete control now yet he still struggled to provide enough work for its inhabitants, enough coin, enough food. But he was making progress, slowing reversing the damage of years of poor decisions but it was an uphill battle. Due to his efforts there were few without homes, without work, but there were still many who took advantage of their neighbors, friends, or family for their own gain. Progress was being made but it was slow.

He crossed into Latom and was briefly disorientated by the abrupt change of scenery. Unlike the other quarters, Latom had dug down into the earth in wide chasms, burrowing into the rocks and carving their homes within. It was originally the quarry where the stone Mycenae's walls were constructed of were mined from, it had later been adapted into homes when a Tainted horde had swept through the kingdom. The steps were perilous to the creatures, far too steep for all but the most nimble and they would tumble into the depths below to splatter on the rocks.

As beautiful as their structures were, he did not descend the stone steps. House Vrachos, a clan on stone masons who supplanted their rivals during the founding of Latom, controlled it with an iron fist. While agreeable enough in some regards, he had been dismayed by the sheer scale of slave labor they used in their construction. Delving into their stone city reminded him far too much of the slave mines of Svellheim and he took any excuse to avoid the unpleasant memories.

With little foot traffic on the surface, he rapidly made his way home. The gardens and groves of trees that usually covered the land were dead or without leaves, the autumn air crisp. He felt as if he walked through a wasteland with each step.

"Help! Someone help me!" a woman's voice echoed up from the ground below. Lykos rushed to the ledge and struggled to push his lethargic magic into his eyes. With a reluctant snap the magic filled his vision.

The dark world below light up in sharp relief as his magic illuminated its mysteries. Multiple levels of walkways and buildings were visible, full of human shapes moving about on various errands. He frantically looked around for the source of the desperate screams. After several nerve wracking moments and several more terrified pleas for aid, he spied a struggling pair in one dark corner.

"Help!" one of the figures wailed once more as the second figure tore at their clothes. Enraged Lykos took two steps back and launched himself through the air, determined to reach the struggling woman before any more harm fell upon her.

He landed on a stone building below and rolled so as to not injure himself. The torchlight illuminated the area poorly and he had to rely heavily on his tired magic to guide his movements as he rushed towards the struggling pair. Leaping from rooftop to rooftop he barely had any time to slide to a halt as he realized that there was no way to jump the next gap whose width and depth were too great to navigate. He looked across the gap and saw the young woman's terrified face, pleading with screams as her assailant assaulted her.

With an angry snarl Lykos turned from the pair and faced the dark wall. He hoped to the Valkyries he had the magic for this or else there would be hell to pay....

"No please don't go!" Angela cried as the unknown man with shining eyes turned away. He took three quick steps and disappeared into the darkness to her dismay.

"Quiet girl, no one is coming to help you!" The man behind her roughly choked her to force her down.

Angela sobbed into the ground and knew that the Citadel guard spoke truth but for a brief moment she had hope that someone was here to end her torment. The wretched man behind her had been harassing her for weeks, always discovering where she was living or working and never accepting her refusals. She had refused his touch for so long but now he took offense resulting in her current predicament.

Angela was a nobody, no family to call her own, no friends to care if she were gone. She turned towards the sky and offered a silent prayer to the Goddesses, their absent Gods, for aid.

"Send me a savior," she whispered. "Send me someone who can protect me and aid me." *Send me a destroyer*, she begged secretly in her mind. *Send me a killer to end this man's life.*

A rough jerk of her hair caused her to cry out once more. "I said quiet girl or I'll slit your pretty throat!"

Angela whimpered as the pain became worse. Through tear blurred eyes she saw something move in the shadows before her. Blinking away the tears she looked up in shock as the shadows before her seemed to ripple angrily, not unlike when a heavy stone is thrown into a still pool of water.

Right before her eyes the man with glowing eyes leaped from the shadowy shimmer. His face was set in a fierce scowl and his hands were held out like claws as he moved towards them, a predator charging his prey. She whimpered in fear but the man with glowing eyes ignored her as he wrapped his claw like hands around the Citadel guard.

With a ferocious tug, the man was torn from Angela causing her to collapse on the ground. Whimpering she turned around in time to see the man with glowing eyes gut the Citadel guard with a knife, before throwing him over the ledge. The Citadel guard's face was completely surprised, as if he wasn't quite sure how this had happened, as he flew over the ledge to disappear forever.

The glowing eyed man slowly stood, turning to face her as an avatar of death. Angela weakly struggled as the figure stepped closer and closer, moving its hands to its neck. Shutting her eyes in fear she begged the figure.

"Please. Please no...."

The feeling of soft fabric surprised her as it fell upon her body. Opening her eyes she saw that the glowing eyed figure had dropped their cloak upon her, hiding her bruised and naked flesh from view. Angela felt a great deal of gratitude towards the figure who she could now see was a normal man, albeit a dangerous man covered in weapons and armor.

"Oh thank you!" she cried as she wrapped herself in his cloak. The glow faded from his eyes revealing a young and handsome face that peered at her sharply. "Thank you my lord!"

"You may keep the cloak. You'll have more need of it than I." The man nodded to her before turning away. With panic Angela realized that the man would leave her here alone.

"Wait!" she called out causing the man to pause. "Take me with you," she begged, grasping his leg.

The man looked at her with pitying eyes. "You would be safer here." She looked up at him desperately.

"Among the monsters? Human or Tainted they are both the same!" she cried. "Please take me with you, I can cook, clean, I'll do anything you want."

The man looked down upon her in pity and indecision. Finally he knelt down so they were eye level and stared into her eyes. Angela tried to avoid his gaze out of respect but with a gentle hand he forced her to stare into those fierce orbs.

"What is the thing you desire most in the world?" he finally asked. Angela quickly realized that this was a test and she knew she could not fail it. She refused to live on the streets anymore and knew that if this man did not take her with him, she would toss her body in the pit beyond.

"To defeat monsters," she tried to claim bravely but knew the moment the words left her lips that they were wrong. "No! Wait!" The man furrowed his brow but said nothing, gazing into her eyes as he patiently waited her answer. Angela spoke after several moments of thought.

"I want to be strong. I want to be able to fight. Those that have wronged me and those that have wronged others. I don't want to watch suffering happen, I don't want to suffer alongside them. I want to be able to stand firm and know that for what I stand for is just. Like you."

The man stared into her eyes long and hard, considering her words. Finally he released her face but she had no desire to avoid his gaze anymore. He stood slowly and her hope begin to flee her body at the thought that he had found her lacking.

"What is your name?" he finally asked. Angela felt a pinprick of hope flare within her chest.

"Angela my lord! I have no family or house to call my own." The man offered her a hand up and she desperately grasped it. Pulling her to her feet he nodded approvingly at her.

"Well met Angela. My name is Lykos of House Talal." She gasped in recognition, those were names she knew well. "I see my reputation proceeds me. You do know that if you follow me, you will face my foes. They will be just as cruel as that guard was and there are far more of them."

"I am prepared Lord Talal." Angela heeded his warning but it would not change her decision. The Goddesses had answered her prayer and sent her a way to strike back at her oppressors. She would seize this opportunity with both hands and not release it until death took it forcefully.

Lykos looked upon Angela as she came to some internal decision. Wrapped in his cloak, bruised and bloodied from the Citadel guard, her body looked frail but her eyes shone with fierce determination. He could respect that.

Earlier this morning he had thought about his inability to aid every person's suffering that he saw, that it wouldn't be feasible to aid so many people lest he be consumed by them. Yet before him stood a woman, whose drive and will matched his own and whose life would have been snuffed out had he not intervened. He realized that he was not in this alone, not even with the inclusion of Angela. His family, his friends, his allies all stood with him in his mission and all fought for the same end.

"Follow me Angela and you will never be weak again." She obediently fell into step behind him, never straying further than an arms length away. And so Lykos led her out of the darkness and into the shining sun.

Chapter Twenty-Nine

The Aviary, home of House Falknor, was impressive if a bit terrifying in Lykos' opinion. The night of the Falknor's Winter Festival had arrived and he and his allies were willing attendants, eager to mingle with the other noble houses. However he found himself far more interested in their home than the festival goers themselves.

Built on the northern mountains in Kremos, the Aviary was built vertically up the cliffs rather than spreading out along the base. Its many stone spires and exposed balconies stood as docking points for their vast fleet of airships and as their family grew they only built higher. As dizzy inducing as heights were, even Lykos was awed by the endless balconies and rooms climbing up into the sky.

The festival itself took place near the base where a large courtyard had been built. Tables of food, performers dancing on kegs, and all manner of party games were strewn about the space. Lykos smiled indulgently as a smattering of children raced by twirling streamers. He turned towards the heavens and gazed upon the glistening stars far above.

"Beautiful," he finally said, staring up into the cool winter night.

"Oh? Me or my home?" Falka's coy voice whispered in his ear. Lykos smirked at her.

"A pile of rocks or the wild storm of House Falknor. That's a tough one."

"Humph and here I was going to offer you a tour after the ball but now you've been mean." Falka mock pouted causing him to laugh.

"My apologies dear maiden for the slight against your honor!" Lykos cried grandiosely as he bowed to kiss her hand. "Allow me to rectify my mistake. You are beautiful tonight."

And she was. Like many of the woman attending the ball that night she had dressed festively. Her deep red dress was accented with actual vines that wrapped around her to entwine in her hair. The overall effect left Falka appearing as a dryad of myth and thus quite the fetching sight.

She laughed at his theatrics and gently grasped his hand. "Allow this wild storm to introduce you to her father, dear wolf."

"Dear wolf? I suppose I should be thankful you didn't name me pawless mutt," he quipped as they moved through the crowded courtyard. Candles were on every surface and great bonfires stood blazing in the three corners, illuminating the night. A lively band played in the center of the space while servants brought in mouth watering dishes of food from the surrounding rooms.

"Pawless mutt?" She considered the name for a moment. "I rather like it, although it is a shame Illusionist Maeve reattached it. I could have given you a hand tonight." Her purring words caused him to snort in amusement.

"Where is your politer half tonight, I would expect Ana to keep your hands full?" he asked, wondering at his friends forwardness. Falka frowned upset and the festive mood lost its cheer around them.

"Ana has taken ill," she reluctantly said.

"I'm sorry to hear that." It was the truth as the former flesh maiden was quite enjoyable to be around once you broke her out her shell. "Is there anything that can be done? You could use one of my healers if you desire discretion."

Falka shook her head. "It's the winter's chill. Not all of us are blessed with magic to warm us during these cold months, we have to rely on the warmth of others." Her attempted jest fell flat as he looked at her in concern.

"The season has only just begun, it will only grow colder still. Let me know if there is anything I can do to help," he informed his friend. Falka gave him a sly smile.

"Trying to get into our bed dear wolf? Or perhaps that should be eager rabbit?"

"How about pathetic fool?" a snide voice cut in. Lykos and Falka looked away to see two women standing in their path. "Such a vulgar display among the youth of today."

"Indeed milady," the second woman agreed demurely.

The two women could not be more eye catching if they had light themselves on fire. The first woman wore dark blue robes with hundreds of tiny crystals sewn in swirling patterns. It would not be worthy of note were it not for the fact that Lykos recognized those gems from his time in the slave mine, their shimmering structures unmistakable. He felt a well of anger rise in him at their presence.

The second woman was shocking for an entirely different reason. Dark leathers were polished to shine brightly upon her body and the woman reveled in the attention she drew. Her cape billowed slightly in a breeze revealing a whip holstered on her hip. Anger burned more fiercely as unbidden memories of being whipped dozens of times rose to the surface. His back stung with half-remembered pain and it was only Falka's voice that brought him out of his memories.

"Lady Emporo, I didn't know we would be graced with your presence here this evening. Or that you'd bring a guest. I would have thought your husband's recent death would have had you in a period of mourning." Falka eyed the pair as one would the corpse of a Tainted beast, with disgusted contempt.

"Oh how could we miss the Falknor Winter Festival? It's the talk of the shipbuilders in the Nero. My husband, may the Goddesses bless his soul, would have wanted me to be happy." Lady Emporo turned and gave Lykos a false smile. "And you must be the new Lord Talal."

He raised his chin. "I am although I can't say I've had the pleasure of making your acquaintance. My requests for a meeting kept being denied. Perhaps you would like to rectify that now?"

He raised his hand, well aware of the slight the woman had given him. Over the past few months he had approached all of the noble houses of note and had been denied repeatedly at the gates of the Emporo Chateau. He only offered his hand now because he knew it was expected of him.

She reluctantly took his hand and allowed him to kiss it although it was obvious to any observer neither enjoyed it. As he looked upon her fine clothing and jewelry a devious idea came to mind. With a sly twist of his fingers he stole one of the rings off her fingers without her notice.

Standing back up he smiled at her and casually placed his hands behind his back. "I was hoping to inquire as to your opinion on my father's actions before he died?"

Lady Emporo narrowed her eyes. "You mean his foolish social revolution?"

"Ah so you are aware." Lykos grinned at Falka who quickly realized nothing good would come of this conversation. Which meant there was no reason to be nice.

"His actions negatively impacted this kingdom because he did not have the stomach to do what was necessary to survive," Lady Emporo snarled.

"One could argue that he was breaking the social mindset that just because something had been done, it must be done again," Falka quipped.

"Slaves served a vital cornerstone of this kingdom long before your father stirred things up! Much like someone has been doing the past few weeks within my territory." Lady Emporo glared suspiciously at him.

He smiled. "Who would have thought that someone might take offense at slavery?" he replied dryly. "What do you think of that Falka?"

"It sounds to me like someone figured out that if our society was dependent on such a deplorable action then this society should fall."

Lady Emporo fumed before them. Her face turned a violent red color that almost matched the hue of Falka's dark dress and Lykos found himself impressed. However he was wary of her companion. The almost silent woman in black was glaring hatefully at them yet it was the gleam in her eye that reminded him of a Tainted. She was dangerous, she was hungry, and she wanted their blood.

"You think you're so clever brat," Lady Emporo spat. Lykos merely raised an amused eyebrow in turn. "Your father went against the established order as well and he had the most unfortunate end. Something tells me you'll follow in his footsteps exactly."

She then cast a significant glance towards her companion to which was returned with a nod. Lykos almost rolled his eyes at Falka with how unsubtle the threat was.

"Well fortunately I don't have to worry about any death threats tonight. That's the beauty about being surrounded by my allies instead of sitting at a table under false pretenses. But I'll be sure to keep your words in mind Lady Emporo."

She trembled with rage at his words but said nothing more to him. "Come Delilah," she said imperiously. "We have better things to do than socialize with riffraff."

As the two woman walked away Falka turned to Lykos and grinned. "Did you hear that, we're riffraff! That's a step up from pathetic fool any day."

"Speak for yourself, I've been riffraff before." He glanced quickly around to make sure the wretched women were gone. "Although look at what I snagged when she wasn't paying attention." He held up a gaudy ring that had a dark emerald in the center. She admired it with glee.

"How did you get that?"

Lykos smirked. "I've had plenty of practice. I think I'll have it melted down and added to a dagger. I rather like the idea of stabbing it in her black heart," he explained.

"Perhaps cut out her tongue and feed it to that Delilah woman. As admirable as her fashion taste was, something about her gave me the shivers. The bad ones."

"Agreed. I think they'll both be trouble in the future but at the present we are at a festival! We should be enjoying ourselves!"

Despite Lady Emporo's interruption the night was still young and Falka and Lykos enjoyed it thoroughly. The young woman introduced him to several of her acquaintances and family members but none was so notable as meeting her father.

"Aha! So this is the man that's been keeping my youngest occupied of late! Come here young man and let me get a good look at you!" Lord Falknor was a big man with a bigger voice, every sentence he spoke echoed around you as if you were in a cavern. He grasped Lykos firmly with both arms and held him steady, although Lykos suspected that was more for the large man as he had been enjoying various alcohols thoroughly.

"It's a pleasure to meet you at last Lord Falknor," he stated respectfully. Lord Falknor would have none of it.

"Now now, none of that! You must call me father!" he shouted in glee. Lykos turned to Falka with wide eyes only to see her just as shocked.

"Father?" he asked weakly. Lord Falknor clapped him on the shoulders before firmly guiding him over to a table full of drinks. Pressing one into each of their hands he nodded gravely.

"Of course! I always hoped my youngest daughter would settle down with someone and it pleases me he is a man of virtue and integrity!" Lord Falknor took a pull from his own tankard and gestured for Lykos to do the same. "Drink up son! You'll need your strength to deal with Falka. She's just like her mother...."

"We're not getting married!" Falka cried out desperately as Lykos' heart began to beat in terror. Unfortunately this conversation was about to get worst.

"Falka's getting married?" Captain Avarc, Falka's eldest brother, strode up with an attractive woman on his arm. "Fantastic, when's the wedding?"

"Good question, how about it son?" Lord Falknor turned towards Lykos who began to wonder if he had perhaps died and gone to eternal torment.

"Lykos' is deciding Falka's wedding?" Captain Avarc asked in confusion.

"I'd expect he and Falka to work it out for themselves but I'd be fine with him choosing," Lord Falknor eventually said. A glance towards Falka was no help, the poor woman was almost catatonic in shock. Thankfully for Lykos' sanity Captain Avarc came to their rescue.

"I thought Falka was with that pretty little number, not Lord Talal."

Lord Falknor's bushy eyebrows rose in curiosity. "What? I thought she was spending all her time with Lord Talal?" The large man turned towards him with a frown. "You can't even keep my daughter satisfied? You'll have to improve on that!"

Lykos panicking heart had slowed down enough for him to think rationally. Staring in open horror at Lord Falknor he saw the shadowy edge of a smirk playing on the man's lips and knew in an instant that he had been had.

"You are the most devious bastard I have ever had the misfortune of meeting," Lykos finally choked out. Captain Avarc and his companion blinked in shock but Lord Falknor broke down in laughter. Falka for her part stared at the group with shell shocked eyes, not unlike a victim of a Tainted Siren.

"Ah Lord Talal, you've ruined my fun!" Lord Falknor said joyfully, not at all torn up about it. "I haven't been this amused since the last time I called my brother's sexuality in question in front of his wife."

Lykos turned towards a slowly recovering Falka. "I know where you get your horrible sense of humor from now."

Falka finally recovered enough to swear revenge against her father but neither of the Falknor men looked too surprise by this. Captain Avarc informed Lykos that the pranks had been going on for years and that the mental breakdowns were usually done in private. He privately agreed and intended to have his own later when he could scream in terror at the thought of being married.

The evening passed by enjoyably and Falka dragged Lykos to the dance floor. He soon found himself passing along the arms of many young women as the eager socialites attempted to get into his good graces. He found the experience unsettling and did not understand why he was drawing such attention.

"They wish to be the next Lady Talal." Falka shrugged when he brought it up to her. He had finally managed to pull away from a Vrachos woman who was almost as old as Illusionist Maeve and had a mind similar to Falka's which was a very perverted mind indeed. "The social status of being a lady in any noble house is immense, especially with so many current lords refusing to take new brides to replace the fallen. My father is in one such situation."

"So they chase after the fresh blood hoping for an easy target," Lykos muttered darkly, eyeing the giggling woman standing all around them. Several of them waved or blew kisses to him. Falka only smiled at his discomfort.

"Oh poor Lykos, so much attention. Whatever shall he do?" she playfully mocked.

"You forget that this time last year I was starving in a mine and breaking rocks with my bare hands. Most of my interaction with other people was them trying to kill me for food," Lykos reminded her softly. Falka grew somber and she placed a hand on his arm in comfort.

"And you'll never have to ever again."

As the party neared its conclusion Lykos spotted a duo that he simply had to bother. Falka laughed off her involvement and bid him goodnight as she desired to check in on Ana Del Rosa before turning in. So walking alone through the crowd, he made his way to greet Lord Sofos and his heir Grimm.

"Gentlemen! It pleases me that both of you could come to the Falknor's Winter Festival!" He surprised the two men by slinging a companionable arm around both of their shoulders. The two men had been speaking with a few minor nobles and the entire group glared at his interruption.

"You seem awfully cheery for a dead man," Grimm spoke through gritted teeth, trying to subtly muscle his way out of his grip to no avail. Lykos' smile only grew wider.

"Grimm! You wound me! Actually you have wounded me. I'm still displeased by your little bloodletting during the Succession Trial. But! This is a new season, new beginnings and all of that. Why don't we bury the hatchet? Hopefully not in my back though," he finished thoughtfully.

"Unhand me you wretched beast," Lord Sofos growled at him. Slapping both men on the back more times than was socially acceptable, Lykos did.

"Ah Lord Sofos I hope we could mend the rift between us. It seems to me we would be better friends than foes." He tried to be personable, in the spirit of the season but Lord Sofos did not appear to bite.

"Your family is nothing but damnation to us all! I would sooner die than aid you," Lord Sofos sneered. "You may have defeated my heir but you have yet to face a true master of combat and strategy."

"Harsh." Lykos glanced at Grimm whose face burned in anger and shame. "I don't know, Heir Sofos was an excellent test of my skill. Perhaps it is you who sell your own blood short."

Lord Sofos puffed up in rage but Grimm reluctantly gave him a respectful nod. "Lord Talal was an exceptional opponent," Grimm replied neutrally. That proved to be the tipping point for Lord Sofos.

"Your mother would be ashamed of you," Lord Sofos snarled at his son who flinched. "As for you Lord Talal, I cannot wait for the day you are made to pay for your fathers crimes!"

Lord Sofos stalked away angrily with his companions but Grimm quietly hung back. Lykos looked at him curiously and noted that the other man was struggling with some internal dilemma. Grimm finally spoke.

"Thank you."

"For what?" Lykos asked.

"You know what," was Grimm's deadpan reply. Lykos smirked but then sobered up.

"Your father won't be around forever you know. You don't have to carry on his banner simply because it's expected."

"Then why do you carry Leon's?" Grimm's reply was sharp and forceful and Lykos considered it carefully.

"Because it isn't his. After I was taken from my family I spent years in a slave mine in Svellheim. I lived, worked, and was a slave in every sense of the word. It was only by chance and the sacrifice of blood and pain that allowed me to escape. It was by chance that I found passage to Mycenae and it was only by the Valkyrie's will that allowed me to reconnect with my family.

"I don't fight because my father brought me up in it or that it's expected of me. I fight because I know what it's like to starve, to know the strike of my tormentor's lash. I know what it's like going to sleep at the end of every night and wondering if I will wake up the following morning. I fight so that no one ever has to live in fear that someone else has power over them. That their life can end on the whims of another!"

Lykos words were honest and raw and he was surprised with himself with sharing such a private part of his life with someone who so recently tried to kill him. But with one glance at Grimm he knew the reason why he shared: Grimm was a kindred spirit.

The glances, the rage, the flinching. Lord Sofos and his son interacted similarly to dozens of guards and slaves in the mines. The clothes and social status may differ but he had no doubt that the man before him faced a different if similar upbringing of misery and torment.

Grimm finally spoke, "goodnight Lord Talal." The Sofos heir turned and walked in his fathers direction as Lykos gazed at his back.

"Goodnight Heir Sofos," he replied wondering if perhaps Grimm could free himself of the chains that bound him. Watching

Grimm's figure being swallowed up by the crowd he had the feeling that life would not be kind nor easy to either of them.

Chapter Thirty

With the alliance with House Agroti firmly cemented, House Talal could now grow its forces from a few hundred souls to almost a thousand. As their training continued Lykos happily assigned them to various posts, patrolling Pyrgos or guarding one of House Talal's many businesses, to give them useful experience. However during this period of growth he was not idle in his own training.

Stepping his training with Illusionist Maeve up several notches, he began to push the limits of his magic to extremes. Holding swords in air through will alone, crumbling a rocky incline with a touch, breathing underwater, or summoning waves of fire or lightning, he found himself improving in leaps and bounds. However it was the creation of a magical golem that he found himself struggling the most with.

Illusionist Maeve could summon five elemental golems with a wave of her hand, each a perfect aspect of the element they were made of. Yet Lykos could only summon a half-formed aspect, regardless of the element, that would tremble and collapse after a handful of heartbeats. Trying and failing for weeks was beginning to take its toll on the young lord and Illusionist Maeve angrily called their lesson to a close.

Trembling with exhaustion Lykos looked a sorry sight, drenched in sweat and his heart beating heavily. Within him his magic seemed to tense and snap back into place, eager to be away from the failed water construct before him. The water splashed harmlessly to the ground and over the side of the stone platform in the Talal ritual chamber.

"My magic feels tense, reluctant," Lykos informed Illusionist Maeve who looked almost disappointed. "Like it's refusing to form the magic of the golems instructor."

Illusionist Maeve tutted. "It is as I feared. Your magic is too resistant to this field. It's not unexpected although it is unfortunate."

"What do you mean resistant instructor?" he asked although he had a small idea what she meant. His magic practically fled from the semi-sentience of the golems.

"Magic is temperamental. It reacts to everyone differently and what may be easy for one person may be impossible for another. Through time, patience, and will power the gap may be closed but that's not an option for you just yet."

"Is that why you're so good at illusions?" Illusionist Maeve still started every lesson by putting him under illusions. Sometimes he would break one only to find himself in an entirely different place. One memorable time he participated in an entire lesson while unknowingly under the influence of an illusion. His mentor had not been impressed and had punished him severely.

"Yes, as well as the creation of these golems and enchanting. The fields are similar to one another, putting magic into another substance. Your talents lean more towards much more direct combat than I favor."

"So I can never learn those fields?" Lykos asked displeased. All three fields were extraordinarily useful and being denied them was vexing. Illusionist Maeve shook her head.

"Not quite. It would just take you years of effort instead of months like it did for me. However I think you can agree that your attention can be better focused on more readily available skills than pursuing those currently beyond your reach."

He scowled but agreed. Without a word the pair left the chamber and climbed the stone steps up into Hearthome.

"How goes Helen's training with you?" Lykos asked, his voice echoing in the stone staircase. Upon her introduction Helen had scornfully looked down upon Illusionist Maeve, unwilling to believe that this elderly woman was infamous the Witch of Kremos Keep. Several painful, humiliating moments later, Illusionist Maeve claimed Helen's reeducation as her priority and abscond with the young assassin to an undisclosed location. The rare moments Lykos saw her she moved with quicker steps, as if she was escaping a dangerous predator. He could sympathize, lessons with Illusionist Maeve often made him feel the same.

"Better than yours. She can't do anything with enchanting or golems but she can at least cast a half-decent illusion." Lykos tried to not grumble as they entered the Talal Manor but judging by Illusionist Maeve's laughter his attempts were lacking. Fortunately a distraction came in the form of one of the new servants.

"Lord Talal? There's an Agroti envoy waiting for you in the western parlor." Lykos nodded to the man and sent him away.

"Let's see what my extended family wants," he muttered darkly as he and Illusionist Maeve entered the parlor. Shawna's uncles, Rolan and Rickard, sat sipping glasses of wine from House Talal's stocks. A quartet of Agroti soldiers stood off to the side with a large wooden crate resting between them.

"Uncles, what can I do for you this fine day?" Lykos asked, making a show of seating Illusionist Maeve and pouring her a glass of wine. Rickard glared at him while Rolan sweated and breathed heavily. The elderly Agroti lord did not look well and Lykos briefly wondered if his health was failing.

"A terrible tragedy my boy," Rolan wheezed as he gestured towards his soldiers. The four men lifted the crate before placing it before him. Eyeing it carefully, and knowing that the guards at his gate wouldn't have allowed anything dangerous in, gave him the courage to open it up.

Inside rested Plower or rather what was left of the giant man. His arms and legs had been cut off, the stumps charred with fire to prevent blood loss. His torso had been cut into multiple times, the wounds deep enough to expose the bone underneath the ripped flesh and muscles. Within the cavity where his organs should have been his limbs had been stuffed, each bearing more horrific slashes. But it was the man's face that was the most horrifying.

Both of his eyes had been ripped out, the cavities left behind hold something far more precious to men everywhere. A glance to the deceased man's mouth revealed where the rest of his manhood had been placed and all of the skin bore thin, bloody lines. The knife wounds could not disguise the sheer horror and pain his face was frozen in.

"Thaddeus' daughter will be inconsolable," Lykos commented absently, remembering how the young woman desired Plower. Belatedly he remembered Lilia, the bar matron of the Beached Mermaid, had seduced the large man and wondered how that had worked out. His comment was ignored by the other occupants of the parlor.

"This was found with the body," Rickard sneered as he threw a bloody scroll at Lykos. Catching it deftly Lykos unrolled it to read:

"Back off from House Agroti or you'll face the same fate!"

It had been signed House Emporo.

"Is this actually a message from House Emporo or is there someone else who's trying to gain our attention?" Lykos asked calmly. Rickard finally exploded in rage.

"This is bloody real you foolish boy! I heard what you did to Lady Emporo at the Falknor Festival and now our head is on the chopping block!"

Rolan spoke up. "Emporo soldiers have begun harassing our farms throughout the kingdom, demanding we pay tribute. What few who had guards reported slaughter and the Emporo burning our crops. Something must be done."

"Agreed," Lykos stated simply as he began to pace.

"Oh the boy agrees! Look how wise he is on his perch far from enemies while we suffer for his stupidity!" Rickard raved. "Let's just go back to our family brother and tell them Lord Talal agrees!"

"Rickard please! This situation is already bad enough without you making it worse," Rolan pleaded.

"I told you this whole thing was a waste of time! He won't do anything!"

"You just told me what happened! Am I supposed to predict every potential disaster that may befall you?" Lykos demanded angrily before drawing in a deep breathe. Letting it go he continued, "Lord Agroti, I'll send some of my forces to secure your farms outside of the Lowland. How is your quarter's security?"

"What a load of tosh! We'll follow this boy to ruin, you mark my words!" Rickard gestured angrily at his brother. Rolan on the other hand merely sighed.

"We're not as well off as I had hoped. Many of the men abandoned their posts when word reached us that their families were being harassed. I have enough men to man the gates but not much else at the moment."

"We should have been protected," Rickard angrily muttered. An annoyed glance at Illusionist Maeve by Lykos told the young lord just how unimpressed his instructor was with the gathered men. He knew he needed to seize control of this meeting before Rickard's rants undid all of his hard work.

"I'll have the men send any wayward soldiers they find your way to return to their posts. In the meantime stop selling your food to the Emporo."

"Stop selling to the Emporo? Are you mad!" Rickard cried out in shock. "That will only make them angrier, we must sue for peace!"

"If you sue for peace you will have given up everything you've lost for nothing!" Lykos all but shouted at the obese man. Rickard and Rolan both reeled back in shock. "If you do not draw a line in the sand and stand firm you will be washed away in their tide. I am asking you to endure so that you may come out of this greater than you were before!"

Lykos took another deep breathe to calm down and allowed the rage fade from his body. "This winter will be cold. The Emporo will need fresh stores to keep their populace happy which means they'll attack you at your gate in the Nero. Fortify the location and allow no foot traffic through of any kind. They won't be able to navigate their army through the other quarters thanks to House Falknor holding Kremos, so they'll have to attack us from the Nero, which allows us to control the location of their assault.

"While they're focused on trying to breach an impenetrable gate I'll be waging a minor skirmish through their territory. With any luck we'll split their forces and this can end without any significant loss of life."

The room grew quite as all those gathered stared at Lykos. Illusionist Maeve and Rolan looked on impressed while Rickard appeared constipated. Lykos decided it was perhaps his most intelligent look to date.

"I'll start arrangements at once," Rolan finally said before wearily standing up. The elderly man was joined by his younger brother who glared at Lykos.

"If this fails, you will regret it."

"If this fails, you'll be dead." Lykos smiled pleasantly at the thought. The man huffed in anger but left with his brother and their soldiers. Lykos finally allowed himself to collapse onto a chair with an explosive sigh. "So what do you think?"

"I think men talk too much," Illusionist Maeve deadpanned. Sometime during the conversation the woman had retrieved her knitting needles and had begun knitting a blanket.

"Do you think my plan will work?" he pressed, wanting to know if she thought he had made the correct decisions.

"Oh of that I have no doubt. You are driven by something other than greed and that's what makes you dangerous. Men can be bought, they can be sold, but a man who believes in something will never cease pursuing whatever cause he champions. He is dangerous."

Lykos frowned. "I do not believe I am that man."

"A year ago you were starving. Now you're about to starve two quarters within this kingdom. Whatever you may think you are Lykos you are dangerous because you have the will and the drive to create change. Whether it be for fallacy or fortune remains to be seen."

Unable to bare her presence any longer he stood and walked away as the soft clicking of her knitting needles echoed in his thoughts. Like the drums of war they echoed unending, heralding blood to be spilled and lives to be ended. Relaying his orders to couriers he walked to the terrace in the garden overlooking Mycenae and pondered his life up until then.

Was he willing to starve others as he had been starved? To slay those who stood before him for their own causes? It was one thing to talk of action, to mindlessly follow the whims and teaching of others, it was another to choose as a free man.

As the questions appeared in his mind so too did their answers and he knew the truth. The kingdom would be righted, his family's honor restored, and no one would ever enslave him again. Nothing short of death would stop him.

Chapter Thirty-One

His plan to isolate House Emporo worked. With the Agroti cutting off their food source the Emporo were forced to rely on the other houses, along with what shipments were still en route from Istani. Neither source of food was enough to feed their large populace and the hungry Emporo turned their attention towards their neighbors in the Lowland.

In the first days of Mycenae the builders were determined to remove as many weaknesses as possible from their defenses. Multiple entrances to each part of the kingdom was deemed dangerous, they reasoned, as it allowed enemy forces multiple avenues of assault. So each quarter they designed and built had as few entrances as possible and tall sturdy walls for the safety of everyone.

The Lowland had three gates, one leading to the wilds outside the kingdom, one leading into the Nero and the other leading into the Riverfront. As the Riverfront was run by House Sofos Lykos had been mildly concerned for interference but reasoned that since none of the houses nearby were House Talal, they should be fine. Hopefully.

But the existence of these few gates allowed the Agroti to form a rock solid defense against invading forces, both human and Tainted. And with a few of Lykos' own soldiers watching the Agroti crops around the kingdom, a large portion of the Agroti soldiers were guarding their southern gate against the Emporo forces in the

Nero. So when the hungry Emporo turned their attentions to the Lowland, the Agroti were prepared.

The first few tribute parties had been sent back with such ease that the Agroti grew quite proud of their martial prowess. They hurled insults and rocks at anyone that passed near the gates much to Lykos' disapproval and were a general nuisance. Their high morale was paired with a loose discipline and he made sure to speak to Adelram that no similar actions occurred within their own forces.

However no one foresaw the Emporo counterattack. All along the double wall separating the two quarters were a series of ballista, there to drive off airborne Tainted. One day they opened fire upon the unwitting Agroti forces without warning. After the initial panic the Agroti returned fire with bows, driving the Emporo from the walls. However the true extent of the attack was revealed as the Agroti turned around.

The ballista arrows had been set aflame and had landed in the Agroti fields. It was at the height of the day and the plains would not flood for many hours so all of the late season crops were dry enough to catch fire. The flames burned hard and fast and many of the Agroti soldiers abandoned their posts on the wall to save as many of the crops as they possibly could.

During this diversion the Emporo raiders struck once more, having counted on their foe to rush to save their crops. Assaulting the lightly manned defenses the Emporo forces slaughtered the remaining defenders and began to try to force the gates open.

Lykos did not know whom but one of the Agroti commanders was intelligent enough to pull their forces from the northern gate to reinforce the southern one. The soldiers had sustained heavy losses but had succeeded in repelling the Emporo soldiers. But it was the weakened situation of both gates that had him concerned.

"We have to reinforce them somehow," Lykos said staring down at a map of the lower half of the kingdom. "Word's been sent that the Emporo ripped apart a few ships to build ladders to try to scale the double walls. They'll never be able to do it but the fact that they're desperate enough to try means we'll have the advantage once we break them."

"There's no way of getting through," Adelram claimed gesturing to the large swath of Emporo territory between the Lowland's southern gate and the Emporo's northern one. "We might be able to cut through Ploio if we are lucky but with how the bloody Nero is designed you'd have to conquer the entire thing to reach the gates."

Lykos grunted. The two men had been pouring over the maps in Leon's study, hoping to find some secret passage into the Lowland so they could reinforce their allies. Yet all of the secret passages they had found were inaccessible to them, blocked by the presence of enemies too numerous to circumvent or kill. So in desperate need of new ideas, he sent a courier to retrieve Falka to see if her knowledge of the hidden areas of the kingdom surpassed these old maps.

The young woman soon walked through the study doors and looked expectantly at him.

"You summoned me my lord?" Her sultry smile caused the aged Adelram to choke but Lykos ignored it with practiced ease.

"Long story short, I need to get to the Agroti's southern gate and the Emporo would not react kindly to my intent." Lykos gestured towards the map he had been examining. "I cannot find any secret passages or sewers that would allow me to circumvent their perimeter. And I was hoping you might know of a way."

"You can't sneak along the double wall?" Falka asked referring to the dual walls that ran between the lower quarters. After the land ceased to provide natural barriers that could be used to Mycenae's advantage, its people created their own. The double wall allowed one quarter to fall while not weakening the neighboring quarter's defensive abilities. A trench, often full of sewage, further strengthened the gap between the quarters. Many criminal elements and common folk of less than respectable intentions used the passes to their advantage as the Citadel guard refused to patrol them.

"The Emporo have too many scouts and sentries for me to easily sneak by myself. It wouldn't matter because I need to reinforce their gate with as many people as I can before it's too late." Lykos was understandably displeased by this. Falka studied the maps thoroughly for a moment before shaking her head.

"All of the passages I know of that would be of help are already on this map. I'm sorry I was not of more help." She shrugged apologetically. Lykos and Adelram sighed before turning back to the maps.

"The longer we wait the more Agroti die and the less likely they are to honor our alliance," Adelram stated.

"I know, I know. It's not like I can just fly over there! I'm a human not a Piercer," Lykos muttered, well aware of the fact that Rickard was most likely raising six kinds of hell in the Lowland at their slow response. Falka perked up.

"Yes you can." Adelram and Lykos stared at her. "Well you can."

"What are you talking about, flight is beyond magic," Lykos said. Illusionist Maeve had shown him how to hover for a moment using air magic but true flight was beyond them. It required too much magic to sustain itself.

"But it's not beyond man," Falka replied with a coy grin. "Use one of my families airships to sneak past the Emporo."

"The Emporo would spot a landing airship a mile away. A few volleys of flaming arrows will cause us to crash and burn before we even get close to the southern gate. We'd have to take the long way round with the airship and that would take far too much time."

Adelram denied shaking his head. Lykos considered her idea before agreeing with Adelram.

"Ah but now you've forgotten the magic factor. My family discovered how to safely fall from a great height with no ill effects. You can fall from far above the Emporo's arrows and by the time they reacted you'll already be on the ground."

"You want to jump out of an airship and use an unknown magical skill to survive?" Lykos asked. The fear of heights he had long thought conquered came rushing back with a vengeance and he had to grip the table firmly to steady himself as he began to feel dizzy.

"Well not me, just you and whoever you choose to accompany you," she replied.

"And why, pray tell, are you not coming with me on this insane idea?"

"I lack the magic needed to survive jumping out of an airship?" she replied sweetly. Adelram spoke up as Lykos attempted to glare her into non-existence.

"I'll start directing our soldiers to the Emporo southern gate. The Vrachos commander owes me a favor so we should be able to move our troops through their territory. Have fun on your mission!" Lykos stared at Adelram in betrayal as Falka dragged him eagerly from the room.

Captain Avarc had docked the Falling Star above the Talal barracks and was eager for Falka's plan. It was a reluctant Lykos who boarded the airship, with even more reluctant Talal soldiers following them. Accompanying him on his suicidal jump was Doukas and Irene. Doukas had lost a quick game of chance with his brother Giles and had sourly agreed to accompany him on this suicidal venture. Irene meanwhile was more eager for their leap, quite willing to learn such a useful skill even if the method was dangerous. Rounding out their group were two of Irene's students and one of Doukas', all understanding the dangerous nature of their infiltration and the mission they were undertaking. As required, all possessed magic to some degree.

"Take us up! Reign in the ropes and set course for the Nero!" Captain Avarc called out as Lykos and his soldiers joined him. "Welcome aboard Lord Talal! I understand you wish to learn to learn House Falknor's method of survival from great heights?"

"Aye captain, I believe it would be beneficial to know for our next mission," he dryly replied. Captain Avarc smiled.

"Indeed. Well the method is actually quite simple. You must embrace the magic within your body to such a degree, they become one."

"What do you mean become one? Our magic is already inside of us," Doukas asked. Lykos too was confused by the distinction.

"It is inside you yes but it's not one with you until you make it so. For the most part our magic rests under our skin, awaiting our call. But with this skill you must infuse every aspect of your body with magic. If you fail to do so, the landing can be quite painful and often lethal.

"Now what I want each of you it to meditate and focus on pulling your magic inwards, instead of pushing it out. It might be difficult for the healers among you as you so often push your magic to aid others than yourself but it is vital for you to do so now if you wish to make the jump."

Listening to Captain Avarc's instructions Lykos tried to pull his magic further inside of him, infusing it with his muscles, bones, and organs. His magic did not resist his orders and with a small gasp he felt his internal organs in a way he never thought possible. He marveled at the sensation of his heart beating like a drum, lungs inflating and deflating like an airship's balloon, and the liquids of his stomach quietly bubbling. Captain Avarc turned towards him.

"Ah I see Lord Talal's managed it! Please describe it for the others so they might know."

"I can feel my bones. Every beat of my heart reverberates through my being. It's like I'm connected to my body in a way I never thought before," he finally explained. It was disconcerting feeling his body in such a manner. Captain Avarc beamed.

"Excellent. Now the greater the fall the more magic you need to infuse your body with to survive. The tricky thing with this magic is that until you actually jump from an otherwise deadly height, you'll never know exactly how much magic you'll need to survive. So overestimate."

Lykos and the others gave Captain Avarc a shocked look.

"Do you mean to tell me that when we jump from this airship we still might not survive?" Lykos finally asked.

"Quite so." Captain Avarc and Falka shared amused glances.

"House Falknor is insane," Doukas surmised. Lykos privately agreed.

They only had a few minutes to practice controlling the magic into the Falknor's Descent as Irene began to call it. However all too soon for any of their liking, they reached the air above the Lowland's southern gate. Assembling on the Falling Star's port side, Lykos and his soldiers looked over the railing to the ground far below them.

"Are you ready for our descent?" Captain Avarc asked joining them.

"Our?" Lykos asked puzzled.

"Of course! You didn't think I'd let you have all of the fun did you? Several of my cousins will be joining to us." Captain Avarc gestured to several grinning men and women who eagerly clutched weapons.

"We welcome your aid." Lykos nodded respectfully before grimacing at the drop. "Everyone ready?"

"No."

"Not a chance in hell."

"You're all insane."

"Well neither am I. You can either join me in jumping off a perfectly good airship to aid our allies who are being slaughtered or you can stay up here and be branded a coward. I'll see you all on the ground," Lykos firmly stated.

And with a wild cry he leaped from the safety of the airship and surrendered his body to gravity.

Chapter Thirty-Two

This is the stupidest thing I have ever done, Lykos thought to himself as the wind rushed past him. He tumbled through the air, unable to control his descent, and began to panic about becoming a smear on the stones far below. His breathing came in rapid bursts as terror set in.

The world grew blurry and gray as he descended to the earth below. The winds buffeted him this way and that as he struggled to right himself in vain. He tried to throw out gusts of wind with magic to steady his descent yet that only made his situation worse. He began to fear that he would not be able to right himself before he reached the ground.

He refused to accept such an outcome. Closing his eyes to the world becoming steadily closer beneath him he turned his focus inwards. He reached for his magic, so strong and reassuring beneath his skin and he let it embrace him, calming him down. His arms and legs stopped flailing through the rough wind and relaxed. The magic infused his eyes and the world was once more visible to his sight.

Lykos briefly wondered if Illusionist Maeve knew of the Falknor's Descent. Infusing his eyes with magic was a useful stepping stone to infusing the rest of his body and it was probably why the process felt so simple to him. His musings were interrupted as he glanced down to see a large mass of blue and green racing to meet him through swirls of yellow.

Tensing his body in a way that felt natural, he felt his heartbeat speed up as the ground was almost upon him. Just before he hit, he prayed to the Valkyries that he would live or if failing that, that they would drop a Tainted Viper on Avarc's head while he slept. Falka's too.

His bones rattled and he almost bite his tongue as he landed harshly on the cobblestone road of the Lowland. He felt the magic rush through him, protecting his bones, muscles, and organs from a messy end on the rough stone work and he allowed himself several relieved breathes that he was still alive. Feeling his heart rate calm he released the magic from his eyes and body and took note of his surroundings.

All around him were Agroti soldiers, paused in their work of reinforcing the southern gate, staring at the man who had just fallen from the sky. He was almost amused to see several of them with mouths wide open, staring at him in stupefaction while others looked up in complete confusion.

"The gates aren't going to reinforce themselves!" he barked, snapping the men and women out of their shock. Many of them returned to their work but kept giving him awed glances as they went about their business. Several soldiers approached him.

"Who are you?" one of them demanded with wide eyes. Lykos didn't allow it to bother him and answered quickly.

"Lord Talal and his reinforcements to secure the southern gate against the Emporo," he replied calmly.

"Reinforcements?" a redheaded woman asked. Lykos simply pointed above him where several black dots were visible descending. "Right you'll want to talk to the commander then, he's by the gate."

Lykos smiled at the helpful young solder who pointed unnecessarily to the gate just beyond them. "Thank you but you might want to move away so my soldiers may land."

"Right." The woman turned away without blinking. "Clear away you lot!"

Lykos stared up at the rapidly descending black dots but was confused by their shape. As they neared he saw each member of his team attached to a large sheet of fabric that billowed above them, catching the wind. And each of them was looking down at him in complete surprise.

Captain Avarc landed nearby and smoothly removed an odd harness from his chest. It fell to the ground and Lykos was interested to see it connected to the large sheet of fabric by thin ropes. Each of the other members of the team also removed similar harnesses, although Avarc's crew had to aid Lykos' forces.

"What are those?" Lykos asked.

"How did you survive?" Captain Avarc asked at the same time.

"What do you mean how did I survive?" Lykos demanded, feeling a slight foreboding at what he was about to hear. Captain Avarc gestured wildly.

"I mean how by the Valkyrie's sagging tits did you survive that fall? I didn't know it was possible!"

"What do you mean you didn't know it was possible, you told me how!" Lykos protested outraged.

"No one's ever been daft enough to actually jump and rely solely on magic! We always use these descent harnesses!" Captain Avarc kicked the mass of leather straps and fabric on the ground behind him. "We only use magic to soften our landing so we don't break a leg or spine!"

"Then why did you ask me if you we were ready?" Lykos demanded angrily.

"So I could show you how to use our descent harnesses!"

Irene and Doukas took the moment to examine him for any injuries. "I can't believe it, somehow the stupid bastard isn't dead," Doukas muttered.

Irene patted Lykos' cheek mockingly. "Well there's always next time."

Lykos however was feeling more than a little annoyed that once more someone from House Falknor had neglected to mention important information until after the fact. "So you didn't know it was possible to survive a fall from that height with nothing more than your magic?" he asked, trying to bring order to his chaotic thoughts.

"I did not but this is grand news! These descent harnesses are such a hassle to pack properly. Your survival has given us a new avenue to explore!" Captain Avarc clapped him on the back in good cheer. Lykos stared at the man, opened his mouth to reply, then shut it with a click. Without another word he strode towards the southern gate.

After all, words could only say so much.

"Who's in charge here?" Lykos shouted as the Agroti forces rushed around, frantically piling barrels and boxes against the battered gates. Large parts of the iron portcullis had been broken and the Agroti had to rely on the battered but sturdy wooden doors for defense.

"I guess I am." The redheaded woman who had spoken to him earlier walked up. "I can't find any of the other centurion's or the commander. Centurion Karen at your service."

"Lord Talal." Lykos briefly grasped Centurion Karen's forearm. She returned his grip with admirable strength. "How do the defenses look?" He looked on in approval as Doukas and his student began to treat nearby wounded. Lykos gestured to Irene to scout the wall and she vanished among the crowd.

"They're holding by straw and prayers." Centurion Karen sighed. "Any advice you can give would be welcome. And any aid more so."

"Relax centurion, we're here for the long haul." Lykos examined the barriers the Agroti were constructing against the broken portcullis. They would not hold long against any determined force who chose to attack it and he wondered why they weren't attempting to replace it instead. "Do you have a replacement for the portcullis?"

"Well yes but we can't get it in place with the Emporo knocking on our door." Centurion Karen gestured towards the wooden barrier that was being destroyed from its far side as fast as it was being reinforced. "We can't do anything until the Emporo are forced off."

"Leave that to me," Lykos said confidently as he turned away. Irene quickly joined him.

"As I was falling I saw that there is a raiding party at the gate with another in a flanking position feeding reinforcements. The Emporo's gate has been jammed open by their forces; it would seem they're rather confident in their success."

Lykos smiled darkly. "Let's explain to them why that's a dangerous motion. Captain Avarc, I need you and your crew to do something for me."

Captain Avarc and his crew smiled in glee at his request and eagerly made off to begin. Lykos turned towards an impressed Irene. "Surprised?"

"More and more as this day goes on," she said simply. "There's a portion of the wall that's been broken. We can use it to drop on the other side of the wall to attack the Emporo directly."

"Good. I want you and your scouts to hold back near the door providing us covering fire with your bows. Doukas' assistant will be with you but try not to die. Doukas!" Lykos shouted causing the man to come over.

"Yes Lord Talal?" he asked expectantly.

"I hope you know how to use that knife on your belt because you'll be with me and whatever Agroti are still alive on the other side. Prepare yourselves for today you face our foe!" Irene led the way up the stone steps to overlook the courtyard that rested between the two quarters. Two lower walls connected them, blocking the outside world off and providing a further defense against invading forces and Tainted. The result was a large courtyard that Lykos hoped to use to his advantage.

Almost immediately archers targeted them and he ordered his forces to take cover. "Over there is the way down Lord Talal!" Irene shouted, pointing to a broken section of wall. A smattering of arrows nearby forced her to take cover lest she be turned into a pincushion.

"Stay up here and try to kill as many of those archers as you can! You just need to distract them for Captain Avarc!" Lykos turned towards Doukas. "When I say now, sprint for that gap. We need to get down there and buy the Agroti some time!"

Doukas nodded shakily and readied himself. Lykos waited until Irene and her archers returned fire before shouting.

"Now!"

The mad dash with a hail of arrows falling too close for comfort was blessedly short and they slid down the slope to the courtyard below. Tumbling behind a pile of stones Doukas gasped in pain and held his leg.

"I think I broke it," he hissed to Lykos. Lykos scowled.

"Can you heal it with your magic?"

"No, not enough time."

Thinking quickly Lykos pointed to several Agroti soldiers trying to fend off attackers while they tried to install a new portcullis. "Then limp to the door and protect them as best as you can!" Without waiting for a response Lykos jumped out from behind his cover into madness.

Blood was thick on the stones beneath his feet and rubble and debris laid everywhere. Dozens of corpses lay still in the pools that formed and fires burned among them. There were a pitiful few Agroti still alive fighting, clustered defensively around what little cover they could find as the larger Emporo force swarmed them. As Lykos looked upon the slaughter he felt his blood boil in anger and he let it fully embrace him.

He shouted a war cry as he fell upon the Emporo soldiers attacking the Agroti defenders. The three men were unprepared for the sudden appearance of a new foe and were quickly slain while their guard was down. Lykos roared defiantly to the sky as the last man fell, attracting the attention of everyone in the courtyard.

"Take heart soldiers of Agroti for your vengeance is at hand! Join me in driving these wretched curs from your lands, your home! And send them back to the pits from which they spawned!"

The remaining Agroti cheered and attacked the Emporo with renewed vigor. But it was a nearby snarl of rage that surprised Lykos. Recognizing the sound from a past encounter he turned with a vicious smile.

"Well if it isn't Heir Kolos!"

Chapter Thirty-Three

L ykos grinned. "Has your father finally let you out to play?"
In the courtyard between quarters, Agroti and Emporo
forces slaughtering one another with wild abandon, there was always time to mock ones foe. Viktor, heir of House Kolos, sneered.
"My father does not know I'm here. I'm sure he'll be pleased when I
bring him your head on a pike."

"Ah so you slipped your leash eh? How fortunate, for me."
Lykos trembled with excitement, eager to face a foe who was once
so vastly overpowering that he had been forced to run. Viktor it
seemed, shared his enthusiasm for the coming battle.

Viktor ran forward, closing the gap between the two men.
Rather than meeting the enraged heir with his sword, Lykos thrust
out a hand sending a fireball to blind him. Viktor charged recklessly
through the flaming ball of magic but was blindsided by several
rocks that he had lifted and thrown with magic. Rather than cap-
italizing on his advantage, Lykos turned to the nearby battling
Agroti and Emporo and aided them against their foes. Slashing and
stabbing his way through the soldiers, Lykos managed to save the
Agroti from being overwhelmed.

"Go aid your brothers and defend the gate! Give your builders
a chance to protect your quarter!" Lykos would have said more
but Viktor had recovered from his attack. With a mighty roar he
jump kicked Lykos in the chest sending both men sprawling to the
ground.

Dazed, he barely had the time to react as Viktor's sword swung down at his neck. Rolling to the side, he grabbed his sword and swung blindly to ward off his foe. Rising to their feet, Viktor and Lykos glared hatefully at one another as they began to circle.

"Father will be so disappointed, I believe he wants to kill you himself. There are standing orders to avoid conflict with you unless you seek it out," Viktor told Lykos who smirked.

"Perhaps your father is wiser than you, knowing that to face me would spell your end," he taunted. Viktor roared and this time Lykos met his charge with steel.

The two men fought through the courtyard, the ground treacherous with blood, corpses, and death. Arrows whizzed past their heads as they threw magic at one another, creating elemental bolts, traps, and other fiendish attacks. Lykos found his every skill tested as he fought Viktor in a proper duel at last. The Agroti men at the gate, reinforced with Doukas casting healing magic, were steadily making way in clearing the courtyard of Emporo soldiers.

Lykos lent aid when he could but the moments were few and far between as he focused more on survival. For all of his improvements and innate ability, Viktor still had spent a lifetime studying combat while he was playing catch up. However skill and ability are not the only factors in combat. Sometimes all you needed was a little luck.

Some of the Agroti that he had rescued repaid the deed in kind, distracting Viktor in an opportune moment. Lykos eagerly capitalized on the distraction and viciously stabbed his sword into Viktor's gut. He gave a terrible scream of pain and Lykos and the Agroti found themselves airborne, thrown away by a wave of magic. Wary, he rose to his feet and eyed his wounded foe.

Viktor grimaced as he held his wounded side, Lykos' strike far too deep for his magic to quickly heal. Both men knew that this battle was over. Viktor began to back away as fast as he could and Lykos stepped forward matching his foes pace.

"Emporo! They have slain your brothers! Attack the Agroti scourge and end their unwarranted attack!" Viktor called out behind him. Lykos swore as the raiding party that had been held in reserve began to fill into the courtyard. As Viktor reached the Emporo gate he called out to Lykos.

"Enjoy your death you bastard!"

"Flee me coward!" Lykos roared. With an angry scowl Viktor left the courtyard leaving Lykos, a wounded Doukas, and the few Agroti left facing a full company of Emporo raiders.

"We've fixed the portcullis!" a voice cried out behind him.

"Fall back to the gate!" Lykos ordered, glancing to the side. To any observer it would appear he was overseeing his men's retreat but in actuality he was examining the setting sun and the low burning fires in the courtyard. The battlefield was full of debris which was perfect for what he intended to do next.

The Agroti dragged the wounded Doukas through the repaired portcullis but noticed that Lykos wasn't coming with them. "Lord Talal! Come quick before they get you!" they called to him.

Lykos shook his head "Close the gate!" he ordered.

"But Lord Talal!"

"Now!"

The Agroti soldiers, eager to be away from the numerically superior force, heeded his orders and closed the portcullis behind them. Lykos was alone with a hundred bloodthirsty raiders glaring at him, eager to avenge their fallen comrades. But as his eyes filled with magic he saw that none of these soldiers possessed magic, that they were just ordinary common folk trained with weapons.

"Emporo soldiers!" Lykos called out before their centurion could give the order to attack. "I will give you one opportunity to surrender yourself to my care. If you deny this boon, you will reap only suffering."

The gathered men and women laughed at his seemingly outrageous demand. As their centurion restored order Lykos shook his head sadly, as if their response had been a grieving widow's wail of sadness.

"So be it." He looked to the dark gate house beyond the Emporo men and nodded his head. With a grind of gears the Emporo portcullis closed as well, locking all of them in the courtyard. The setting sun's light vanished beyond the horizon, cloaking the area in shadows.

"Prepare to die," Lykos stated calmly as magic pooled in his hands.

Rorric was a swordsman of no particular skill. His family had served as soldiers in the Emporo army for years and the most action they ever saw during that time was against Tainted plaguing their convoys at seas. However in the past few months that upstart Lord Talal had shaken the kingdom, creating and filling a need of bloodshed that was previously unknown to the young man. He enjoyed forcing himself on others, taking what he wanted, killing who bothered him. He enjoyed life.

He was not enjoying his current situation.

He had marched into a courtyard with the rest of his raiding party, expecting a glorious battlefield of rich foes he could mug and torture. Instead he saw a singular man staring defiantly at them all, unafraid of the large force outnumbering him a hundred to one. And the foolish man had the gall to demand they surrender? Absurd.

Rorric jumped as the iron portcullis leading into the Nero slammed shut behind him. A glance to the men on either side of him revealed that they didn't know what was going on either. However it was a whisper behind him that caused the blood to drain from Rorric's face.

"Prepare to die," the voice whispered in his ear. A sharp pain erupted from his belly causing him to gasp and glance down. A sword was impaled through body, held by the man who moments before had been clear across the courtyard.

"What are you?" Rorric whispered, blood bubbling from his lips. His killer's cold stare revealed no answers. With a grim look the man yanked his sword from Rorric's body painfully causing him to scream in pain.

As Rorric collapsed to the ground the man stepped forward among the raider's ranks. Before his eyes the man stood like a demon, throwing out fire and lightning, shaking the ground with explosions. Water leaped from barrels to make footing treacherous, steel severed limbs with terrible ease. The raider's screams soon joined Rorric's as the solitary mage moved through their ranks like a scythe through the wheat.

"We have to get in there!" Irene shouted as Doukas wrapped her leg. An Emporo archer managed to hit her exposed leg while she and her scouts retreated from the wall. She had felt relief when the Agroti soldiers had fallen back but that turned to anger when Lykos had not accompanied them. She was unsuccessfully arguing with Centurion Karen about retrieving the foolish man.

"I don't have nearly enough men to fight against another raiding party! By the Goddesses, we'll be lucky to even hold this position!" Any response Irene had to that was cut off by the sounds of men and women screaming painfully. The Agroti turned fearful eyes to the barricaded gate, the battered wood doing little to dampen the terrible sounds. Rumbles of earth, thunder, and steel soon joined it.

"What's happening over there?" Centurion Karen called up to the soldiers manning the gate. "You there, what's going on?"

The gatekeepers did not respond. They stared with slack jaws at whatever hellish activity was bringing out such terrible screams. Frustrated, Irene sent her two scouts to the top of the wall to report what they saw but once they stood overlooking the courtyard, they too stared. Worried that perhaps some foul magic was at hand paralyzing her scouts she ordered several soldiers to retrieve their fellows without looking at the courtyard. However it was all for naught as when the soldiers reached the top of the wall the ghastly screams stopped and a heavy silence filled the air.

Irene and Doukas limped over to the gate. "We need to check on Lord Talal," Irene stated with concern.

Centurion Karen reluctantly agreed, "open the gate! You four with us."

The group approached the gate and their hasty barricade was pulled apart enough for them to squeeze by. The portcullis was raised and torches brought forth, illuminating the dark courtyard.

It was a massacre. Dozens of men and women lay strewn about, deep slashes and stab wounds perforating their bodies. Some of them were killed by fire or stone and one man looked as though a giant had smeared him along the wall. The stone underfoot was thick with fresh blood and in the center stood a solitary figure.

Lykos, Lord of House Talal stood over his slain foes, covered in their blood. Not a scratch was on his body as he casually cleaned his bloody weapons with a crimson cloth. It was a disturbing realization when the group realized that the cloth had once been white. He took note of the arriving group.

"Excellent you're all here. Centurion, have your men pile the Emporo bodies outside their gate, on the Nero side. Captain Avarc of Falknor should be clearing out any further soldiers in their gate house so you should see about reinforcing him and securing it for our use. Irene, I need your scouts to run along the wall on the Nero side to see how far the Emporo fortifications are and how much space we can safely claim. Doukas, you still haven't healed your leg? Hop to it man, we'll need you before this night's done."

Throughout Lykos' entire speech not one of the gathered men or women blinked or acknowledged his orders. After several moments of silence he took note of the fact that none of those gathered were moving.

"If you would prefer to wait for the Emporo to mount another assault upon your home that's fine too," he reminded them with a hard edge. With wide eyes Centurion Karen snapped a reflexive salute and began to order her soldiers to follow his instructions. Irene and Doukas approached him slowly, similar to how one would approach a wounded Tainted eyeing you as its next meal. Their movements were so ridiculous he almost laughed but contained himself.

"Are you alright?" Irene asked gently, unsure as to his mental state. He raised an amused eyebrow at her.

"Are we to play doctor? And here I thought you didn't return my interest."

She narrowed her eyes. "Well you're still sane if a bit crude. What passes for your sanity anyways."

"What happened here!" Doukas cut in, gesturing to the massacred Emporo forces. "How did they all die?"

Irene and Doukas stared at him as he slowly, lovingly cleaned his weapons. He made sure to pay extra attention to the Talal crest carved into each of their surfaces, making sure to remove every drop of blood. Finally he sheathed them and looked at his impatient subordinates.

"I killed them."

"You killed them," Doukas muttered angrily. "There must be a hundred soldiers here Lord Talal!"

Lykos merely stared at the enraged healer. "And?"

"How did you kill them? The feat alone will be sung by bards throughout the kingdom by weeks end," Irene asked.

"I politely asked them to surrender."

"And when they told you to shove that where the sun doesn't shine?" Doukas asked.

"I explained to them very calmly and rationally that they made a mistake."

"You stabbed them all repeatedly didn't you?" Irene groaned. Her only answer was Lykos' entirely too satisfied grin. "What about their mages? One would think they'd object to that happening." She gestured towards the soldier who had been smeared along the wall.

"There weren't any, which is concerning," Lykos replied with a frown. Despite the presence of Viktor, there were no mages within the Emporo raider's ranks. Both companies should have had at least one mage attached to them, to provide magical support in any conflict. Either House Emporo didn't wish to chance losing a valuable mage against a foe such as the Agroti or they were engaged elsewhere. As Lykos watched the moon rising on the horizon he knew not which answer was more worrying.

Chapter Thirty-Four

When morning dawned Eliza, Lady Emporo, expected to have word that the Lowland was under Emporo control. Her people had been suitably motivated after all, her late husband had been discovered dead with an Agroti flesh maiden and when combined with the Agroti's recent refusal to sell food to the Emporo? Well her common folk were practically begging to be allowed to take up arms against the agricultural house.

So it was an unpleasant surprise when she woke up in her lover Delilah's arms that a courier was not standing patiently by with reports of their success. As she roused herself and her lover, she heard frantic whispers from beyond her bedroom door.

"Enter!" Lady Emporo barked in a clear tone, displaying her nakedness without shame as she stood. Several moments of silence passed before the door reluctantly opened revealing a frightened man.

"Good morning L-Lady Emporo." She did not take the man's stutter as a good omen nor his refusal to gaze upon her body kindly.

"What happened?" she demanded forcefully, accepting a light robe from Delilah who was already garbed in her own.

"The raiding parties failed to report in this morning my lady." The man's trembling body was beginning to grate on her nerves. "A scout was sent. He returned word w-with...."

"With what?" Lady Emporo glided forward, grasping his face with her hand so she could stare into his terrified eyes. "Tell me now!"

"The raiding parties were slain to the last!" he gasped out as her fingers began to crush his face. With a howl of rage her fingers were ablaze, searing the flesh of the courier causing him to scream. After a moment of intense heat she released the man who collapsed to the stone floor dead, quietly burning to a crisp. With intense eyes Lady Emporo flung her hand at the thick wooden doors, a blast of wind knocking them open with a bang. Two of her guards were standing with the scout who bore the message.

"What did you see?" Lady Emporo demanded, advancing on the terrified scout. It took Lady Emporo a moment to realize that the man wasn't afraid of her, no he was afraid of what he had seen at the gate.

"Centurion Lionus sent me to check in on the raiding parties this morning my lady. Upon arrival at the northern gates in the Nero I discovered the reason why no word had been sent."

"Well out with it man before you join my foolish courier," Lady Emporo threatened. The man winced but barely gave the now charred corpse a glance as Delilah began to flick her whip in well practiced motions.

"Outside the gates was a massive mound of corpses! The two raiding parties you sent had been brutally cut down by the Agroti! They now man the gates on both sides of the courtyard between the Nero and the Lowland."

Lady Emporo gave a vicious nod to Delilah who gave a bloodthirsty smile to the terrified scout. With a flick of her wrist, her whip wrapped around his neck and coursed with electricity. The poor man fell to the ground as the cruel woman electrified him to death.

"Remind the men what happens when they attempt to withhold information from me," Lady Emporo ordered the two guards who wisely chose to remain silent. With an obedient bow one of the men walked off to remind her soldiers why her family had held control of two quarters for decades. Ignoring the remaining guard, Lady Emporo turned towards Delilah who was cleaning her whip, peeling charred flesh from its coils.

"Do you have any idea how the Agroti managed to fend off our forces dear? Our spies told us that there were barely enough soldiers to protect their farms, let alone man the outer walls."

Delilah hummed in response. "Someone must have sent aid my lady. Some unknown ally that managed to sneak reinforcements past our lines. Perhaps the Sofos? They are in an opportune location to provide aid, especially if it would indebted another house to them."

Lady Emporo considered her lovers words before agreeing. Turning to the remaining guard she fixed him with a firm stare.

"Send men to the Agroti farms outside the Lowland. I doubt they'll know anything but we need to remind those fools in the Lowland who has the power here." The guard nodded before walking away, leaving the two woman alone once more. "Delilah my love, could you use your contacts to discover what happened?"

Delilah caressed her lovers cheek. "Of course my lady."

It was much later in the day when Lady Emporo was sitting down for dinner that useful information finally became known. One of her guards walked over to whisper in her ear so as to not disturb the violinist playing off to the side. However Lady Emporo's shriek of rage caused the woman to cut an awful note by accident.

"Talal!" Lady Emporo screamed, her magic rattling the table in front of her. With a mighty heave she flipped the heavy wooden table onto its side, sending its contents scattering across the floor. Delilah choose this moment to walk in.

"Ah I take it you've heard the same news I have then?" she calmly asked while dismissing the guards and violinist. It spoke of the scale of Lady Emporo's rage that none of them questioned her order. Lady Emporo breathed heavily as veins popped out on her face.

"If by heard you mean that there are Talal soldiers at every Agroti farm from here to the Citadel walls then yes! If by heard you mean that those men did not take kindly to being questioned and fought violently, even killing, my men then yes! If by heard you mean that infernal Lord Talal is meddling in our affairs then yes."

"It gets worse," Delilah said while recovering an unbroken bottle of wine. Pouring herself and Lady Emporo a glass she held it out for her lover to take, who merely walked away. Huffing in displeasure, she followed her through the halls.

"My love do not allow the child to cause you such emotions. They're unbecoming for someone of your stature," she gently chided. Lady Emporo fumed silently for a moment before remembering her lover also had news.

"What did you discover?"

"Lord Talal reinforced the Agroti's gate himself. Apparently he dropped in from an airship."

"How did an airship get close enough to the lines to provide support? I thought our archers had been positioned all over the walls."

"You misunderstand me my lady. When I say dropped, I mean he jumped from high up in the air and fell to the ground. The archers had no idea he was up there until he was already on the ground."

"....He's mad," Lady Emporo muttered, finally taking the glass of proffered wine from Delilah.

"He's desperate. He has to protect his allies lest they leave him with nothing. I would have thought the warning we sent would have scared him off but this gives us an opportunity." She maneuvered closer so that Lady Emporo was backed against the wall.

"Go on," Lady Emporo ordered as she ran her hand over her lovers face.

"Right now he and his allies are fortifying against us. They will start attacking the Nero soon, claiming retribution for our raiding parties. So we find allies of our own to defend ourselves against the cruel warmonger Lord Talal."

Lady Emporo snorted. "Kolos is in no position to help us. Not with the amount of gold he's been spending outside the kingdom. Goddesses know what he's up to. House Miles could be useful if we could pry them away from their internal affairs...."

Delilah silenced her lover with a lingering kiss. "I was thinking more along the lines of someone closer to the Agroti and Falknor lands."

"Agroti and Falknor lands?" Lady Emporo was puzzled before realization struck. "House Sofos! They hate the Talal more than anyone."

"And thus they'll be all the more eager to attack the young Lord Talal who has conveniently placed himself in a quarter he cannot leave without being accused of abandoning his allies."

"You are brilliant my dear." Lady Emporo clinked her glass of wine with her lovers and the two woman laughed as their plans came together.

Lord Sofos was all too eager to ally with House Emporo in their domination of House Agroti. All they had to do was mention that Lord Talal was currently trapped in the Lowland with no escape and the man was practically foaming at the mouth to get to the young lord. It merely confirmed in their minds that men were the weaker sex, so easily distracted, so very controllable.

They worked out in short order what their plan of attack was. The Emporo would lay siege to the Agroti's southern gate, while the Sofos would begin attacking their northern one. Because the Falknor lands had such a height advantage, Lord Sofos would have to sneak as many men as possible into their quarter so they could seize control of the Falknor gatehouse. Otherwise any prolonged assault would be doomed due to the superior defenses of Kremos Keep which was situated above it.

Which is when Delilah provided a solution. They would create a contract with Andrea, the Goddesses "Prophet" and head of the Acolytes. She would send her assassins to wreck havoc in the Falknor ranks, for a small exchange of gold of course.

Both Lord Sofos and Lady Emporo agreed. In three days time they would assault the Agroti with their joined forces while House Falknor would learn the error of aiding their enemies. While all three were disappointed they could do nothing about Pyrgos, with it so far away, they were content with the knowledge that with the death of Lykos, that everything would be made right again.

Lord Sofos returned to his home in the Riverfront, admiring the many waterways and fountains his family had added over the years. The land was rich, fertile, and beautiful and it was known throughout the kingdom that the purest waters, freshest air, all belonged to House Sofos. Entering his sprawling home, Arachnis found his son training under the watchful eyes of his soldiers.

"Ready to bring honor to our house?" he asked his son imperiously. Grimm lowered his sword as he nodded to his father. "Excellent, you'll be leading our attack on the Agroti."

Grimm raised his eyebrows in surprise. "I wasn't aware we were in conflict with the Agroti?"

"They're allies with Lord Talal," Arachnis explained to his son. "Who is currently trapped in the Lowland unable to leave. It's the perfect opportunity for you to get revenge for your mother's death!"

Grimm glared down at the floor. "Thank you for the opportunity father," he replied with false sincerity. And then in a quieter voice he muttered to himself, "I wonder why you can't get your revenge without dragging the rest of us into it."

"You're welcome son. I know you'll bring honor to our house." Oblivious of his son's words, Lord Sofos gestured for Grimm to follow him. "Now pay attention. You'll be leading the men in a charge through the gates in three days time. Listen to your centurions, they will provide you valuable feedback in your quest to kill that wretched stain on Mycenae's history."

Grimm continued to listen as his father told him how best to invade the Agroti. How to make an example out of those who rose up against him. How to use violent and bloody displays to ensure order. How much fear to instill in the populace so that they do as you say the moment you tell them to but not so much that they would try to rebel. They were oft repeated lessons from his childhood, only now that he was a man they had grown far more graphic and detailed as his father's speech grew more eager.

How to pose corpses to achieve the proper response. How many people should be flogged a day to keep the people beat down. How it was acceptable to kill those who disagreed with your methods. It was the last one that always prevented Grimm from speaking his mind. He was unsure if familial loyalty would apply when it came to his father's revenge.

He sometimes wondered what his mother had been like. To listen to his father's stories she was some magical princess that everyone in the kingdom loved and worshiped. Looking at his father he somehow never quite believed him, no woman that pure would marry a man that cruel. Grimm would never know for sure as she had died soon after he had been born, cut down by an errant sword.

According to his father she was an innocent bystander in Leon's Rebellion. Grimm doubted that anyone back then had truly been innocent. Leon's vendetta against slavery was well document-ed, a peculiar quirk for a lord most had thought until he had begun waging war against half of the kingdom to support it. All too quickly the rest of the noble houses had been swept into it and House Kolos had emerged the victor. But which side had she stood on?

Grimm knew his father was firmly for slavery. He could list all of the reasons why slavery was needed, necessary even, for their way of life to continue. However if Grimm's mother was as pure as his father claimed her to be, he doubted that she would have supported that view. He cursed himself for these thoughts. He cursed Lykos while he was at it.

They had been happening more and more since the young lord had begun making waves in Mycenae. Perhaps the other noble houses would ignore it but Grimm could tell that Lykos was just like Leon. Give him a cause to fight for and he would destroy the opposition, failure was not an option nor was death. And now Grimm was the opposition. He hadn't fared well against the other man in the Succession Trial but this time he would have an army to aid him. But so would Lykos....

As Lord Sofos left his son to prepare for the invasion, only one thought was running through his mind. Did he obey his father's words and orders or did he choose for himself what was best for him?

Chapter Thirty-Five

Before the sun rose on the third day Grimm met with his army of five hundred soldiers at the Lowland's northern gate. He had given his centurions their orders the previous evening, giving them a route to "patrol" as to not arouse any suspicions from anyone watching the Riverfront. It was a needless precaution: the few Agroti who manned this portion of the wall were asleep at their post.

Shaking his head at the Agroti's slovenly lookout he marched his soldiers through the courtyard, causing the few farmers who were awake this early to stare at them with wide eyes. Grimm smiled reassuringly at them.

"Relax Agroti, we are meant to be here. We're on our way to help at the southern gate!" His relaxed manner seemed to put the Agroti at ease. He smiled in amusement to himself at his words. One could argue that they were accurate, if misleading as to who the actual beneficiary was. Regardless of his personal musings his centurions directed the movement of his soldiers through the gates. Despite the efficient and quiet manner the men and women moved with, it was not long before one of the Agroti guards took note.

"What's going on here?" one of the bearded men demanded, squinting in the weak torch light. "Ain't nobody who comes through here this early normally."

"Ah well this is a normal circumstance you see." Grimm nodded respectfully to gatekeeper as they stood next to each other.

Clapping him on the shoulder he continued. "We're invading you see and I need to get my men through the gate."

"Invading?" the man asked dumbfounded. Some of Grimm's soldiers stopped to aid him but he subtly gestured them to continue moving.

"That is correct good sir." Grimm eyed his soldiers then the Agroti gatekeeper. He wondered how many of his men he could get through the gate before the befuddled man noticed.

"Why would you invade us?" he asked incredulously

"It's nothing personal against you! Nay we're after a man House Agroti has been harboring," Grimm replied. Almost all of his forces were through the gate.

"But we don't have no criminals here! We're good folk!" he protested earnestly. Grimm gave him an exaggerated look of examination.

"You check all those who enter your quarter?" Grimm pressed. Was the man truly that simple?

"Yes sir!" Was the proud response.

"And no funny business or sneaky people have been about?" Goddesses help this daft man.

"Nay sir!"

"Well you seem like a good man gatekeeper." Grimm patted him on the shoulder reassuringly as the rest of his soldiers moved through the gate. "So I'll trust your word on this one."

"Thank you sir! Feel free to go through if you'd like. Watching the morning tide was always a favorite of mine when I was your age."

Grimm smiled. "I might just do that." What tide could be happening in farmland anyways? Preposterous. "You have a nice day gatekeeper."

The gatekeeper nodded to himself in satisfaction, pleased that he had done his job and that everything was right in the world. He waved goodbye to the young heir and returned to his duties at protecting the walls of the Lowland, ignorant that he has just allowed a hostile army to walk through his post.

Grimm quickly caught up with his centurions and ordered for them to make haste through the farmland to the Agroti Homestead. As the only significant building of defensive value in the entire quarter, seizing it would allow them almost total control over the Lowland and thus its people. Finding Lord Talal would be a simple matter after that.

As they marched through the endless fields and groves Grimm thought of the battle that was to come. Lykos, Lord Talal Grimm reminded himself sternly, would most likely be among his troops at the southern gate. The Agroti had been making bold raiding parties into the Nero, distracting the shipbuilders from their duties, and stealing supplies. Lord Talal would be there, causing the most havoc possible.

"Hello down there!" a voice called from afar. A stone pillar, one of many they had passed on their march, was on the far side of a nearby river. On top of it sat Lord Talal, waving at the five hundred soldiers under Grimm's command in the damp morning air.

"Fancy seeing you here Heir Sofos!" Lord Talal called out without any concern. Immediately one hundred archers drew arrows and took aim at the unconcerned lord, whose position had not moved in the slightest. "Out to enjoy the fresh morning air as well?"

Determined not to be outdone by the infuriating man Grimm responded glibly, "oh I woke up today and thought it was a smashing day to enjoy a walk through the land. What better place to take a stroll than through an orchard?"

Lord Talal nodded sagely. "Won't you come up and join me for an early morning chat?" He gestured to a stone pillar on Grimm's side of the river. Grimm eyed him incredulously before shrugging.

Ordering his men to stand down he climbed to the top of the stone pillar.

Sitting himself carefully on its rough surface he turned his gaze to the object of his hunt. "So what brings you out here Lord Talal? One would have thought you'd be raising nine kinds of hell among the Emporo."

"I fancied a rest. One can only kill so many Emporo soldiers before one gets tired of the bloodshed."

"Funny I thought you Talal lived for causing chaos and death."

He frowned. "That might be one perspective but I like to think that I'm working for the betterment of our people. However there are those who would see me fail to suit their own selfish purposes."

"Spoken like anyone who desires power."

"Quite so."

His easy agreement shocked Grimm. "You don't disagree?" he asked incredulously.

"Power is needed for change. Whether for good or bad, change needs power, a driving force if you will. You could throw an army at an objective but if you do not give them something to fight for then they will most assuredly fail."

The two men sat in silence as the sun's light touched the mountain's peak far above. Grimm's forces relaxed and partook of some of the fruits on the sturdy trees all about them, a few climbing the tall frames to reach their bounty. It was Lord Talal who broke the silence.

"What do you fight for Grimm?"

For honor, Grimm almost said. *For family*, he thought. But in truth the answer was both greater and lesser than that. His entire life he had heard stories about how his family's honor was called into question with the death of his mother in Leon's Rebellion. That she was one his secret supporters who was helping him in his madness. However he could never find it in himself to believe those words often spoken by rival houses and decried by his father.

"For my mother," he finally said. Lord Talal hummed in thought.

"For your mother," Lord Talal repeated slowly, watching the water rush underneath them. "I'm curious if you know what I fight for?"

Grimm considered the man in front of him. An unknown heir who had appeared out of nowhere last year, reportedly killed the Stultus and if the Emporo were to be believed, was single handily responsible for the disappearance of their slaves. "For freedom?" Grimm eventually decided, remembering their conversation at the Falknor Winter Festival.

Lord Talal continued to look down in contemplation. "In the beginning, I only wanted to be strong so that others would never hurt me. I wanted to be able to live my life without having to worry about a dagger finding my heart in my sleep or starving if I didn't steal food.

"I was a slave once. For years I toiled in those mines. I had to do truly cruel things in order to survive, I had to forsake parts of my humanity that I didn't have a name for, not yet. And when I finally escaped I wasn't concerned with helping others, I was only worried about surviving the next part of my life. I broke into the Talal manor and was discovered almost immediately by Shawna who told me that I was her son. I didn't believe her despite logic dictating otherwise, it seemed too perfect, the kind of thing that always happens in stories but not real life. The very next day I intended to run away to continue my existence in solitude but the Valkyries had another plan.

"I saw a woman with a small boy who would not leave him even though neither could survive. She stayed with him despite the fact that it would mean her death. I would know, I later found their bodies, half-eaten by Tainted Gnawers in a sewer underneath the kingdom. They weren't worth a proper burial to anyone, so the guards had just thrown their bodies away." His tone was scornful.

"I returned to the manor because I wanted to be stronger, I wanted to be more powerful, I wanted to be able to fight without fear. I returned because I remembered what it was like every night to be nothing and I refused to go back to that if given the chance for more. So I returned.

"Shawna did not care for my reasons. In her mind her son had returned and that's all that mattered. I could be the most terrible person in the world and she would still love me. And then she told me about my father and his rebellion.

"It spoke to something in me. The truth, the simplicity. It resonated inside of me and for the first time I felt like I belonged there. That I was a Talal. I didn't take up my father's cause because of familial duty, I continue it because I believe in it! I fight so people like that woman and that boy don't suffer and die because no one will help them. So that anyone may be free and stand tall! I don't fight for my father's memory, I fight to be the man I wish would have helped me when I was enslaved!"

As Grimm listened to his words the morning light inched down the mountain towards them. His story and history were interesting and did explain a lot why the man was so driven towards freeing slaves. And he reluctantly found himself admiring the drive that burned in the other man.

"You fight for those who can't." Grimm nodded in respect. Lord Talal looked up from his contemplation to return it.

"And for the fallen," Lord Talal answered.

"For the fallen," Grimm agreed.

The two men sat in silence, each lost in their own thoughts as the dawn finally ended and day truly began. Grimm became aware of his centurions at the base of his stone pillar glancing up to him worryingly.

"Heir Sofos? Are we not to continue on our mission?" one of them asked. Grimm shook his head.

"Our mission was to find Lord Talal and there he is." Grimm gestured unnecessarily at the lord who mockingly waved. The centurion sputtered.

"Well yes but aren't we supposed to kill him?" The man pressed. Grimm grunted in displeasure before turning towards Lord Talal.

"I suppose." Grimm stood and stared at the smiling Lord Talal. "Doesn't feel right fighting you when you're so outnumbered though."

"I agree. I think you should turn around and return to the Riverfront instead of facing such overwhelming odds," Lord Talal suggested. The centurion's laughter set off the soldiers under their command and Lord Talal was treated to the sound of five hundred voices laughing at him. "How about this. You and I engage in a battle of skill to decide the matter. If you win you may do with me as you wish."

Grimm snorted in amusement. "And if you win?"

"I want your personal surrender. You have my word that you will not be harmed under my care, nor that I will parade you around as a spoil of war."

"And my soldiers?"

"The moment you admit defeat I will do everything in my power to ensure their well being," Lord Talal vowed. Grimm considered his proposal much to his centurion's ire.

"My lord! We could just simply capture him now!" they protested.

"Something about this situation is wrong," Grimm told them. "He is sitting here, supposedly alone, and all he wants to do is talk

to me and duel? Send out scouts to make sure we're not being surrounded, I'll play his little game."

Turning his attention back to Lord Talal, Grimm called out to
him, "what shall our duel be? To be the first to knock the other off
their stone perch? Perhaps a duel of arrows?"

Lord Talal shook his head. "We both have magic and we have a
river. The contest I propose is thus: using our magic we must make
the largest wave possible. The stones will mark our success."

Grimm pondered the odd duel but was content the terms.
"Shall we begin?"

Lord Talal gave him an amused smirk. "You may go first. Take
all the time you need to prepare, you'll only get one shot," he challenged.

"I'll only need one shot," Grimm retorted.

Breathing in deep he reached for the magic within him. Lord
Talal didn't know it but Grimm had always had an affinity for water
during his studies, mastering it much faster than any other element at his tutor's instructions. This duel would end in his favor he
vowed as he began to push his magic into the river below.

It started small, the fast moving water below was not eager to
rise from its endless descent but Grimm's willpower would not be
denied. The more the Sofos heir pushed his magic into the river,
the higher the waves rose. He began to feel strained as he pushed
his magic but he was determined to win this contest, this battle of
strength with his foe and so he persisted.

Finally, with one last tremendous push, he caused the river to
rise halfway up the stone pillars the two men were on. Behind him
his men cheered at his feat, praising his strength. So assured they
were in their victory they were disquieted to see Lord Talal politely
clapping his hands, as if the feat was only mildly impressive.

"Well done Heir Sofos," he congratulated Grimm who was
breathing heavily. "That will certainly be a feat to match."

"Right," Grimm replied lamely. "Well your turn now."

"Would you like a moment to catch your breathe?" Lord Talal asked sincerely.

"No!" Grimm reddened. "I want you to throw your pitiful wave so we can end this farce!"

"Very well." Lord Talal closed his eyes and placed his hand upon the stone in front of him. Grimm eagerly watched the waves beneath them for movement, determined to see who between them was stronger, but the water remained unchanged. After several disappointing moments he glared angrily at Lord Talal.

"Well are you going to summon a wave or not?" Grimm asked crossly. Lord Talal neither opened his eyes or moved his hands as he replied.

"Patience Heir Sofos. I am bringing the water to us," he calmly replied.

Grimm huffed as he sat back down on the stone pillar but heeded Lord Talal's words. After several more moments he noticed something odd about the water below. The water level had dropped considerably from when he had created his wave and was getting lower with each breathe. It was then Grimm and his soldiers heard a sound in the distance.

"Does anyone else hear thunder?" one woman asked. It was a close description but it sounded wrong to Grimm. In fact it almost sounded like a waterfall....

Snapping his head towards the south Grimm saw a large moving shape on the horizon. It was large, frothing, and fast as it moved along the grove lined river. Never before had he seen a sight such as this and he was rooted on his stone perch in awe as it sped towards him. Closer and closer the shape came and with a terrified start he realized that it was a wave of huge proportions, taller than a man.

Looking back at Lord Talal, he realized that the man must somehow being doing this although the amount of power needed would be immense. He began to feel the faint tremor's of fear at the thought of going up against such power, Lord Talal would swat him down like a fly! The wave approached ever closer, ever louder, sounding like an unending waterfall rushing forwards. With a start Grimm realized his men were in the path at the same moment they did.

With shouts of panic and terror the men began to scale what trees they could. Two of the Sofos' mages, cousins of Grimm, tried to create earthen walls to shield them from the oncoming wave, pulling earth and rock from the ground beneath them. But all of their preparations were for naught as the wave was quickly upon them.

The water struck Grimm's pillar, far above his own mark, throwing a wall of spray high up above him. However that screen of water could not hide the waves devastation upon his forces. As he gripped the stone in terror he watched in horror as his cousin's earthen fortifications were blasted into nothing, the water not even slowed in the slightest as it swept forwards. The few dozen who had managed to climb trees were safe from the waters below but watched in horror as their fellow soldiers were crushed into their haven's stout trunks by the harsh waves. And many more were simply picked up and carried away screaming by the monstrous wave.

All around him Grimm could see the Lowland flood as the wave Lord Talal summoned swept across it. His mouth was slack as he took in the sheer scale of what had just been done, all in the name of a duel. With wide eyes he turned back to Lord Talal, expecting to find the man panting in exhaustion but to his awe he was calmly examining his handiwork.

"Not as high as usual but it will do," Lord Talal calmly shouted to Grimm over the rushing water. "It should go down in an hour or so."

Grimm had many thoughts running through his mind as the morning sun shone brightly upon them, illuminating just how far the wave had gone. However looking at his waterlogged soldiers grasping the trees desperately he found his anger surging forth.

"You promised no harm would come to my men!" Grimm demanded angrily. Lord Talal gave him an unimpressed look.

"I said no harm would fall to your men the moment you admitted defeat," Lord Talal retorted sternly. "You have yet to concede the duel."

Grimm angrily stood and flexed his hands as he stared at the infuriating lord. He wanted to stab, burn, drown, flay that insufferable bastard! But looking at the large lake that had rapidly formed around them he knew he was beaten. There was no way he could match Lord Talal's feat.

"I yield," Grimm whispered.

"What was that Heir Sofos?" Lord Talal asked.

"I yield!" Grimm cried, falling to his knees. "Please save my men."

Lord Talal rose to his feet. "Sadly nothing can be done for the soldiers who have already been swept away. But for those of us who are still here...."

Lord Talal raised a hand to the sky and sent forth a ball of fire. It flew high into the air before exploding powerfully, echoing over the land.

"For those who still remain help will be on its way," Lord Talal said. "For what it's worth, I am sorry that your men died."

Grimm said nothing. A few minutes passed before several long boats appeared, cutting through the water using long poles to push them along. Agroti soldiers lined each of the boats and they called out joyfully when they spotted Lord Talal.

"Fancy a bit of a swim this morning Lord Talal?" they shouted with glee as they pulled up along side. He smiled indulgently at them.

"Those early morning walks, who can resist? Especially not these ladies and gentlemen." He gestured to the waterlogged and scared Sofos soldiers clinging to their trees. "Would you take them secure lodgings? We'll transfer them to somewhere else as soon as possible."

"A fine haul Lord Talal, we'll do that," the Agroti soldiers agreed before retrieving the Sofos soldiers. Some of them had to be forcibly removed from their trees, so great was their terror of the water, while others willingly dove into the safety the hulls promised. Finally it was just Grimm who remained on his stone perch. One of the boats pulled up along side and within it stood Lord Talal offering a hand of aid.

"You'll be coming with me Grimm. We have much to discuss."

Reluctantly he grasped Lord Talal's arm and pulled himself onto the boat. He was Lord Talal's prisoner now and he didn't know if that was better or worse than returning back home to his father.

Chapter Thirty-Six

"**A** nd now we burn the flesh of our dead so they may return to dust...."

Lykos watched as Lord Falknor lowered a torch to Ana Del Rosa's still form. She lay upon a wooden pyre built in the center of the Aviary's courtyard, surrounded by the small number of people who had known her: Captain Avarc and Falka's other brothers and sisters, Shawna who was being supported by Adelram as she wept great tears. And trembling by his side was a devastated Falka who clutched Castalia and Kavar, Ana's mother and father, as she watched her lover's body burn.

Ana's death had only happened earlier that day. Still recovering from the winter chill she had been safely holed up in the Falknor home or so they had thought. For the Acolytes had not been idle while Lykos and his allies had waged war.

They had infiltrated Kremos thoroughly, placing themselves close to targets of extreme importance to House Falknor. Friends, lovers, companions, no one had been safe from their reach. Ana had been laying defenseless in bed when one such assassin came upon her. With a quick thrust of their blade, she had died.

Other pyres were being light in the courtyard, illuminating the night. Despite the quick reactions of the Falknor soldiers and healers many of the victims could not be saved. House Falknor honored their deaths in the custom of their house, granting this ceremony to all those who died in a sign of solidarity. Dozens of bonfires light up the night, chasing away the bitter winter chill. Ash mixed with snow before Lykos' eyes and he reached out to grasp Falka's cold hand in his own as Castalia and Kavar moved off to hug their surviving daughter Elanor.

"They will pay," he promised. The words were unnecessary, both of them knew that they would make the assassins regret this day. But Lykos was already thinking about who had wielded those assassins and reluctantly realized he was already at war with the most likely suspects: Houses Emporo and Sofos.

"She was always so surprised by everything. The little things like servants preparing her bath or cooking a meal for her always seemed to shock her. She told me once she thought she had fallen asleep, that this was all some terribly wonderful dream. Her family was free, she didn't have to sell her flesh for coin, and...." Falka trailed off as tears fell from her eyes.

"You," he finished simply. What meager comfort his words and presence provided was not enough as Falka screamed and fell to her knees in the soft snow underneath. He joined her and hugged her close, wishing that he could take her pain away but knowing he could not.

They knelt in the snow as the pyre containing Ana's body cracked and burned, collapsing in on itself. He thought of the young woman. How utterly relieved she had been when he and Falka had rescued her family. The many evenings the trio had spent relaxing after they had rescued other families of slaves. It was truly because of her that he managed to rebuild the Talal army and he vowed to not forget her sacrifice.

The quiet ceremony would have gone on for hours as the observers waited for there to be nothing but ash to be scattered to the wind had a Falknor soldier not run up panting. The man skidded to a halt next to Lord Falknor and began to urgently whisper into his ear. His eyes grew potent with rage as the man continued to speak and with a snarl he walked over to Lykos.

"There's a large force of soldiers marshaling at our southern gate. They're most likely Emporo soldiers hoping to use the funerals to their advantage."

"Cowards. They can't even allow us a day of peace to bury our dead," Lykos snarled as he rose. "Shall we repel them?"

Lord Falknor nodded and caressed Falka's head as she cried. Lykos gently pulled her to her feet and guided her over to Shawna who hugged the young woman close to her. "Stay with them, please?" Lykos asked Adelram who nodded.

The two men quietly walked away, their anger brimming at these interlopers who dare present themselves. Several squads of men fell into step as they boarded Lord Falknor's personal airship, a truly mammoth vessel that dwarfed Captain Avarc's. Its twin airbags lifted the mighty vessel into the sky as Lord Falknor ordered his men to man the ballista: prisoners would not be taken this night.

They flew in silence through the chilly air until they were above Kremos' southern gate. Lord Falknor pulled his ship a fair distance away, allowing them to circle the ledge the Emporo had stationed themselves on. However something about how poorly defensible their position was raising the hairs on the back of Lykos' neck.

"Something's not right Lord Falknor," he told him as the man issued his orders.

"What do you mean Lord Talal?" Despite the relative youth of Lykos the older lord trusted his opinion, especially in combat.

"They're sitting on a ledge, exposed, against the one noble house who possesses a fleet of airships? It's either a trap or something else." He brought magic to his eyes and felt it take effect. With magic enhanced sight he looked upon the gathered soldiers by the gate and saw the truth. "It's not House Emporo."

"What do you mean not House Emporo?" Lord Falknor asked. "Is it House Kolos? That is the Reliquary beneath us, it was once their responsibility."

Lykos shook his head and allowed the magic to fade. "It's House Prodotis."

"What? Why the blazes are they all the way over here? We have few dealings with the swamp dwellers, certainly none that require this amount of their soldiers at our gates." Lykos could only shrug.

"We should go down to see what they're up to." At Lord Falknor's incredulous look he justified himself. "We're not at war with them and they're neutral. It might benefit us."

Lord Falknor stared long and hard at the gathered Prodotis men, whose silent vigil in the snow remained unchanging. The aged Falknor lord gave a sigh and reluctantly ordered his men to land near them.

"Aye it might. But something about this feels dangerous Lord Talal. Mind their swords and especially their words." Lord Falknor cautioned.

"I will Lord Falknor, there is no doubt about that," Lykos agreed. As they approached the Prodotis forces they heard shouts of panic. It was reasonable he thought, it was a dark night and Lord Falknor's airship moved silently through the air. Presenting their starboard side, Lykos and Lord Falknor approached the railing.

"Ahoy down there!" Lord Falknor called out. "What business do you have at the base of my walls?"

"That would be my doing Lord Falknor." A hooded figure stepped through the ranks of armed soldiers. Her voice, for it was a woman, was enchanting to Lykos and he found himself hanging onto her every word. "I actually came here to entreaty with you for an introduction to Lord Talal but the Goddesses smile upon me. He is here."

"And who has come to see me?" Lykos was thankful for the dark night for his cheeks burned red at the siren's words. With a flip of her hand her hood fell revealing hair as blonde as sunlight framing a womanly face. He found himself drinking in her features like a man drinking water for the first time. The enchanting woman bestowed a beautiful smile upon him.

"I am Lady Prodotis although you may call me Lilith."

"Your home reminds me of my own Lord Falknor. We've cut into the cliffs at the edge of the swamp although we dug in deep rather than up as your family has." Lady Prodotis shared with her host. Lord Falknor had permitted the lady and some of her guards entry into his home so that they may conduct talks away from the freezing chill of winter.

"Ah yes, I remember now. You have the most fascinating wall carvings in all of the kingdom. Even the Vrachos rarely find minerals such as those that adorn your walls," Lord Falknor complimented her back as he handed her a drink. Lykos could not help the frown that crossed his lips, Lord Falknor was almost flirting with the woman.

He shook his head. The woman was beautiful, there was no getting around the fact. She possessed a woman's figure and combined with her voice it was a devastating combination to his relatively inexperienced mind. He had to restrain himself several times from bragging or being overly courteous. Fortunately Lord Falknor was much more practiced in the ways of women and had easily taken the reigns in this discussion.

The older lord politely escorted Lady Prodotis through his home while Lykos walked awkwardly behind them. He had hoped neither had noticed but judging by the resigned glances of Lord Falknor and the bemused smiles of Lady Prodotis, it was a foolish hope. Thankfully he could pretend he didn't exist while the pair spoke.

"Perhaps I may give you a more in depth tour next time you visit," she demurred. "You as well Lord Talal, I would greatly enjoy spending more time alone with you."

Even Lord Falknor blushed at the blatant invitation in her tone. It took Lykos a deep breathe to muster up the courage to reply. "I'm not sure I'd survive an evening alone with you," he finally managed to say.

Lady Prodotis laughed joyfully. "Such a wicked tongue on you. I think it's a shame that it's wasted on these political games we must play," she sighed regretfully.

"Ah yes politics. Like taking a stroll through half of Mycenae with a squadron of guards Lady Prodotis."

"I'm not sure how those are alike Lord Talal." Lord Falknor cut in with a smile. Lady Prodotis laughed once more.

"No I understand Lord Talal's comparison, although I must insist you call me Lilith," Lady Prodotis said coyly. Lykos found keeping his blood in his head a challenge.

"I insist you call me Lykos then Lilith." He smiled and Lilith shared one of her own.

"Well I've been watching your lordship quite closely since the Succession Trial. Fighting off all of those challengers, why it gave me the shivers." She shook her shoulders much to her audience's interest. "You're a man of honor Lykos, you fight for the common folk, the slaves. You're a man who could have anything he desired yet you give away practically everything. You are someone worth coming closer to," the woman practically purred those last words.

Struggling to keep his mind off more carnal topics Lykos tried to focus on a safe topic. "And what will you do once you get closer Lilith?"

She gave him a small smile. "I am aware of your war with House Emporo and how they've attempted to subjugate the Agroti. And now they've dragged House Sofos into their foolishness. You are a mighty warrior Lykos but you cannot be everywhere at once. So I offer my soldiers to aid you in conquering House Emporo."

"That is a very generous offer my lady but I fail to see what you gain from this arrangement," he politely pointed out.

"I get to aid the rising star of Mycenae before he reaches his apex. I'm sure my generosity now will be repaid in various concessions once the kingdom is yours."

They spoke for several hours on the possible concessions they might gain should Lykos prevail in his task on freeing Mycenae from House Kolos' choking influence. He outright refused to give the Nero to the Prodotis, justifying that House Falknor had a far more pressing need to repair and maintain their fleet of airships. A series of discounted trade deals pacified the cunning woman for the time being but she did manage to get him to agree that the terms would be discussed further, at a later and more intimate date.

Lord Falknor offered her a room for the night but she gracefully declined, stating that she would return to the Marsh to marshal her forces. She bid the two lords goodnight and swayed out of Lord Falknor's study leaving the two men alone.

"She is dangerous," Lord Falknor finally said.

"Aye, that she is," Lykos replied, thinking how inexperienced she made him feel. He was by no means ignorant of the female body but something about the older woman seduced him in a way he never had been before. It was unsettling and exciting in equal turns.

"Did you notice how she focused first on me before moving in on you?"

Lykos pondered Lord Falknor's question for a moment before nodding. "It was as if she thought you were the one giving the orders in this little venture of ours, that I was a puppet."

"Aye. Lilith is a rose dipped in poison. We should tread carefully lest we prick ourselves."

Lykos again nodded in agreement before smirking. "I notice she didn't give you permission to use her first name Lord Falknor."

"Jealousy doesn't suit you Lord Talal. Watch that one, she's dangerous," he cautioned.

"Of course but I'm more concerned about my virtue being in danger than my life."

"Funny, Falka led me to believe that had been lost long ago. Someone named Plower?"

Chapter Thirty-Seven

Lykos studied the chess board before him, the wooden surface and pieces smoothed over years of use. Everything had minute imperfections that had never been repaired yet added character to the pieces they adorned, each one had its own story. He made his move and glanced up.

"Not that this isn't enjoyable but are you ever going to tell me why you requested to see me Grimm?"

They were in Grimm's temporary prison in the Aviary, a room without windows yet lavishly decorated. Grimm might be a prisoner but he was still the heir to a noble house and that afforded him certain luxuries. Although Lykos thought the small library along one wall was a bit much.

"Do you still refuse to tell me how you summoned that titanic wave Lord Talal?" Grimm asked formally as he studied the board, his brow furrowed in concentration. The chess game had been Lord Falknor's idea, a method of building camaraderie with the young heir while they attempted to recruit him over the past week. It was an ongoing process.

"And spoil the most exercise your mind has gotten in years? I think not." His mocking reply was met with a scowl as Grimm blocked his bishop with a pawn.

"Then you can wait until I've beaten you." The two men remained in companionable silence for several more turns before

Grimm hesitantly spoke. "Has my father asked about me? Does he know that I'm alive?"

Lykos carefully considered the trap that Grimm had laid with his queen. His own was in danger but so was his king. He finally spoke as he sacrificed his queen to move his knight over to protect his king. "We sent word a week ago that we had you in our custody. Someone pulled your families forces away from the Agroti gate and are now solely focused on breaking down Kremos' front door."

"But he hasn't said anything?" Grimm pressed. Lykos shook his head.

"No." Grimm deflated before his eyes and Lykos felt pity for the other man as they continued to play. He could not imagine how Grimm must be feeling at the moment but perceived it to be a combination of abandonment, betrayal, and loneliness.

"Check," Grimm said simply, moving his queen up. Lykos calmly blocked it.

"What would you do in my situation Grimm?" he asked.

"If you mean the game I would surrender. If you mean real life, I would also surrender. Check by the way," was the dry reply. Lykos chuckled.

"Just give up?" he asked using his king to take Grimm's bishop.

"You'll never win so you might as well save yourself and others the suffering. It would be the honorable thing to do. Check."

Lykos moved his king sideways to safety. "That seems like it would be too easy."

Grimm shrugged as he moved his queen. "It's easy to fight. You simply have to go against what everyone else is doing."

Lykos frowned. "I disagree. It takes will power to go against something, it is difficult to stand against the rivers flow. But that resistance is where we show our strength." He pushed forward a pawn.

"But would it not be more difficult to lay down your arms, to stand in the path of a sword knowing that you could move but don't? Especially if by your own action you could save and prevent pain in others? Check."

"There are different kinds of strength. And while personal sacrifice is important and respectable there is another more valuable aspect that applies to this game and this war." Lykos moved his king further to the side.

"Oh and what is that? Checkmate in two."

"Perseverance. Check." Lykos moved his pawn forward, placing Grimm's king in check.

"What?" Grimm looked down at the board in shock. His pieces were heavily focused around Lykos' king and remaining knight but by his own king stood one of Lykos' pawns. "Fine." Grimm made a motion to take the pawn with his king but Lykos stopped him.

"My bishops." Lykos pointed to the far corner of the board. "My thanks for moving your pieces out of the way."

Grimm realized with shock that his opponent would win the game next turn with the creation of a new queen. Lykos, despite being outnumbered and outclassed by Grimm's own pieces, had won. Frustrated he knocked his king over and glared at the grinning Lord Talal.

"Now what was the information you were so keen to share?" Lykos asked as he relaxed back into his seat.

"What do you mean we have a spy?" Giles demanded angrily.

"I mean exactly what I say, someone has betrayed us," Lykos repeated calmly as he stared at his gathered allies. Meeting in the dining room of the Aviary he looked down in contemplation. "Someone told our enemies about my presence at the Agroti's southern gate last week and how I defeated the Emporo raiders."

"It wasn't Heir Kolos who gabbed his gob?" Adelram asked gruffly. Lykos considered the question for a moment before shaking his head.

"Viktor wasn't meant to be there. He was just sating his need for bloodshed when I intervened. If his father found out we were both there House Kolos would have waged open war on us for me wounding its heir. I think we can safely determine he kept his mouth shut as we aren't all dead."

"So who is the spy then, did your little informant say?" Falka spat. Still grieving Ana's death she was not the most stable emotionally. In lieu of any Acolytes to personally blame she became hostile anytime Grimm was brought up. Unfortunately as they were both in the same building that was quite often.

"He claims he doesn't know whom but that they were someone there that night with me. That narrows it down to Irene, Doukas, and the Agroti."

The expected explosion occurred as accusations and denials were hurled left and right. Giles stood protectively by his brother, both angrily shouting at Helen and Irene who returned with equal rage. Falka and her father were angrily arguing with Lord Agroti and Rickard across the room while poor Demos cowered behind them from the noise. Soon everyone else was swept up into the shouting match and weapons were being drawn. With a deep breathe Lykos raised his hand and clenched his fist. Immediately a shock wave of air exploded from his hand, throwing everyone back against the walls. Dazed, they were ill prepared for him to begin shouting at them.

"I will not have my friends and allies pointing fingers and weapons at one another! We are here to discover the truth of the matter not tear each other apart!" Lykos stared hard at his allies as they slowly rose to their feet. "Someone has betrayed me and I want to know why. Rolan! Irene! Doukas! Front and center!"

The three slowly approached Lykos as if he were about to leap forward and rip out their throats with his hands. He waited impatiently for them to stand before him before continuing.

"Lord Agroti you are in charge of the men there that night, what information can you share?" Lykos asked the frail old lord.

"My builders were repairing the gate and my soldiers manning the wall. With how hectic that night was I doubt any of them could have spared the time to spy on top of their duties."

Lykos quirked an eyebrow at that but turned to the next suspect. "Irene?"

The woman appeared startled but answered, "you ordered me to provide covering fire from the ramparts. I was shot through the leg and retreated to gain medical assistance."

Lykos nodded and turned towards Doukas who spoke without being prompted. "I was with you the entire time. I injured my leg during our descent into the courtyard so I protected and healed the builders while you had your duel with Heir Kolos." Something about the ease in which he spoke prickled Lykos' senses and told him he was lying. But before he could press on that suspicion he was interrupted.

"It's obvious who the spy is! It's the girl!" Rickard shouted from the side, spittle flying from his lips.

"What are you talking about you obese little man?" Helen demanded. "It must have been one of the Agroti!"

"Ha! All of my men were accounted for during and after the battle, can the same be said for your little huntress friend?" Rickard heatedly replied. Giles cut in.

"My brother was with them the entire time too! And Irene was up on the walls with enemy archers, she could have easily passed along information!"

"No I didn't!" Irene turned wide, terrified eyes to Lykos as the accusations piled up. "I swear on my life I didn't!"

"Meaningless words girl!" Rickard stomped forward pulling out his hammer. "You must have done it!"

"No I swear!" Irene begged as she backed away. Giles stepped up behind her and grabbed her arms, trapping the woman in place.

"Let go of Irene you oaf!" Helen shouted as she moved forwards. Doukas blocked her path.

"Don't call my brother an oaf, he's capturing the spy!"

"Move cretin!"

"ENOUGH!"

Lykos voice echoed through the small room, bringing it once more to silence. However before he could speak Rickard once more befouled the air with his voice.

"You must do something about this spy Lord Talal or else my brother and I shall withdraw our support!" Lord Agroti weakly nodded next to his brother. Lykos gave the two men an unimpressed look.

"No one, I repeat no one in this room save I is allowed to decide what happens to anyone. Is that understood? Giles, release Irene." Giles opened his mouth, paused, then closed it releasing a trembling Irene from his grasp. Lykos stepped forward until he stood over her and felt horrible for what it was he was about to do.

"Irene for your betrayal I banish you from my home, my house, and my heart. Begone from my sight and never return." Tears from her eyes fell in great rivers at his words. "I can't believe I ever took you for a midnight stroll in my mother's garden."

His parting statement confused the young woman but it was disguised by Helen smacking him viciously across the face. "You utter bastard. Were it not for the Valkyrie's will I would end you where you stand."

Lykos said nothing as shame and anger warred inside him but he persevered. "Guards," he called out evenly. "Escort Irene from the quarter."

Irene was dragged away roughly by two Falknor soldiers. In ones and twos the rest of his allies vacated the room, some of them giving him respectful nods and other scornful condemnation. Lykos could not decide which made him feel more awful.

That night Lykos stood on the terrace of his home, overlooking the kingdom alight with a thousand fires as it slept through the winter chill. The garden his mother had so lovingly taken care over the past year lay under a foot of snow, the beautiful flowers hidden from sight. *Living undead they were, living dead we are*, Lykos thought bitterly.

Two sets of footsteps echoed behind him. Without turning he knew who they would be.

"I had hoped you would get my message." He turned around to see a furious Helen and a miserable Irene. "I'm glad you came."

"You have some nerve!" Helen spat stomping forward raising her hand to slap him again. With a harsh motion it fell, stinging his cheek far worse than the cold. "Irene would never betray you and you know it!"

"Irene?" Lykos spoke softly, stepping around Helen to make his way to the downcast woman. "Irene?"

"I didn't do it," she whispered. "I swear I didn't betray you."

"Irene look at me, please?"

"I swear I didn't do it." She almost became hysterical repeating herself as she looked up into his eyes. He cut off her words by placing a finger upon her lips.

"Irene I know you didn't betray me," he told her. Behind him Helen gasped.

"What do you mean you know she didn't betray you? Then why the hell did you banish her!" she demanded, grabbing his arm angrily in case she needed to inflict more violence.

"Because I couldn't prove her innocence." A tear fell from his eye. "I know you aren't the spy Irene because too many times I have offered you my heart, offered you my confidence and you always turned me away. No spy would ever turn away the opportunity to get closer to their target, to gain their trust in such a manner. That is how I know you did not betray me. But I couldn't let the alliance fall apart. We're trying to build a better world and to do that we need allies. With Rickard so focused on you he hid the truth from everyone by accident: the true spy is Doukas."

Helen exploded. "Then why didn't you tell everyone that!"

"Because he doesn't have proof," Irene's rough voice answered in understanding. "Doukas betrayed us and he doesn't know how."

Lykos nodded. "And because I don't know how I can't stop it from happening again."

"Balderdash! You could have stopped this! You could have ordered everyone to do the right thing! You could have killed him!" Helen shouted, her words echoing in the night.

"At what cost? To turn myself into a tyrant king? I would have to rule through fear, through total control, and I would not be able to honestly say I worked for the betterment of this kingdom if I so brazenly ignore our basic rights! Our allies would abandon us and the wolves at our door would tear us apart."

Lykos paced angrily, kicking the snow. "Do you think I wanted to banish Irene? Action had to be taken lest someone else make the choice for me. I am trying to make the best of a horrible situation so my friend wouldn't die, lynched by a mob of her former allies and friends!"

He fell to his knees in the cold snow and wept. The two women stared at the weeping man before them and knew he spoke the truth. Irene joined him in the snow and wrapped her arms around his head, holding him close with tears of her own falling to the ground. Several long moments passed before she spoke quietly.

"I was engaged to be married once, I think you would have liked him. He was strong and caring just like you were. We were out patrolling the forests beyond the kingdom's border when we were set upon by a Tainted Horde. We fought and prevailed but a Tainted Viper had sneaked up behind me. He saw it and saved my life at the cost of his own."

The pair knelt in silence in the cold snow as Helen looked on. Lykos finally shifted and stood, helping her to her feet. "I never knew."

"Few do. The past must stay in the past lest we lose sight of our future."

Irene and Lykos remained quietly standing, staring mournfully in each others eyes as Helen looked on awkwardly. Finally it was too much for her and she spoke, "this is all well and good but how do we prove Irene's innocence?"

"I need Irene to find out how our enemies communicated," Lykos replied. "Somehow they knew what happened almost as quickly as it actually did and that is an advantage I will not allow."

"Why does this sound so reasonable and so horrible at the same time?" Helen muttered.

"What would you have me do Lord Talal?" Irene asked formerly. He gave her a sad look.

"I have no right to ask this of you Irene and I'm sorry but I need your help. I need you to return to the Acolytes. That order has ties to our enemies and I need you to infiltrate them to find out how they're spying on us."

"This is a horrible idea!" Helen all but shouted but Lykos quelled her with a glance.

Irene breathed in deeply before nodding. "I'll do it."

He gave her a sad smile. "Thank you."

Irene returned it and touched his cold face gently. "In another lifetime you would have made me a happy wife," she said sadly.

"In another lifetime you would have made me a happy husband," Lykos agreed. As snow began to fall above they leaned in close and shared a tender kiss farewell.

Chapter Thirty-Eight

Lykos did not talk to his mother about Irene's banishment. Shawna would give him disproving looks in the evenings when he joined her for meals and he could not bare it. He all but moved into the Falknor Aviary to be closer to the war he was waging upon Houses Emporo and Sofos, sneaking into his own home for lessons with Illusionist Maeve. It was an odd situation.

Since Grimm's capture the Sofos forces had made increasingly unsuccessful attempts at breaching the gate. Kremos Keep was aptly named, raining fire and arrows upon would be invaders. With the Falknor airships denying passage and the Agroti barring the south, the Sofos were effectively trapped within the Riverfront, unable to leave or interact with the rest of the kingdom safely.

Which simply left the Emporo arrayed around the bay. With the Prodotis applying pressure along their own southern gate, Lykos' army pushing in from the east from Latom, and the Agroti pushing down from the north, now was the perfect time to strike and capture the Nero.

The Nero was the most recently built quarter in the kingdom and its stone walls lacked the more extensive fortifications of older sections of Mycenae. The only significant modifications done were the many iron grates that allowed the ocean tide to sweep through them and water the Lowland with the tide. Because of this, the entire Nero was elevated, with the great ocean sweeping under their buildings every morning and evening. The left over space was dedicated to shipbuilding, the buildings above containing hooks and machinery to build the vessels below. It was in the Nero where most of the Falknor airships and all of the Marsh's boats had been constructed.

Which was why it was necessary that they conquered it before charging the Emporo stronghold. Rebuilding and maintaining airships was time and space consuming work thus they needed the Nero's preexisting infrastructure to support their efforts. Otherwise the campaign would be a long and exhaustive affair with an elevated death count. Lykos was keen to avoid that.

Marshaling at the Agroti's southern gate Lykos, Doukas, Falka, and Captain Avarc studied a map of the Nero provided by Centurion Karen. All around them Agroti soldiers and Captain Avarc's crew were busy arming ballista or sharpening weapons, preparing for the blood that would soon be spilled.

"We need to capture the two major shipyards here and here along with this barracks here if we wish to hold the Nero." Captain Avarc pointed to several spots on the map, the closest to the eastern gate that led to the main Emporo territory.

"The barracks make sense, they'll be able reinforce themselves all across the quarter if we don't take it, but why the shipyards Avarc?" Falka asked her eldest brother. Captain Avarc sighed.

"With all the troops we've been transporting around, the extractions under fire, and general wear and tear from use, our airships are hanging on by a thread. Our craftsmen cannot perform the necessary maintenance for our fleet in Kremos alone so we desperately need more experienced hands. Otherwise our airships will have to be grounded for our own safety."

"What will happen if we can't get the shipyards?" Doukas asked curiously.

"Airships will start falling from the sky," Captain Avarc grimly replied. The news was sobering.

"Very well. I'll lead the assault on the barracks to knock it out. Falka and Captain Avarc will both lead assaults on the shipyards, do whatever is necessary to gain control of them. Centurion Karen, you'll help Falka with taking her shipyard, try not to let her die." Lykos ignored Falka's protest as he continued to study the map of the Nero.

"What about me Lord Talal?" Doukas asked.

"You'll be with me. If taking the barracks becomes a battle of attrition like I fear it will be I'll need your healing abilities. Captain Avarc, will you need more men in addition to your own?"

Captain Avarc thought for a moment. "I wouldn't say no to any extra aid but whoever you send will have to be able to fight without damaging their surroundings. I'd prefer not to lose a shipyard due to foolishness."

"I contracted the services of a squad of Air Rattlers, I'm sure they'll be more than happy to raise a little hell," Centurion Karen offered. Captain Avarc and Doukas whistled in surprise.

"How did you get them into the kingdom? I would have thought the Acolytes would have stonewalled you," Doukas asked with interest.

"I once dated an Emporo sailor who showed me a way. Caught the bastard showing it to another girl a week later. Still it's been useful," Centurion Karen replied with a smirk.

"What's an Air Rattler?" Lykos asked. Falka too looked confused and turned attentively towards the redheaded Agorti who dutifully explained.

"It's not surprising you've never heard of them, most of the time they stay near Istani fighting off pirates. They're mercenaries who specialize in air magic."

"More like infamous," Captain Avarc muttered rubbing a scar on his wrist. "Came across one at a bar once. She didn't take kindly to my attention."

"What did she do?" Falka asked bemused.

"Summoned a whirlwind of broken glass," he muttered darkly.

"That doesn't sound too impressive, I can do that," Doukas boasted.

"She had such fine control over it that she could use the glass to bore a hole through solid wood." Captain Avarc lifted his sleeve to show dozens of crescent scars all over his arm. "She nearly shredded my arm to pieces."

The group winced in sympathy at the painful mental image. "Well let's hope she's not among the Air Rattlers Karen has contracted." Lykos smirked at Captain Avarc. The other man scowled but refused to rise to his bait.

"If you don't need the Air Rattlers Karen, Captain Avarc will take them," Lykos told her firmly.

"We should be fine." Centurion Karen calmly stated. "There are only enough for the two of us since they work in pairs though. Sorry Lord Talal." He waved away her apologies. While he would have appreciated the extra support, he knew taking the shipyards was vital to the war effort.

"Damn right we're fine!" Falka said winking at the centurion. She had been less expressive since Ana's funeral and Lykos was pleased that his friend was slowly returning to her old self. But there was a wariness there now that she was aware this war was real and taking lives. He pitied his friend but would not voice it, he knew she would not appreciate it.

"Excellent. If everything goes to plan, we'll have control of the Nero before lunch."

"Nothing is going to plan!" Doukas shouted as he hid from a barrage of arrows. They had been leading a squad of Agroti soldiers through the Nero when disaster struck. Stuck between two buildings, with the slow moving ocean beneath them and a wall of burning wagons blocking their way they were taking fire from Emporo archers. The archers had been stationed on the roof of the two buildings and were raining arrows upon the unprepared Agroti soldiers.

"I know that, there's no need to keep repeating yourself!" Lykos snapped as he threw another bolt of lightning up at the roof. As tempting as it was to simply light the wooden buildings on fire, it would spread too quickly to contain, burning large portions of the quarter and harming far too many innocents. Thus he choose to throw bolts of lightning whose destructiveness was relatively manageable. Or at least that's what he told himself after he blasted a chimney to pieces.

"Well how are we going to get out of this then?" Doukas demanded, doing his best to make sure no Agroti died from their wounds. The amount of wounded was steadily increasing as time went on and he was struggling to keep up.

Lykos cast his eyes about for an escape route but none revealed themselves. The doors and windows to the buildings on either side were barred and the wagons still burned ahead of them. The alley they had walked down had not ended in a bridge as they had hoped but a small overgrown garden that overlooked the ocean below. As he looked at the garden he thought of a wonderfully dangerous idea.

"Doukas, I need you to light the garden on fire!" Lykos called out. Doukas looked up from the arrow wound he was healing on a moaning Agroti swordsman with an aghast expression.

"Are you mad!" Doukas cried. Lykos grinned savagely.

"Very!" He sent several bolts of lightning to distract the Emporo archers. "Now Doukas!"

Doukas muttered angrily but did as he was told. He threw several large fireballs at the trees and bushes behind them. The blazing warmth chased away the winter chill as Doukas cast more and more fireballs at the plants.

"Everyone over the ledge!" Lykos ordered. Shouts of dismay met his ears. "It's either into the ocean or death by pincushions! Now move!"

With great reluctance the Agroti forces ran through the burning garden with Lykos and Doukas covering their retreat with lightning bolts. The Emporo archers had difficulty seeing them as the flames sent up great billows of black smoke, obscuring the air and their sight. Sending one last burst of lightning to scatter a group of exposed archers, Lykos and Doukas leaped from the garden into the ocean below.

Cold. A cold so dastardly and insidious that it wormed its way into your body to clutch at your heart with icy tendrils. It sapped Lykos' strength but he pushed the paralyzing effects away with an ease gained from years spent in the frozen north. Kicking his feet, he swam to the surface and with a gasp of air broke it.

"Swim to the other side!" Lykos needlessly ordered the soldiers as most of them had already begun swimming as fast as they could. He quickly pursued them, eager to get out of the chilly water. After several moments that felt far longer than they should have been, he found himself being pulled onto a stone platform.

Ignoring his chattering teeth Lykos created two large fireballs in his hands, illuminating the dark area and warming his body. Around him the Agorti clustered, trying to get close to the warmth. Haggard and chilled, they did not look the most ferocious of troops but they had fought with Lykos at the Agroti's southern gate and had something most soldiers were famed for: the willingness to go on despite the risk of death.

"Did we lose anyone?" Lykos asked. The Agroti sounded off around him.

"We lost a dozen my lord," one of them answered, rattling off their names. Lykos closed his eyes when he realized he knew none of them, that even the ones living were virtual strangers. The only person he knew was Doukas who was a traitor. Wait, where was Doukas?

A splash alerted Lykos and the Agroti. Despite the chill that slowed their limbs the soldiers reacted admirably, raising weapons to the waters edge. There lay Doukas, clutching a blue Agroti corpse, his breathe releasing great bellows of mist. With quick motions the Agroti pulled them both out of the water.

"It's Henry," one of the Agroti spoke up coldly, identifying the man Doukas had brought with him. Doukas quickly conjured flames of his own to warm himself up.

"Out of the frying pan into the ice, you don't do things by half Lord Talal." Doukas' chattering teeth and blue lips fit in with the frozen faces of the Agroti soldiers. Lykos was reminded of frozen slaves huddling around each other for warmth. Shaking his head he banished the memory.

"Now what?" the same man asked, glaring at them. Lykos pointed to the stone work above them.

"Once you've warmed up we'll be climbing along the undersides of the buildings. We need to be quick before the tide arrives this evening," he ordered as he examined the water line below them. It was already rising.

Lykos and Doukas kept the flames going for several minutes as the soldiers warmed and dried themselves. However it was exhausting for the two magic users and far too soon for their liking the two men quenched the flames. It was time to move.

The stone supports of the Nero's many buildings possessed enough handholds that the journey was almost simple. It was still fraught with danger: algae covered stone made grasping treacherous while rogue waves occasionally struck from below, soaking the climbers. The waves were the biggest danger they faced as one unfortunate soul found out. A wave surprised him causing his grip to falter and his head burst upon the stone pillar below, staining the seam foam red with his blood.

Still Lykos and his soldiers trudged on, climbing underneath the Nero towards the barracks. Every so often he would chance detection by popping up to the street level to double check their location. Fortunately there were no impassable obstacles on their journey to the barracks and they reached them before night fell. The waves crashed uncomfortably close, sending up icy spray to freeze the already soaked men and women. They clutched with desperate fingers, determined not to fall to their deaths in this watery tomb. Lykos surveyed their target.

The barracks were a series of elevated buildings, rising higher than those surrounding them, to gain an unimpeded view of the quarter around them. It was an ideal spot to watch over the Nero and it would have to fall from Emporo control if Lykos and his allies wished to maintain any semblance of power here. A quick examination of the building revealed scores of patrolling soldiers, all heavily armed and armored, displeasing him immensely.

Hammond, the Agroti who had been promoted from the remaining soldiers to act as their leader, crouched next to him. "Are we to capture or destroy this barracks?"

Lykos frowned. "Preferably capture so we could station our own soldiers here. We could just burn it to the ground but I'd rather not chance the fire spreading to the other buildings unless we have to."

"Figures," Hammond muttered. "So what are we to do?"

Lykos wished he had Irene or Helen with him. With just a few assassins this location could fall to their control in a matter of hours but instead he had banished Irene and sent Helen to harass the Sofos. He would have to make do without.

"Hammond, take Doukas and your soldiers and find a secure spot to hole up in. I'm going to sneak in and try to find the Emporo commander. With any luck," Lykos was beginning to hate those words, longing for the day where he wasn't constantly outnumbered or outmatched, "we'll be able to end this with little bloodshed."

"Yes Lord Talal," Hammond replied. With a few quick and quiet words he led his soldiers off with Doukas in tow.

Examining the barracks revealed one dark corner where only two soldiers were, quietly talking in the night. Reaching out with his magic and hoping that such a distance was not too far, Lykos slashed his hand. Relief flooded him when the portal slid into creation and he carefully stepped through, appearing behind the two men.

"Did you hear the rumor?" one of them asked. Lykos remained in the shadows, wondering if something important might be said.

"That the farmers are amassing an army to sweep us all to the side? Absurd," his companion replied.

"No the one about the new Lord Talal. Supposedly he banished some whore from his forces for betrayal. Lady Emporo placed a reward for any information leading to her capture."

"I'll stay away from anyone driven from that loon's service. He believes slaves should be free! Barking mad that one."

"Aye."

The two men walked away as Lykos pondered their words. Irene had been asked to share any information she could with Helen but not to do so if it risked her exposure. He had to trust her ability to stay safe as aid could not be offered without alerting their enemies that their spy was under suspicion. Shaking his head to clear his thoughts he began to sneak through the barracks, hoping to find someone in charge. It was only several tense minutes before he struck gold in a large room full of maps and weapons where two men stood talking.

"Send a legion to reinforce the north-western shipyard," a slight man ordered. "Instruct Haverforth that he's in charge and not to bollocks it up as he did with the defense of the northern gate."

"Yes sir Commander Ulric!" The second man hastened to carry out the now named Commander Ulric's orders and scurried through a side door. Lykos smiled grimly to himself as he eyed his opponent. Just as he prepared to enter the room and strike the man down another soldier rushed in from the opposite door.

"Commander Ulric! There are intruders!" he cried in alarm. Lykos growled in anger as the two men rushed from the room. Knowing who was to blame he followed carefully.

He followed them to the parade grounds in the center of the barracks. There Doukas and the Agroti soldiers were being held captive and Hammond stood several paces away, held at sword point. Lykos was further angered to see the soldiers had been roughed up but was delighted to see Doukas with a broken nose.

"How did you get so deep into our territory Agroti?" Commander Ulric demanded as he neared, his hands resting on his belt as he swaggered forward.

"Go shove your head in a Charger's ass Emporo scum!" Hammond spat. Commander Ulric's backhand lifted the man clear off his feet to land in a heap.

"Mind your tongue before I remove it," Commander Ulric sneered as he turned towards his soldiers. "How were they discovered?"

One of them pointed at Doukas. "They were hidden behind some crates rather well but his leg wasn't concealed when one of the squads marched by. It was easy capturing so few men," she finished boastfully.

Commander Ulric was unimpressed with her boast and growled causing her to flinch. Lykos for his part was glaring at Doukas, trying to decide who he would kill first. Sadly it was no true choice and he knew he had to attack Commander Ulric to save the Agroti soldiers. Moving closer to strike he was almost ready when disaster struck.

A soldier walked into the yard at just the wrong time and saw him crouched in the shadows of a crate. He dashed forwards and Lykos was ill prepared when the man's meaty fist collided with the back of his head, throwing him out of cover and disorientating him.

"Commander there's another one!" the soldier cried out as Lykos tried to focus his eyes.

"Lord Talal! Seize him!" Commander Ulric ordered as he drew his Sword. Lykos suddenly found himself surrounded by soldiers and steel. Thinking quickly he slammed both fists into the ground sending out a minor shock wave with magic into the packed dirt. It exploded into a cloud of dust blinding the soldier's vision and allowing him to strike out at them.

"Agroti! Rise! Rise up and fight the invaders of your home! Fight against the burners of your fields! Fight against the Emporo!" he roared as he killed the soldiers around him. Breathing heavily he was surprised when the dust around him settled quickly. Once his vision was restored his eyes narrowed in anger at the sight before him.

Many more Emporo soldiers had filled the training grounds and had each taken an Agroti soldier hostage, knives to their throats as they stared with glee at Lykos. Commander Ulric had Hammond by the throat while three soldiers stood over Doukas who bled from a wound on his temple. A glance at the ground around Doukas revealed several butchered Emporo soldiers necessitating their excessive attention. Lykos was grudgingly impressed.

Commander Ulric bowed mockingly towards him. "Well met Lord Talal. An impressive display that will be repaid tenfold upon Pyrgos if you do not surrender to me now."

Lykos slowly turned, taking in the training grounds. Too many soldiers, too many hostages, too little time. He knew he was in a dangerous position and must tread carefully lest it be his end. But as he looked upon the Emporo soldiers who kept glancing at everything, expecting another man to pop out of no where, a devious idea came to him.

Lykos gave a short mocking laugh as he crossed his arms, as if he were completely at ease with the world around him. The gathered men and women looked at him as if he were insane, even more so at his answer. "Haven't you figured it out?" he asked with a devious smile.

"Figured out what?" Commander Ulric demanded.

"How my men managed to get so far into the Nero, this barracks, without drawing your attention?"

"We found them!"

"After we already got in. And have you figured out how I managed to get so close to you in a barrack full of your forces?" Lykos asked as if sharing a secret with a confidant. He gestured all around him at the training grounds full of men and women who began to glance around in paranoia.

"Trickery no doubt," Commander Ulric muttered as the soldiers grew uneasy all around them.

"An interesting trick wasn't it? A man appearing from no where in your most heavily secured building? But it does pose an interesting question: if one man could do it, why couldn't ten?"

Lykos carefully, gently used air magic to brush the necks of some of the soldiers, almost tickling the backs of their necks as they nervously held their hostages. He smirked.

"And if ten men could do it, why couldn't a hundred?"

He swept the air behind a few men to his left before doing the same to those behind him. All around the yard he carefully pulled the air, never enough to move anyone but always making it seem as if an invisible person moved closely behind them.

"What sorcery is this?" one of the Emporo soldiers asked in terror.

"I feel a knife!" another of the soldiers cried. All eyes snapped to him. "There is a knife to my throat!"

"I feel one too!" cried another. All over the training grounds the Emporo soldiers began to claim to feel non-existent knives held to their throats, their own paranoia inventing an enemy they could not see. Lykos smiled at his plan working so perfectly.

"Commander Ulric?" he asked pleasantly. "My Archons and I will accept your surrender now. Or would you prefer to foolishly die in a blaze of glory?" He choose the name randomly, knowing he needed something to name the fear their minds were creating, to make it real. It worked as more soldiers began to whisper frantically.

Commander Ulric gnashed his teeth furiously as he looked at his terrified men. He glared at Lykos who merely looked back at him without concern. Making his decision Commander Ulric nodded.

"For the Emporo!" he cried, driving the dagger into Hammond's chest. Hammond fell with a gurgle as Lykos watched in fury. Summoning his magic he hurled a bolt of lightning that struck Commander Ulric's armor clad chest directly. With a scream of pain and terror he fell to the ground as he was electrocuted to death. Lykos quickly whirled to the Emporo soldiers.

"If you move you die!" he cried out as several Emporo made to follow their commander's orders. He delicately brushed their necks with air magic, hoping that his bluff would hold strong. Fortune smiled upon him and allowed him to breathe easily as the Emporo soldiers quickly dropped their weapons.

"Agroti, secure the Emporo soldiers. Archons if any Emporo tries to leave you have my permission to eliminate them in any manner you deem fit," Lykos ordered his invisible and non-existent soldiers so as to not arouse suspicion. The Agroti were confused but obeyed his orders quickly, locking the Emporo forces in the bunk room. The group joined him as he closed Hammond's eyes.

"Lord Talal? Why didn't you simply use your Archons to kill them all?" one of them asked. Lykos gave her a wry smirk.

"There aren't any Archons," he told them with a great deal of satisfaction. "It was all a bluff."

"But some of them said they felt a knife at their throats!" one of the Agroti protested.

"I knew I felt someone's hand!" another insisted.

"I could hear talking I swear!" another claimed. More and more of the Agroti began to claim to feel the existence of the invisible Archons. Finally Doukas spoke up.

"Soldiers of Agroti, Lord Talal is obviously trying to keep their existence a secret! A force such as these Archons is only a boon if no one knows about them." The Agroti nodded in realization, nodding and winking to Lykos in an exaggerated manner.

"Of course Lord Talal!"

"We won't tell anyone about the Archons!"

"Your masterful oration skills saved our lives!"

Lykos shook his head in frustration. At least the barracks fell he thought grimly. In the distance he could see two green fireballs launched high up into the air, signifying the capture of the two shipyards. With glee he sent his own up to join them.

The Nero was theirs.

Chapter Thirty-Nine

I f Lykos had expected to be met as liberators of the innocent he would have been disappointed. The morning after capturing the Nero he awoke to find a multitude of riots occurring throughout the quarter. The liberated slaves eagerly took up arms against their former captors, forcing him and the Agroti to police them lest they get too rowdy and as for the common folk? They hated being occupied.

He could empathize. Prospering under one house only to be conquered by another had to anger more than a few but he was just not prepared mentally to handle the riots. Their forward momentum ground to a halt as they were forced to deal with the troublemakers, putting out fires that threatened the safety of all. It was an exhausting affair.

The news wasn't all bad. With control of the shipyards Captain Avarc was able to begin repairing the damaged airships. As soon as the ballista along the walls were taken care of, their air fleet could begin dropping troops all over the Emporo controlled quarter of Ploio. However they had to get through the rioting common folk to take the gates first.

"So how many Archons are there anyways?" Doukas asked for the third time that morning as they dispersed another rioting crowd. He had been aggravatingly interested in the fictional warriors Lykos had created, believing them to be real flesh and blood. It was beginning to grate on the young lord's nerves.

"Not as many as I would like," he answered honestly, wishing that the mythical warriors of his own invention were in fact real. He had heard many whispers throughout the ranks of Agroti that the Archons walked among them, silently on the watch for foes. If he had known how the rumor would have spiraled out of control he would have found another way, a few flesh wounds would have been preferable to the headache of dissuading others. Glancing at the attentive Doukas, he changed the subject. "I received word from Adelram earlier. Giles is performing exceptionally well at maintaining order in Pyrgos."

Doukas chuckled. "Sounds like him. He always was a stickler for the rules. He's still hoping that the other noble houses will recognize House Dumas as nobility in Mycenae."

"I've often wondered why. You came here a few years ago didn't you, from Svellheim?" Lykos questioned as the two men moved towards the south, to the gate leading into Ploio.

"Aye. Our family was heavily invested into the slave trade, capturing and kidnapping common folk from the roaming villages in the north. Save for the Tainted eating a few of the "stock" every once in a while it was a lucrative trade and my family prospered."

Lykos' eyes narrowed. "So why did you stop?"

"Giles. He's a big softy. When dad tried to get us into the family business as lures, basically bait for the wandering tribes, he threw a big fuss."

"A big fuss huh?" Lykos asked dryly as they made it to the gate. All around them Agroti soldiers prepared ballista and weapons in preparation for the coming assault. He was pleased to note that they moved quickly due to high morale with their recent victory.

"Aye." Doukas confirmed. "Broke two of our uncle's necks and beat our father black and blue. I'm sure dear old dad would have pursued us if I hadn't broken his legs too."

"Glad to know you're loyal to your brother," Lykos remarked, spying Centurion Karen making her way to him.

"Of course, someone has to look out for the big guy," Doukas assured him.

"We have a problem," Centurion Karen informed Lykos in lieu of a greeting.

"When don't we?" he asked rhetorically. "What happened?"

"I've just received word from the Lowland. The Falknor are no longer occupying the sole attention of the Sofos. Raiding parties have been probing at our northern gate while scouts have been spotted everywhere else along the walls."

"Unfortunate." Lykos pondered the situation for a moment. "Do we know how long we have before they launch an attack?"

Centurion Karen shook her head. "It could be anytime between an hour ago to next year. We're too far away to assist in a timely manner so Lord Agroti wants us to maintain our position and send our spare units to reinforce the north."

"If it helps in any way," Doukas interjected, "I think we should listen to this request. With the Nero we've blooded the Emporo's nose enough that they should back off from facing us."

Lykos scowled. "If we give the Emporo time to recuperate we'll never take Ploio. We have to strike now if we want to end this conflict without a terrible loss of life later. We need to press our advantage here while we can."

Centurion Karen stared at Lykos in silence before replying, "very well. I'll send word to Lord Agroti that we're beginning our attack on the Emporo. I hope it's the right decision."

"Not what I would have done but you're the one in charge." Doukas gave a grim smile as his eyes flickered over the rooftops. "You don't believe the Prodotis and your forces in the east can handle the Emporo?"

"It's not that. Lord Sofos is dangerous but arrogant and we have his heir. He won't risk us killing Grimm so this is just to test us. Lady Emporo and Delilah on the other hand want to control or eliminate House Agroti and kill me. They're a much bigger threat that needs to be neutralized."

Centurion Karen looked thoughtful at his words. "I never thought about it that way. Glad to see the stories about you contain a kernel of truth."

"Stories?" he asked bemused. Doukas snorted.

"Between destroying the Sofos incursion and your capture of the Emporo barracks the bards are weaving incredible tales of your skill. Don't let it go to your head, I heard most of those Sofos soldiers survived and are currently getting fat in the Agroti jails, right Red?"

Centurion Karen glared. "Mind your tongue. Lord Talal, I'll prepare the men." Both men watched her walk away.

"You really shouldn't play with fiery centurions Doukas," Lykos warned. The man laughed.

"It's good to rile her up. It makes her heart beat faster, it'll help keep her alive."

Lykos privately agreed but wasn't about to admit it. Doukas was not a man he felt comfortable around nor did he intend to be charitable. Because of his actions he had been forced to send Irene far away for her own safety after all. He became aware that Doukas had said something.

"Care to repeat that?" Lykos asked blankly. Doukas nodded to the rooftop behind him.

"Do you have any soldiers stationed on the rooftops?"

"What? No, they should be all at the wall getting ready." Lykos stepped to the side so he could keep both Doukas and the roof in sight. Sure enough on one of the rooftops was a hooded man staring down at them. "Who goes there!"

His shout caused the man to spring forward off the rooftop. With the man closer, he could see his clothing was adorned with markings of the Acolytes. He immediately became wary and prepared himself for combat.

"Die heathen scum!" the fanatic shouted, throwing a hatchet at him. Lykos, more than prepared for such an obvious attack, found his balance offset by Doukas who tried to push him to the side.

"I'll save you Lord Talal!" he cried. His attempted rescue only succeeded in burying the hatchet deep into Lykos' shoulder causing him to fall to the ground. As he fell wounded the Agroti soldiers quickly gave chase to the assassin who vanished down the street. And as his vision faded to black he realized that the hatchet had been poisoned.

Lykos woke up feeling stiff, sore, and immensely displeased. He opened his eyes to find himself laying on several worn blankets and Doukas standing over him casting healing magic.

"Never, ever, push me out of the way," Lykos ordered roughly, his voice croaking unpleasantly. Doukas blinked in surprise.

"You're welcome for saving your life," he said snootily.

"It wouldn't have needed saving if you hadn't pushed me into the hatchet," Lykos retorted as he forced himself to sit up. Looking around revealed the Agroti still busying themselves with preparations.

"That edge was poisoned!" Doukas tried to justify.

"Once again it wouldn't have mattered if you hadn't tried to *help* me. You've wielded a sword before, you know to never trip a swordsman," Lykos angrily replied. Doukas trembled as he looked down, in either shame or rage Lykos knew not, but when he next spoke his voice was calm.

"Of course Lord Talal, I'll remember that for the next time."

"See that you do. Now help me up," he ordered. Doukas complied and they set off slowly in search of Centurion Karen. Quickly spotting her by several ballista on the wall he ascended the stairs, leaning against the stone heavily as he climbed. Whatever poison that had been used on the hatchet had sapped his strength and it was slow to recover.

"Lord Talal, should you be on your feet?" Centurion Karen greeted when she saw him. He gave her a wry grin.

"Probably not but these gates won't take themselves."

She looked surprised. "You still want to aid us despite your injury?" she asked incredulously.

"Of course. I'm here, I'm alive, therefore I will help."

"Well, I suppose you could take command of the ballista. Tell them where to focus their fire and they'll lay it to waste."

"Wonderful. Doukas keep Centurion Karen alive and don't push her into any hatchets," Lykos ordered. Both Doukas and Karen growled but consented to the order. With a nod they walked off leaving him to look over the ballista crews.

Each ballista required two soldiers to properly man it. They would pull the crank in unison, tightening the tension until it was almost ready to snap. Then after moving the contraption to aim at the target they would release the heavy metal bolt to rain destruction upon their foes. The ballista were excellent at keeping the airborne Tainted at bay and could be easily modified to attack airships or gates. He looked forward to using them to break open the Emporo defenses.

He did not have to wait long for down below Centurion Karen had marshaled her forces and began to march towards the gate. Lykos nodded to the soldiers nearby. "Ready your ballistas and take aim at the Emporo gate." He waited until their calls of ready could be heard. "Fire!"

"Aye sir!" The soldiers cheered as a dozen metal bolts dashed through the air and struck the reinforced gate. The thick wood splintered explosively under the hail of metal as it punched through.

"Reload!" Lykos ordered. The soldiers hastened to obey, turning the cranks on the machines quickly. He watched as Centurion Karen led the soldiers below against the remains of the wooden gate, ordering men to pull at the shattered remains. Eager hands grasped the splintered wood and began to heave while a peculiar fact made itself known to Lykos: the Emporo had not lowered their iron portcullis.

Frowning in thought he gestured to a courier. "Run to Centurion Karen as fast as you can. Find out if she neutralized the Emporo portcullis and if not let her know they they haven't dropped it."

"Of course Lord Talal!" The man bowed before sprinting into the chaos below. Lykos continued to stare at the raised portcullis, unease pooling in his belly. Something wasn't right about how easily the Agroti were taking the gate. Meanwhile the Agroti forces below finally succeeded in pulling open the wooden gate and began to stream through in a relentless wave.

Centurion Karen and Doukas led the charge through the gates with several squads of soldiers following them closely. The clash of steel and screams of violence were heavy in the air and in one terrible moment Lykos saw the trap they had just sprung. He watched in horror as the Agroti courier he had sent crossed the iron portcullis and in slow motion the heavy iron fell upon him and several Agroti soldiers.

Their death was not swift. They laid pin underneath the heavy iron, impaling them on thick spikes. They began to scream in pain as the horror of their death struck them for while they weren't dead yet they soon would be. It was a gruesome sight and Lykos felt sick. Centurion Karen, Doukas, and the few Agroti with them were cut off from reinforcements or retreat against the vengeful Emporo. But the trap was not done yet.

A terrible cry sounded from behind. Whirling about he could see a mob of vengeful common folk, waving improvised weapons and torches as they advanced upon the rear of the Agroti forces. He was trapped as well.

"My lord the ballista are ready! Your orders?" a soldier asked. Lykos only had one choice.

"Agroti!" Lykos roared over the courtyard. Silence fell in an instant as hundreds of men and women turned from the portcullis to stare at him. Lykos pointed to the gate leading into the Nero. "Defend your flank!"

A precious few moments were wasted as the Agroti stared at him dumbfounded. It was not until the enraged Emporo common folk began to pour into the courtyard that the Agroti soldiers rallied and attacked back. Lykos turned to the Agroti next to him. "Where are all our mages?" he demanded.

"They followed Centurion Karen my lord!" she stammered. He snarled. He did not have the strength to melt through the metal gate while his arm healed, thus he was incapable of aiding Centurion Karen and Doukas. However he eyed the armed bastilla carefully.

"Can we use the ballista to shoot a hole through the wall?" Lykos asked eyeing it. If it were built the same as this side he doubted it.

"I don't believe so my lord." she answered. "The spikes will just get stuck halfway through."

"Valkyrie's tits, we can't go over, we didn't build any ladders. And it's too high to climb." Lykos angrily glared at the side walls of the courtyard. When the Emporo retreated they had ripped out the wooden stairs, a feature they were designed with for this exact reason. Lykos wished whatever architect of that feature died painfully.

Architect. The word echoed in his mind as he stared at the Agroti swarming the Emporo common folk. The hairs on the back of his neck raised as his heart began to race. Someone was watching him.... There!

On the Emporo wall across the courtyard stood the man, the Architect, that he had seen talking to Helen in the Grand Temple, the same man he had seen all those months ago after he escaped the mines. His inhuman eyes were trained on Lykos from his broken perch, watching him keenly, and he felt as prey before a hunter. He stared into the Architect's eyes for only a moment but felt as if he had seen the whole breadth of creation. It was unsettling to experience and then it was over. The inhuman man was gone but he had given him an idea.

"Make a ladder!" Lykos cried to the soldiers arming the bastilla. They looked at him in confusion. "Launch the metal bolts into the walls! Put enough of them at an angle and our soldiers can climb up and over the wall!"

"Aye Lord Talal!" The Agroti eagerly began launching metal bolts across the courtyard and to his immense satisfaction they stuck true to the wall. It would take several volleys for the ballistas to make a suitable ladder however and Lykos hoped that Centurion Karen and her men could hold out long enough.

"Keep at it Agroti, I want our soldiers on that wall quicker than a Tainted Piercer in flight!"

He watched impatiently as the Agroti subdued the rioting common folk, those still living being tied up and taken to the barracks to be secured. The remaining Agroti began to climb the makeshift ladder the ballistas had made, attacking the archers House Emporo had stationed there to man them.

Lykos found himself participating in a part of command he had previously never considered, namely that of a leader who merely oversees the fight rather than one who participates in it. The swing of a sword, a fireball to the face, those were skills he prevailed at. However the frantic tedium of ensuring hundreds of men and women did as they were told was an experience he was not enjoying at all. He was glad he had Adelram to handle this aspect of the Talal forces while he led from the battlefield.

Still as the day went on and news of Centurion Karen and her men's survival reached him, Lykos and the Agroti soldiers were heartened. Even the news that Doukas was still alive could not dampen his spirits for the fall of the Emporo was at hand.

Chapter Forty

The invasion of Ploio was well underway. Its streets were filled with broken barricades and blood stains as Lykos and his allies fought the Emporo soldiers for control. The rich common folk of Ploio did not muster the resistance their Nero brethren put forth, a fact Lykos and his allies were thankful for as this conflict was already bloody enough. More effort was put forth to liberate the slaves, whose sudden freedom left many dazed and confused.

Lykos and the Agroti had managed to claim the territory leading up to the river but had been stonewalled from crossing by the Emporo soldiers. Adelram had swept south, hugging the quarter's walls and had connected to the Prodotis forces who had managed to gain a foothold at their joined gate. Lykos could admire the abilities of the Emporo commander for holding off three separate incursions into their home, even if it did make his life more difficult.

One such difficulty was how to break the Emporo lines so they could move on to the Emporo Chateau, take it, and end this conflict. Which was why Lykos had traveled through the war torn quarter to meet with Adelram and the commander of the Prodotis forces, Commander Withers, to discuss their options. The trio met in a building abandoned by the Emporo during the invasion.

"We could always moon the purse pinchers and leave them here to rot." Commander Withers was a crude man with an angry face and Lykos found himself disliking the antagonistic man almost immediately. It did not help that Commander Withers reminded him strongly of the slave overseers he had the misfortune of experiencing throughout much of his life.

"I will not suffer an enemy to live," he firmly stated, staring Commander Withers down. The man reddened but scoffed.

"That's all well and good but my men are running on scraps. Even with the wealth we've plundered from the Emporo they've grown tired of this conflict," Commander Withers said.

Lykos looked at him furiously. "What do you mean the wealth you've plundered?" he demanded. Adelram too looked displeased as Commander Withers looked at them in surprise.

"Of course? Otherwise morale would be far worse."

Lykos ground his teeth. "Who informed you that we were plundering from the Emporo?"

"Well no one. It's just what we've always done," he said in surprise.

"You steal from those who haven't done you any wrong?"

"Honorless mongrel," Adelram muttered. Commander Withers glared at them both.

"They're our enemies! Everything up to and including death is on the table!" The Prodotis commander justified with the air of a man who knew he was correct. Lykos was not willing to concede.

"Not only is that wrong, we are not here to pillage a people whose only crime is to serve House Emporo!" he began but Commander Withers interrupted snidely.

"Is that why you've butchered half of their people?" he demanded, stepping into Lykos' personal space. "You nobles, you can never leave well enough alone!"

Lykos was taken aback at the sudden vehemence, especially from an ally. "What are you talking about?"

"You oh so special noble houses! We're just toys for you mages, lording your fireballs and lightning bolts over us. Twisting our minds with illusions for your own sick amusement," Commander

Withers spat. Lykos almost violently retaliated before reason returned to him.

Had he not thought the same once? Growing up in the mines and walking Mycenae's streets, he had heard whispered stories of magical lords and ladies waging violent wars, destroying Tainted hordes, and accomplishing great feats. He too had been envious and fearful of the mages for they had been elevated to the status of gods among men. His own recent feats and how they were whispered among the Agroti came to mind. Was he any different?

Adelram did not have any doubts. "You will respect the noble houses or I'll turn you inside out with my bare hands. I'm sure Lady Prodotis would be interested to know your thoughts on her own house," he finished darkly. Commander Withers laughed.

"Threats of violence? You're just as bad as the Emporo."

"We are nothing like the Emporo," Lykos countered angrily.

"Just because you freed a few slaves doesn't make you a Goddess. Look at this building." Commander Withers gestured to the ransacked room they stood within. It showed signs of burn damage, its structure only just standing despite the destructive force's best attempts. Lykos could make out the remains of chairs, tables, and couches all over the room. "This used to be a flesh palace. I can guarantee no one here ever did anything to either one of you or the Emporo! Your forces," Commander Withers poked Adelram in the chest, "burned it down when a few Emporo soldiers took refuge within!"

Lykos looked at Adelram who shifted uncomfortably. "There are casualties in every war," he finally said.

"Enough. Adelram we do not harm innocents regardless of them providing aid to our enemies. Withers, we do not steal from them! Regardless of it being common practice we are not here to fill our coin purses! Is that understood?" Both men muttered under their breathe and Lykos slammed his hands on the burnt table. "I asked is that understood!"

"Yes Lord Talal," both men dutifully replied.

He sighed. "How are we going to reach Lady Emporo and force her to concede?"

Adelram spoke up promptly. "We need to break the morale of the Emporo forces somehow. Some show of force that would allow us to sweep through their territory."

"We could start executing civilians," Commander Withers suggested. At Lykos' disgusted look he quickly explained, "threaten to execute them! They wouldn't want their families to suffer."

Lykos shook his head but it was Adelram who voiced his thoughts. "No that would only push them into attacking us. A show of force is our best bet."

Looking between the two men Lykos was struck with an idea, hating how it would prove Commander Withers correct. "What about the Emporo Bazaar?"

The Emporo Bazaar was a magnificent building, lovingly carved out of the finest stone, built with the richest timber, and decorated with the most finely woven tapestries and statues the kingdom of Mycenae possessed. It was the pride of House Emporo and the common folk who worked in it everyday. Adelram had managed to capture it early in the war and spent a large bulk of his time keeping it under his control from desperate Emporo incursions.

And Lykos just threatened to burn it to the ground.

He actually sent several couriers to the Emporo lines to deliver a message: "Surrender or I burn down the pride of House Emporo." Each of them had been given further orders to explain which pride that was as Commander Withers pointed out the egotistical Emporo would believe it to be the entire quarter. Lykos and Adelram had agreed and the order was given.

"Do you really think it will work?" Commander Withers and Centurion Karen stood near to Lykos as they stared towards the make shift barricades on the street. He deliberately stood inside bow range while his two companions stood several steps into the safe territory. It was Karen who asked the question.

"Yes," Lykos said simply, for in his mind nothing else needed to be said.

"Depends on how much Emporo pride and greed rules them," Commander Withers stated as Adelram walked up.

"The deadline has been reached Lord Talal." Adelram made a point of stopping just behind Lykos. "Want me to give the signal to start lighting fires?"

"Aye." Lykos nodded, his gaze never leaving the barricades. Adelram turned and bellowed an order and three huge bonfires were set ablaze outside of the Bazaar. Almost immediately he saw movement on the barricades as a squad of archers let loose panicked arrows. He remained impassive at the arrows that landed all around him, courtesy of subtle nudges with air magic he employed.

"Nicely done," Adelram complimented. It was one of the few magical techniques that the older man had taught him instead of Illusionist Maeve. It usually required too much concentration to pull off in a timely manner but with the distance between him and the archers, he had more than enough time to react. Several more volleys followed but with each wave being turned aside the time between them grew longer until finally they stopped.

"And now they'll open the barricade," Lykos stated calmly. Indeed the hasty wooden fortifications were being pushed open from the other side, revealing many grim faced men and women. They began a slow, reluctant march towards Lykos who stood without reacting to the large group of soldiers. Behind him his commanders and centurions began ordering his soldiers to their places in their fortifications. Finally the group arrived.

"Lord Talal I presume?" The apparent spokesperson was a middle aged woman with several interesting claws running down her neck. "I'm Commander Lexis, the leader of the Emporo forces. We," she took a deep breathe, "we surrender."

"I accept," Lykos stated graciously. He would pay her the respect she had earned. He nodded towards Adelram who began to order the Talal soldiers to relieve them of their weapons. "So long as you're calm, reasonable prisoners we won't be forced to do something we all will regret. It is a rather nice building."

"Thank you Lord Talal." Commander Lexis and her soldiers followed Adelram as he led them to their temporary housing. Lykos intended for this war to end tomorrow one way or another so holding the Emporo forces long term would be unnecessary.

An Agroti courier ran up and began to whisper urgently into Centurion Karen's ear. The redheaded woman paled so much Lykos wondered if she would pass out from blood loss. She waved the courier away and quickly approached him.

"The Sofos have launched more and more attacks against the Lowland. It's gotten to the point where they're just hurling fireballs over the walls, trying to do as much damage as possible." The commander was rarely so frantic as she was now and he agreed the news was quite dire.

"Return to your people. House Talal and Prodotis can secure the Emporo now and I'll deal with the Lady Emporo tomorrow. Once I'm done I'll join you and the Agroti and we can put a halt to House Sofos' attacks."

"Thank you Lord Talal! May the Goddesses give you strength," Centurion Karen said. With a final nod goodbye she whirled around and began to issue orders to her soldiers.

Lykos turned back to face the abandoned barricade. Just through the wooden fortifications he could see the Emporo Chateau in the distance, almost glowing in the sunset. Tonight his soldiers would secure the quarter and tomorrow he personally would end Lady Emporo.

Chapter Forty-One

Wood met metal as a dozen Talal soldiers battered a ram against the Chateau's gates, rattling them in their place. Lykos stood behind them, casting fireballs occasionally to weaken the metal as his soldiers did their best to knock down the obstruction to their final goal: House Emporo.

Clang. Clang. Clang.

Lykos observed the soldiers Adelram had trained for him. Their strong backs and rough hands could have been mistaken for any common man in the kingdom but he knew the truth. These were a few of the many former slaves they had liberated from this very quarter over the past few months.

Clang. Clang. Clang.

He supposed it was poetic that the former slaves should now overthrow their former masters. It was morbid amusement that filled him when he realized that just as the masters were led by another, the former slaves were led by another like themselves. The world truly did have a sense of irony.

Clang. Clang. Clang.

The gate would fall. Lykos knew it, his soldiers knew it, and the members of House Emporo cowering in their home knew it yet still none exited to challenge him. He wondered how many he would have to kill today. The only two he knew for sure would die were Eliza and Delilah, they would not be allowed to escape justice.

Clang. Clang. Clang.

Were it not for common sense he would simply burn down the Emporo Chateau. That would spur the common folk of Ploio and Nero into open revolt and he was keen to avoid fighting a vengeful populace more than he had to. The Stultus had been universally hated but the Emporo? They were beloved.

Clang. Clang. Screech!

The eyes of all those gathered snapped to the gate as it was knocked from its position. The metal had torn free of the wall and the Talal soldiers cheered as they rushed onto the grounds. Lykos followed at a careful, measured pace, determined not to rush about excitedly. Calm and collected was the image he sought to portray, the center of a storm.

The grounds were beautiful, decorated with rose beds and rare trees. But he only had eyes for the house itself as his soldiers trampled the prized gardens. The beauty of the house was also wasted on those who cared not for the finely carved water spouts or detailed panels of carvings. As Lykos and his soldiers approached the doors they swung open to reveal Lady Emporo and Delilah.

The clothing of the two women could only be defined as obscene. Lady Emporo's breasts hung free of her light robe, which barely concealed her lower half. The material was sheer and done in varying shades of white, darkening and lightening as it flowed around her body. Delilah's clothing couldn't contrast her lover's more. Leather, polished to a dark shine, covered her body. But it wasn't any less sinful as it was pulled tightly against her skin, highlighting every inch and curve she possessed was thrown into sharp relief. The Talal soldiers with Lykos gave great exclamations at their wardrobes but were quickly marshaled into position by their female counterparts.

"Lord Talal, you broke my gate," Lady Emporo sniffed disdainfully.

"You killed my friend," Lykos countered, referring to the Agroti champion Plower.

"Who?" she asked quizzically.

He looked at her in disgust. "You don't even know his name do you?" he asked. She looked down condescendingly.

"I don't associate with the rabble like you do." The gathered Talal soldiers began to mutter angrily. "Control your mutts Lord Talal or I'll have Delilah do it for you."

"Lady Emporo, for your crimes of killing my friend, waging unjust war against the Agroti, and for the practice of slavery, I demand your surrender!" Lykos ordered to the cheers of the soldiers with him.

"Quaint." Lady Emporo turned towards Delilah. "Take care of them my love. When you're done playing with Lord Talal, bring him to the ballroom."

"Of course my lady," Delilah said demurely. Lady Emporo turned and retreated into the house as she pulled out her whip. "I can't wait to break in my new toys."

Lykos narrowed his eyes in anger as he realized that she meant him and the Talal soldiers. He turned to the Talal soldiers. "Stand down."

"Giving up so easily?" she mocked. The leather clad woman shrieked in rage as she dodged a fireball he had tossed her way, singeing her hair.

"Hardly. However your lady sent my friend back to me in pieces. I feel it to be fair I do the same to you," he explained as he pulled out a very special dagger.

"What an adorable little blade! Do you plan on trimming my nails for me? Remember I like them long so I can gouge out the eyes of fools," she mocked as she shook out her whip. The long cord had many sharp metal attachments on the end that made him wary.

"You'll find out if you're a good girl," he said stepping forward.

"But I've been so naughty." Delilah smiled innocently as she matched him pace for pace. "So what does that get me?"

"The same thing!" Lykos roared lashing out with his magic. The blast of air surprised her as she was launched backwards to land in a heap. He wasted no time rushing forward but was driven back by several sharp glances of the woman's whip across his upper arms. Roaring in surprise and pain Lykos reared back allowing her to stand to her feet.

"You may have struck first but first blood goes to me boy!" Delilah crowed. Lykos snarled and sent several fireballs at the dominatrix. Despite the restrictive appearance of her tight leather clothes she nimbly dodged the flames. Then to his surprise she sent several of her own that he narrowly dodged. "Bet you weren't expecting me to have magic!"

Lykos growled but continued to throw magic, hurling blasts of lightning, fire, and air, all of it being countered or dodged by the vile woman. Delilah gave as good as she got and he found himself resorting to creating earthen barriers for protection. After a few tense moments going back and forth the two combatants created gusts of wind, pushing forward at each other, trying to overpower one another to no avail. The magic built and reached a crescendo and suddenly reversed, pulling them forward to collide painfully. They collapsed dazed and confused on the ground.

Lykos swung his dagger blindly but heard the snap of a whip by his ear. Acting on instincts bred in the mines of Svellheim he rolled to the side and away. When his vision cleared he saw a disbelieving Delilah staring at him and the whip in her hand.

"You've felt the touch of a whip before haven't you! You fear its snap! You've been someone's plaything before!" she exclaimed with a deranged look in her eye. He cast his eyes about for anything to aid him and saw a broken fountain spraying water. Reaching towards it with his magic he gave the spraying water a boost and it soaked the pair of them.

"I cannot wait to bend you to my will like I did to Lady Emporo!" Delilah exclaimed, paying no heed to the water soaking her clothes. She raised her whip to strike him but found her motions hampered. "What is this!"

The water had soaked through her leather clothing, severely restricting her movement but he had pulled at the magic once more. Ice began to form on her limbs as the heat fled her body and it confined her in place. Lykos picked himself up off the ground and launched himself at her, sending them both to the ground in a tumble of limbs and broken ice. He dropped his dagger and wrestled the whip from Delilah's struggling hands and angrily struck her face.

"I am no ones pet!" Another strike to the dazed Delilah's face. "I am no ones slave!" Another strike sent her limp. "I! Am! Free!"

He wrapped the whip around Delilah's neck and pulled it tight. Her eyes widened dramatically as she scratched desperately at his hands to no avail. He had her in his grasp and he was not letting go.

Her struggles slowed further as the air was cut off from her body. Her hands fell limply to her sides as he continued to strangle her, not letting up for a moment. When her body moved no more he grabbed the dagger from where it laid and stabbed it violently into her heart.

As his breathing calmed he looked around him. The Talal soldiers were all standing around him in silence as they stared at the victor of the duel. Removing the dagger from Delilah's corpse, Lykos rose to his feet to stand equal to them.

"Well fought Lord Talal!" The soldiers began to cheer. "Down with the masters!" they cried. Lykos felt a warm feeling in his chest at their cheers.

"I once lived as a slave," Lykos began, his soldiers quieting at once, "fighting for scraps, a place to sleep, the right to live! Now I stand before you as a lord! I have gone from having nothing to having everything and will you my brothers and sisters stand with me as we discover what tomorrow holds for us?"

The cheers of the Talal soldiers were more beautiful than any garden of roses or finely carved statue in his mind.

Lykos kicked open the doors to the Emporo ballroom, sending them into the walls with a mighty clatter. Gathered in the room, holding what appeared to be a party, were the many members of House Emporo being waited upon by slaves. Lykos paid them no mind as he led his soldiers in through the busted door, pleased with how this day had gone so far. The fact that he was also dragging Delilah's corpse by her whip, which had been tied around her neck as a noose, was merely the cherry on top in his opinion.

The shouts of shock and surprise were kept to a minimum as the Talal soldiers dispersed through the crowd, herding the Emporo members to the sides of the room while the slaves were absorbed into their own ranks free of chains. At the far end of the room, sitting upon a chair more fit to be called a throne, was Eliza staring in horror at the remains of her lover.

"My beloved!" she cried as she rose from her chair. Lykos said nothing as he dragged the corpse closer before depositing it at her feet. "What have you done to my beloved?"

"Well she was a wild animal so I put her down," he replied dryly. He mentally prepared himself for several more useless minutes of banter before being able to kill her.

"Die!" Eliza screamed as she lunged forwards, launching fireballs at him as fast and plentiful as the falling rain. Lykos was badly burned before he managed to roll away and into cover behind an ornate pillar. Rising, he was surprised at the sheer amount of rage the woman possessed for her fallen lover and wished once more that he had simply burned the home to the ground.

"Lady Emporo, I relieve you of your title!" He tried to follow the proper rules of house conduct but she was making it difficult, what with the unending streams of fireballs. His cover was destroyed by one particularly large blast and he found himself exposed.

"Die you parasite!" Eliza roared as she sent a wave of lightning at him. He tried to roll underneath it but was caught in its arc. With a pained grunt he was thrown against the far wall where he laid stunned for just a moment. While there he had the painful realization that unless fortune favored him he was most likely going to lose for Lady Emporo's skill with magic vastly surpassed his own. As demonstrated by the fact that she began to throw around several elements simultaneously.

Instinctively Lykos broke the delicate tiles underneath his feet and created an earthen barrier for protection. Hiding behind the low earth wall as streams of fire, lightning, and ice soared through the air above him he looked about for anything to aid him. Spying Delilah's corpse he decided that it was his best option and made to move towards it but Lady Emporo was not going to allow that so easily.

With a wave of her hand she summoned four elemental golems: fire, earth, lightning, and water. They moved to stand vigil over Delilah's body, prepared to defend her until their destruction. Lykos noted that the exertion of creation appeared to have tired out Eliza who was panting off to the side where an almost invisible fifth elemental, one of air, stood watchfully by her side.

He scowled angrily. The magic and skill needed to create five elementals, and all of different aspects, was immense. Dispelling them would be no easy task because even though he could simply attack with other elements, the magic would feed them making them stronger. But then he wondered if he could use that to his advantage.

Sending forth a stream of fire towards the elementals, the fire elemental stepped forwards as expected. Lykos activated his magical sight and was pleased to see it absorbing his magic and becoming stronger as he fed it. Despite his constant attack, the other elementals made no move to assist their brother, and the fire elemental burned hotter and taller as his attack went on.

Lykos was the first to notice due to the magic within his eyes. As he fed magic into the fire elemental so too did its power grow, sending out waves of insufferable heat. The heat pounded upon its fellow elementals and with his enhanced eyes he could see them weakening. His plan was working.

It was the air elemental, despite being the furthest from its fiery brother, that fell victim first. In a great burst of flame the air elemental ignited surprising Eliza, her family, and the Talal soldiers.

"What just happened?" she demanded. Everyone's attention was drawn to the water elemental, whose watery surface was boiling and turning to steam. In a gush of steam the water elemental evaporated. "No!" Eliza realized with horror what he was doing.

The earth elemental's skin cracked and burned as it was reduced to ash and all that was left was the towering fire wrath, with great wings now augmenting its form and its much smaller brother made of lightning. Eliza tried to end her fire elemental but found the magic no longer answering to her. The magic he had thrown at the fire elemental to grow it had been absorbed, forcing its allegiance to switch. He now controlled the towering fire elemental.

Eliza roared with rage and sent her final elemental, the one made of lightning, against the flaming elemental demon under his control. When the two figures clashed, bolts of lightning and gushes of flames erupted, forcing the House Emporo members and the Talal soldiers to duck lest they be killed. Eliza and Lykos had no time to dodge such attacks, so focused as they were on controlling their elementals, and thus were burned savagely.

The two elements were locked in combat, neither gaining the ability to overpower the other as they fought. Lykos felt tremors of exhaustion wrack his body as the struggle went on, his control over the fire elemental slipping and he knew that if he did not soon find a way to end this conflict he would die.

The two elementals had not moved from their position near Delilah's body and it was the still form of that wretched woman that gave him another idea. Using his last shred of control over the fire elemental he had it send a gout of flame which caused her body to burst into flames. The fire elemental roared at its new found freedom but its exhalation only lasted but a moment before Eliza saw what had happened to her love.

"!!!" Her scream of rage was as magical as it was verbal and it shredded apart the two elementals and threw everyone to the ground dazed. She rushed to the side of her fallen love and tenderly stroked the burned face as tears fell.

Lykos had been thrown once more into the wall and slowly rose to his feet, burned, bruised, and bleeding but still alive. Across the room he saw Eliza kneeling over Delilah's body and he drew the dagger he had killed Delilah with. It was this dagger that he had melted Eliza's stolen ring into so long ago and it was time to return it to its owner.

He staggered across the room slowly under the watchful eyes of House Emporo and his soldiers, all of whom were shaken by the blast as well. He paid their frightened eyes no heed as they watched him for his only goal was to end the threat that was Eliza. Stopping behind her he listened to what she was whispering.

"We were so close my love, so close. We should have been able to defeat him and his allies but we failed. Oh how I long for your touch my love...." she whispered pitifully.

Lykos thrust the dagger through her back and into her heart. With a final gasp the woman fell on top of her love, joined once more together in death. Releasing his grip on the weapon he stood and looked casually around the room. With slow steps he walked to the chair that Eliza had been sitting in, the chair more fit to be called a throne. He sat and stared out upon the ballroom.

Gashes and burn marks ruined paintings, columns laid smash and cracked all around the space. The smooth stone tile was melted and warped in places and had been torn out in others. The Talal soldiers moved to stand in position around the room as the members of House Emporo walked towards him. Slowly, many unwilling, the gathered members of House Emporo knelt before him in surrender.

The death of one man can lead to hundreds, Lykos thought as he contemplated the fate of Plower. The large man had been jovial and a worthy fighter but as he sat upon that throne staring at the kneeling House Emporo he realized Plower was much more important. He had been an ally, a friend, and the men and women before him were party to those who ordered and facilitated his death.

Rage rose within him but he ruthlessly crushed it. You could not live for the dead. To do so would be to promote folly and he liked to think himself better than a fool. He nodded firmly to the Emporo and gestured for them to rise.

The battle for House Emporo was done.

Chapter Forty-Two

Lykos eyed the two women before him and pondered the choice he had. On his left stood Kiara, looking disdainfully down upon him from her greater height, further increased by how far she had stuck her nose up. On his right stood Amentha, much more stout than her twin sister with an additional burden upon her front: she was with child.

It took a few pointed questions to determine that the child was one of the few remaining Stultus offspring in the kingdom. The remaining bastards had either been killed during the Succession Trial or fled when it became obvious that they would never regain Pyrgos from House Talal. Amentha had feared that he would kill her and her child and thus had been reluctant to share the identity of the father but Kiara had outed her.

That choice was actually simple for Lykos. He would never kill Amentha or her child but neither women knew that. The real question he was pondering was which of the two sisters, who both claimed to be Eliza's heir, should be elevated to Lady Prodotis. Amentha was the younger but already pregnant with a heir who would be recognized by the other noble houses as noble birth. Kiara was the elder but the ease at which she revealed the identity of her sister's lover bothered him, she was either a social climber or uncaring towards blood and he did not desire either kind of person in a position of power over others.

"Amentha." The pregnant woman looked at him with frightful eyes. "You'll be the new Lady Emporo."

"What!" Both women were shocked albeit for different reasons. Rage burned in Kiara's eyes.

"But I am the elder sister!" she argued.

"Aye," he said, "but your sister is already pregnant with a child that the other houses will recognize. I expect both of you to run House Emporo."

Amentha looked confused. "You want us to both be Lady Emporo?" He shook his head.

"No. I expect you to listen to your elder sister's advice and to put your house in order. My allies and I will be watching closely."

Kiara spun around and stomped away with as much rage as a lady of a noble house was allowed to display. Amentha grasped both of his hands with her own. "Oh don't mind my sister Lord Talal. She always assumed that Aunt Eliza would pass the headship to her. Thank you for this opportunity my lord!"

He had been surprised when the members of House Emporo had knelt before him after he had killed Eliza and Delilah. Even more so when they requested that he choose their next head. It had taken several days of questioning to determine which one would be the most acceptable and willing to aid him in achieving his goals.

Most of House Emporo, and the common folk living in their territory, possessed slaves to some degree. At first Lykos wanted someone whose morals and ideals matched his own but quickly realized it was a fools errand. All of the members of House Emporo possessed slaves and willingly used them. So instead he examined how they treated their slaves and narrowed his choices down to the twins who had already been groomed by the former Lady Emporo. That Kiara betrayed her sister so easily only made the choice that much easier.

"There is one more thing Lady Emporo." He smiled as Amentha's face light up in excitement at the new title. "How many mages does House Emporo have ready to serve?"

She looked puzzled. "Only a dozen of my family have magic Lord Talal. Eight of those have been recalled to the Citadel, two are currently serving the Acolytes, and my sister and I are the last."

Lykos was shocked. "Only a dozen? You must have three or four times that number in your family."

Amentha shrugged. "Most of my family prefers to exercise material wealth instead of training their body or magic. I think my younger cousin Salvador was the last one to have his magic awoken. We threw a fantastic ball to celebrate! I had the most lovely dress...."

"Yes thank you," he interrupted, having no desire to hear about the evening in question. "Thank you for your time Lady Emporo, could you go over your estate and make sure everything is in order?"

"Of course Lord Talal." Amentha bowed as well as she was able to, mindful of the small human growing inside of her. She glided from the room leaving him alone with his thoughts.

Did every noble house truly have so few mages? And if the Citadel had recalled eight Emporo mages to its walls, what were they doing with them? Why had they not returned to defend their home? The questions were troubling in their implications as he left the ballroom.

"Was that wise?" Captain Avarc asked, rising from the wall he had been leaning against. "Kiara looked ready to spit fire when she stormed past."

"So she didn't actually spit any? That's a shame I was hoping to burn some of these atrocious paintings," Lykos replied as they walked through the Emporo home. The ugly frowns, frozen in time, stared down upon them. "Was it wise? Probably not but I need someone at least neutral to our ideals and Amentha is our best chance."

"Aye but a woman scorned and all that. It would be prudent to not keep such a lengthy list of enemies," Captain Avarc cautioned. Lykos hummed in agreement. The two men were joined by Commander Withers who grunted in greeting.

"Lady Prodotis demands the Nero in compensation," Commander Withers stated without preamble. Lykos and Captain Avarc both stared blankly at the man. "For our contribution towards eliminating the Emporo threat," he explained.

"Bold words from a house who did little actual fighting," Captain Avarc countered. Commander Withers swelled in anger.

"We fought just as hard as you did Falknor and we deserve compensation if we're not allowed to pillage the quarter!"

"Wealth," Captain Avarc sneered. "You parasites, is that all you care about?"

"No we also like blood, care to share your own?" Commander Withers stepped closer, laying a hand on his sword. Captain Avarc matched the motion and blood would have been shed if Lykos had not intervened.

"Enough," he ordered calmly, stepping between the two men. "Withers, how many shipbuilders does House Prodotis posses?"

The commander looked puzzled. "None we always just buy more boats from the Nero to replace our stock."

"So you want to put an entire quarter, that we've just conquered, in control of the things keeping your families and resources safe?" Lykos stated slowly, trying to impart just how foolish the demand was.

"Well we'd oversee them!" Commander Withers tried to defend their demand. Captain Avarc snorted.

"How would you know if the boat they just built for you was watertight? Despite our airships spending most of the time in the air we often land them in water. Our sailors have experience in performing repairs to keep our ships afloat while you Prodotis just allow your ships to sink."

Lykos cut in. "House Falknor will be taking over running the Nero. If Lady Prodotis desires to learn shipbuilding then she is more than welcome to talk to House Falknor concerning that matter. A strong relationship between the two houses is possible. Encouraged even."

Commander Withers gritted his teeth but nodded. "I will go inform my lady." Lykos and Captain Avarc watched the fuming man leave.

"Why do I have the feeling something very unpleasant is about to happen?" Lykos asked Captain Avarc who looked at him in confusion. Just as he opened his mouth to reply Commander Withers returned escorting Lady Prodotis.

"Lord Talal, I understand you've denied my humble request." Lady Prodotis pouted as Lykos and Captain Avarc bowed respectfully in greeting.

"Lady Prodotis, I was unaware that you were nearby. Welcome to the Emporo Chateau!" Lykos gestured to the home around them. She obligingly looked upon the decor.

"Well met indeed but don't you go distracting me," she mocked scolded him. "I greatly desire those shipyards."

"I am sorry to disappoint you Lilith but House Falknor would be better suited to oversee the Nero's shipyards. They posses the manpower and knowledge needed to oversee the Emporo shipbuilders to ensure no foul play occurs," he explained apologetically.

"I suppose there's nothing I could do to change your mind?" Her smile and implication made him blush but he remained firm. "Now about killing Delilah, I don't hold it against you at all."

The change in conversation threw him for a loop. "Killing Delilah?"

"Of course, I understand it was a necessity. Poor girl could never choose correctly. Why once she had two young lords fighting for her affections and she choose the one who died of a heart attack! Such a shame."

"Did you know her well?" he asked wondering what he was missing. Her head twitched quizzically as she looked at him.

"I would expect so, my sister and I were quite close once upon a time."

"Oh your sister!" Lykos coughed embarrassingly. "Right, your sister. Yes, sorry for killing her. Killing your sister," he finished awkwardly as the trio stared at him.

"Thank you Lykos for your kind words," her dry tone made him cringe at his mistake. "Sadly a number of months ago my sister and I disagreed at how best to improve our house's standing within the kingdom. She believed gold and thus the Emporo, were the best choice."

"And yourself Lady Prodotis?" Captain Avarc asked neutrally.

She smiled coyly him. "Sometimes you have to get a little dirty." Lykos enjoyed the sight of the older, more experienced man blushing at the sensual woman's words. Although he did wonder at her meaning. Delilah had used Eliza to control House Emporo, starting a war between them and House Agroti. Lykos wondered if Lady Prodotis wasn't doing the same to him now.

"Are you sure I couldn't convince you to spare me the Nero dear Lykos? I would take excellent care of it," she tried once more.

Lykos narrowed his eyes, his suspicion only tempered by the fact that as a lord of a house he too would do the same as Lady Prodotis if their circumstance were reversed. "I'm afraid not my lady, House Falknor has already been promised their shipyards. Yet there are no quarrels between allies, I'm sure we can gift you something that you desire."

Lady Prodotis very obviously eyed Lykos in a manner causing all three men to shuffle uncomfortably. "House Falknor will be making many airships I think. My house will be pleased with the increase business in the sale of our swamp gas. That, along with maintaining the levies through the Emporo canals, should keep them pacified."

Lykos spied the obvious concession demand and answered easily enough. "If House Prodotis desires to maintain the tolls on the canals I'm sure the Emporo will comply."

"Thank you Lord Talal, I hope to get in touch with you soon. Come Withers." Commander Withers obediently followed his lady as they exited the Emporo home. Captain Avarc turned towards Lykos.

"That woman made me feel as if I were inexperienced child."

Lykos nodded. "Yet I still find her utterly captivating. Often the most beautiful things are the most deadly."

"Well said my friend."

"Lord Talal! A message from the Agroti!" A Talal courier approached the duo rapidly. Lykos took the proffered scroll and unwound it. As he read the message from House Agroti, his face darkened slowly as the message sunk in. Finishing it he threw the message angrily towards a surprised Captain Avarc and began to pace in thought. Captain Avarc read the letter out loud:

"Lord Talal of House Talal. I have the unfortunate duty of informing you that Lord Rolan has passed away, the stress of war too much for his strained heart. As per Agroti law the lordship passes to his brother Rickard who has declared an end to our alliance with House Talal. Your forces are no longer allowed within our borders or allowed to patrol our farms. This is not a call for war but rather neutrality, we have no desire to continue your fight. Sincerely, Thaddeus Steward of House Agroti." Captain Avarc looked towards the angrily pacing Lykos. "Well this is unfortunate. I wonder why Rickard ended the alliance."

Lykos dismissed the courier before answering him. "He's never wanted to aid me. Every action I've taken he's opposed in some manner and now that he has the power to control the Agroti, he'll use it to be a royal pain in the ass. He's probably already barred the gates leading into the Nero."

Captain Avarc considered their options. "We could always use our air fleet to capture them. Install someone controllable like we did here."

Lykos was already shaking his head. "We are not tyrants. So long as he doesn't raise up arms against me or mine I am content to let him rot in the Lowland. We have the Emporo now and we can focus on House Sofos to end this blasted conflict. Let us return to your home and talk to Grimm."

"As you will it Lord Talal." Captain Avarc bowed his head and the two men departed.

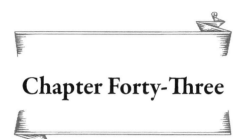

Chapter Forty-Three

Lykos twisted through the air, his opponent's sword swishing through the space his head had just vacated. Feinting forward he twirled his sword to the side and downwards, intending to trip his foe and force them to submission. But with a clang of steel and a shower of sparks his thrust was parried and he found himself defending furious strikes. He saw his opponent overextend and with a jab of his elbow struck them.

"Why do you always go for my face?" Grimm asked as he stumbled backwards to buy himself some time. "Trying to make me hideous so you have a chance with the ladies?" Lykos snorted in reply as he advanced quickly, bringing his sword to bare. Grimm blocked the blow sluggishly and failed in forcing him back, finding himself once more on the stone floor without a weapon. The Talal lord stood over the Sofos heir with the blades rested heavily upon the latter's neck.

"I yield!" Grimm cried and Lykos stepped back calmly with the weapons lowered. He rubbed his neck as he glared at the grinning lord. "I am no common swordsman but even I can see how you slew the Emporo at the Agroti's gate. Your blade work is only topped by your skill with magic."

Lykos acknowledged the compliment with a modest nod of the head. After securing House Emporo under his banner he had returned to Kremos, determined to end House Sofos' siege upon the quarter. He had worked tirelessly these past few weeks, talking and dueling with Grimm in order to convert him to his cause and it was slowly working. However Grimm needed a push to join him wholly and completely and Lykos pursued it eagerly.

Both men had acknowledged the fact that they had never had a proper duel, the Succession Trial having been interrupted by other combatants and the less said about their river duel the better, thus they did not know which of them was the better fighter. After stealing Grimm's sword from where it was being held, as Lord Falknor had been firmly against the idea, the two men gleefully began to duel and wreck Grimm's prison cell.

Lord Falknor had not been amused.

Lykos appreciated these little duels with Grimm although it rapidly became apparent that he was the superior swordsman. However he took it as an opportunity to challenge himself, using only his left arm or no hands and on one memorable occasion with his arms already tied up, and found the exercise to be enjoyable. Once Grimm got over the fact that he was outmatched, he too found himself enjoying Lykos' company.

"So what shall we talk about today Grimm?" Lykos asked, sheathing his sword and taking a seat at the chess table. Here the two men were much more evenly matched with the games often ending in draws or narrow defeats. Grimm joined him at the table.

"You could always tell me which one of your allies will be visiting me after you leave today. If it's one of the Dumas brothers or Helen I ask that you leave me the sword," he joked.

"Cheer up, she poisoned me when we first met. Your first encounter went remarkably better than my own."

"She threatened to castrate me!" Grimm protested in outrage. Lykos chuckled fondly at the memory.

After a week of only talking to Lykos, Grimm had begun to get antsy and had taken to bothering the servants bringing him food. Nothing violent but his vocal demands for information had caused more than a few mild panic attacks among the staff and Lord Falknor had stepped in. As Lykos could not be there all day, he did have business interests to watch over, raids to conduct, and training with Illusionist Maeve to do, many of their allies had taken turns to watching the young heir.

Helen and Grimm had disagreed on the proper form of address for the Valkyries. Helen's northern roots showed in her address where as Grimm was insistent on calling them Goddesses, both ignoring that they were merely two different names for the exact same thing. The resulting fight had alerted the guards who narrowly prevented the assassin from gutting the young heir. The look of terror on his face when Lykos had next seen him was something that still caused the occasional chuckles.

"But the next time you two talked it went well!" Lykos argued as he moved his knight. Grimm glared as he countered with his own.

"She gave me a six hour lecture on why the spirits should be honored in life!"

Lykos merely grinned in amusement. "Why are you so wary of the Dumas brothers?" he asked curiously, wondering if Grimm too saw Doukas as suspicious. Grimm grimaced in remembered pain.

"Giles insists on wrestling and Doukas is perhaps the most caustic healer I've ever had the misfortune of being healed by."

"At least your nose isn't crooked anymore."

"Yes at least my nose isn't crooked anymore. Wait, what?"

The morning passed easily for the two men, who despite their once status as enemies had found an easy camaraderie during their talks. But as with every day that had ended this past month, their conversations turned towards Lykos and the war.

"Why do you hesitate?" Lykos asked Grimm as servants brought in the midday meal.

"My father has told me my entire life how my mother died in your father's rebellion, an innocent bystander cut down for senseless war. Would you not be hesitant if our positions were reversed?"

"I would be hesitant of anyone's words in your situation," he answered honestly as he stood up grabbing Grimm's sword. "However I would try to keep an open mind to the facts of the situation."

"Oh and what facts would that be?" Grimm asked sullenly, reaching for the fresh bread.

"That I've been a prisoner for almost two months and that my father has not once asked for a cease fire," he replied before walking out the door. Grimm's hand fell from the bread as the heavy wooden door was secured once more.

Lykos sighed heavily as he walked along the stone hallway, intent on taking an airship back to Hearthome for his next lesson. Lykos and Lord Falknor were hesitant to simply invade the Riverfront for despite all of Lord Sofos' hostility, they did capture his son and kill many in his service. But the constant attacks on the gate were beginning to wear on the populace of both quarters and if something wasn't done soon there would be riots in the streets.

"How is the murderer today?" Falka spat as she joined him in his walk. He glanced at his friend and frowned. She had become withdrawn and angry without the distraction of a fight, liable to snap at even close friends or family. While he could understand her anger he longed for the return of his friend and thus had allowed her behavior towards his prisoner. That would end now.

"Why don't you ask him yourself?" Lykos offered Grimm's sword to her. She looked down at it as if he had just offered a Tainted Viper. "Take the afternoon watch."

"I'm not going to watch him! And I'm sure as the Valkyries not going to give him a weapon!" she protested angrily. He gave her a hard stare that caused her to flinch.

"I understand that you're still grieving Ana's death," her face turned sorrowful immediately, "but your actions are rude, petty, and quite frankly childish."

Her face rapidly filled with wrath. "You dare think you know my sorrow! To know what I am going through!"

"I dare!" he roared back, stepping closer. She reared back but he did not halt his advance, staring at his friend with hard eyes. "You are not the only person whose lost someone of great importance to you!"

"Well who have you lost in this war!" Falka cried, tears falling from her eyes. "Why am I the only one who has lost someone?"

"I lost her too." She looked up at him through watery eyes. "Everyday I miss Ana and not just because of how happy she made you. She was exactly how I imagined a younger sister to be, always curious about everything around her, eager to experience new things. The world became a darker place without her in it."

He wrapped her in a hug and held her as she cried. He then whispered into her ear, "remember when Shawna first served her tea?"

Falka nodded and hiccuped. "I thought she was going to faint!"

"And then when Adelram showed up and demanded to know why someone had drank his?"

"Ana panicked so badly that we both claimed to have drank his. And then he chased you around the garden with a stick. She giggled so much that she fell out of her chair." Falka hiccuped as she rubbed her eyes free of tears.

"All of you seem to be fond of chasing me to inflict violence upon me. I almost feel unwanted."

They shared a laugh and parted. He gently stroked her cheek and glanced at Grimm's sword in his hand. "Do you blame Grimm for Ana's death?"

"No." Falka fidgeted with the edge of her dresses sleeve. "Yes. I don't know! He's a Sofos!"

"Yes he is. He was also in another quarter entirely when assassins murdered their way through your home. Assassins contracted by his father and Eliza. No one should carry their father's sins."

"They hold you to yours," Falka muttered.

"And I rise above them. We do not need to sink to their level of pettiness in order to prevail. I want you to talk to Grimm and realize that he is just as much of a victim as you are."

Falka growled. She ranted. She glared and threatened to enact nasty retribution against him but he remained firm in his decision. He needed Grimm on his side and he need Falka to not want to murder a potential ally. Holding out the sword once more to her he gestured for her to take it. Reluctantly her fingers closed around the cold steel.

Falka stepped into the room that had been Grimm's cell for weeks and her eyes immediately fell upon him. The young man was laying on the bed, gazing up at the ceiling and had not turned when she had entered.

"So which Dumas brother is watching me today? Giles? Doukas? Wait whoever entered doesn't stink so it must be a woman. Demos? Don't tell me it's you Helen I don't want to argue with anyone today."

"My name is Falka."

Grimm's head perked up to stare at her. She stood as still as stone by the now barred door clutching his sword in one hand, trembling ever so slightly. He studied her face with an intensity that bordered on obsession and that almost caused him to miss her next words.

"And I want you to die."

In a blur of movement she crossed the room in a series of bounds and held his sword to his throat. The pair stared deep into each other's eyes, one in resignation and the other in anger, and the moment stretched across heartbeats. He stared up at her trembling form and finally spoke.

"Very well." His quiet acceptance did not sit well with her. She wanted a fight, to rage against an enemy, the person who had caused Ana to die! Yet standing over him, a blade held to his throat, she only felt empty. With a savage cry she thrust the sword downwards.

"Did you really have to destroy my pillow?" he asked in amusement as feathers flew through the air. Falka sank to her knees and collapsed against the wall next to Grimm's bed.

"That utter bastard," she whispered. "He knew I wouldn't be able to do it."

"Lord Talal?" Grimm asked as he slowly sat up. He eyed the sword pinning his pillow to the bed but ignored it in favor of Falka. "Sounds like Lord Talal."

"I am going to kill him," she muttered darkly. Grimm slowly slid off his bed until he was sitting next to her on the ground.

"Definitely Lord Talal," he commented dryly. They remained in silence, each consumed by their own thoughts. He began to fiddle with his hands and glanced at her out of the corner of his eye. "So why do you want me dead?"

It took several long moments for her to answer and only then it was after she shook her head causing her hair to obscure her face. "Someone very dear to me died from the assassins your family contracted."

Grimm clenched his hands. "I'm sorry I didn't know-"

"Of course you didn't know!" She scrambled on top of him and began to beat him with her fists. "You don't know anything because you're worthless! You were just doing what you were told and you never even hurt anyone! Thanks. To. Lord. Bloody. Talal!" Each word was punctuated with a smack to Grimm's face who looked quite dazed at the sudden assault. But just as quickly as it began it ended and she curled up on the floor next to the startled Grimm.

"My name is Grimm, I'm-" he tried to bring some semblance of normality back to the situation by introducing himself properly but she interrupted.

"Heir Sofos, I know," she muttered crossly.

"Right." Grimm eyed her curled up form and contemplated rubbing her back to provide comfort. Somehow he doubted that was the correct course of action and instead settled for gingerly examining his bruising face. "You hit quite hard."

"You should shut up," she warned however Grimm had decided to leave his sanity on the bed with his impaled pillow.

"Falka is an interesting name, similar to House Falknor in fact. Considering the crest sewn into your dress I think it would be safe to presume that's your house." He ignored Falka's growling as he continued, "you're either a younger member or from one of the cadet branches otherwise I'd be more familiar with your name and face. But I suppose the real question is why are you helping Lord Talal watch me?"

At Lykos' title Falka stopped trembling with rage. Quietly pulling herself off the floor, she moved away from her spot and began to pace the small room. Grimm hastily stood to move out of her way, standing in the middle of the room to watch her never ending circle. She began to speak.

"I always desired a little adventure. I'm far too low on the right to succession to ever be notable which allowed me more than a little leeway when it comes to my actions. Running around with criminals and flesh maidens, my family put up with my adventures so long as I didn't do any real damage to our name. I took advantage of such a view often, stealing trifles or learning how to duel from father's soldiers."

She smiled wistfully in fond remembrance. "That's how I met Lykos actually. It was at the Stultus ball before we killed them. I was just there to see what treasures I could steal away and if I was caught? That's what the sword was for. But then I saw him.

"He was out of his depth, it was obvious to anyone watching him. No one would give him the time of day so when he left the party I followed. And what a marvelous meeting we had. We both threatened to kill the other within seconds before recognizing a kindred soul in the other. With all the distrust of thieves, we joined forces to rob the Stultus blind.

"I always wondered why he never asked me why I was trying to steal from the Stultus. I stole because I was curious and frustrated and I wanted something more from life. But even back then he only stole for a purpose, to live, to survive. He stole because he refused to die. He refused to yield to the suffering that he had experienced before he broke free from his chains. To him it was never a question of morality or joy, it was necessity and he was and will always be willing to do what ever is necessary to survive.

"It made me feel petty. I am skilled with the blade, in theft, and all the skills a lady is required to know. Yet for all my skill, many greater than his own, I still found myself lesser to a man who knew his purpose in life. I desired that purpose, I was envious that he knew what he wanted."

Falka never stopped her endless pace as she circled Grimm, who had been lulled into a false sense of security by her monologue. Thus when she suddenly grasped the sword still impaled to his bed and whipped it around to once more touch his throat, he flinched in surprise.

"What is it that you want I wonder?" she asked as she circled him, the tip never leaving his throat. The young heir was intelligent enough to keep eye contact with her, rotating so that his back was never exposed to the weapon in her hand. "You know what Lykos wants, he is frightfully honest about his intentions, and I help him because out of everyone I have ever met in my life he was the first to state his desires, then ignore them."

Grimm stopped in surprise while she continued to trace his neck. "What do you mean ignore them? He's raided dozens of slave pens over the last year!" he protested.

Falka shook her head at his misunderstanding. "The night I met him he was determined to rob House Stultus blind and I was receptive to that request but then we met them. They were vile men, horrible humans who were an insult to me, Lykos, every noble in the kingdom and just like that his intentions changed. He was no longer content to simply steal from those wretched men, not after their deplorable behavior towards me. They were marked for death because they were crude, vulgar creatures.

"We followed them through the estate." She smiled manically. "I killed more guards than him back then although he's worked hard to catch up recently. We found them torturing Ana. I wanted to rush in but Lykos always preferred a more stealthy, clever approach. He used his magic to great effect that evening although he couldn't quite stop one of them from slicing one of his hands off."

"Wait!" Grimm cried out and she paused with the blade to the side of his neck. Turning to face her he continued,"House Stultus died around a week before the Succession Trial. Do you mean to tell me he fought with an injured arm? How?"

Falka smirked. "He's just as much flesh and blood as you and I and while his skill with magic is exceptional, there is one thing that separates us from him, an ocean wide gap. Care to guess what it is?"

"He's bloody suicidal?" Grimm muttered and for the first time in weeks Falka truly laughed.

"He is driven. And that is why I stand with him. No matter what obstacle gets in his way the moment you give him a goal he will achieve it no matter the cost. When he says he will free the slaves and bring this kingdom to peace, he will.

"But this brings us all back to you. He wants you to help him but I don't know why. All I see before me is a pampered heir whose first true battle in the war led him to being outsmarted by his enemy."

"He summoned a tidal wave!" Grimm protested. She merely gave him an unimpressed look as if he were an idiot.

"Regardless, you gave in. You had no drive, nothing to stand for, nothing to believe in. So that's what I ask you Heir Sofos, what is it that you believe in? What is the burning desire in your heart that you feel earnestly every single morning when you wake, that keeps you up at night? What will you fight for, die for, kill for!"

Falka raised the sword as if to strike but Grimm was prepared, lunging forward to knock the weapon from her hands and tackling her to the ground. She scratched at his face with her fingers and he retaliated by biting them forcing her to stop. He tried to pin her to the ground but she broke his nose and the pair split apart breathing heavily. They paused for one long moment, glaring and sizing the other, before lunging forward together once more.

They destroyed the room. Grimm's sword laid forgotten under a broken desk, courtesy of Falka kicking him into it. The broken bookshelf lay with its books spread torn all over the floor from when he brought it down upon her. The bed had been flipped, the sheets used to block improvised weapons, and feathers covered the ground. And collapsed in the middle of the room lay two bloody figures groaning softly in pain.

"You're better than Lykos," Grimm complained as his magic worked slowly at healing his injuries. Despite not using it to fight the fiendish woman who possessed no magic of her own he found himself often outmatched by her ferocity. She gave him a bloody grin.

"You're not." She rolled unsteadily to her feet and examined her bloody hands. "Although you do bleed more than him."

"Ha ha," he deadpanned as he leaned against the destroyed bed watching her. "Is Lord Falknor going to call your guards in to drag me to the dungeons for hurting you?"

"He might give you a reward for landing a hit on me actually. He did spend a great deal of coin on my tutors when I was young." She scooped up his sword from where it lay. "Think about it."

"Think about what?" he asked.

"What do you believe in? Rest well Grimm." Falka knocked on the heavy wooden door which was opened without delay. The two Falknor soldiers were not even fazed to see a bloodied Falka leaving with an exposed blade and she passed quickly under their gaze.

"Goodnight Falka." Grimm replied softly, almost too quietly for her to hear. The raven-haired woman gave him a soft nod before walking away silently. The two men briefly stared into the damaged room but reached for the wooden door without comment. As the door shut Grimm sat there quietly, his wounds still dripping blood despite the efforts of his magic. He had a lot to think about.

Lykos stepped off the airship and nodded to the bloodied and bruised Falka. "Good morning my friend. I do hope you didn't break my prisoner too badly."

She gave him a mocking smile and his heart leaped at the familiar sight. "Lord Talal, we have company," she said gesturing behind him. He turned and was intrigued to see a haggard Grimm standing at attention in torn clothing and without chains. Lykos raised his eyebrow to ask the silent question: *Are you with me?*

"Lord Talal, I Heir Sofos pledge my support and aid to you, to bring peace and justice to this kingdom. My sword shall rise for you, my magic shall shield you, and my House will heed your call." Grimm knelt before him. "I am yours to command."

Lykos smiled in satisfaction and turned to Falka who wordlessly tossed him Grimm's sword. "Rise Grimm," he commanded. Grimm did as he was bidden and Lykos tossed him his sword. "There is work to be done my friend."

Chapter Forty-Four

"I knew you were suicidal but this is just insane," Grimm told Lykos as they walked through the dark streets of Kremos. It was a cool night, the bitter chill that had been sapping the kingdom finally broken, although the snow and ice still remained. As such the streets were empty of people to witness the sight of Grimm leading a chain bound Lykos towards the Riverfront.

"Your father told you to kill me. Imagine how happy he will be to see that you've instead managed to capture me and are bringing me home to face his wrath," he replied all too happily for the umpteenth time.

"Utterly insane," Grimm repeated shaking his head. Lord Falknor had especially been displeased to learn the details of Lykos' plan, calling it unnecessary and dangerous. The Sofos forces would never be able to breach Kremos' gate due to its superior fortifications and the Emporo blockaded both them and the Agroti from the south. Ignoring them until they decided to be reasonable seemed to be the much more intelligent plan to Lord Falknor. Falka also sided with her father but further questioning revealed that she only wished to go along with them on their suicidal venture and was put out at not being invited.

Captain Avarc was the only one who understood the genius of his plan although he believed it would have been just as effective with him as the bait. Lykos put his foot down and instead asked the older man to personally look after his mother Shawna in case this did turn for the worst. Reluctantly Avarc had agreed.

So in the bitter morning Lykos walked through streets bound in chains that looked secure but were actually loosely tied about his wrists and chest. Grimm carried his sword in one hand while "pulling" him along with the other. Sometimes he just yanked the chain for his own amusement, causing Lykos to stumble theatrically.

Finally the two men made it to the quarter's gate and passed through without incident. The Falknor soldiers looked at them in amusement and he made sure to make a show of being a reluctant prisoner.

"Oh woe is me! I've been captured," he pretended to swoon as the soldiers laughed. "The mighty Heir Sofos has captured me."

"I'm glad you're enjoying yourself. You do realize the guards might simply turn you into a pincushion with arrows once they see you right?"

"Such terrible threats! Have mercy on me!" Lykos cried mockingly. Grimm gave an extra yank of the chain causing him to stagger. Lykos smiled but allowed himself to be pulled into the courtyard at the base of Kremos. Before them stood the gate leading into the Riverfront, manned by Sofos soldiers who looked at the pair with growing interest.

"How did you summon that titanic wave Lykos?" Grimm asked suddenly as they stared at the heavily guarded wall. Lykos gave him a sly smile.

"I didn't."

"Don't try to deny it, that was no illusion. Even Illusionist Maeve would have been incapable of such a feat."

"I didn't summon it," Lykos stated firmly, his eyes dancing with mischief. Grimm sighed in frustration.

"Then where did it come from?"

"The ocean."

"....What?"

"The Agroti water their fields using the tides of the ocean every morning and evening. As you saw it's an impressive sight capable of great destruction. I merely waited for the sun to rise and nature did the rest." Lykos could not help but laugh at the shocked look on Grimm's face.

"I'm really surprised you didn't know this, I mean you've lived next to the Lowland your entire life. Didn't you ever see or hear it?" Grimm looked down as he burned red in embarrassment.

"You seriously didn't know this did you?" Lykos asked rhetorically.

"Shut up," Grimm said.

"I will never let you forget this."

"Shut up," Grimm said slightly more forcefully.

"Not ever."

"Shut up," Grimm hissed, eyeing the motionless gates before them.

"Falka will be very amused to hear this."

"I swear if you tell her I'll kill you."

Lykos chuckled quietly to himself as Grimm pulled him forwards. The heavy gate before them swung open and several Sofos soldiers rushed out to level spears at them.

"Halt! Who goes there?" the leader asked.

"Heir Sofos with his prisoner, Lord Talal," Grimm replied and the gathered Sofos soldiers began to whisper excitedly.

"Heir Sofos? I thought you were being held prisoner my lord?"

"I was. I escaped and was fortunate enough to capture this miscreant." Grimm smirked as he tugged on the chain tied to Lykos. "I must make haste to my father for our fight ends this day!"

The gathered Sofos soldiers cheered and formed up around the two men. As one, they marched into the Riverfront, Grimm pulling his "unwilling" prisoner along. However Lykos was thankful for the tugs as they allowed him examined the Riverfront territory covertly.

It was beautiful. As its name suggested rivers were plentiful here, crisscrossing the quarter in a intricate maze of water. The buildings lining the water were held up by sturdy stones and covered in artfully carved wood. He could understand why the quarter was famed for its relaxing atmosphere, even during the winter. The few civilians they saw had pleasant expressions on their faces, unconcerned with the skirmishes being fought just steps away from their houses.

It set his nerves on edge with how wrong it felt.

Peering deeper he could see the suffering he saw in all parts of the kingdom. The beggars being hustled away by patrolling guards, the slaves cleaning the stone streets and buildings obediently. For all the beauty of the Riverfront, it too carried the disease that the plagued the kingdom and he vowed to cut it out.

However he felt calm as even more soldiers joined them on their trek to Grimm's home. He did not believe himself foolish enough to take Grimm's change of heart at face value, he had been attacked far too many times for that. But glancing sideways towards Grimm's face told him all that he needed to know about the situation: Grimm was resolute and determined. Only time would tell if he followed the plan or if he would be forced to kill the other man before killing his father.

"He won't surrender you know," Grimm whispered to him as they marched.

"I know," he replied softly.

Grimm sighed heavily. "So he's to be put to death then?" he asked rhetorically.

"Locking him in a cell for the rest of his life might have been acceptable were it not for your family's rules on succession," Lykos said apologetically, knowing that if a Lord Sofos lived his heir was honor bound to free him. The two men lapsed into silence as Grimm's home appeared before them and he felt his heart quicken in anticipation. It was time to see if his trust in Grimm was well placed. The majority of the soldiers remained outside but two of them escorted them into the sprawling building.

Despite living so close to the outer edge of the kingdom, House Sofos had a history just as ancient as House Talal's, and the many statues, paintings, and tapestries decorating the entry hall reflected this. Many of them depicted events Lykos had seen dozens of times over within Hearthome and he wondered at just how much of their history was shared. His reflection was cut short however, at the appearance of Arachnis.

The man was unwashed, his beard unkempt, and heavy bags under his eyes. Yet despite this, a satisfied smirk crossed his face at the sight of his son dragging Lykos by chains. The man stepped forward and threw his arms wide in exaltation.

"At last my wife's spirit can rest!" he cried. "Guards take Lord Talal from my son."

As they reached out to grasp his arms Grimm cut in. "Nonsense, leave us at once," he ordered sharply. The two men gave Lord Sofos uneasy glances but he waved them away, staring at his son in confusion.

"I only desired to help you my heir," Lord Sofos claimed as he stared at his son in confusion. "I sent you to kill the offspring of that monster and instead you captured and brought him home! I am so proud." He turned towards Lykos. "As for you warmonger, you've met your match at my hands! I will make you pay dearly for my wife's death all those years ago."

"Yes father, tell me again how did mother die?" Grimm asked, bringing his father's attention back to him.

"Grimm?"

Grimm dragged Lykos along as he marched towards his father. "I've thought about all the stories you've told me, all the lies you've spoken."

"They weren't lies!" Arachnis protested.

"I've thought long and hard over my upbringing, pondered deeply on the words you've spoken yet it wasn't until I was in the clutches of my supposed enemies that I saw the truth! That you are the monster you always claimed Leon to be!"

"Preposterous!" Arachnis spat, his eyes mad. "I have only ever looked out for you, raised you!"

"Then tell me the truth! So we can finally end this." Grimm shook Lykos' chains meaningfully and a cruel smile crossed Arachnis' face before fading into sorrow.

"Your mother and I disagreed on how to handle Leon's little war. I wanted nothing to do with him, why should I care about the suffering of others, I have my own to look after but she wanted to help. We fought and she," Arachnis' breathe hitched, "left me. She left me here wounded and went to go find Leon, that bastard, to heal him after his battles!

"It was an insult! An embarrassment, to have my own wife leave me to aid another man. I had to pretend to the other houses, our own family, that she had taken ill but everyday I feared the truth getting out. I knew something had to be done, far too many months had already passed, so I sneaked out of my own home in the dead of night, like a criminal! And I went to find her. And find her I did!" Arachnis spat.

"She had laid with him! And the proof was in her swollen belly! That wretched beast had laid with another man's wife and fathered offspring!" Arachnis grew red with fury. "I returned to this house and ordered the bitch killed! She betrayed our marriage oaths, she betrayed my trust, and she tried to drag our house into

Leon's wretched rebellion! The only thing she ever did right was birth me a heir that I could claim as my own!"

Grimm punched his father square in the mouth. Unfortunately this was with the hand holding Lykos' chain causing him to join Arachnis on the floor. Grimm drew his sword and stood over the two men, staring down at them with the fury and rage of one who had been raised in lies.

"You are weak and pathetic," Grimm told his father furiously. "I have always wondered why you demanded so much more from me than you ever would have been able to do. It was because your magic was worthless, your arms weak, and you hated the fact that my father was not you. You could have raised me as my mother's son but instead you tried to turn me into you. Any last words Arachnis?"

"Your mother would be disgusted by you, you bastard," Arachnis tried to claim. With a savage roar Grimm's blade fell, piercing his father's heart. The man struggled briefly before succumbing to the strike.

"And she would have done that to you years ago." Grimm spat on Arachnis' corpse as Lykos slowly lifted himself from the floor, removing the chains as he rose. "Of all the things to learn here tonight, being your half-brother wasn't what I expected."

"Not quite," Lykos stated absentmindedly. Grimm's head whipped around to stare at him. He cringed at his impulsiveness. Too late to keep quiet about it now. "At least I'm not sure on my end."

"What do you mean?" Grimm asked puzzled.

"Well, when I was in the slave mines I was told my parents had been killed during the raiding party. I had thought that my entire family had been killed up there in the north until I came down to Mycenae and touched the Talal awakening stone. That's when Shawna claimed me as her and Leon's son. So I don't truly know if we are brothers or cousins or something else. The Talal blood could come from anywhere."

Grimm was silent for a long moment in thought and Lykos wondered what he would do with this information. "It doesn't matter. You're my brother, if not by blood then by battle. You brought the truth to my eyes, have given me a reason to fight, as far as I'm concerned that makes us family."

Lykos nodded gratefully. "With your father dead you're clear to take over House Sofos." His statement brought a frown to Grimm's face.

"I'm not the true blood heir though. By rights it should pass to my uncle Fernuclus."

"Would he be amiable to our goals?"

Grimm answered without hesitation, "no, if he were Lord Sofos he'd try to kill you for suggesting taking away the source of his workforce. He and my aunt run all of the flesh palaces in the quarter and slave labor is his main source of income. If he controlled House Sofos I imagine it'd only become worse."

"As far as I'm concerned only three people know that you're not actually of Sofos blood. One of them is dead, another isn't sure they themselves are of Talal blood, and the last is you."

Grimm considered his implied proposition. "This doesn't solve how I'll deal with my uncle or anyone else who uses slaves in the quarter."

Lykos shrugged. "The same way the Emporo are dealing with it. They may hire on any of the former slaves for their workforce but they aren't allowed to abuse them any longer. Anyone who tries will find themselves made an example of."

"Isn't that harsh?"

"As far as I'm concerned anyone taking unwarranted privileges with another does not deserve mercy."

Chapter Forty-Five

L ykos once more found himself at a ball and was beginning to wonder if this is what his life would consist of once he finished ridding the kingdom of slavery. The event was being held at the Emporo Chateau to celebrate the spring season and that the trade routes to Svellheim were safe once more to transverse. He shuddered at the thought of ever willingly returning to the frozen kingdom.

Still the party was in good cheer as House Emporo celebrated not being burned to a crisp by his army. Here and there members of the conquered house glared at him but he bore it in good humor, they had lost after all. Grimm's voice cut into his thoughts.

"So what do you think of Falka?" he asked nodding towards where the raven-haired woman was being circled by a group of giggling children. Lykos smiled slightly at his transparency.

"I think that while children like her, she's growing quiet vexed with them herself," he replied.

"Well yeah but she's still good with them," Grimm complimented her. Before their eyes the woman in question was dragged into yet another dance with the little rascals.

"Thinking of the future already?" Lykos tried not to laugh at Grimm's surprised expression.

"No! No. Not at all! Well maybe just a little. No, certainly not!" Grimm protested as Lykos lost his silent battle and chuckled at the denials.

"Well before you get too far ahead in planning your wedding, you should find out if she's even amenable to the idea," he suggested.

"Grimm's being married? Oh you must tell me everything!" a pleased female voice cried out from behind the two men. Standing there was the new Lady Emporo, Amentha, whose swollen belly had grown since the last time Lykos saw her. Grimm's horrified face at the sight of her gave him a devious idea.

"Well he certainly hopes but you see he's been having some problems my dear Amentha." He leaned closer to her in a collaborative manner as Grimm stared at him in utter horror. "I'm glad you're here my lady for you see Grimm desperately needs the opinion of a woman! Perhaps you could take him aside and explain the missing facts for him?"

Amentha smiled knowingly at him. "Of course my lord! Attend me Lord Sofos and I shall explain to you everything you need to know." Grimm was probably unaware of being dragged away, so focused he was on Lykos' betrayal. With soft chuckles Lykos waved goodbye mockingly.

"Are you enjoying tormenting our newest ally?" Giles asked as he stepped forward with two mugs of mead in his hands. Handing one to Lykos the large man continued, "probably for the best. The poor lad needs to toughen up some."

"You're right, I should assign someone to double check his skill." Giles puffed out his chest with a proud look on his face. "I'll ask Illusionist Maeve to do it."

Giles' chest fell and he scowled. "You're a cruel man Lord Talal."

Lykos raised his mug in salute before taking a long pull of the honey flavored drink. Smacking his lips, he became aware of peculiar acrid taste mixed in that felt most wrong to his tongue. Turning to Giles he opened his mouth to speak when a nasty bout of nausea racked his body.

"What did you just give me?" he managed to choke out, as his stomach roiled painfully. With no small amount of terror he realized he had been poisoned. He dropped the poisoned mead to the floor, causing it to shatter and splash everywhere.

"I don't know! I gave you the mug Doukas gave me!" Giles cried out to his alarm. His shout attracted the nearby party goers attention and Lykos began to feel his limbs lose their strength. "Doukas! Get over here!"

As Lykos knelt weakly he became aware of several approaching figures. Soft hands grabbed his arm and began to drag him across the floor. Giles stepped forward and grabbed his other arm, and the pair of them half-carried Lykos from the ball room.

Finding himself deposited on a couch he saw Falka and Giles staring down at him in concern. His eyes unsteadily focused on Falka as his head began to pound with each beat of his heart. "Falka I need you to get Shawna somewhere safe. Adelram too. If you can try to get Illusionist Maeve to protect them that would be great."

"Lykos you aren't going to die," she argued. He could feel his magic trying to find and burn out the poison but it was moving too slowly to save him. He felt true dread when he realized he was going to die.

"Lord Talal!" Lilith hurried towards him with Doukas by her side. "What happened?"

"He's been poisoned! Quick Doukas, save him!" Giles ordered his brother. Lykos felt a tremor of alarm and tried to protest but his strength was rapidly fading. He was unable to prevent Doukas from checking his health.

After several grim moments the healer spoke up. "I can't do anything. I recognize the smell of this poison, it's the Huntsman's Bane. The only known cure are Tainted Tears."

Lilith perked up. "We are most fortunate!" She stepped forwards and reached for her bodice, undoing the top few knots.

Lykos would have been much more interested in the view had poison not been coursing through his body at the time. Undoing the last knot, she removed a small vial that was being held between her bosom. Handing it to Doukas she began to retie her dress.

"Hurry up and give it to him you fool!" Falka demanded of him when it became clear the healer was still staring at Lilith's exposed flesh. Snapping out of it, he approached Lykos who began to struggle, not wanting the possible spy and traitor near him. However the healer paid his struggles no mind and poured the Tainted Tears down his throat.

Tainted Tears were an exceedingly rare ingredient that were incredibly difficult to harvest. Tainted do not often cry, their bodies well armored and hardy, thus torturing them until tears fell was impossible. In fact the only known time for Tainted to cry was during the full moon and getting close enough to collect them was an exercise in insanity due their combative nature. Regardless the thick blackish liquid was more valuable ounce for ounce than gold and those who survived harvesting even a few encounters lived well.

That Lilith had such a vial on her person tonight was indeed "fortunate".

Lykos could not stop the thick liquid from being poured into his mouth nor stop himself from swallowing it. The liquid was not foul as he expected and though dazed he was reminded strongly of raspberries. Warmth bloomed in his belly and without warning he found himself doubling over and vomiting streams of black gunk. However with the black gunk's appearance, his magic began working much more effectively in removing the poison from his body and he rapidly regained his strength.

"Gross," Falka said as she moved out of the way. Lykos gave her an annoyed look but privately agreed, the foul substance on the floor was quite offending to be near. Blessedly he was done and wiped his mouth.

THE RISE OF LYKOS

"That was thoroughly unpleasant." Realizing that his father had died to a similar poison, if not that exact one in particular, he questioned Doukas, "why didn't you have the antidote?"

"We were at a party with our allies, I didn't think I'd need my kit!" he protested. Lykos gestured to Giles to pull him to his feet.

"Start. And tell the rest of our healers to do the same. Skills are only useful when the needed tools are on hand." He swayed momentarily before regaining his balance. "Did anyone see you drag me out here?"

"A few of our allies but for the most part everyone was preoccupied with the ball Lord Talal," Giles answered. "With any luck they'll just think you were drunk."

Lykos grunted and turned towards the patiently observing Lilith. "My thanks for your Tainted Tears Lilith. Your assistance was most timely."

The edge of suspicion in his voice did not go amiss by Lady Prodotis. "I have several vials hidden within my bodice. If you would like you could examine me much more thoroughly at a later date my lord," she finished flirtatiously.

Any response by Lykos was cut off by a deep voice. "You certainly have a much more hardy constitution than Leon. Or perhaps you're simply lucky that your allies aren't as useless as his were."

Lykos and his allies turned to the doorway to see Alithis and a distinguished looking man missing one eye. He gave a small frown: it seemed it was finally time to meet the man who murdered his father.

"Lord Kolos I presume?" he asked thankful for the weight of his weapons at his waist. Stepping around Giles he examined the man who had killed Leon and forced his mother to be a captive in her own home. The man's fine robes did little to conceal the armor underneath, shiny black scales of some wretched Tainted beast protecting him. Yet there was an air of ozone around the man as if lighting had struck recently. With barely any effort he examined Lord Kolos with his magic.

A storm raged underneath the man's skin, endlessly raging. Lykos was reminded strongly of a hurricane beating harshly upon a mammoth rocky cliff: an unstoppable force meeting an immovable object was an apt description of his magic. Alithis in comparison was closer to Lykos' own yet as he allowed the magic to fade from his eyes he knew both men were beyond him magically at the present. There was a bitter taste in his mouth not caused by the poison as he thought about how much stronger, faster, more powerful he needed to become to fight his foes on fair ground. But between the mines and Illusionist Maeve's teachings he knew to never fight fairly.

"Lord Talal, I was hoping we could have a chat." Lord Kolos' voice was strong as he gave the silent order for everyone to leave the room. Alithis pointedly opened the door and stepped through it as Lord Kolos examined Lykos with his singular dark eye. Lilith and the Dumas brothers quickly fled the room but Falka stepped closer to him.

"So chat," she challenged. Lord Kolos' gaze switched to her for a fraction of a second and Lykos witnessed the effect of magic on someone without it. Falka shuddered and took half a step back, as if pushed by a gust of wind. He wondered if he had a similar effect on people or if Lord Kolos was simply using his magic for extra effect.

"I'll meet you in the library Falka," Lykos quietly suggested. She gave him a small nod and skirted the room around Lord Kolos. As soon as she crossed the threshold Alithis shut the door, leaving them alone.

Lord Kolos admired the puddle of black gunk on the floor for a moment before twisting his hand. A flame shot from his hand faster than Lykos could react and struck the puddle, rapidly burning it to a crisp. Then the much older, very dangerous, lord smirked at him, his eye darkening in amusement when he saw that Lykos had leaped out of the way and drawn his sword to attack.

"Put that away boy," Lord Kolos ordered before nodding to the singed floor. "A curious aspect of using Tainted Tears is that the resulting puddle will turn into acid and burn through whatever medium it touches. I think we'd both like this conversation to go uninterrupted."

Lykos slowly, unwillingly, sheathed his blade. The older lord had cast magic far faster than he thought possible, faster than even Illusionist Maeve, and he worried that if Lord Kolos attacked he wouldn't have time to defend himself. It was a troublesome thought.

"It's fascinating," Lord Kolos said as he stared at Lykos.

"What is?" Lykos asked through ground teeth.

"Your face. You have the same dull gleam of stupidity in your eyes that your *father* possessed before he met his unfortunate end." Lykos felt a brief flash of anger before he ruthlessly crushed it.

"A man will always focus on what he wants most," he taunted, deliberately stepping into Lord Kolos' blind spot that Leon had created. Lord Kolos frowned but turned so that he remained in view.

"I see you're just as lacking in manners and forethought as your *father*." A small smile crossed Lord Kolos' face. Lykos frowned at the strange inflection Lord Kolos put on the word father.

"What's so amusing?" he asked.

Lord Kolos began to laugh mockingly. "You've managed to convince everyone your Leon's son when I know your not!"

Chapter Forty-Six

Lykos felt shock, horror, and panic in rapid succession at Lord Kolos' proclamation. Belatedly he tried to school his expression but the damage was done.

"Don't try to deny it. I already know the truth as I always have. Nothing happens in this kingdom without my knowledge or permission." He smirked at Lykos whose thoughts began to race a mile a minute, possible plans to flee the kingdom, killing the man in front of him, all passed through his mind in an instant. He forced his panicking heart to slow as reason made its way through his mind: Lord Kolos wanted something.

"What do you want?" he asked, his face and voice dead.

"You've been an exceptionally useful tool, Lykos." Lykos briefly burned with anger at the presumed familiarity and insult. "Taking up your *father's* cause, removing the stain that was House Stultus, conquering the Emporo. I could use a man of your talents."

"I would never join you!" he shouted in denial.

"Why ever not? You owe no allegiance to a man you've never met, who doesn't share your blood. Shawna? The woman's insane, always was! I have a vision for this kingdom, united under a single banner, and your father almost ruined it by upsetting the balance."

"Freeing slaves is upsetting the balance? Piss poor system that is reliant on the broken bodies and blood of others," Lykos spat. Lord Kolos shook his head, almost as if he were disappointed by his answer.

"So narrow minded. You must broaden your mind! The happiness of a few must be sacrificed for the good of many!"

"So narrow minded," Lykos shot back mockingly, the whip scars upon his back twinging uncomfortably. "How easily you sacrifice others for a false good. Perhaps you should try sacrificing a little for your vision."

"I lost my eye!" Lord Kolos furiously replied.

Lykos gave the man a mocking, unimpressed look. "Oh no, I'm Lord Kolos and I lost an eye to a man I poisoned under false pretenses. Oh woe is me." He was pleased to see his little comment broke Lord Kolos' mask. Gone was the commanding presence and in its place was a feral beast, almost frothing at the lips.

"Join me," Lord Kolos ordered. Lykos found himself being forced upon by the older man's magic in the same manner he had to Falka. "Join me or die!"

Lykos felt the crushing waves of magic upon him and pushed back with his own, the two men engaging in a contest of wills. However it quickly became apparent that the difference in magic was too much and he felt himself begin to weaken drastically. He feared that Lord Kolos was too powerful for him to beat by strength alone and he was losing more and more magic each moment in this contest. The magic of Lord Kolos was all but ordering him to submit and he found his will crumbling towards its suffocating force. His strength had been all but broken trying to resist the man's magic when an old memory resurfaced.

During the Succession Trial he had faced Bart who summoned a mighty storm. He could not make any headway into the fierce winds and instead had built an earthen shell to weather the storm in. In a mad moment of desperation, Lykos believed he could do the same with his magic here.

Instead of pushing outwards with his magic Lykos pulled it in, tighter and tighter, until it was once more within his flesh. Immediately Lord Kolos' magic filled the gap and moved closer but Lykos focused on all of his hatred and desperation into the simple goal of not resisting but simply enduring.

Lord Kolos' magic was an unstoppable force as it hammered upon the immovable object that was Lykos' will. The young man had survived the frozen slave mines of Svellheim, the brutal streets of Mycenae, and he was damned if he was going to yield to this single man. He resisted that impossible force with the will that had kept him alive all of these miserable years.

Their magic clashed violently causing the air to grow hot and furious around them. The elegant decorations were torn from the walls, the wood panels cracking and splintering, and the candles within the room flared brighter as the mages met in a battle of wills. Lykos glared defiantly into Lord Kolos' eye.

"No."

Lord Kolos snarled, "submit!"

"No."

"Obey me!"

"No!"

"OBEY!"

"NEVER!"

The magic in the room reached a critical point and exploded, launching the two men back into the walls. Wild magic tore through the room, further destroying it and covering them in debris. Lykos groaned but grinned because he had discovered an important fact at the end of their face off: Lord Kolos could be beaten.

It was a pyrrhic victory, both of them had succumbed to the attacks devastating effects, but Lykos realized the gap between them wasn't insurmountable. With enough time and practice he could narrow the gap between them and beat Lord Kolos. Because he did want to beat him now. Forget the thousands of men and women still enslaved in the kingdom, forget the rise of crime and hatred within the kingdom. Lord Kolos tried to enslave him with his magic and that was something he would not ever allow. He refused to ever be enslaved again and the man slowly recovering across the room had attempted to do just that. Which is why he would die.

Lykos pushed the broken bookshelf off his back and lunged towards the still recovering Lord Kolos. Grasping his sword he drew it with one smooth motion and brought it down but struck nothing but air. Lord Kolos sat with an outstretched hand, holding him back with magic even as he recovered from the backlash. Lykos was grudgingly impressed.

"You have more of a fight in you than Leon ever did." Lord Kolos stared at him with an appraising eye. "It's a shame we are destined to meet as enemies."

"You can't hold this up forever." Even as Lykos pointed this out the magic holding him was weakening, slowly allowing him to move forward.

"I don't have to. You're going to leave me be." The one-eyed lord's smile was cold.

"And why would I ever do that?" Lykos grunted as he stepped forward shaking in exertion. Weakening or not it was like stepping through swamp water. Lord Kolos rose to his feet to watch his approach with interest.

"Because if you waste time attacking me you might not get to save your little friend in time."

Lykos halted and twitched his hand dangerously. "What did you do?" he demanded.

"I sent Alithis after the Falknor brat. She might even still be alive, the accomplished swordsman she is, but he does have the advantage of magic."

Lykos glared. He had often dueled Falka as a way to keep his skills sharp and found himself constantly challenged by her sharp reflexes and brilliant mind. Only his magic allowed him to keep up with her and if Alithis had been trained from a young age as she had been, then his friend was in peril.

"I will kill you," Lykos vowed.

"You'll try. Certainly not tonight though." Lord Kolos smirked one last time and the oppressive magic fell away, allowing him to move once more.

Yet he stood still. He had a choice before him, one that only he could see, happening in the time between heartbeats. Should he raise his sword to strike at Lord Kolos or run to aid Falka, who was most assuredly still fighting Alithis? If he sacrificed his friend he could strike a great blow against the corruption of this kingdom but he'd have to live with the knowledge that he let Falka die.

That was unacceptable.

As Lykos strode towards the door Lord Kolos shook his head in mock pity. "Perhaps you have some relation to Leon after all. Neither of you are willing to sacrifice lesser beings for your gain."

Lykos paused with his hand on the door handle. "I would be proud to claim Leon as my father. He understood that sometimes you must give up your vision of the future for the safety of others. Until we meet again Lord Kolos."

Lykos bolted through the halls of House Emporo, trying to ignore the sounds of the music and revelry in the distance, frantically looking for library. Rushing past startled servants and party guests he almost didn't hear the clash of steel on steel behind a set of double doors. Kicking them open, he brandished his sword.

The library was wrecked. Paper fluttered through the air in spirals, caught in a whirlwind created by the two dancing figures in the center of the room. Alithis and Falka traded blows but in an instant Lykos could see his friend was tiring while Alithis looked fresh and strong. With a roar he leaped into the fray.

His sudden appearance surprised both combatants and he rained blows upon Alithis to buy Falka time to recover. His target was not caught flat footed for long however and returned them violently. He found each blow shaking his arm and desperately called upon his magic for aid, steadying his limbs and aiding his flagging strength. Falka rejoined the melee.

"What took you so long?" she shouted as she attempted to pin Alithis' leg to the floor with her rapier. The man rolled and retaliated with a fireball that she barely dodged.

"You always complain about being bored, I thought you might like a challenge!" Lykos replied as he sent a fireball of his own at Alithis. The man merely grinned as it splashed harmlessly upon his chest, which was clad in the same Tainted scales that adorned Lord Kolos.

Lykos was worried that despite with his assistance he and Falka were still being stonewalled by Alithis. The man was exceptionally skilled with the blade and kept pace with both of them. He used his flagging magic when he could but it was easily countered by the well rested man whom Lykos was beginning to hate. They were being defeated.

Just as he began to feel the faint traces of panic within Falka shouted, "blind him!"

Obeying without hesitation, he launched a blinding bolt of lightning straight into the ceiling, dazing both of men. He could hear Falka panting beside him as she rushed forwards and with a cry boldly jump kicked Alithis in the chest. With a startled shout he flew through the air and crashed through the window leading outside.

"You alright?" Lykos asked, stumbling over to Falka who lay where she fell, gasping on the ground. Her dress was torn but he saw little blood, a testament to her agility and dodging ability. Pleased to see her in one piece he offered her aid.

"Now that we've defenestrated my attacker would you care to tell me who he was and why in the Valkyrie's names did he want me dead?" she asked. She grasped his offered arm and together they pulled her to her feet.

"Alithis is his name and as far as I know you were a target of opportunity."

"Wonderful, that makes me feel important at least."

Any further reply was cut off by the sound of rushing footsteps. Lykos and Falka looked around at the wrecked library and quickly realized it would be best to not be here when they arrived. Grasping her arm he led her to the now opened window and climbed out onto the ledge.

"Do you think anyone even noticed we were gone?" Lykos asked, looking out at the undisturbed guests. The ball was still going on without any interruption and they had easily slipped back in through the open balcony doors.

"No it appears as though your poisoning, battle with Lord Kolos, and our battle with Alithis went entirely unobserved." Falka muttered sarcastically. Unfortunately for her it went over his head.

"Good, good. I'm all out of magic until I can rest so no more quick getaways." Falka was about to reply when an Emporo guard rushed into the ballroom shouting loudly.

"Lord Talal wrecked the library!"

"Quick think of a getaway," she hissed as the crowd began to mutter excitedly. Lykos knew he didn't have the magic to create a portal and their corner was regrettably lacking in exit paths. He would have to improvise.

"What are you-!" Falka began to ask when Lykos cut her off with his lips meeting hers. She stood stock still while he kissed her, eyes wide open as his lips left hers.

"We need to make a scene," he whispered into her neck. He leaned up to kiss her once more when she pushed him off, knocking him into a servant whose tray clattered to the ground, drawing the attention of everyone in the ballroom.

"Get off me you great oaf! Were the three times on the balcony not enough for you?" An outraged expression crossed her face but Lykos could see her eyes shine with amusement at her act.

"How can I help myself around such an exquisite body? Why look at you my dear!" Lykos slurred his speech and leered at her dark blue bodice. A sharp slap sounded through the air and he found himself looking surprisingly to the right of Falka at a rather interesting statue of a Tainted Charger in its exploding glory. He turned back to her and balked at seeing genuine rage in her eyes. "Now now, no need for-"

His words were cut off again as another slapped forced his head to look at the now amused crowd of party goers who no longer had any suspicion towards his actual crimes. He tried once again to speak, "now I know I've been rude-"

He managed to duck her next slap and grinned happily at her before her surprise stomp on his foot caused him to hop comically around in circles. The laughter of the crowd around them only deepened as he allowed himself to trip over the same servant he had crashed into, sending them both to the ground. Apologizing profusely to the man, he subtly gestured to Falka that it was time to leave.

"I'm leaving and I expect to never see you again!" she declared while stomping off into the crowd who parted for her. He hurriedly rose to his feet leaving the servant to clean up his mess and ran after his companion.

"Let me at least walk you home darling," Lykos said as he saucily winked at a young woman from House Miles on Falka's other side. Falka merely glared at him as the crowd around them watched them leave in amusement. Exiting into the fresh night air they drew in deep relieved breathes.

"That almost ended badly."

"With your acting ability? I'm surprised we weren't clapped in irons."

"Says the woman whose did her best to knock me out."

"Oh trust me you'd know if I tried to knock you out." They shared an amused smile as they examined the well kept grounds around them. He decided to share something he felt was of great importance.

"I had a choice," he told her, "on whether or not to leave you to face Alithis alone. But it wasn't even a choice because I knew I couldn't let you die, you mean that much to me. You're my friend, my first friend, and that means a great deal to me. I used to think about having friends when I was in the mine. They wouldn't steal my food or hurt me, they'd help protect me. I found family in Shawna and Adelram and an ally in Maeve. But you were my first friend. Thank you Falka."

She smiled at him and he smiled back. "You're my friend too Lykos." However a sudden, blinding pain below the belt dragged him to his knees. She had punched him violently in the crotch!

As he knelt groaning, she leaned over him. "However if you ever kiss me without my permission again I'll do that again only with my knife!" She then leaned down and gave him a kiss on the cheek. "Have a goodnight!"

Falka swayed away leaving him to stare after her, partly in shock but mostly in amusement. However only one thought came to mind.

"Good luck with your choice in women Grimm."

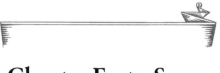

Chapter Forty-Seven

Lykos was pleased to be living in Hearthome once more. Due to the conflict in the north western part of the kingdom he had only been able to spend small portions of his time in his home and he had been looking forward to continue the fight against slavery within the kingdom and by extension House Kolos. However he hadn't expected one part of command: logistics.

He longed for the days where he could just rush into a warehouse, magic and sword carving a path through guards. Instead he spent much of his time meeting with his allies and commanders, planning troop movements and defense patterns for the territories under their control. And once a week he met with all of his allies to get on the same page.

"This is a waste of time!"

Lykos glared at Kiara, who was his connection to House Emporo. Amentha's pregnancy had progressed too far for her to easily travel forcing him into interacting with her infuriating sister. He had more than once considered the option of arranging an "accident" so he would no longer have to deal with her.

"We should capture the Lowland now that we surround them on all sides!" she continued, gesturing to the map of Mycenae on the table they had gathered at. Lykos briefly looked at the other occupants of the room.

Adelram was giving her a blank stare, a warning sign he knew to prelude a violent response from the normally restrained man. He was there as the direct link to House Talal's army, a force that Lykos was using to protect their various interests around the kingdom. Next to him sat Captain Avarc and Grimm, representing Houses Falknor and Sofos respectively, who were largely ignoring Kiara's outburst as they plotted patrol routes along the Reliquary border.

Lykos was pleased Grimm had seized the title of Lord Sofos, although he had assigned a cousin to act as a steward while he was away from his quarter. Grimm and Lykos had briefly been concerned that someone in House Sofos would challenge his rightful placement, as he was truly a bastard of House Talal, but the change of power had gone through easily enough. Apparently the late Arachnis had not told anyone of his wife's infidelity.

The last member of their little gathering was Commander Withers, representing House Prodotis' interests. The sour man glared sullenly at everyone and everything and often argued with Adelram and Lykos on the best methods to employ.

"House Prodotis seconds House Emporo's proposition," Commander Withers intoned causing Avarc and Grimm to groan.

"They are neutral to our conflict and have made no offensive movements towards any of us. So why are you two so desperate to attack them?" Lykos asked Kiara and Withers.

She huffed. "Their territory is so underdeveloped that it's an insult to this kingdom. Why with the space available Emporo artisans could make such magnificent works of art, sprawling chateaus and gardens lining the waterfront."

His skin crawled when he realized what the Emporo wanted. Their elite wanted bigger and grander homes than the ones they already possessed and the large "empty" space in the Lowland was enticing to their desires. That the fools were ignorant of where their food came from was not surprising, the powerful were remarkably narrow minded. Lykos nodded to Commander Withers to hear his thoughts, and through him House Prodotis.

"Our army is hungry for some form of reward for their part in taking the Emporo territory. We were denied the Nero and the traditional looting and the men have grown discontent."

"Bloody pirates," Adelram muttered.

"The Nero was never yours as a reward, House Falknor is much better equipped to utilize it," Captain Avarc told Commander Withers.

Kiara laughed mockingly and glared at the airship captain. "And it's not yours either Falknor scum. House Emporo will recover its territory one day."

"Enough," Lykos forcefully cut in before the words devolved into violence. "Kiara we are not violating the neutrality of a house just so the Emporo can build themselves summer homes. Withers, control your men. We do not pillage from the good folks of this kingdom."

Neither answered but silently fumed. He thanked the Valkyries for small favors as he turned back to the main matter at hand: how best to strike at House Kolos while continuing their overall mission to free the remaining slaves within the kingdom.

"Can we take the Reliquary?" Lykos asked the room at large. Captain Avarc gave Commander Withers and Kiara a glare before answering.

"We could but it would be pointless. Between House Falknor controlling the airships and House Prodotis in charge of the canals, we can easily move anywhere in the kingdom save the Citadel. The Reliquary doesn't have any strategic importance in the grand scheme of things, unless you want to go tomb raiding."

Captain Avarc instead tapped the symbol representing the Grand Temple which rested between the Citadel and Kremos. "We should eliminate these assassins."

"Speaking of past insults?" Kiara shot nastily. "If we are not annexing the Lowland then we should look towards Latom and Aspida. Both are dangerously placed against our forces and your home as well Lord Talal."

Lykos considered the map. While Kiara spoke the truth, the two quarters weren't quite that deadly of a threat. To get into Pyrgos from Aspida you had to cross an exposed bridge, which couldn't be circumvented by climbing down the mountain due to the large gap between the two quarters. To attack Pyrgos from Latom was also folly as it was literally an uphill battle with no cover. With the Falknor airships he never need worry about a siege upon his home either as they could just fly in the supplies they needed. However now he was curios to Avarc's reasoning.

"Why the assassins?" Lykos didn't disagree with the danger they represented but he hoped that there was logic driving this objective.

"The Citadel has one and only one gate leading in and out of itself and that gate opens into Naos. Only a few minor houses have any residency there because the main focus of power is with the Acolytes. If we wish to establish a blockade, or even siege, on the Citadel we will need Naos under our control."

"Control we could just as easily get taking Aspida. The Five Families ruling it haven't been receptive towards our talks and taking their land would be an example to others," Commander Withers claimed. Only Kiara nodded in agreement to his words.

Adelram spoke up, "I think we should be hesitant on declaring war on just anyone, especially those who have been neutral to us. I agree with Captain Avarc that we should focus on the Acolytes."

"Agreed. We don't need unnecessary fights and I would prefer less blood to be spilled as we repair this kingdom." Commander Withers scoffed at Lykos' words but said nothing. He was well aware of the man's opinions of the noble houses but disagreed: if you had the ability to help others you had the obligation to do so.

More harm is done in doing nothing than those who try to better the world.

"So you plan on poking a nest of Vipers? That seems bloodless," Kiara muttered angrily.

"It's a sound plan," Grimm countered. "We can only make our walls so thick and have so many guards. Limiting assassins, especially those who can use magic, is a worthy goal."

"Aye. Adelram?" The older man snapped to attention under Lykos' gaze. "Marshal our forces. I want them taking over the smaller temples throughout the kingdom before we move on their main one in Naos. That should help limit the number of daggers at our back while we move forward. Captain Avarc, we're going to form up in Kremos before marching into Naos so we'll need your airships to ferry our troops nearby."

"Why aren't we just using the airships to deposit our troops on top of the temple?" Kiara asked snidely.

"Because the assassins man the ballista all over the quarter. I'd like to avoid wasting dozens of airships in a fruitless assault," Captain Avarc answered easily but Lykos could see Kiara grind her teeth in frustration.

"Kiara, Commander Withers. Your soldiers shouldn't be needed for the assault on the temple but I would like for you to increase your guard on the edges of the kingdom. I've received reports on an increase in Tainted activity."

And that was worrying. Avian Tainted harassed the Falknor airships over the kingdom all the time but other than one or two lone wanderers large Tainted generally avoided the walls of Mycenae, preferring to roam the countryside. In fact the last time Tainted had been this close to the kingdom was when they had hunted Lykos outside the walls after he had crashed a year ago. And determined Tainted could get past those walls if they truly tried.

It took several more hours to hammer out an exact plan, full of troop movements, who did what, and how best to secure Naos after taking it. Lykos felt a small tremor of excitement, the path he had set out on was nearing the end and soon they'd be able to rest and rebuild. He dismissed his allies and examined the map of Mycenae as they vacated the room. He quickly became aware someone had not left.

"Commander Withers! What can I do for you?" Lykos asked the man who had not moved from his seat.

"I carry a message from my Lady Prodotis. She respectfully requests you do not antagonize House Kolos so publicly again as it makes our work much more difficult."

He stared at Withers in confusion. "Lady Prodotis," he spoke carefully, "is concerned that I am unduly antagonizing House Kolos?"

"Yes." Commander Withers nodded, pleased that he understood.

He did not understand. "She does know that we are at opposing them yes? That we wish to break their power on the kingdom?"

"Of course but that doesn't mean we shouldn't be uncivilized."

"Uncivilized!" Lykos' shout almost woke the dead. "We're talking about a man who met with my father under false pretenses, poisoned him, then locked my mother up in her home for almost two decades. How is any of that civilized?"

"Well that was in the past! Circumstances always change. Why Lady Prodotis had to spend several hours talking Lord Kolos down at the end of the Emporo ball last week just so he wouldn't react negatively."

Lykos froze in anger. When he finally spoke each word was low and dangerous, the magic in his body angrily leaking forth and rustling the maps on the table in front of him. "What do you mean she spent several hours talking him down?"

Commander Withers felt Lykos' magic and tried to feebly push back with his own but the enraged lord refused to yield. Pushing forward, Withers was pinned painfully to his chair. Gasping, he spoke, "she did! Apparently he threatened to enact drastic actions against you for your insult. Lady Prodotis was most displeased with you!"

Lykos pushed down with his magic, cutting off the struggling man's words. He stood from his seat and advanced menacingly towards Commander Withers.

"Make one thing clear to dear Lilith. Lord Kolos and by extension House Kolos are our enemies. We should not be placating, calming down, or negotiating with those who have already proven to us that their word, their honor, means nothing! Lilith is displeased with me? I am furious with her! And be sure to tell her that!"

He grabbed Commander Withers by his cloak and hauled him to his feet. Shoving the man towards the door, he watched with angry eyes as Withers raced from the room, eager to be gone from the furious mage. He turned back to the maps with unseeing eyes.

Why was Lady Prodotis talking to Lord Kolos? It rubbed him the wrong way and he began to wonder if they were in league together. He thought back to the Emporo ball and how he had been poisoned. It took only a few questions to Illusionist Maeve to confirm just how difficult Tainted Tears were to gain and how odd it was for Lady Prodotis to have the only cure to an exotic poison on her person.

He shook his head in frustration. They lived in dangerous times, it should not be surprising that people took precautions. And it was perfectly reasonable for her to talk to Lord Kolos to calm him down after their argument, he was overreacting.

Right?

Chapter Forty-Eight

The shadow war being fought against the Acolytes was going well in Lykos' opinion. Adelram had trained the soldiers for House Talal well and Lykos took this time to get them used to taking orders from him. He would lead groups of various sizes against a variety of targets, learning firsthand how best to use his soldiers, their capabilities, as they raided Acolyte temples. It was dangerous work but he felt it necessary to build respect and trust between himself and his soldiers. Adelram agreed.

"They need to know you won't send them needlessly to their deaths. Because one day you might have to and you need them to go without hesitation," he grimly told him after the young man had watched one of his soldiers die in front of him. Illusionist Maeve was more brutal in her explanation.

"They are numbers. With magic you or I or our enemies could lay waste to an army. So to stop us they send two armies. These men and women are nothing but fleshy walls to buy us mages time."

He took both of their words to heart and hardened his own further. There was nothing he could do for the dead but learn their lessons so that those still breathing might survive. He was not so foolish as to believe that the day would never come where he would have to sacrifice his soldiers. However he hoped that it was far into the future and that he went with them, so he would not have to live with the knowledge.

There was one area where the fight against the Acolytes was dragging. Lykos had begun to use his commanders for their original purpose, pulling them away from instructing recruits and moving them to leading various offensives all over the kingdom. There were complications of course but none so bad as Doukas.

Lykos had been determined to keep the potential damage the spy could do to a minimum, a laughable goal considering the man was partially in charge of teaching healing, but his brother Giles had been quite vocal in his protestations at Doukas not being given command of soldiers. He had originally given Demos command but the energetic woman was a poor fit for the position, unable to muster the ruthlessness needed to be a good leader. Giles had pointed out Doukas' many accomplishments and abilities and the trio involved had agreed that he was the better choice. So Lykos reluctantly gave the spy command.

And was not surprised when reports of failure began to appear. Any plan Doukas was included in inevitably failed as overwhelming forces pushed them back. He could see that Doukas was too savvy to allow the Talal soldiers to die, the man's profession was healing after all, but the number of wounded and failed objectives began to stack noticeably. Adelram was pleased when he ordered the end of these missions as finding willing troops to go with the "cursed" commander was becoming difficult.

However he had gained enough traction to go for the big prize: the Grand Temple in Naos that he had met Helen in so long ago. The Acolytes had pulled back and he seized the opportunity to marshal his forces in the nearby Kremos for the final push.

The day of the attack arrived and he met with his commanders at the Aviary. The dizzying height was advantageous, allowing them an unimpeded view into Naos down below, although Lykos made sure to stay clear of the ledge. Despite knowing he was able to use magic to save himself from the fall, he had no desire to experience it without cause anytime soon. He turned to face the men and women in the room.

Adelram was leaning over a map with Lord Falknor, the two men discussing where they could deploy their airships effectively. Even though the repairs had been completed on the fleet, Lykos had been sour when he realized that they would remain largely unused in this conflict. The assassin's watery nature, slipping through the cracks when the going got tough, relegated the majestic ships to transportation roles.

Giles and Doukas were talking quietly in a corner while a nearby Helen glared at the pair. The assassin had never quite forgiven either man for their part in Irene's banishment and Lykos had quickly assigned her to spreading awareness for their cause in neutral temples. Through her work he had swollen his ranks noticeably with skilled fighters, saboteurs, and assassins. However the chip on the young woman's shoulder was a mile wide and she appeared oblivious to Demos' one sided conversation with her.

Giles and Doukas conversation devolved into an argument, drawing the attention of those gathered.

"I'm just not feeling well today!" Doukas protested.

"Nonsense, you just need a little blood letting to feel your normal self!" Giles slapped his smaller brother on the shoulder. Lykos approached the pair.

"What's wrong?" he asked. Giles gestured to his brother and Lykos examined the man closely. Doukas was unusually pale and sweat wet his brow heavily. But it was the almost frantic nature of his actions that interested Lykos.

"Doukas claims he's not feeling well which I think is absurd! He just needs to go kill some assassin scum and he'll be right as rain."

"I've felt ill all morning brother!" Doukas protested.

"Have you treated yourself?" Lykos asked.

"Of course!" he replied offended.

"He hasn't," Giles stated firmly. Lykos gave the brothers an unimpressed look.

"Demos!" The bubbly young women snapped to attention. "You have a patient." Lykos stepped to the side, gesturing to the glaring Doukas.

"Aye Lord Talal!" Demos chirped as she began to examine her patient. Lykos watched with interest as a web of magic appeared in her hands. Like illusions and summoning, he had no skill with external healing and watched with sharp eyes as Demos skillfully checked Doukas' health. The web of magic flexed in peculiar manners as it touched him at various parts of his chest and head. With a clap of her hands, the magical web vanished.

"Well as far as I can determine he's just stressed my lord!" she chirped happily. "He's combat ready."

"Good." Lykos turned towards Doukas. "You'll be with me at the front Doukas. You too Giles."

"Gladly Lord Talal." Giles' smile was a stark contrast to his brother's frown.

With little fanfare the group left the room and joined the Talal soldiers assembled in the Falknor courtyard. As soon as Lykos made his appearance, the lounging soldiers leaped to their feet to stand in orderly rows at attention. Silently pleased with their quick response, he addressed them.

"The Acolytes," Lykos said the name distastefully, "have perverted the Valkyries in the name of greed and personal power. Today we will finally strike a devastating blow against their numbers and bring honor back to this kingdom! We will eliminate the blights on this kingdom one evil at a time and work towards a world we can all live together in, in peace!"

The soldiers cheered and bashed their weapons on shields, howling their support to the wind. Lykos smiled in satisfaction and gave the order to march. Quickly and efficiently they began their march to Naos and the Grand Temple within. Lykos and Giles quickly made their way to the head of the procession with a reluctant Doukas in tow.

They made it through the Falknor territory without incident, the early morning invigorating them as they walked. Exiting Kremos through the gate Giles laughed heartily.

"They have no one manning the gates!" He pointed out with glee. "It's as if they don't have the soldiers left to man their defenses!"

"Aye it appears that way," Lykos agreed thoughtfully. He thought of the temples they had taken over the past few weeks. The defenses had been heavily fortified but lightly manned and the rare magic user he had faced had been easily defeated by superior numbers and skill. Unless the mythos of the legendary assassins had been grossly exaggerated, their strongest fighters were being held in reserve. The real question was why?

"Lord Talal, please! I'm really not feeling well." Doukas was sweating heavily as he practically begged. He glanced at the nervous man beside him out of the corner of his eye and nearly swore out loud when the man glanced up almost too quickly to notice.

It began to click into place. The reason why the temples were so easily taken, Doukas' nervousness, the unmanned gates: they were walking into a trap.

He held up his hand and the soldiers behind him obediently stopped. Giles appeared confused while Doukas was relieved that their progress had been halted. Helen and Adelram joined the trio at the head of the progression.

"Why have we stopped?" Adelram asked gruffly.

"A feeling," Lykos replied, glancing up the street towards the now visible Grand Temple. "Helen, Adelram. Take a portion of our forces and watch our flanks, I don't want to be trapped. Giles and Doukas will remain here while I go to scout ahead personally."

"I won't allow you to go by yourself-" Helen began but he waved her off.

"I'll be taking a dozen archers, I'll be fine."

"-and I'll still be going with you. The Valkyries claimed you as their champion, thus I will watch your back," she finished firmly. He considered the dangerous woman for a moment before nodding in agreement.

After pulling a dozen archers from the assembled soldiers, they began to scale the buildings on either side of the street. While tempting to simply create a portal to transverse the distance between the ground and the roof, pulling the twelve archers and Helen along would have been exhausting. While physically demanding, recovering from the exertion of climbing would be much easier than using magic so the choice was easy.

Pulling himself up onto the wooden slats that made up the building's roof, he lay low upon the slope. Just an arm's length away were several assassins, the harpies on their shoulders revealing their affiliation, waiting patiently. He held up his hand to silence his forces as they joined him on the roof.

Helen whispered into his ear, "a scout group I think but where are the rest of them?" Lykos frowned at her words and looked carefully around. It took him a moment but several familiar shapes began to appear all around them. He carefully pointed them out.

"We're surrounded," he said quietly, unwilling to give away their position. The assassin's position made sense, the superior height would allow them to rain hell upon the Talal forces below. Just in his line of sight alone there were dozens of rooftops with a handful of assassins each and he had no doubt there were more laying in wait on the ground below. They were trapped.

"What are your orders Lord Talal?" one of the archers asked quietly. There was fear in the man's eyes but Lykos was pleased to see the gathered men and women were calm. He examined their position for a moment. Save for the assassins just beyond the low wall, it was relatively well defended with plenty of cover. Firming his lips, he nodded and began to explain his intentions.

"We can't leave these assassins up here. Helen and I will clear this roof while you and the rest of the archers begin to clear the other rooftops with your arrows. Keep them as far away as you can, they excel in medium and close range combat."

He did not wait for the man to answer as the noise would no doubt alert the assassins nearby. Instead he leaped from his crouch, drawing his sword, and diving for the closest assassin. The man gurgled in surprise as he stabbed him from behind, flinging his dying body at another assassin. The assassins were slow to react as he fell upon them and were further unprepared for Helen to join him.

Lykos was dimly aware of his archers firing their bows, their movements smooth and efficient as they fired upon their nearby foes. Many assassins fell to their arrows but many more rose up from their position and moved to engage across rooftops.

One of the Talal archers fell as a poisoned dart found her throat. A young man took a knife to the back meant for one of his fellow soldiers, dead before he even hit the rooftop. Said soldier died to a leaping assassin, his twirling blades flicking blood in an arc as he moved to engage Helen. Lykos fought furiously, kicking another assassin off the rooftop. The man flew screaming through the air and he did not pause to listen to the crunch as he impacted the stone street below. The man's death throes alerted the rest of their forces below that they had run into opposition.

Lykos ducked a wild slash from a woman covered in burn scars and cursed his lack of foresight. Captain Avarc's airships would have been more than enough to pin the assassins to the roof, especially with the Talal forces waiting below. Ballistas or not he vowed to never underestimate a foes abilities so much again that he would not attack with everything he could muster.

Despite the best efforts of his archers, he found himself relying heavily on his sword as more assassins joined them on their roof, focusing on protecting his soldiers from their deadly weapons. Helen began to use the corpses piling up to block the leaping assassins in mid air with magic, sending both corpse and the living to crashing on the ground below. It was exhausting, grisly work, but after several frantic minutes the rooftops were quiet. The trap had been overcome.

Wearily, Lykos led the remainder of his forces to the ground. There were many more bodies on the ground than those Helen had sent and it appeared his prediction had been correct. While the assassins waited above, their soldiers ambushed the Talal forces from all sides, hoping to slaughter the unaware men and women. But thanks to Doukas' nervousness and Lykos' paranoia, the vast majority of his forces had survived with few wounded.

"Trash seemed to fall from the sky!" Giles called out to them as they rejoined the rest of the Talal forces on the ground. The gathered soldiers laughed. "It would seem some heavenly figure took affront to their presence."

"So it would seem." Lykos bore the chuckles with good humor. "Perhaps we should move so we don't draw unwanted attention ourselves?"

"As if any force could stand up to us!" one of the soldiers called out and the rest began to cheer. Lykos smirked but did not cull their enthusiasm, feeling they would need the boost for when they took the Grand Temple.

It took several minutes for his commanders to restore order and have the dead pulled to the side. After taking the temple proper burials would be arranged for the deceased but until then they could only assign a guard to watch over the dead. In an orderly fashion Lykos led his forces in a march towards the Grand Temple. All along the street doors and windows opened and curious faces watched them with solemn eyes. In the alleys dark clothed figures hustled away, disappearing into the shadows as his army advanced, no doubt fearful of their might. Lykos paid neither group any mind. He was not there harm common folk or to chase down petty criminals, he had a bigger prize to take.

The Grand Temple loomed before them and he immediately knew something was wrong. There were no guards manning the many entrances, no one moving in and out of the building. With wary steps, he drew his sword and moved carefully through a doorway. The last time he had been here the building had been bustling with people and full of weapons. Now it was empty, the furniture had been tossed around if not outright destroyed and the walls and floor were pockmarked with damage. And everywhere were bodies dripping with fresh blood.

"What happened here?" Helen asked in surprise. She nudged one body with her foot. "This was Alaric, one of Andrea's most trusted lieutenants. It looks like someone ripped open his chest but how? He was so skilled in blade and magic?"

"He was," a soft voice called out. Lykos and the others pointed their weapons to the source of the voice as a figure stepped from the shadows. The woman's face was hard and freshly scarred, as she looked impassively at the gathered Talal forces. It took Lykos a moment to realize this dangerous woman was Irene, brutally damaged and healed over time, but Irene nonetheless.

"Irene," Giles growled. Lykos and Helen both took a step forwards as Giles gripped his sword tighter. "You have a lot of nerve showing your face here. Allow me to end the traitor's life Lord Talal!"

"Giles, still as dim as ever." Lykos' neck prickled unpleasantly at the sheer disgust and contempt in Irene's voice. It felt unnatural to hear such a tone come from her. Under his gaze she straightened slightly. "I have completed the task you have given me Lord Talal."

His eyes sharpened as those gathered were shocked into silence. With a steady hand Irene reached behind her and grasped something. All around Lykos arrows were drawn but he held up his hand. She brought the object out slowly and held it out for them to see. Grasped in her hand was Andrea's hair, which was attached to her decapitated head. The expression on the dead woman's face was one part anger, one part surprise and he glanced at Irene for an explanation.

"May I introduce Andrea of House Vrachos, the former Prophet of the Goddesses." Lykos gave the decapitated head a dark smile.

"A pleasure to meet you but let's not get ahead of ourselves," he returned his gaze to Irene, "we have much to discuss."

Chapter Forty-Nine

Why can't things ever be simple, Lykos wondered idly to himself. He had sent the Talal soldiers to secure the surrounding area as the fewer eyes to witness what was to come the better. Giles and Helen stood ready to trade blows while Doukas himself was nervously glancing at the still figure of Irene. The woman in question was coolly gazing at Lykos who was beginning to wonder if he should just give up the day and return to bed to let the Valkyries deal with this mess.

He had quite willingly revealed to his commanders that Irene was in fact, not the spy. Having expected some outburst from the more volatile men and women present he was pleasantly surprised that fireballs did not immediately begin to fly. He was even more surprised when the normally calm and pleasant Demos charged at him with a scream of inarticulate rage. He was not quick enough to prevent her vicious slap to his face nor her follow up punch to his jaw. Fortunately Helen stopped the raging healer before she could utilize her knife upon his delicate organs.

With a fresh appreciation that Demos was a trained killer despite her preference to healing, something he should truly have remembered considering she was a former Acolyte, he turned to Helen. "Thanks."

"Don't mention it." She smirked. "I would have let her smack you a few more times but she drew a knife. I figured erring on the side of caution was wise."

"Right." He looked up at the upset Demos who was pinned to the wall with several of Helen's knives holding her aloft. "Nice right hook Demos."

Demos had the grace to blush but the glare quickly returned to her face. "You made me think bad thoughts about Irene for months and you're only now telling us she wasn't the spy?"

"Well yes."

He dove to the floor as Demos literally screamed, sending forth a wave of air magic and wrecking the room even further. He laid dazed on the floor as she panted heavily from her spot on the wall.

"Okay you can let me down now, I'm good," she chirped to Helen. Helen gave her friend an admiring smile and quickly pulled the knives holding her up away. With casual grace Demos regained her feet and began to hum contently.

"What the hell is going on?" Giles demanded as he gripped his sword tightly. "I thought we established months ago that Irene was the traitor!"

"It was a ruse." Lykos brushed the dirt from his hands and clothes as he stood up. "I've actually known the identity of the spy the entire time."

"What!" Giles shouted as Doukas became deadly still.

"Of course," Lykos continued, pretending to be oblivious to the tense Doukas. "However with the speed of the communication between my defense of the Lowland's gate and the attack on House Falknor, a more important issue arose: how did they talk across the kingdom faster than we can physically travel?

"Even with magic I couldn't travel that great of a distance that quickly. Not even with my knowledge of the waterways and secret passages. No the Acolytes have somehow figured out how to communicate while being on the opposite ends of the kingdom and I wanted that knowledge. But then reason left us!

"I had hoped that by revealing the spy's existence to my allies and commanders that prudence would allow us to act quickly. That we could defeat our foe and gain their advantage for ourselves. Instead I had to watch as fear mongering and a mob mentality made my allies abandon all common sense! And in the end I was forced to make the best of a horrible situation, only created by the lack of any proof!

"I banished Irene. I sent away a woman I cared for deeply and then had to ask her later that night to go spy on our enemies! To go somewhere where none of her friends, none of her former allies, me! Where none of us could aid her! All to find some Valkyrie forsaken proof!"

Lykos' magic writhed inside of him almost painfully, begging to be released but he kept it under rigid control. He fixed dark eyes on Doukas who began to tremble in terror before him as all eyes in the room turned towards him save one. Giles instead turned towards Lykos in denial.

"Lord Talal! You cannot be serious, my brother would never betray us!"

"He did," Irene countered firmly.

"He did not!" Giles objected vehemently.

"He did and I have proof." Silence filled the room as everyone turned focused on Irene.

"That's not possible!" Giles sputtered.

"Irene." Her eyes snapped to Lykos and he felt a chill as the once beautiful eyes gazed at him coldly. "What did you find?"

She pulled a strange device from her hip pouch. A palm sized crystal had been wrapped in several wires with several smaller crystals glowing softly at various places. As he watched the device glowed softly and the smaller crystals began to orbit the larger one slowly. It was a fascinating and exciting device and he knew incredibly valuable. He wanted it.

"Andrea called them volka. Some enchanter from the far north went insane several years ago, claiming the Goddesses spoke to him and taught him how to craft them. He did so and through blood, treachery, and betrayal the plans fell into Andrea's hands. The large crystal in the center provides the power while the smaller ones provide the connection. Holding one in your hand allows you to speak over any distance, including between kingdoms."

"This is a fantastic device!" Helen muttered excitedly, moving closer to examine the volka. "I always wondered how Andrea gathered information so quickly."

"Indeed this can benefit us greatly," Lykos agreed.

"Yes, yes. It's a magnificent toy," Giles said impatiently, "but how does this prove my brother's guilt?"

"Because this volka is special. It was Andrea's personal device and each one of these crystals went to a specific lieutenant and she had a very *pleasant* way to gain your attention." Irene smiled nastily as she twisted the device. For several moments nothing happened but soon the smell of burning leather filled the air.

"Congratulations it makes a nasty smell," Giles mocked as Doukas gripped his side painfully. "This is absurd Lord Talal, end this farce at once!"

"The device does not smell," she deadpanned.

Giles sneered. "Ridiculous, come brother we will find our fortunes elsewhere!"

Any reply Doukas was to voice was cut off by his pained cry. The robes on his left side smoldered and as he pulled at the smoking cloth an object fell from their folds. There laying on the ground before all was a softly glowing volka.

In a flash Helen had to be restrained by Lykos as she lunged, blade drawn, at Doukas who immediately tried to bolt from the room. Demos once more surprised everyone by tackling the fleeing man to the ground and binding him with earth magic. The only ones to remain stationary were Irene, whose icy glare never left Doukas, and Giles who stared at his brother in shock.

"Let me at him!" Helen screamed as Lykos struggled to restrain her. "He must die!"

"And he will!" Lykos shouted causing the assassin in his arms to still. "But not by your hand. He's done far more harm to others in this room."

She reluctantly nodded and he allowed the assassin her freedom. "You're lucky filth, I would have made your suffering a thing of nightmares," she spat at Doukas.

"Please my lord, you don't understand! I had to!" Doukas tried begging, struggling against Demos whose magic bound him tightly. Lykos scoffed.

"A traitor is a traitor. Whatever your reasons you chose not to trust us and you directly contributed to the death of several of my friends. And the forced banishment of someone very dear to me. No your death is at hand it is merely time to decide who wields the blade."

Lykos ignored Doukas' cries for mercy as he looked at Irene and Giles. Irene was arguably the wretched man's most harmed victim but as the last living member of House Dumas Giles had right by law to wield the blade, and to remove the stain of his brother's actions from their family. However one glance at Irene and he knew his choice.

"Irene? Would you do the honors?" For a long hard moment she stared at the cowering man before she slowly shook her head.

"I have enough blood on my hands. I do not wish to add his to that river," she quietly said.

"I understand." With a smooth motion he drew his sword and beheaded Doukas, causing his head to go flying. It landed with a meaty thump, eyes wide opened in surprise as the rest of his body collapsed to the ground. He was almost amused to see the mouth open and close slightly, as if he was trying to speak some last secret but no sound came forth. Finally he was still.

Giles collapsed as sobs wracked his frame, staring at his brother's corpse. Lykos stepped back, allowing the man to grieve, but kept his sword drawn in case he needed to defend himself. It was unneeded however.

"Lord Talal?" Giles spoke roughly, his voice thick with tears. "I know he does not deserve it but could you honor my brother? For the man he once was?" At once he knew what the man wanted and he glanced towards Irene to see her reaction. The woman stared impassively at them and he truly regretted what had been done to his once friend.

"Because he was your brother," Lykos finally replied, flicking his wrist. A fireball flew out from his hand and landed on Doukas. Flames immediately rose from the body and began to burn through the enchanted robes adorning his still form. Giles wept harder and Demos knelt beside him to offer comfort.

"Do the volka always burn when called upon? Seems like it wouldn't be very stealthy," Helen asked as she played with Doukas' device. Lykos was not surprised to see her uncaring towards Giles' suffering, nor the traitor's funeral. Despite knowing he should rise above such pettiness, he too turned his back on the improvised funeral and joined Irene and Helen.

"It was a modification added by Andrea. If she used it, it meant that you were supposed to answer as soon as possible." Irene winced as she rubbed her side. "It is unpleasant to experience first hand."

"Thank you Irene," Lykos told her sincerely. For just a slight moment he saw her eyes soften and glimpsed the broken shell of a woman within. His heart beat uncomfortably within his chest as he looked into those sorrow filled eyes.

"You would have done the same for me," she finally replied. He tried to give her a smile but failed.

"Will you come back?" he asked.

"You banished me remember?"

"Forget the banishment. Forget the kingdom. Forget everything. I never should have asked this of you and I will spend the rest of my life making it right."

"We all make a choice dear Lykos." She gave him a sad little smile. She held out two scrolls to him. "The instructions on how to make more volka and some information you should know."

He reluctantly took the scrolls from her and placed them securely on his belt. "You will always have a place at my table," he finally told her. Irene gave him another sad smile and then once more walked out of his life.

Chapter Fifty

Spring had sprung upon Mycenae with wild abandon, thawing frost and melting snow drifts. Already fresh growths of plant life were springing up all over the kingdom and Agroti farmers could be seen in each quarter tending to their fields. The fresh air promised new beginnings....

"You should apologize!"

And bitter realizations.

Lykos was happily back at Hearthome in Pyrgos, Shawna and Illusionist Maeve welcoming him back warmly. At least he liked to pretend the fireballs Illusionist Maeve sent his way were out of affection and not of any real ill intent. Although that did not explain her cackling.

"I am not going to apologize to an enemy Lilith," he stated firmly. He was meeting with Lady Prodotis on the terrace overlooking the kingdom and despite the last of winter's chill touching them, he found his skin burning under the sun's harsh glare. He had awoken this morning to find a message from his ally requesting an audience and if he had known what she wanted to discuss he would have returned to his slumber.

"You slighted him and his house! There will be dire consequences if we do not mend the rift between Houses Talal and Kolos!" she pressed as he observed the kingdom below.

"Mend the rift? He poisoned my father, plunged this kingdom into an era of crime and slavery, and personally tried to enforce his will upon me with magic! The rift is as wide and deep as the ocean below!" Lykos countered, repeating an old argument.

"Nonsense a bridge can be built between your two houses and peace can be brought back to these lands." He stared at her in disbelief. "Oh don't give me that look! Kopanos is a reasonable man!"

Lykos spoke firmly and clearly. "Lord Kolos is a violent, dishonest, beast who is not to be trusted for he cannot be reasoned with. I will not sue for peace, I will not repeat my father's mistakes in dealing with that wretched man."

Lilith's eyes sharpened momentarily before she switched tracks entirely. Stepping closer to him she caressed his arm and smiled seductively. "There's no need to act rashly my lord, perhaps we could find some way to come to an agreement?"

"My decision is final Lady Prodotis," his sharp tone actually made the woman take a step back in surprise, "and if there is nothing else that needs to be discussed I have other matters to attend to today."

Lady Prodotis quickly composed herself. "Very well Lord Talal I will make my exit. I do hope I'll see you at my ball tomorrow though?"

"Of course Lady Prodotis I wouldn't miss it for anything." Except perhaps a bloody battlefield. At least there the enemies were honest and open about their intentions. "I shall see you then."

She gave him a regal nod and exited through the garden, leaving him alone with his thoughts. Reaching for a pouch at his waist he pulled out the second scroll Irene had given him, the one with vital information. All that was written on it were two lines:

Unmarked barges have been making their way through the canals to the Citadel each night.

An ally of House Talal is consorting with House Kolos.

Scowling Lykos returned the scroll to his pouch and made his way into his home to seek out Illusionist Maeve. He needed advise and violence and the old woman promised both.

"Again. How sure are you of Irene's information." Illusionist Maeve was sitting on a chair she had forced him to carry into the Talal ritual chamber. Despite his hope for a proper mages duel between them, she instead had him conjuring representations of each element. It was an exercise any competent mage could perform and many used it to test and measure their skill and power.

With a twist of his hand he conjured a ball of fire to orbit his body. "Positive. I would trust her with my life."

"Then you've learned nothing," she harshly replied.

"On the contrary I like to think I've learned a lot."

"You're a trusting fool."

"I trust those that have never betrayed me." A sphere of water rose from the gushing water below and joined the fire circling him. Lykos breathed out slowly as the strain upon his mind of holding two conflicting elements began but he ignored it with practiced ease.

"You banished her, cast her out, and you trust the information she gives you?" Her condescending tone was a tad mocking he decided. He began to slowly feel along the stone and earth walls for the next sphere.

"She was innocent and helped identify the traitor and his method of communication." Lykos had pulled Giles back to the Talal barracks while the man grieved for his fallen brother. While Giles had assured him that he had no knowledge of his brothers treachery, he choose to be cautious in trusting the last Dumas. Just not with Irene.

"So she couldn't be bitter towards her former allies and plot their demise?" Illusionist Maeve asked as he pulled a large clump of dirt from the walls to join the fire and water. The "easy" three elements done he focused now on summoning air and lightning.

"No," he stated firmly. The wind in the room picked up as he focused on creating a mini tornado. The tiny cyclone began to twist around the other three elements but he focused to keep them firmly separated.

"Then which of your allies is most likely to betray you?"

"All of them." Illusionist Maeve actually smirked at that, not that he noticed. "But paired with the first bit of information the obvious answer is House Prodotis. Unmarked barges on the waterways they supposedly control? That's more alarming than a Tainted Charger in a pub and there has been no talk of it. Something is happening and my thoughts do not bring me comfort."

"So what will you do?" His eyes narrowed as a ball of lightning formed in between his hands. Sparks shot out, threatening to break free of his control, but he kept it ruthlessly in line as it joined the other elements orbiting around him.

"I'll crush my enemies, grind them into dust and light the remains on fire," Lykos answered decisively as he brought the five orbs closer to one another. He pressed them tight against one another, never allowing them to mix, as this was the true purpose of the exercise. Maintaining the separate elements under these circumstances for more than a minute was impossible for most Citadel mages according to Illusionist Maeve.

Lykos wondered if he could reach three minutes this time.

"Good. Leon always was too lenient with his foes. Oh he would kill you if you cast magic at him, shot an arrow, or raised a sword but he would allows his foes to surrender. So many men and women were allowed to escape justice because they were spared death...." Illusionist Maeve trailed off in thought.

Lykos said nothing so great was his concentration on his task. Time passed agonizingly slow and he wondered how long it had been. Tremors began to wrack his body despite the lack of physical exertion but he did not feel exhaustion. His magic and body felt stronger than ever and he reveled in the feeling. Finally the exercise proved too much for his mind and his control slipped.

Water evaporated, stone shards exploded outwards, and lightning sparked. His armor deflected the worst of it while Illusionist Maeve simply waved the elements away from her frail form. He breathed in slowly reveling in the feeling of his magic relaxing in his body.

"Just over five minutes," she told him quietly. "Congratulations."

"On what instructor?" he asked curiously. Rare was it that Illusionist Maeve offered positive feedback and he was mindful of a trap.

"I have nothing left to teach you. You're free to study the depths of magic yourself now." He rocked back on his heels at his mentors words. He was done? The mere thought seemed absurd and he voiced as much.

"Do not mistake this for meaning you know all. You do not and you never will. However we've reached the point where you can no longer grow under my tutelage. This last exercise was to gauge your understanding, skill, and control of magic and you've passed beyond all expectations. Now it is time for you to practice and refine your technique."

"My technique?" Lykos inquired. Without any warning five perfect spheres appeared around Illusionist Maeve, each following their own orbital path. Looking closer Lykos could see their surface an ever shifting pattern of snakes, constantly slithering but never touching. He thought of his chaotic summonings, how he needed to take elements from what was already there, and felt the burning desire to one day match her feat.

"What will you do now? Would you like to command troops once more? I'm sure I could convince Lord Falknor to give you your old posting at Kremos Keep back if you'd like."

The elderly woman shook her head. "My fight is done. You will be my last student, my last chance. Fix this kingdom, burn it, do something but do not ever be like the rest of them, those sheep. I allowed myself to be the pawn of others for too long and it almost ruined me. Do not make my mistakes." Illusionist Maeve cracked a smile on her wrinkled face. "As for what I'll do, I've talked to that boy Grimm. He has a brothel that needs a new overseer and spying on the youth making their own mistakes will do this old woman some good."

Lykos smirked. "Never change Maeve."

Chapter Fifty-One

"This cloak itches."

"Grimm."

"And it's an ugly color."

"Grimm."

"I don't know why I even have to be here, she's your ally."

"Shut up Grimm."

They stood on the boardwalk leading up to the Prodotis home. Ahead of them was a line of other party guests, each waiting their turn to present themselves and to enter. Grimm had invited himself to accompany Lykos on this errand when he had discovered who was going to meet them there but decided complaining what the best way to pass time.

Wishing Falka would get here faster Lykos examined the Prodotis home carved out of the cliff. Like House Falknor, House Prodotis had chosen to utilize the mountains for their home although their decision was also for practicality considering the marsh resting below. He realized with some amusement that far up on the cliff above them rested Hearthome. He briefly wondered if this had been intentional but was distracted by Grimm pulling his sleeve.

"She's beautiful." The adoration in his voice alerted Lykos to Falka's arrival. Turning around he privately agreed, Falka looked magnificent in her sweeping blue dress that waved in the gentle wind. The swamp gas did detract from her appearance somewhat though.

"Aye." Lykos gave his friend a warm smile as she joined them.

"Lykos," she greeted warmly. "Grimm! I did not expect to see you here tonight."

"Oh Lykos insisted I be here tonight." Lykos gave an oblivious Grimm an unimpressed look. "He's been complaining all evening waiting, well you know how he is."

Falka winked at Lykos. "I do. Why once I had to kill all the Stultus guards for him!"

"I killed some," he angrily countered. She merely smiled.

"And I killed some. And then some more. And then a few more after that. I think there was another group after that as well wasn't there?"

"Let's just go," Lykos grumbled, walking towards the now empty Prodotis gates. Sharing a laugh Falka and Grimm flanked him on either side, all three mindful of loose boards that could trip them. As they approached the gate a large woman in mail and plate armor blocked their path.

"No weapons allowed within my lady's home. Disarm yourselves or be turned away," she ordered. Lykos looked to the left and right theatrically, noting that none of the other party goers had left their weapons with the guard. With narrowed eyes he turned back to the smirking woman.

"If it's a question of money-" he began before he was cut off.

"I've been well compensated this evening," she smirked as she brushed a bulging pouch hanging from her belt, "and I do not lack in coin. You have nothing to offer me Lord Talal. Either forgo your weapons or leave my lady's grounds."

Lykos gave Grimm a glance who nodded back with a grin. Sauntering up to the taller woman Grimm gave her what he believed to be a charming smile and what Lykos privately thought made him look constipated.

"Lovely lass I would be greatly honored if I could bestow a kiss upon your hand this evening!" he began grandiosely. The woman stared at him blankly.

"You want to kiss my hand?" she repeated dumbly. He looked pleased his attempt at seduction was going so well.

"Yes, I would consider myself to be blessed by the Goddesses to kiss your hand!" Anything else he was about to say would go unheard as the woman delivered a savage right cross to his face with her armored fist. The surprised Lord Sofos fell to the ground stunned. Falka shook her head in disappointment.

"Never send a man to do a woman's job," she muttered under her breath as she approached the guard. Leaning close to her ear she began to whisper several interesting and provocative things causing the guard to blush heavily. Grimm looked up at the pair impressed and aroused and Lykos nudged him with his boot to stand up and cover himself. Embarrassed, Grimm stood and wrapped his cloak tightly around himself as Falka finished her one sided conversation.

"So won't you be a dear and allow me and my friends entrance?" she asked sweetly. The guard nodded furiously and breathed raggedly.

"Of course my lady!" The woman stood aside and Falka led her two companions into House Prodotis' home. Lykos nudged Falka to gain her attention.

"I only have one question." She raised a questioning eyebrow towards him. "I can understand the need for the pillows, mead, and the belts but what would you need eight scribes for?"

Her answer made the trio laugh into the night however their mirth quickly subsided as they entered the ball room. The room was carved deep into the rocky mountain and the many stone pillars were covered in carvings depicting Tainted being slaughtered gruesomely. But these beasts were merely decoration to the true monster in the room for opposite of Lykos stood Lord Kolos talking to Rickard of House Agroti.

Slowly Lykos advanced into the room, his eyes sweeping from side to side as he examined the occupants. Houses Vrachos, Miles, Agroti, and Kolos were well represented while only a minor amount of Lykos' allies were present. Although he wasn't quite sure he could label Kiara of Emporo as an ally.

"What a friendly looking bunch," Falka commented as a servant approached with glasses of wine. Lykos waved the man off and ignored how the servant gave the trio a sniff of contempt.

"It's almost like everyone who wants you dead or at least don't care if you live, is in this room right now," Grimm commented impressed.

"Does that still include you?" Lykos asked dryly.

"It changes from day to day. Today I feel inclined to aid you."

"Your loyalty is deeply appreciated."

"As entertaining as you two are, I'm off to go complete my assignment Lykos," Falka interrupted.

Grimm shot them both an inquisitive look. "What assignment?"

"While I distract our hostess Falka is to sneak into Lilith's private chambers and find any evidence of betrayal."

"Lilith? Lady Prodotis!" Grimm hissed furiously. Glancing around to make sure no one could overhear them, he protested, "you cannot send Falka to face off against the Prodotis guards alone!"

"Thanks for the support," Falka gave him an unimpressed look. "But I intend to sneak past them, not announce my presence."

"It's still too dangerous!" he weakly pleaded to Lykos. Falka began to turn red in anger but Lykos spoke firmly.

"Agreed." Falka and Grimm turned, giving him a look of betrayal and relief respectively. "Which is why you'll cause a distraction for the guards while Falka gets her work done."

Falka nodded reluctantly while Grimm considered his order. "I suppose just killing the lot of them is out of the question?" he muttered rhetorically.

Lykos almost agreed out of reflex but caught the words before they left his tongue. Opening and closing his mouth several times, each time his answer changing, he finally decided on a course of action. "Do whatever needs to be done."

Grimm nodded before turning to Falka. "Shall we my lady?" Lykos could hear a slight tint of possession in his voice as he offered her his arm.

"Try not to get yourself killed," Falka told Lykos, taking Grimm's arm and pulling him away. "Step lively Lord Sofos we have a villainess to plunder!"

Lykos turned his attention to the ballroom and the occupants within. Here and there he could see hostile faces watching him from the crowd and he considered the pros and cons of simply killing them all with sword and magic. Waving away the rather insistent servant offering wine once more he briefly considered who would enable him to cause the biggest scene and thus distraction. However with a smirk on his face and a quick, bold stride he knew exactly who to approach to cause the biggest threat in the room; he made his way to Lord Kolos.

The many nobles parted quickly before his gait and the room quieted noticeably as he approached the one-eyed lord. A soft, feminine figure joined him on his journey through the jeweled and finely clothed hordes of beasts within the room.

"Lilith." Lykos' smirk became a full blown grin and he knew he must look quite demented as he determinedly walked towards Lord Kolos.

"Lykos!" She attempted to pull him to the side but he ignored her touch quite easily. "Perhaps we should talk to some of the other guests first, there is no need for an interaction between yourself and Lord Kolos just yet."

"Nonsense! You've been telling me for weeks to meet with him as a friend and to mend our conflict! Perhaps it is time?" She actually paused in disbelief at his words, stopping to stare at him in bafflement.

"Really?"

"No." His grin only became wider as adrenaline began to pump through his veins. Lilith frantically caught up to him.

"I thought I had ordered no weapons to be allowed?" she asked, gesturing to the sword on his hip. "Give me your sword Lykos, it will make the guests nervous."

He blatantly eyed the weapons upon each of the nobles around them, as well as the armored guards lining the walls. She huffed in frustration.

"Come Lykos, let us dance!" she exclaimed gaily grabbing his hand. She succeeded in turning him partly and instead of resisting he simply spun, launching her into an onlooking nobleman.

"My apologies Lady Prodotis but I seem to have two left feet," Lykos commented, never halting in his walk. Finally he arrived next to Lord Kolos and Lord Agroti who both glared at him in stony silence.

Contempt filled both men's eyes although Lykos knew not which was less surprising. Lord Kolos, obviously, desired to control the kingdom and his actions to free the slaves usurped that dream. Lord Agroti was simply greedy, especially with the ease in which he had moved in on his deceased brother's lordship. So knowing it would infuriate both men, he neglected to give the traditional nod of respect and spoke with gusto.

"Rickard! Glad to see you've managed to tear yourself away from the Lowland. And Kopanos! You've left your lofty tower. Well isn't that interesting? The man who rules the highest part of the kingdom talking to the man who rules the lowest! Aren't these events simply grand? You never know who you'll rub shoulders with!"

"Brat," Rickard sneered in contempt. "You have a lot of nerve showing your face after abandoning House Agroti."

"Says the man who refuses to honor the pact his house made with my own," Lykos countered without hesitation. Rickard swelled impotently with rage but Lykos ignored him, turning to Lord Kolos. "Nothing to say tyrant?"

The crowd murmured at his bold accusations, surprised that he would dare insult Lord Kolos to his face. The man for his part merely looked at him as one who would examine a particularly interesting rock.

"I try not to allow the opinions of my inferiors bother me overly much, I have much more important matters to pursue." The crowd laughed appreciatively at his words but Lykos' rebuttal was already prepared.

"Like whipping slaves, stealing land, and poisoning those who oppose you?" The whispers almost became a riot at his bold accusations and Kopanos' stare once more became cold. Rickard for his part seemed to realize the danger of his situation and backed out of it slowly, not wanting to draw either lord's attention. Lykos and Kopanos stepped closer and laid their hands on their respective weapons.

"I also offer mercy. Shawna has felt my kindness these past years," Kopanos' remark had the crowd whispering as Lykos flushed in anger. Knowing that those present had condoned his mother's prolonged banishment and imprisonment he switched tactics.

"I am rather surprised you showed up tonight. Considering how I've been burning out your assassin's these past few weeks."

A look came to Kopanos' eye that Lykos did not like. It gleamed with a light that told of hidden knowledge and a mocking amusement at watching a fool dance without knowledge for an audience. It told him that he was missing something crucial about the situation and he loathed being ignorant. Kopanos shrugged carelessly at him.

"I was due to do it myself soon anyways. They were becoming unruly." Kopanos looked beyond him for a moment. "Viktor, put that dagger away."

Lykos turned slightly to see a fuming Viktor with a raised dagger standing three paces from him. The young man glared at him but turned to Lord Kolos. "Father please?"

"No," he said shortly. "You're making a fool of yourself and House Kolos." Lykos was amused to see the man so furious at his heir's actions, the surrounding nobles watching the interaction with eager eyes. Viktor growled as he sheathed his dagger.

"Good boy," Lykos mocked as he insultingly turned his back on Viktor. "Probably for the best considering last time I sent him running with his tail between his legs."

"Why you little-"

"Heirs often disappoint their lords," Kopanos said evenly, ignoring his son. "Leon at least had the decency to succumb to the greater good."

The persistent servant once more offered his tray of drinks and Lykos at once understood his purpose. The wine was poisoned, from Kopanos or Lilith it did not matter which, and he was to die in front of the nobles of Mycenae as a demonstration of power. Such a shame for them that he refused to yield to their desires.

Reaching his hand out towards the servant the man obediently proffered his tray in relief, presenting it with satisfaction. Lykos took a fragile glass from the man's tray and raised it towards Kopanos.

"How about a toast?" Kopanos looked at the glass with sharp eyes but composed himself. That answered who poisoned the wine.

"Of course Lord Talal, what should we toast to this evening?" The words were mocking, as if he were bestowing a great honor upon Lykos. *In a way it was*, he thought. Giving him free reign to say what he pleased in such a public forum was a great boon to him and his cause.

"Freedom," Lykos said smartly. "After all is it not the duty of those such as we to better the lives of those who serves us? Should we not free them from being slaves to starvation and danger? To those who would do them harm? So I stand before the good nobility of this kingdom and raise this toast to us and to those who serve us: all men deserve to be free and we shall bring that freedom to them."

The range of emotions that Kopanos' face cycled through was truly fascinating to watch for Lykos. Anger, rage, disgust, contempt all flashed in quick succession on the one-eyed man's face before settling on anticipation. Raising his glass mockingly in agreement the two men drank the wine with their audience slowly following suit. Cool, dry wine slid down his throat and Lykos could smell the barest edge of a familiar poison. He drained the whole glass.

Kopanos began to smile, his own glass gripped lightly in his hand. "Excellent wine Lord Talal?"

"Not a terrible vintage but the poison ruined the glass," Lykos replied examining how his magic tried to burn the poison out. It was ineffectual and it quickly began to tire itself attacking an enemy that wouldn't end. He briefly wondered if he had a death wish, after all purposely poisoning yourself in a room full of potential enemies is not the action of a sane man.

"You knew the glass was poisoned?" Kopanos asked in astonishment. Lykos gave him an unimpressed smile as he felt the strength start to drain from his limbs.

"Oh but of course."

"So why did you drink it? Do you think you can overcome it unlike so many before you? Like your father?" Kopanos taunted. Lykos' smile was as dark as a Tainted's soul.

"So you would toast to freedom," Kopanos reddened in rage but Lykos quickly continued, "and so I could do this." He crushed the glass in his hand, the glass shards cutting deep into his skin. Focusing on his magic he felt how it feebly tried to burn the poison out of his system, exhausting itself. Instead of fruitlessly trying to fight it, he guided it, pushed it towards the open wound on his hand. Wrapping the poison in his magic was a difficult task but he enforced his iron will upon it and was rewarded. Before the eyes of everyone watching he pushed the poison out, it turning his crimson blood black as it splattered on the floor where it quietly sizzled. The crowd murmured excitedly as he stood proudly, not dead, before them all, his wounds slowly closing and cutting off the now poison free blood.

The technique was something he and Helen had theorized after his second poisoning. While magic could be used to neutralize most poisons a few were too vicious to overcome. However their little work around was to not neutralize the poison but to merely contain it. Once done it could be removed through any open wound. Helen would be pleased to hear of the effectiveness of their technique and would undoubtedly try to name it after the Valkyries.

Kopanos sneered but then growled in rage at what Lykos had just done. The most terrible weapon of assassin's within the kingdom had just been publicly beaten, easily so, and it would now lose its effectiveness locally. Word would spread on a way for anyone with magic to combat poison and now it would only be useful on common folk, the least important citizens of the kingdom. As the excited nobles began to whisper Kopanos roared.

"You will die boy! And it will not be gentle nor kind! I will make you beg for death for decades before granting you its sweet release!" He began to stalk through the crowd, it parting before his wrath.

"You don't have a good record at killing me Kopanos of Kolos," Lykos spoke softly but his voice captured the attention of everyone present, including Kopanos who paused trembling in rage. "In fact every time you have tried to end me I've only gotten stronger. So keep trying, make me stronger, so that when I end you, you will know you created your own demise."

Lord Kolos gave a snarl of rage and left the room to the excited whispers of nobles. Lykos became aware of the silently fuming Lady Prodotis beside him.

"Is something the matter Lilith?" Her face was pinched in anger, ruining her make up, but he did not think she was aware of that fact. She gave him a frustrated look.

"Why must you make things so difficult! I've worked so hard on bringing peace to this kingdom and now you've ruined it all-"

He cut her off before her rant could build. "Contain yourself Lady Prodotis. There will never be peace between that man and I, not until one or both of us is dead. Remove from your fantasy the possibility of him and I being allies and act as the ally you claim to be. Falka, Grimm. So good to see you both."

Falka and Grimm rejoined him and greeted Lady Prodotis. The woman huffed and walked away without another word leaving the trio alone.

"Did you find anything?" Lykos asked Falka. The raven-haired woman nodded angrily.

"Another of those communication devices Irene found. I left it behind though as I thought it would be suspicious if it disappeared tonight."

"Agreed," Lykos murmured but his thoughts were miles away. Lilith had not been alerted of Irene's reappearance nor of the evidence she had procured. There was no rational reason for her to have a volka nor for her keeping it quiet. Combined with her choice in party guests and actions a rather alarming fact had made itself clear to Lykos: House Prodotis was not an ally.

Chapter Fifty-Two

"I demand an audience with Lord Talal!" Lykos looked away from the tea he was pouring Shawna as they caught up. The soldiers stationed near the house were crossing their spears in front of Lilith, denying the infuriated woman entrance to the garden. He waved them aside.

"Good morning Lilith. Come to enjoy the view?" He gestured towards the edge of the terrace. Past its vista Mycenae was blooming with new growth as spring descended upon the kingdom. It was a fantastic view and he could finally appreciate why House Talal had laid claim to this peak when Pyrgos had been settled.

"What is wrong with you!" Lilith shrieked. Shawna shot the younger woman a disappointed look.

"So rude," she sniffed in disdain. Lykos' look of amusement only fueled Lilith's ire.

"My keen grasp of the human psyche is telling me something is upsetting you. Please make yourself comfortable and tell me all about it," Lykos suggested, gesturing to an open seat. She ignored it.

"Why must you be so difficult! Why can you not simply end your feud with Kopanos?"

Lykos pretended to give it a considering look. "Mother, do you think I should befriend Kopanos of House Kolos, the man who abuses the people of this kingdom, poisoned and killed your husband, and who kept you in isolation for the worst part of two decades?"

"I sometimes fantasize about feeding him his remaining eyeball before throwing him off the highest tower of the Citadel," she replied while daintily sipping her tea.

"That's," he paused to give it a moment of thought, "honestly tempting." Privately he was pleased such a bloodthirsty response had come from his mother. Lilith was not.

"You barbaric war mongers!" she screamed. A small gust of wind began to blow through the garden as her magic reacted to her emotions. "I have worked tirelessly to mend bridges, to build trust with House Kolos and you have swatted it away time and time again!"

"Trust?" Lykos asked incredulously "I wouldn't trust that man if he told me the sky was blue! But while we are on the subject of trust, let's talk about you."

"Me?" Her eyes widened in surprise at the accusation. He was pleased to see a small hint of fear in her eyes before she suppressed it.

"Yes you," Lykos drawled. "For an ally of mine you seem awfully determined to place me in the same room as my enemy, without any means on defending myself."

"Preposterous!"

"Oh? So your soldier was not ordered to confiscate the weapons of myself and my allies and leave us defenseless and at the mercy of our many enemies? The ones you had so graciously invited to your ball and allowed their weapons?"

"You were perfectly safe! It would have been a sign of good faith to go without your weapons-"

"It would have been a sign of foolishness. The only reason why I even walked out of your home without being turned into a pincushion was because I poisoned myself." He tried and failed to pretend that statement was perfectly reasonable. "Besides if it was a sign of good faith Kopanos should have forgone his weapons as well. Poisons as well."

"That's not the same thing," she protested.

Shawna spoke up. "Yes, allowing my son to be poisoned is perfectly reasonable but Goddesses forbid you take away that murderer's dagger. Should be tossed to the Tainted at the gate...."

"That does not excuse your actions at my ball last night! I have never been so embarrassed and in my own home no less."

"And your continued actions have worn on my nerves long enough Lilith. Our alliance has born little fruit and you must decide if you wish to continue being my ally." He stood from his seat and placed a hand on his sword. "Choose: Talal or Kolos. Me or Kopanos. Now."

Lilith huffed, in anger or fright he did not know, but she glared at him through narrowed eyes. "I helped you conquer the Emporo!"

"You did nothing. Adelram did more with the Talal forces, negotiating their movement through the Latom with the Vrachos, than you did conquering Ploio! Choose Lilith."

She opened her mouth, to continue the argument no doubt, but shut it with a click. "Very well. I shall think on this. I'll send word of my answer tomorrow."

Lykos raised an eyebrow at the power play but decided to ignore it. Regardless of her choice she would never again be considered an ally. Neutrality from him was the best she could hope for. He nodded and bade her farewell.

"Goodbye Lykos. Goodbye Dowager Talal." Lilith left the garden as quickly as she had entered and tranquility was restored.

"What a nasty piece of work," Shawna told him. "Ladies used to be respectful and honorable, you could trust their word. I wouldn't trust that hussy to tell me which end of a Tainted Charger has the explodey bits."

"The entire Charger can explode," Lykos told her with an indulgent smile. "Although I think it might be more for its hatred of humanity than being prodded with an exceptionally pointy stick."

"Adelram never forgave you for that did he? My cousin always knew how to hold a grudge." He rested back into his seat as Shawna prattled on, telling a story he already had heard a dozen times before. Today was one of the few days he had to relax and he wasn't going to let anything ruin it.

"Lord Talal!" One of his soldiers rushed forward panting heavily. "We're being attacked!"

"By who?" he demanded rising to his feet.

"Houses Kolos and Prodotis my lord!"

Damn.

Chapter Fifty-Three

I will never allow a potential enemy to live, Lykos vowed angrily. Report after report, bloody soldiers from all corners of Mycenae trickled in giving the same news: Prodotis and Kolos forces were marshaled outside of the Pyrgos' gates to the displeasure of Houses Vrachos and Miles respectively. Not that either one put up much of a fight.

When Lykos had gifted the rivers to the Prodotis to be under their control it allowed them almost complete access to the kingdom. Pyrgos and Kremos were the only defensible positions remaining due to the stark height difference between them and their neighboring quarters and by that extension the Riverfront was buffered. The rest of the kingdom was suffering while they held out.

"We controlled over half the kingdom and now we're down to less than a fourth!" Lykos snarled as he slammed his fist into the wooden table before him. With him was Adelram and Illusionist Maeve as they compiled the various reports of enemy movement. "How did we not see this happening?"

"The Prodotis have complete control of the rivers, they could move a whole army and we wouldn't even know about it. Moving their forces and House Kolos' wouldn't be outside the realm of possibility," Adelram answered. Illusionist Maeve waved her hand dismissively.

"Possible or not it doesn't matter. We've been hoodwinked and the only thing to do is learn from it and move on to killing the bastards."

"Agreed." Lykos nodded respectfully to his mentor. "I've already ordered our soldiers to secure the gates leading into Latom, with our elevation they'll never fall. The bridge into Aspida on the other hand will only be able to hold off the Kolos forces for so long before they secure it. We need reinforcements."

"Can you use the volka to contact our allies?" Adelram asked.

"I don't know, can we Illusionist Maeve?" Lykos pointedly asked annoyed.

Illusionist Maeve began to mutter harshly under her breathe. Adelram looked at her in disbelief. "What am I missing?" She glared at the grizzled man but reluctantly began to pull several volka from a pouch at her waist. "You never gave them to our allies!"

"I was testing their capabilities as well as seeking ways to improve them! They're crude if effective tools and their full potential is so much more than mere communication. With enough time I think we can use these crystals to link minds, true mental-"

Adelram cut her off. "That's very fascinating but entirely unhelpful at this point. We need to get word to our allies to counter this threat. Goddesses we don't even know who we can trust."

"Yes we do." Lykos tapped two sections of the kingdom. "Grimm and Falka, and by extension their families, will aid us. The status of the Emporo is unknown but considering they're in the way of the Prodotis and the Prodotis are at our gates, it's safe to assume they're in no position to aid us."

"Not that they would be willing to," Adelram commented. Lykos hummed in thought.

"The way I see it I need to get to Kremos. From there I can rally Houses Falknor and Sofos and we can attack the Prodotis and Kolos forces from both sides." He grabbed the volka and placed them in his own pouch. "And it would allow me to deliver these in person, a courier would never be able to reach them safely and being able to talk to our allies is vital."

"Well what are you waiting for boy get going!" Illusionist Maeve barked.

Getting out of Pyrgos was actually rather easy for him, he merely used the water passage he, Falka, and Ana Del Rosa used the previous year to rescue slaves. The freezing water sapped the strength from his limbs and slowed him but he willed himself to continue, knowing that time was of the essence. Exiting under the waterfall he ground to a halt at the terrible scene before him.

Screaming and ransacking was rampant in Ploio, terrified Emporo common folk fleeing anywhere they could as Prodotis raiders moved through them like a wild Tainted Horde. Fires burned here and there as the Prodotis forces worked their evils upon the terrified men, women, and children. The sight sickened him as it was all too familiar.

In the mines he had witnessed much and the needless cruelty always struck him as wasteful. Fighting for the scare food, a small dry patch to curl up to rest, these were constants in his life growing up. And the things humans did to one another.... his blood boiled in rage at the terrible things that have been done, are being done, will be done.

So it was with great reluctance he turned from the chaos and made his way to the gate leading into Latom. Even with magic he couldn't restore order to the kingdom by himself so it was with a heavy heart he employed stealth to reach his allies. Sticking to the shadows he made his way through the gate without incident, blending in with one of the crowds rushing into Latom. Spying Prodotis raiders up ahead, he ducked his head and moved closer to a nearby cart. He passed by without incident.

Latom's layout meant that few buildings were on the surface and that moving through it to the Reliquary or Pyrgos was a simple endeavor. However it was also perfect for an army to set up a camp with strong fortifications, each cavern carved out of the rock created trenches to obstruct any attackers. With the Agroti farms and orchards decorating the land, supplies were abundant and an army in siege could remain for months. However Lykos had no intention of remaining in Latom.

Along the northern edge of the quarter were a series of drains leading into the sewer system beneath the kingdom. However more important were the secret passages that led into Lykos' least favorite part of the kingdom: the Catacombs.

Hundreds of thousands of skulls gazed without blinking at him. Tainted Gnawers and Vipers scurried and slithered over the bones of the long dead, making nests in the remains of their foes. He felt ill at the sight of a trio of Vipers slithering through the eyes and mouths of the dead as he walked past them, their hissing warnings ignored as he made his way through the maze of the dead. His goal was simple, he needed to get to Kremos so he could rally his allies.

But first he had to make his way through this morbid path, the dead his only companions. Thousands upon thousands of men, women, and children had died in Mycenae since its creation and not all burial rights consumed flesh and bone in purifying fire. Most were stripped of their skin and muscle and organs, the matter burned away and kept as ashes by mourning families. The bones of the dead were "gifted" Lykos thought with a sneer, to the foundations of the kingdom, to strengthen them. The macabre practice had been in place for centuries.

But not the noble houses, he thought as he stepped carefully around a pool of stagnant water. Those of such rich blood would not be content to be buried with the common folk, the ones they lorded over. Above him, on the surface of the Reliquary were great tombs for each house and within them hundreds of souls rested. The mere thought that they were the only ones allowed to breathe the fresh air left a sour taste in his throat for he was harshly reminded of the mines of Svellheim.

The Tainted did not attack him as he walked through the darkness, the small flame conjured in his hand chasing shadows. At first he was content to not challenge his good fortune but he quickly realized he was being herded by the Tainted along certain paths. Swarms of Gnawers obstructed stairs, Vipers formed impassable walls blocking side passageways, and he was led ever downwards by them. But since his path remained consistent, ever onward to Kremos, he allowed humanities most hated foe to corral him.

A bright light appeared before him which did not belong. Quenching the flame in his hand he walked forward into it to find himself in a vast place that should not have been there, illuminated by glowing purple fungus on the walls. Where solid rock and dirt should be was a vast hole that led deep into the earth, its depths unknown. All around the room Tainted creatures rested and Lykos realized that this was their nest, underneath the kingdom. He knew he could not allow it to remain and drew his sword and prepared to call upon his magic.

The rasp of steel echoed through the cavernous space and the Tainted all turned as one to face him. Firming his mouth he stepped towards the closest swarm of Gnawers when a low rumble filled the cavern. All movement stopped as the ground began to shake and he looked around wildly trying to find the cause. However his eyes were drawn to the pit in the center of the room.

Slowly a massive form began to rise from the darkness. Pitch black scales, darker than the surrounding darkness, were thrown into stark contrast with the bones of dead humans caught in the grooves between them. And still the mammoth creature rose higher and higher, its presence nearly reaching the roof of the chamber before finally halting. And then it roared.

The earth shook and Lykos felt the power of magic in the air. But this was not human magic but the foul, twisted magic of the massive Tainted Viper in front of him. It spoke of eons of suffering, pain, and rage and it was all directed towards humanity. Towards Lykos. *The Titan Viper*, he named it in his mind, turned its face towards him and glared at him with hostile eyes larger than a man. It roared at him once more and he was nearly driven to his knees by the strength of its magic.

He had to kill this he realized with dread. Never before had he seen a Tainted so large, never before had he killed something this size. The doubts crept into his minds as the thought of failure consumed him. Falka would die. So would Grimm. That the Titan Viper had not already broke the surface, attacked Mycenae mattered not, it would now. It would take his entrance to its home as a challenge and it would respond in kind, killing Falka, Grimm, Adelram, and Shawna....

No.

Lykos felt the oppressing magic snap and realized his doubts had been caused by the Tainted in front of him, attempting to defeat him without ever attacking. It roared again, the stone around the cavern rattling, shaking, and in some cases floating as it was touched by the Tainted's magic. But he roared back an answering challenge and with three quick steps leaped towards the beast with his sword raised high.

"What was that?" Falka asked Grimm as the ground began to rumble. Barricading Kremos from the Kolos forces in the east had left the pair paranoid, the sudden attack surprising them both. But the natural defenses of Kremos held strong and now they were discussing their next possible move with Falka's father.

"Perhaps an earthquake?" Grimm replied as the ground ceased its tremors. Lord Falknor opened his mouth to respond when a shock wave of magic shook the earth.

"That's not an earthquake! To arms! We're under attack!" Lord Falknor cried to his soldiers. The trio rushed through the quarter as masonry cracked and broke all around them.

"Who's attacking us?" Grimm shouted after pushing a flesh maiden out of the way of a falling brick. The woman screamed in terror but the trio did not halt their rush through the quarter.

"Not who, what! It's a Tainted!" Lord Falknor replied, his wrinkled face flush with exertion. "Pray to the Valkyries that we can kill it before it breaches our defenses."

"A Tainted is doing this?" Falka shouted before asking the more pressing question, "Tainted have magic?" Lord Falknor stumbled as the ground shook more violently than any yet. A vicious, muted roar could be heard and felt in some nearby place.

"Yes!" Lord Falknor answered as Grimm helped the old lord to his feet. "If a Tainted grows large enough, lives long enough, they can start influencing the world like we can! This will not be an easy fight."

Great roars were now audible, the ground shaking as if some giant had grasped the world with both hands violently, and the common folk of Kremos were fleeing away from the mountain as loose stones fell. Falka, Grimm, and Lord Falknor reached an intersection in the road when the world quieted around them. "Is it over?" a Falknor soldier asked to everyone, anyone.

The ground beneath the man burst upwards, throwing stone, dirt, and rock everywhere, and while he disappeared into that storm his screams did not. Dust filled the air as the ground shook more violently than any quake before and from that cloud of dust a dark shape emerged. Stretching taller than the buildings lining the street rose a Tainted Viper whose girth rivaled those same buildings. When it finally stopped rising the ground stopped shaking and it gave a terrible roar of magic and air that knocked all gathered to the ground. And then it began to thrash angrily against the buildings.

"Clear the area! Aim for its eyes!" Lord Falknor cried pointing to where one of the Viper's eyes had been ripped out, the gaping hole oozing thick liquid. Grimm sent a fireball that splashed harmlessly against the Tainted's thick scales, knocking loose what he was shocked to realize were human bones.

"It's too strong my lord! We need to evacuate the quarter and call in the Citadel guard to take care of it!" one of Lord Falknor's men shouted to him. The Viper's thrashing had become almost frantic as it smashed its head into the ground, not even paying any heed to the hail of arrows the Falknor soldiers sent.

"I wish Lykos were here!" Falka cried as another of her arrows missed the beast's eyes. Suddenly the monstrous Viper halted its thrashing and threw its head straight up into the sky. A gurgle came from its massive maw and it fell, fell, fell to the ground below, crushing several buildings in its way. A sad sigh of air escaped the Viper's mouth as its body rested and the oppressing magic in the air dissipated.

Slowly Lord Falknor approached the collapsed beast, climbing over a partially destroyed pub to reach its head. Up close the huge creature's body was even more shocking, the hundreds of bones stuck between the scales no less frightening. He looked into the gaping hole in its head where an eye had once been before moving to the other side to look into the remaining one. No hellish light shown from those dark depths.

"It's dead," he said dumbfounded to Falka and Grimm who had joined him. "How did it die?"

As if in response a soft glow grew in the Viper's eye. Lord Falknor scrambled backwards, terrified that the beast might still be alive and rise from its position to slay them all but he needn't have worried. The glow in the Tainted's eye grew brighter and brighter, not their natural hellish light but a cool blue. And then the eye popped.

A wave of heat and goo exploded outwards, missing Falka who sensibly hid behind Grimm. The two men had no such luck and received a face full of the foul smelling liquid. So distracted as they were by the explosion they almost missed the person exiting the Viper's eye. There, covered in gore, stood Lykos.

"I think this might be one of my better entrances," he stated calmly as he stepped out of the eye. Falka wrinkled her nose.

"But you stink."

"I do. However few things catch the attention like casually slaying a Titan Viper."

"We're calling these things Titan Vipers? Sounds like someone is overcompensating." Anything else Falka might have said died in her throat as the Titan Viper slowly began to slide backwards, falling back down into the hole. Just as suddenly as it appeared, the Titan Viper vanished.

Lord Falknor seemed to finally snap out of his shock. "Lord Talal! Your timing is impeccable. House Falknor is in your debt."

"And I intend to collect," Lykos calmly replied. "Our enemies have stepped from the shadows and now it's time to strike."

"Our soldiers and airships are yours to command but what about Houses Miles and Vrachos? They both have an army sitting upon their doorstep and we don't known if it's by their will or not."

Lykos began to wave his hand in front of Grimm's frozen face, the man still staring in shock at where the dead Tainted once lay. Curious, he looked between them but could not see what was so fascinating about the disappearance of a slain beast. Shrugging he turned back to Lord Falknor. "I will have to meet with them directly. It will be the best way to determine the truth of the matter."

"Going to where the armies of our enemies are gathered to find allies?" Falka smiled coyly. "Sounds fun."

Lord Falknor rolled his eyes at his daughter. "Yes fun. I suggest sending a courier to Houses Agroti, Miles, and Vrachos to meet in the Lowland to discuss current events. With what those events are they should come running."

Grimm finally snapped out of his shock. "I am never going be able to beat you am I?" he asked Lykos.

Lykos smirked. "Never."

Chapter Fifty-Four

The Agroti council chamber was full of loud voices arguing and the echos were beginning to grate on Lykos' nerves. The Agroti were there in force, a dozen members sitting in chairs throughout the chamber, as were Lord and Lady Vrachos who insisted on having their guards present for their protection. The real issue was House Miles.

House Miles was actually made up of five lesser houses whose extensive blood feuds almost ransacked the kingdom before Leon's Rebellion. During one of there rare moments of peace- in actuality a moment where they all had swords on each others necks and they were in real danger of going extinct- one of the houses had the intelligent idea to marry into each others families, to forcefully bring them peace. No one was pleased with this decision but all agreed that it would be the only way to ensure they don't perish in mutual destruction over more arguments. So House Miles was born.

With their odd number of houses it was decided that the new noble house would rule by majority opinion, with each member house having to vote lest they sacrifice their voice. However underhanded deals, blackmail, bribery, and extortion were common practice among their number so the little power the quintet had amassed was poorly wielded.

Five pairs of lords and ladies had showed up to represent the interest of House Miles and had spent the last hour arguing fervently over inconsequential issues. And throughout it all the Prodotis representative Commander Withers smirked at Lykos from his seat next to Alithis.

"Your daughter scorned my son!"

"Well he shouldn't have been showering the serving wenches with his seed!"

"You're one to talk, any new bastards among the Entari?"

"Butt out Sulfra scumbag, don't think I don't know you've been laying with my mistress!"

"Ha! She begged me for a real man to show her pleasure."

"Is that why she was knocking on my door?"

On and on it went and Lykos was fast losing his patience with the arguing lords and ladies. Rickard sat upon his throne like chair, grinning in glee at the sour expression on his face causing the young lord to finally snap.

"ENOUGH!" His voice drowned out the squabbling men and women and all were surprised to be interrupted "What is the hold up? We need to discuss the actions of the Prodotis and Kolos and you're arguing about who had sex with whom!"

The lords and ladies looked down abashed before Lady Ilic spoke up. "We're trying to determine who the spokesperson of House Miles will be in this meeting."

Lykos' control almost slipped and he narrowly withheld the urge to draw his sword and begin slaughtering the fools. Taking in a long deep breathe he blew it out slowly to calm himself down. Spying the smirking Commander Withers had him take another deep breathe. "Lady Ilic you're in charge of House Miles for the duration of this meeting." Spotting several angry faces he quickly continued. "And if you wish to argue that you can leave and your interests remain unspoken for."

That last bit of information was thanks to Illusionist Maeve. One of the worst scenarios for any member of House Miles was being forced to remain unspoken, to be silenced in their internal politics. More than one conflict had been avoided by the mere threat although some members still acted out despite that. Illusionist Maeve herself was one such member and hadn't been able to speak with her family in years.

"Now that everything is settled, perhaps we should discuss the reason why we are all here today?" Rickard's jowls warbled unpleasantly as he spoke. "Lord Kolos and Lady Prodotis are currently waging war against the impertinent Lord Talal and to do this they've occupied Aspida and Latom, held by my dear allies Houses Miles and Vrachos respectively. Now...."

Lykos narrowed his eyes at that new bit of information as Rickard rambled on. An alliance between the three was beneficial as it would allow him to gain their support in one swoop. However the same was true for his enemies which meant that this meeting could decide the war. He returned his attention to Rickard as he finished speaking.

"....We will now hear from the honorable Commander Withers, representing the interests of Houses Kolos and Prodotis."

Commander Withers rose to his feet and stood in the center of the room. "Friends! I am pleased to see you all in good health for these past few months have been trying on us all. There has been hunger, war, and cruelties that our peaceful kingdom hasn't seen in decades. And who is to blame for these actions?

"Lykos of House Talal! Just like his upstart father this fiend is determined to bring chaos and misery to this kingdom. He will bring this kingdom to ruin and he will drag us all to ruin with him! I ask you, would you throw in your lot with him? To throw away our decades of tradition? Or will you denounce him and raise your arms with us so that we might live in unison once more!"

A round of applause echoed through the room as several members of the audience applauded. Rickard clapped his hands lightly, nodding slightly at Commander Withers in agreement. He cleared his throat and gained everyone's attention. "What a passionate display. And now the opposition?"

Lykos paid no mind to the lack of respect, instead choosing to focus on the other men and women present. He rose from his seat and stepped down to the stone circle. Narrowing his eyes at Commander Withers, who did not vacate the space, he nonetheless turned his attention to his audience.

"Lies. I have heard naught but lies from this Viper since the moment I first met him. You name me a fiend? I name you a coward."

Commander Withers glared harshly at Lykos. "I speak only the truth! Why I-"

"You had your right to speak commander and now you will respect mine. Or do you only obey some of our traditions?" Their audience murmured in approval at his brazen approach. Commander Withers huffed and crossed his arms.

"When House Stultus fell I participated in the Succession Trial for the right to safeguard Pyrgos, a trial I prevailed in. When I took up the lordship of House Talal I went before you all and offered the hand of friendship. I have made overtures to each of your houses, respected all of your rights save one.

"I have not abided the law of slavery. I lived for years as a slave in the mines of Svellheim and when I was free, when I discovered who I was and the power I wielded, that we all wield as nobles! I knew I could not put anyone in that position, not even my enemies! And so I took up my father's banner and pushed as he did, for the rights and freedoms for all who call Mycenae home.

"Some of you opposed me. Some of you didn't care. But all of you have directly felt the touch of my actions, for better or for worse. I come before you this day not to ask you to die for me but to fight for this kingdom! I want you to help me build a kingdom where the strength and honor of a man is not traded like a bag of goods to be sold to the highest bidder.

"Commander Withers states that I am bringer of chaos and I agree! I will disrupt any system that thinks the oppression of a portion of the whole is valid. I will break any system of order that relies on such a viewpoint, I will oppose it in every fashion!"

The only sound in the room was the steady drip of water to the floor. The gathered lords and ladies watched him with careful eyes and he realized he might have just made his situation far worse by challenging the very system they had profited from. However he would not take back his words even if it did make him more enemies today, he had done far too much and gone too far to ever forgo his own conscience. However not all of those gathered were shocked into silence.

"You're as irreverent as always boy," Rickard sneered. The obese man looked to his fellow lords and ladies. "I think we can skip the debate, House Agroti is voting for war against House Talal."

Not surprised in the slightest, Lykos turned towards Lady Ilic as she hastily conferred with the other members of House Miles. As they talked Commander Withers moved closer to him.

"I will make you bleed for those lies."

"Oh commander, your fantasies always were the stuff of dreams."

"Mark my words Lord Talal," Commander Withers spat at his feet, "if I don't kill you Alithis will."

Lykos had almost forgotten Alithis' presence, the man's face blending in with the dozens of other men and women in the room. He sat calmly in his chair, his gaze unblinking upon Lykos. Noticing his attention the man sneered and Lykos knew that he had yet another enemy to deal with. That will be a problem for future he thought as he had more pressing concerns to focus on now.

"House Miles votes for trial by combat!" Lady Ilic's voice cried out. "We will side with whichever participant prevails!"

"House Vrachos seconds. We wish to see the skill that won the Succession Trial." Lord Vrachos echoed quickly. Rickard gave Lady Ilic and Lord Vrachos an ugly look but bowed his head.

"So be it," he spoke. "Lord Talal and Commander Withers will fight where they stand. Neither man may leave the stone circle or he will forfeit his claim and be branded a coward for the rest of his days! Begin!"

Lykos immediately threw his elbow out, aiming to strike Commander Withers on the jaw but was met with a blade clattering off his arm guard. Scowling with the realization that the man had prepared while the nobles spoke, he drew his own sword to block a swipe at his head.

In the circle the two men danced, their weapons swinging back and forth. Neither could use their magic easily, by the time a hand was raised their foe had moved and a swing of the sword was incoming. So instead they traded blows as sweat began to pour from their limbs, occasionally locking blades to try to overpower one another.

Lykos strained against their locked blades with all his might but Commander Withers would not budge an inch. The man glared into his eyes and whispered, "did you hear what I did to Lady Emporo? She declined my lady's offer of friendship so I cut that bastard out of her and strangled her with own child's remains! Kiara will make a much more acceptable Lady Emporo in the new order!"

"You are vermin Withers, I will cut you down into little bits and feed you to the Tainted at the walls," Lykos growled.

Commander Withers snarled and disengaged, twirling his sword to the side. Lykos ignored the obvious trap and instead tried to step to the side to force his opponent closer to the edge of the circle. His foe matched him and Lykos stepped to the side to avoid being forced out himself. He growled at the stalemate he was in and he knew he had to do something desperate if he were to succeed.

Stepping closer to Commander Withers the man matched his steps and both men were locked once more at the edge of the circle. Only this time Lykos allowed the commander to push him towards the edge. Caught off guard, Commander Withers hands were outstretched in the wrong moment as Lykos swung his sword up, cutting them off cleanly at the wrists. Withers bellowed in pain, falling to his knees as his mind registered the injury. Lykos stepped calmly away from the edge of the circle and stared down at him.

"May your soul never find rest," he stated hatefully. With a long sweep of his sword he beheaded the fiend, sending his head flying through the air. As a finishing touch Lykos kicked the handless, headless corpse out of the stone circle where it began to stain the water red with blood. Flicking the blood off his blade he looked up to see the gathered lords and ladies applauding and cheering his victory, save two.

"We ally with House Talal," Rickard reluctantly declared as his family cheered around him. However it was the second man who had Lykos' attention. Alithis rose from his chair, his hand upon his sword, staring at him with intense eyes. Everyone else looked on, wondering if there might be more bloodshed to be had. For a long moment they stared at one another before the Kolos representative nodded reluctantly.

"I will go inform Lord Kolos of this development." The restrained anger in his voice was music to Lykos' ear. Now to deal with the armies surrounding his home.

Chapter Fifty-Five

Having gifted several volka to his allies, Lykos found directing the movements of his forces across the kingdom to be greatly simplified. With Grimm leading the Agroti and Sofos to retake Ploio and the Marsh and Lord Falknor and his children pushing through the Reliquary to Latom, Lykos began to push through Naos to Aspida. With Houses Agroti, Miles, and Vrachos allied with him, the Prodotis and Kolos forces were quickly finding themselves unable to mount a serious offensive against his home.

Lykos and his allies struck like lightning against the Kolos and Prodotis lines, their fortifications facing the wrong way as they found their rear vulnerable. By the end of the first day he had reclaimed much of the lost territory and he was pleased to receive word that Lord Falknor had forced House Prodotis from Latom. The narrow tracks of land worked against the swamp dwellers as the Falknor air fleet leapfrogged their forces over the gaps with ease.

But with the rise of a new day Lykos was determined to force House Kolos from its position in Aspida, forcing them away from his gates entirely. Pulling his own volka out of his pouch he used it to contact Adelram within Pyrgos.

"Lord Talal." Adelram's stern voice and words alerted Lykos that some of his soldiers must be present. "Your forces are ready."

"Excellent, I'm making my way to the front lines now. Have we determined who's in charge of House Kolos' forces Commander

Adelram?" The volka spun slowly in his hands, always pointing one end towards where Adelram must be. Lykos noted the possible tracking implications to be tested later.

"An old friend of yours, Heir Kolos, has been heard shouting at the pass. He can't cross it thanks to our archers but some of the common folk have been complaining about the noise."

"Well we can't have that," Lykos remarked dryly. "When I give the signal open the gate from our side and take theirs."

"Of course Lord Talal." The volka stopped spinning as Adelram closed the connection from his end. Stowing the device Lykos continued walking through the sea of grim men and women who joined him from House Miles as they readied to drive the invaders from their home. Approaching the fortified crossroads that separated the respective forces, he found Lady Ilic talking to Lord Entari as they directed their soldiers. Approaching, he overheard part of their conversation.

"Mikaelson is still as arrogant as ever," Lord Entari told Lady Ilic. "He refuses to allow us to train our soldiers in how to forage in the wilderness. What if we had to siege one of the other kingdoms? We'd perish!"

"So I can count on your support on the next vote? I'm sure we could find an.... agreeable compromise."

"Compromises.... Can be enjoyable. My wife had been so distant lately it will be enjoyable to have company once more."

"I see we understand one another my lord. Perhaps we may get to know one another better after this dreadful event is over."

"Hopefully a great deal better sooner."

"Lord Talal! Are you prepared to help rid our lands of these interlopers?" Lady Ilic curtsied when she noticed him standing there. Lykos idly wondered if she thought she was being discreet but decided to pay it no mind as the internal politics of House Miles did not interest or concern him.

"I am. Do you have any further questions about the plan?" He hoped she did not considering the number of times he had to repeat himself explaining it to her and the other members of House Miles last night.

Fortunately it seemed some information finally stuck. "I do not Lord Talal. I'll go ready the archers for our assault."

Beside her Lord Entari nodded. "And I'll go ready the swordsmen." Lykos restrained the urge to roll his eyes as the lord and lady went off together in the wrong direction. Gesturing to two nearby couriers he gave them the orders to alert the soldiers that now was the time to strike.

Despite the lack of leadership, the centurions of House Miles effectively directed their soldiers into charging the Kolos lines. Lykos followed behind their stampeding charge, the clash of metal and man always a few steps away from him, but not one of House Kolos' soldiers stepped close enough to him to be a threat. The highly trained soldiers of House Miles were more than a match for the demoralized men and women of House Kolos, cut off from their home.

A little over two hours later he found himself nearing the gate that led to the pass into Pyrgos, where the last forces of House Kolos were rallying. Through the mass of man and metal he could see a frantic Viktor bellowing orders to no avail, the gatehouse he had seized being the last fortification he possessed against Lykos. And when he saw Lykos....

"BASTARD!" Viktor's roar echoed along the stone streets, silencing and drawing the attention of everyone. "You will pay for this scum!"

Lykos turned to the closest centurion. "Kill any who do not surrender. Leave Heir Kolos to me."

"Yes Lord Talal." The man saluted before issuing his own orders, rapidly organizing House Miles' forces. In unison, the orderly lines marched towards the fortified Kolos position, their shields raised high to protect them from desperate arrows. The sound of metal on stone, coming from all directions, drove the point home to many of soldiers of House Kolos who trembled in fear at the sound. First one, then two, then dozens of them threw down their weapons at the feet of the advancing army.

"Cowards! Pick up your weapons and kill them!" Viktor ordered, throwing a fireball at the advancing column. The fireballs set aflame several wooden shields but were ultimately ignored by the bloodthirsty men and women holding them. "Kill them or be punished!" Lykos shook his head.

"Surrender!" Lykos called out to the fearful soldiers. "Surrender and no harm will come to you. You have my word."

"A word of a liar is nothing! I will not surrender Talal!" Viktor roared but around him the soldiers of House Kolos shared uneasy glances. The clatter of steel echoed as the last of them dropped their weapons. Viktor looked furious.

"I'll have your heads for this! I'll have your families strung up and stoned for this betrayal. Talal!" Viktor whirled to face him. "I will not surrender, you will have to come and kill me yourself!"

For a moment he thought about ignoring the challenge. He could easily order the soldiers of House Miles to advance on the lone heir and slay him. Magic or not the odds were not favorable to Viktor. However he felt the adrenaline racing through his system and decided that killing Viktor, a thorn long in his side, would be an excellent way to end this day.

"I accept." Whatever words Viktor was going to say to him died as a fireball flew towards him. Ducking it quickly, Viktor was not prepared for the suddenly much closer Lykos smashing his first into his nose breaking it. With a howl of pain he went down but he did not stay that way. A hail of fireballs left his hand, forcing Lykos to dodge lest he be burned.

Drawing his sword Lykos slashed at the recovered Viktor. The steel clanged as it was deflected and Lykos quickly used his magic to pull water from the well nearby, soaking Viktor. Raising his hand to send a bolt of lightning at the soaked heir, he was quick to pull it back as Viktor's blade slashed wildly through the air. He was not quick enough to spot the feint however and felt the cold bite of steel slash through his unprotected side.

"Ha! Not so tough now are you?" Viktor mocked as Lykos howled in pain. Trusting his magic to heal his wound, Lykos attacked furiously, raining blows upon the startled heir. But Viktor was not caught off guard long and began to slip in attacks back. Lykos was not bloodied again from those furious strokes but more than one blow was caught on his leather armor, bruising the flesh underneath. However Viktor then made a foolish mistake.

Forgetting the water soaking his form, he summoned a ball of lightning to throw at Lykos. A single spark from that ball, a sensation that most mages ignored with ease, suddenly became a conduit for the most excruciating pain he had ever felt as the ball of lightning was conducted into his flesh. The man sizzled and jerked as his muscles spasmed before falling to the floor with a groan.

Lykos could not help but laugh at the ridiculous manner in which his opponent defeated himself and many of the soldiers of House Miles joined him. Sheathing his blade, he kicked Viktor in the side to draw his attention. "Will you surrender Heir Kolos?"

Viktor spat in his face. He wiped it off with a grimace. "I guess it's time to kill you then but first I want to reenact a little scene our fathers did years ago."

Viktor gave a pained chuckle. "You want me to poison you? Done."

"Oh no Viktor not quite. You see my father took something from your father and I intend to take the same from you." Lykos drew a dagger as Viktor's eyes widened in realization. "Yes that."

"No! Don't! Please don't! Lykos, Lord Talal please I beg of you!" Viktor screamed as the dagger was slowly pushed into his eye, not deep enough to kill but more than enough to remove the sensory organ. Lykos carefully carved out the eye taking care to move as slowly as possible to prolong Viktor's torment. With a plop the remains of Viktor's left eye fell to the stone floor beside his head. Turning Viktor's head to watch, Lykos ground his boot into the remains, destroying any hope for saving it.

Turning to the bloodthirsty and cheering soldiers of House Miles who were watching over the grim and fearful faces of the captured Kolos soldiers Lykos spoke to them. "Think I should take his other one?" The answering cheer made him turn back to the whimpering Viktor with a dark and hungry smile. "You shouldn't have attacked me Viktor."

Lykos raised his dagger to plunge it into Viktor's right eye but was met with a concussive blast of air in the chest. He flew through the air before crashing into a wall, the hard stones making spots dance before his eyes. Struggling to his feet he tried to catch his breathe as the world slowly swam back in focus.

Alithis glared hatefully at Lykos from his place beside the moaning Viktor and the wind picked up around him as it reacted to his magic. As his cloak was tugged by the wind, Alithis coldly examined the now fearful soldiers of House Miles and their hopeful Kolos captives. Lykos rose to his feet.

"Alithis."

"Lykos. Lord Kolos sends his regards."

"I'll send him his son's remains."

"No you won't," Alithis stated calmly, his observation of his surroundings complete. Lykos began to step forward, his hand going to his sheathed sword.

"And why won't I?"

Alithis clapped his hands together and a portal appeared underneath Viktor, sucking him out of sight. He smirked at Lykos. "Because he's already gone."

"I will kill you Alithis," Lykos vowed. "I will kill you all."

Before Alithis stepped into the portal leaving behind the captured Kolos soldiers, before Lykos struck the stone with his sword a moment too late, he said three words:

"You will try."

Chapter Fifty-Six

Lykos looked at the battle damaged ballroom of House Prodotis with contempt. By the time he had traveled down to the Marsh Grimm and Falka had already broken the quarter's defenses and laid siege to Lilith's home. The resistance they faced had been negligible as most of the Prodotis forces were already either captured from their failed siege on House Talal or during their pillaging of the Emporo. It was a dark day with thunderclouds covering the sky and Lykos found the weather fit his mood perfectly.

He had already stopped in Ploio to relieve Kiara from her ill gotten position of Lady Emporo. Throwing her to the mercy of the common folk she allowed to be harmed had seen to her quick and brutal death but it did little to alleviate the guilt he felt as he looked upon Amentha's spiked head. Or the bones of her unborn child nibbled clean by Tainted Gnawers.

The other members of House Emporo had either fled or been killed in the pillaging leaving their quarter unattended to so Lykos asked Commander Lexis and Giles to restore order. The large man was still withdrawn from his brothers betrayal and execution and Lykos hoped that the busy work would help him heal.

However now he had to deal with *her*.

"Unhand me you beasts! Don't you know who I am? I'm Lady Prodotis, ruler of this quarter!"

Lykos turned to watch Lilith be dragged through the once majestic doors of the ballroom in chains. The woman looked vastly different from her normally beautiful self, her hair askew and matted, makeup smeared, and clothes torn and burned. The black eye and bloody cheek showed that she had not yielded quietly or easily to his soldiers. The two soldiers forced her to her knees before him.

"Hello Lilith," he quietly said gaining the attention of everyone. His soldiers, the former slaves held captive throughout the kingdom, stood tall and proud along the walls, alert for threats. Grimm and Falka ceased their quiet conversation while a nearby Demos used magic to mend a soldier's bloody arm. A few minutes ago it was detached and Lykos was painfully reminded of his own amputation at the hands of the Stultus. His scar twinged in remembered pain but he shook it off to focus on the present.

"Lord Talal," Lilith tried to smile prettily for him but the missing teeth did little to aid her appearance, "I'm so glad you're here, there has been the most dreadful misunderstanding."

"Has there?" he asked calmly while watching Grimm and Falka out of the corner of his eye. He was almost positive Grimm had just bet Falka something.

"Yes! I have been a most loyal and ardent supporter of your cause since the very beginning! I have tried explaining this to your soldiers but they seem to be under this strange impression we are enemies."

"Preposterous," Lykos deadpanned. Her eyes brightened noticeably in glee that he was seemingly so agreeable.

"Just so! Why I was trying to tell them I had important information to share with you but they wouldn't hear of it."

"Indeed? Would it have something to do with the unmarked barges making their way to the Citadel these past few months?"

Lykos enjoyed these moments. This was a moment where one person, Lilith, believed her falsehoods to be considered truth and thus were getting into the groove of spinning a tale. That was when another person, himself, throws them off balance causing them to become extremely surprised and dumbfounded by the knowledge of the second person. Lilith was currently imitating a Tainted Diver, whose gaping maw was a crass joke among sailors.

"The barges?"

"Yes the barges."

"You know about the barges." Hysteria began to color her voice as she realized the valuable information she thought she was hoarding was not in fact hidden.

"Yes." Lykos waited a long moment for her to say something but it appeared she had be rendered mute. "Well if you have nothing more to say on the matter...."

"I do!" Lilith cried. "I have a lot to say on the matter."

Lykos waited expectantly for the woman to talk but she did not. "Well?" he asked in an effort to end this waste of time.

"This information is proof that I am willing to serve you my lord!" Lilith sketched a partial bow from where she knelt on the stone floor. "And that I may better serve you as an ally than a prisoner." The manacles jingled meaningfully on her slim wrists. Lykos almost rolled his eyes.

"See about finding the keys to those manacles. They need to be checked." Lykos gave a meaningful glance to one of his soldiers. The woman winked impishly.

"Yes my lord!" she began to rummage through her pouches with great exaggeration, looking for the elusive key. Lykos turned back to Lilith who staggered to her feet, holding out her hands expectantly.

"Well Lilith? Your information?"

The soldier approached Lilith's outstretched hands and began to fiddle with the manacles. "House Kolos forced me to allow those barges through. They have all sorts of odds and ends in them. Crates of magic crystals, food, weapons. I think he's stockpiling for when you lay siege to the Citadel. You have him running Lord Ta-lal!" she explained eagerly.

"That is all that was on those barges?" he asked with doubt on his voice. Lilith huffed with how slow the soldier was with her manacles.

"No. Some of them had mercenaries from outside the king-dom. I tried to talk to one, he was quite odd. He didn't speak at all. I say what are you doing to my bindings woman, you're supposed to be taking them off not tightening them!" she cried out as the mana-cles were indeed tightened. The soldier shook the manacles secure-ly before stepping back to her position. "You were supposed to take these off you bloody idiot! Lykos tell her!"

Lykos gave Lilith an even look, examining the woman who had just ordered him in front of his own soldiers. Turning to the sol-dier he gave the woman holding her chin up defiantly an evaluating glance. "Did you find a key soldier?"

"I could not find the key my lord!" she answered proudly.

"Excellent," Lykos replied.

"What?" Lilith shrieked.

"But I did check the manacles my lord and I found them loose! So I tightened them." the soldier happily explained. Lykos nodded in approval.

"Excellent job," Lykos realized he knew her name, "Angela. I'm pleased to see you've managed to excel in my service."

"Thank you my lord!" Angela practically glowed happiness.

"Lykos this farce has gone on far enough. Release me so we can begin planning our revenge on Kopanos and ruling this kingdom."

"Oh Lilith there is only one thing your mouth is useful for." Quick as lightning Lykos drew his sword and stabbed it through her open mouth. Removing it smoothly, Lilith slumped to the floor dead and he looked down upon her form with a smirk. "Accepting every sword in the kingdom."

"Ha I knew it!" Grimm cheered. "Pay up Falka!"

Lykos watched amused as Falka reluctantly passed him several gold coins. "You bet against me Falka?"

"I bet that you'd use magic to kill her," she answered grumpily. "I was hoping you would immolate her in fire."

"Perhaps the next one. Well she was the last of the recognized Prodotis excluding some bastards in the service of the Citadel. Still none of them will be allowed to take over the Marsh as I'm gifting it to House Falknor."

Falka looked surprised but then understanding dawned in her eyes. "Now that House Falknor controls the Marsh and Nero we can make as many airships as we like. Our air fleet can grow without restraint."

"Just so. Grimm I want your forces to help my soldiers to secure the waterways of the kingdom. It's not just taking over the levies that needs to be done, I want each and every single warehouse in Mycenae searched. Any remaining slaves are to be freed and any of those mercenaries Lilith mentioned are to be captured or killed."

"I'll begin at once. Dinner later Falka?"

"Why not, I'm in a good mood." She smiled mischievously at Grimm who grinned. Lykos waited for him to leave before turning to Falka.

"Giving him a chance?"

"I still miss Ana Del Rosa but Grimm's not a bad man. Nor is he hard on the eyes."

"He might be hard on other things." He ignored her slap on his arm as they stared out the broken balcony to the quarter beyond. "We've come so far Falka."

"We have."

"Our journey together started with us agreeing to rob the Stultus." He gave his friend a smile.

"You know we never did do that. You had to go and get your arm cut off."

"Hand."

"Same thing." Falka's eyes glowed with fond amusement. "We've had so many adventures. I wonder how ours will end?"

"I do not know my friend but I know this: we are not done quite yet. Now come, your brother Avarc invited me to meet his new betrothed and I'm sure you have many embarrassing stories to tell her."

"Now that you mention it, there was this one time...."

Chapter Fifty-Seven

"Lord Talal sure knows how to throw a party." Demos swayed happily from side to side as she listened the music. Her companion for the evening was not so joyous.

"He's thrown better," Giles grunted. Lord Talal had thrown a small gathering for his close friends and allies, a way for them to blow off some steam before they took the battle to House Kolos and ended this war. As far as Giles was concerned it did not matter if Talal or Kolos ruled the kingdom, just so long as he was able to establish House Dumas within Mycenae.

"I thought this was the first party he's held? Unless you're counting the Stultus ball he crashed."

Giles smirked. "Actually I was thinking about when I went with him to recruit Plower as House Agroti's champion."

"I know that look. What manner of mischief did our lord create?"

"Well we found Plower easily enough, drinking his sorrows away with that vile swamp ale the Marsh is so fond of. Lord Talal employed a little of his famed diplomacy...."

"Lord Talal hit him didn't he?"

"Don't interrupt. This was actually one of the times where he tried talking things out with his opponent. Plower didn't like Lord Talal's face or something and charged him. They're fighting, smashing tables and chairs, and Plower starts putting holes in the boat."

"I thought you were in a pub?"

"The boat is a pub. Everything floats in the Marsh, now pay attention. The boat sinks so we go to a new pub and Lord Talal and Plower start drinking and burying the hatchet. As the evening drags on the bar matron catches Plower's eyes and he asks for some aid in wooing her. So Lord Talal goes straight up to her, looks her right in the rack, and compliments her eyes. Now that I think about it Lord Talal might have been groggy the following morning because of the mild concussion she gave him."

"How simply horrible! I can't stop laughing."

"It gets better. The next morning Falka asked me to place an illusion upon her to make her appear like Plower. It wasn't my best work but with how hungover Lord Talal was he was in quite the sorry state when he woke up in the larger man's embrace."

They laughed merrily at the story and the night drew on....

On the other side of the room Lykos eyed the laughing pair with suspicion. "They're laughing about me."

"Don't be absurd," Falka countered, "they're laughing at you."

"How does that distinction matter?"

She screwed up her face in thought. "Give me a moment I'm sure I'll think of something witty."

"If they were laughing at Lykos shouldn't they be pointing at him?" Grimm commented idly.

"No," she denied determinedly

"Well let me know what you decide, I'm just dying to know. Hello Helen, I'm glad you could make it. Care for some wine?" Lykos gestured to a nearby bottle the three friends were drinking from.

"No. Lykos, Irene passed along some news that's disturbing in its implications. Do you have somewhere we can talk in private?"

"Speak your piece, both Falka and Grimm have my trust."

"Fine. I don't like how quite House Kolos has been," Helen said leaning in closer. "Irene sent word that Viktor's offense at the Pyrgos' gates was entirely on his own prerogative, his father was furious that he acted without orders and took their army out of the Citadel. So if House Kolos and its lord weren't behind Viktor's ill fated siege, just what are they up to?"

"It's not easy moving resources quickly," Grimm offered. "The only reason why we can do the movements we have is because we've had total control of the waterways and Falknor air fleet. They could still be marshaling their army."

Falka bit her lip as she thought. "But the Prodotis held those waterways and aided Viktor's troops. My father placed a tariff on transporting Kolos goods once he allied with Lykos and none of our captains would have gone rogue. So considering they've been able to move freely for months I think Helen is right, something is wrong about this situation."

"Is that what your gut is telling you?" Lykos asked Falka, trusting her instinct completely.

"House Kolos is hiding something, something so big that they feel it could turn the war entirely in their favor. The question is why would they let you conquer the rest of the kingdom while they waited? The Citadel guards have barely harassed us when you consider their numbers."

Lykos frowned in thought. "Helen could you let Irene know I would appreciate any more information that she finds? She hasn't spoken to me since...."

She nodded in understanding. "I'll let her know now. Watch your back," she advised.

Lykos turned to Grimm as she left. "Have you had any difficulties taking control of the waterways?"

Grimm's slight hesitation sent alarm bells ringing through his mind. "Yes and no. We've taken control of the levies without issue but...."

"But what?" Lykos prodded.

"But I've had more than a few patrols simply vanish when they checked in on various warehouses."

"Blast." Lykos was furious. "You should have brought this to my attention the moment it happened!"

"Every once in a while a patrol will disappear only to turn up a few days later, hungover! I had thought this was similar, soldiers celebrating the end of the campaign but Helen's information shed a new light on everything. I think those mercenaries Lilith talked about are killing the patrols."

"Tomorrow you and I will be going to deal with this threat. It's time for this kingdom to know peace."

"I'll be coming along as well," Falka said. "It's been far too long since you and I have cracked skulls together Lykos and this promises to be an enjoyable endeavor."

"So long as you don't do the same thing you did during our first slave raid, I'm fine with that."

"Lykos!"

"Ah to be young again." Lord Falknor smiled at his daughter's outraged face. "Although I do wonder why Lord Talal is determined to wind her up so?"

"It keeps them young," Adelram grunted as he sipped his ale. "Let the tots have their fun while they can. Before they know they'll be old and weary like us."

"I don't know who you're calling old young man but if you don't mind your tongue I'll have it cut out," Leandra, the former Lady Agroti, threatened. Lord Falknor laughed, knowing the widow of Rolan was jesting.

"Perish the thought! How else would I partake of those delicious blueberries you grow?"

"No one will be eating my blueberries anymore. Rickard, the brat, had the gardeners rip them out! Some nonsense about moving past my late husbands shadow or some rot. Shawna! My dear, it's so good to see you again."

Shawna and her mother exchanged hugs while Lord Falknor moved to Adelram's side. "It's a shame Lord Talal didn't remove Rickard from the field when he had the chance. The man's been more of a pain than the Tainted at our gates," he whispered. The aged commander shook his head.

"Lykos is many things but a kin slayer he is not. Despite my best efforts...."

"Adelram! Where is your fabled honor?" Lord Falknor inquired. Adelram gave a decidedly sadistic smirk. His form shimmered briefly to reveal Illusionist Maeve sitting on top of a bound and glaring Adelram. "Ah I see. Greetings Illusionist Maeve, your skill is as impressive as ever. I was displeased when your house recalled you from your post at Kremos Keep. Comfortable Adelram?"

"I greet you Lord Falknor. And as for you Adelram." Illusionist Maeve hopped off her perch and prodded Adelram's earthen bindings with her cane, dissolving them into nothing. "Think you can call me a witch behind my back with impunity do you?"

"I'll call you witch to your face you wretched woman!" Adelram growled as he rose to his feet. He whirled on Lord Falknor. "And you! You know me! She got my voice all wrong as well."

"I couldn't tell," Lord Falknor's succinct drawl made them all laugh. "I've always been envious of your little illusion tricks Maeve, I've never quite had the knack for them."

"You lack imagination, the most vital element in creating an effective illusion. It is no insult, your house may be recent in Mycenae but I've heard of your families exploits in Svellheim. Your ancestor's ingenuity is what allowed for those mines to be carved so deep into the earth."

"And why we left."

"Just so. Your youngest daughter though shows promise in the art of imagination. It's a shame your awakening stone was stolen, I would have enjoyed tutoring her in magic as I did your other children."

"Ah yes, I seem to remember someone exploding us a new wing. Did you see how Avarc managed to carve out the floor under the library...."

Shawna sat contently next to her mother as the party went on, watching happy guests partaking in food, drink, and merriment. It warmed both of their hearts to see those that they cared for in such a manner. Her eyes lingered on her son Lykos as he and Grimm acted out a story for Falka's amusement.

"It's the mother's curse," Leandra told her matter of factually, following her gaze to her child. "It's the mother's curse to watch her children grow up and discover they no longer need her. It's even worse for you with how little you knew your boy before he took up Leon's cause."

"You sound so bitter mother. Come to regret shunning your only daughter because you and your husband lacked the spine to stand true to your beliefs?" Shawna did not mean to sound so bitter but being abandoned by her own family for close to two decades was a harsh punishment for anyone.

"I regret many things in my life and however much I wish I cannot change them but I'm here now Shawna. Please let me be a mother for you."

Shawna was quiet for a long time as she considered her mother's words. "I forgave you a long time ago," seeing her mother's pleased smile she quickly continued, "because I knew that the thought of your actions would torment you long after. Speak to me as if I were your daughter and I will speak to you as if you were my mother but do not believe anything has changed between us."

"....I suppose that's all I could ask for."

Any further conversation was cut off as Lykos called for everyone's attention. "Allies. Friends. Family. We are almost done. Our foe has been cut off from all possible escape, denied every ally, and now cowers behind ancient walls in order to avoid our wrath! Tomorrow we end the threat that is House Kolos once and for all!"

Short and to the point, his toast roused the party guests and they drank heartily. Shawna captured her son's eyes from across the room, offering him a smile and raised glass of her own when a sharp pain stabbed through her chest. Looking down she was shocked to see a sword sticking through her chest, dark blood dripping from its edge.

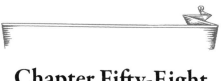

Chapter Fifty-Eight

In one terrible moment Lykos saw Kopanos' plan, the web of lies and deceit binding him tighter with each action he took. That cunning man would not face him until the end, long after he exhausted his forces against lesser foes and then when his forces gathered to relax and recuperate, that was when Kopanos would strike.

Right at the heart.

All around his home gray clad soldiers appeared, illusions falling from their bodies like water. Their blades fell without mercy onto his allies, friends, and family, slaughtering them left and right. Lord Falknor, Lady Agroti, and so many others fell to the assassin's blades but the most terrible for him to witness was his mother Shawna dying by the hand of Alithis.

As bodies fell around the room and the screams began Lykos raged. "To arms! Kill the invaders!" he ordered, lunging towards Alithis with the intent to kill. A gray clad soldier stepped silently in his path so he sent a blast of air to throw the man into the wall. Instead of having the intended result, the man grasped the wave of air and sent it back at an unprepared Lykos, throwing him across the room to crash into a table. Dazed and confused he looked up to see the man advancing, sparks dancing from his fingertips. The smell of ozone in the air was his only warning before a bolt of lightning left the man's hands.

Rolling to the side Lykos acted quickly, throwing two knives which impacted solidly into the man's chest. However the constitution of mages proved true; the man merely staggered to the side. But the distraction was all Lykos needed to rush forwards and behead him with his sword. Snarling in rage he saw that Alithis had not moved from his position, his sword still buried deep into Shawna's chest. Catching his eye Alithis gave a savage smirk before ripping the sword out of her frozen form. She slowly fell.

"No!" Lykos cried leaping across the room. Cradling her fallen form in his arms, he tried in vain to rouse her. However it was a futile effort for her eyes were sightless, her breathe was still. Shawna was dead. And standing over the pair was a laughing Alithis.

"The bitch is dead," he jeered as Lykos trembled in rage. "And now you'll be too!" His hand rose and a wave of heat and air exploded in front of Lykos, sending him once more through the air. This time his flight was not arrested by sturdy wooden construction, instead the wooden wall of his home barely halted him as he was thrown violently into the garden. He rolled until he hit the stone fountain, coming to a painful stop against the solid masonry. He moaned as the pain of cracked bones hit him.

Dazed he rose slowly to see Alithis climb through the new hole in his home. Lykos grasped his sword and swung at him but his senses were still jumbled from the explosion and subsequent flight. Alithis batted it away with ease and smashed his face with the pommel of his sword. "Any last words Lykos of House Talal?" Alithis asked mockingly.

Lykos, gasping for breathe, gestured for him to lean closer so he could whisper into his ear. Obliging a dying man's last request mockingly Alithis was unprepared for him to stab a dagger into his stomach, twisting it violently. He fell backwards and tripped over debris.

"I'm going to kill you," Lykos gasped as both men staggered to their feet. Alithis gave the dagger buried in his gut a disgusted sneer before pulling it out. "I will make you pay."

"You first." Alithis and Lykos raised their weapons, prepared to fight to the death, but were interrupted by more explosive blasts from Hearthome. Both men turned to see Falka, Grimm, Giles and several of Lykos' soldiers jump out of the ruins before it went up in flames. Alithis, seeing he was outnumbered, snarled, "this isn't over." He slashed his hand, creating a portal on the ground beneath his feet. Gravity did what it was meant to and the assassin who killed Shawna slipped out of their grasp.

"No it's not," Lykos said, turning from the location of the portal to his burning home, the Citadel looming ominously in the distance.

"Those soldiers all had magic-" Falka began.

"Where the bloody hell have they been hiding?" Giles interrupted "I would have thought they'd be all over the kingdom raising hell on us."

"They are."

"What?"

"They are all over the kingdom. Look." Falka pointed towards the terrace. Gathering at the edge they looked on in horror as the kingdom below them burned. Screams and shouts of terror sprang up periodically, flashes of light and fire blooming into existence all over Mycenae. Falka looked through a telescope she had on her belt. "More of those gray clad soldiers but none of them are baring the Citadel's mark. What do you think Lykos? Lykos?"

Lykos was not staring at the scene of destruction happening all over the kingdom. He was watching his home slowly burn to the ground before him, the flames consuming the body of the woman who took him into her family.

"Why is no one fighting back, we have armies at our disposal," Giles asked. It was Grimm who answered.

"And they have magic."

"So do we!"

"They *all* have magic."

Grimm spoke the truth and it was clear to all how severely out-classed their armies were, how outclassed an entire kingdom was against such a force. Whole buildings crumbled into debris as the gray clad soldiers brought their magic to bear. It was a terrible sight to behold and it showed no sign of stopping.

"What do we do Lord Talal?" Angela, one of the soldiers who managed to escape, asked. Lykos turned slowly and she flinched by the raw hate that burned in his eyes.

"Sound the retreat."

"Retreat? To where? There's no where left to go!" Giles ex-claimed.

"Retreat from the kingdom."

Deathly silence met his order. "Lykos you can't be serious," Fal-ka protested, "the wilderness is too dangerous!"

"I am."

"But why? We can muster our allies, fight back! Reclaim our homes and land!"

"Our allies are scattered, our foe planned for this exact eventu-ality. We can either stay here and die or we can retreat and live to fight another day. For a day where we can win."

For those were their only options. It was all part of Kopanos' plan for Lykos to clear the kingdom of any potential threat to this assault, eliminating the factions who would have resisted. The Acolytes crumbling from within, the noble houses extinct or allied, it was all part of a grander plan with him being a pawn. And now the only two pieces left on the field were Talal and Kolos, Lykos and Kopanos. And Kopanos thought he had him trapped.

Ignoring the protests of his allies he turned to the Talal soldiers under his command. "Angela. Send out word to all of our soldiers, our common folk, everyone. Tell them to make their way to the Lowland and Riverfront to escape. Tell them to grab anything that might be useful, food, weapons, medicine, and that if they aren't with us when the moon is at its apex then they will most likely not see dawn. Go now!"

At his order his soldiers scattered from the garden yet Angela remained. "Lord Talal, what will you do?"

"Providing a distraction to buy our people time to escape. They burned down my home, it's only fair I return the favor."

"Well I'm going with you my lord!"

"No you aren't Angela. I need you to go to the Lowland to deal with Rickard. If he doesn't let us take the food we need, kill him."

"I understand Lord Talal," Angela stated unhappily.

"Well you're not getting rid of me. These bastards killed my father," Falka stated firmly. Grimm nodded firmly beside her.

"I guess I'll help you too," Giles muttered. Lykos gave the last Dumas a sharp look but kept any reservations he had about the man after his brother's betrayal to himself. Instead he gave his home one last look, imagining it whole and not burning. With a small sigh he turned away.

"Then let's move."

He led through the ransacked Aspida, the buildings freshly shattered as the gray clad soldiers ripped their way through it. Stopping by one such soldier whose head had been unluckily crushed by a flying rock, he examined the body. Pushing back his sleeves he found thick, rope-like scars circling both wrists.

"He was a former slave," Lykos stated decisively, "or rather he might still be a slave. These scars are from the manacles tearing into the skin over years."

"How do you know?" Falka asked softly. Lykos wordlessly pushed up his own sleeves, revealing slightly smaller scars on both of his wrists. Despite knowing his status as a former slave, the harsh reminder was sobering to the free spirited woman. "Not anymore."

"No, never again." Lykos stood up and resumed his pace. They had been walking for several minutes through Aspida yet had only come across the deceased. Their nerves caused them to jump at every flickering shadow, each crack of burning wood. Tainted Gnawers and Vipers swarmed from the shadows and began to eat the dead, oblivious of the still living humans just feet from them.

"We should split up," Giles suddenly declared. His sudden speech caused the other three to jump, their weapons twitching in their hands. "At this pace we won't ever find anyone let alone draw their attention away from those retreating. We split up, find the soldiers, and raise the alarm."

Lykos reluctantly considered the wisdom in his words. While it would be easier for them to find their foes it also drastically reduced their strength, making finding those soldiers more dangerous. Just as he was about to decline a shrill scream rent the air. The quartet swiftly rushed towards a dark alley, flashes of light illuminating it. Within stood a trio of gray clad soldiers, butchering their way through a family of six. Already the father lay on the ground, a hole burned through where his heart should be, and his eldest son desperately reached for his father's fallen sword.

Lykos and Grimm charged forwards, their swords raised to strike at the back of two unsuspecting soldiers. Something gave away their presence however and while one soldier continued to attack the family the other two smoothly turned about and fended off their strikes. Lykos and Grimm moved smoothly around one another, each strike driving back their foes, each block protecting the other, but the two soldiers they faced matched them in speed and skill. The shrill screams beyond let the duo that this fight could not drag on much longer if they were to save the rest of the family.

"Falka, Giles attack!" Lykos ordered, not feeling their presence behind them. No arrows or magic flew over his shoulders as he barely stopped a sword strike from impaling Grimm. "Attack damn it!"

"Falka this is no time for games darling. If this is about what I said earlier I'm sorry!" Grimm cried out, sending out a fireball at one of the soldiers. The man barely grunted at the impact as his partner doused it with a small blast of water.

"You hear that Falka, he's sorry! There's no need to punish me for his stupidity!" Lykos was growing worried that no snarky response was forthcoming but could not chance a glance behind him as the two soldiers were relentless. "Blast it. Grimm roast them!"

"Roast them? I'm a bit busy for that!" Grimm's arms were a blur of motion as his sword danced from side to side, blocking feints and lunges. Lykos let his guard slip for just a moment, just one heart beat to send a blast of lightning from his hand. The soldier, thrusting his blade into Lykos' side, had no room to dodge as he was blasted at point blank range into his partner. Grimm quickly thrust his hand forward, fireball after fireball leaping from it and dousing the two men in flames. They struggled only briefly before succumbing to the blistering flames.

Lykos looked away from the flames to see the last soldier watching them, a curious tilt on his helmeted face. Before Lykos or Grimm could attack, they swiftly turned to the side and opened a portal, vanishing from the alley. And on the stone beyond, their blood pooling in cracks, lay the family slain to the last.

"We were too slow," Lykos said regretfully before hissing. The wound on his side burned with fresh pain and a quick glance confirmed that even with magic it would not heal quickly. "Grimm, I need your help." Lykos gestured towards his wounded side.

"You know I'm horrible at healing." Grimm examined the wound which fortunately wasn't gushing blood.

"I know which is why I need you to cauterize it." Lykos gritted. If given enough time the wound would heal but burning it would help direct his magic into repairing the internal injuries, his damaged muscles, first. A burn would not kill him, a hole in his side would.

"Right well grind your teeth." Grimm advised before putting his hand on Lykos' side. A sizzling sound and searing pain caused him to howl into the night as flames bathed his side. However a short moment later it was over, Grimm's fire cauterizing his wound shut and the badly burnt skin was the only trace of any prior injury. Already he could feel his magic redoubling its focus on his internal injuries and breathed a sigh of relief as the pain became manageable.

"That's going to scar you know," Grimm told him.

"I thought you knew I collected them."

"You collect lots of things; enemies, strays, insanity."

"Speaking of strays where are Falka and Giles?" Both men grew sober, turning to the mouth of the alley to see neither missing person. "We need to find them."

"Agreed. I don't know who trained these soldiers but it wasn't at the Citadel. The number of sorcerers in Mycenae that are as strong as they are can be counted on one hand. Our campaign would have been much more difficult if they had been fielded from the start."

"It would have been impossible." At Grimm's inquiring look Lykos explained his theory of Kopanos planning the entire thing. Both men bore grim frowns as they walked quickly down one of Aspida's streets. "It's why I gave the order to abandon the kingdom. There is no way we can survive here. Distance and time are what we need."

"Time?"

"Time. These soldiers came from somewhere and they've been or are currently slaves. Which means at some point they came from Svellheim."

"Slavery occurs in all three kingdoms," Grimm argued.

"Call it a feeling then. I doubt Istani would be willing to part with their slaves, they need them to maintain their massive water kingdom. Svellheim though? There are enough slaves up there to build a dozen armies and still not empty the mines. The real question is how do they all have magic."

"Yes, it runs in families," Grimm stated matter-of-factly. Lykos was reminded of how his own magic was awakened in the slave mines, being trapped in the cave in and touching the crystals that lay all around him. Doubts began to cloud his mind, of being a Talal and the gift of magic in general. However they quickly fled at the sight before him: Viktor flanked by half a dozen soldiers with Giles standing over Falka with his sword raised high.

Falka was furious!

Being taken prisoner by the oaf Giles was an insult, doubly so since his intelligence was of no great note, but being brought to Viktor? The brat! She ground her teeth knowing the larger man had only succeeded in capturing her thanks to his magic. It still vexed her that no matter how talented she may become with a blade, magic would always trump her skill.

"Well what do we have here? A wayward bird and a, I'm sorry I don't know who you are."

"Giles of House Dumas Heir Kolos."

"I'm not familiar with House Dumas.... Giles."

"We were a minor house in Svellheim before our fortunes ran afoul. We immigrated to Mycenae to search for grander riches."

"And then you fell in with House Talal," Viktor spat hatefully. His hand fluttered almost unconsciously to touch his new eye patch.

"Regrettably so." Falka rolled her eye at how thick Giles was laying it on. "My brother and I were waylaid by Lord Talal's promises for aid in gaining wealth and status for our house here. It was a lie."

"Ha! Your brother sold us out to assassins and here you stand dealing with his enemy! Is it no wonder that Lykos has not rewarded you, you backstabbing fool?" Falka mocked. Giles grew red in rage and struck her harshly in her stomach, driving her to her knees. "Your arm is weaker than a child's." She felt her taunt would have been more impressive had she not be gasping for breathe.

Viktor gave the pair a considering look before nodding to himself. "Giles of House Dumas. Execute this insurgent and you may serve me. I'm sure you'll find the perks far more enjoyable than anything Lord Talal could offer."

Giles and Falka glared into each others eyes, daring the other to look away first. He averted his gaze and nodded. "Yes my lord." Drawing his sword, he stood over Falka with his weapon resting lightly upon her neck.

"Before we kill me," Falka spoke quietly, "could one of you hold my hair? It'll make it easier for the traitor to kill me if his target isn't obscured. He always had such poor aim you see."

While Giles sputtered in anger and denial Viktor merely rolled his eyes. Gesturing to one of his soldiers he said, "very well. Who am I to deny a dying woman's last wish?"

The silent soldier took her hair with rough hands and pulled it taunt, forcing her slim neck to be visible above the collar of her cloak. The cold steel of Giles' sword touched her gently. "You always were a prick Giles. Of course if rumors were true you have an exceptionally tiny one yourself...."

Giles roared and lifted his blade high into the night. Falka listened closely to the singing metal as it slashed through the night air, waiting to hear the pause of the steel reaching the top of its arch. And when the weapon began its descent she acted, pulling her head back so suddenly that the soldier's hands, gripped so painfully in her hair, were pulled with them. Giles' descending sword missed Falka's head, her hair, and sliced clean through the soldiers' wrists.

Leaping to her feet, she pulled her sword from the cursing Giles' waist and stabbed it into another soldier's heart before he could react. Removing her blade, she twirled it artfully, eyes dancing from soldier to soldier, wondering which would make the mistake of attacking her first, when she felt it. The cold steel of a sword stabbing deep into her back, through her lungs, and out of her chest.

"That was rude," Viktor's voice whispered in her ear. As Falka fell once more to the ground she could see Lykos and Grimm running towards her, their faces furious with anger and loss. As the world around her dimmed she hoped her two dear friends would kill Viktor, Giles, their soldiers and not join her in death themselves....

"Falka!" Lykos and Grimm cried out as she was stabbed. Their cry drew the attention of the remaining four soldiers, their weapons drawn instantly and palms glowing with gathered power. As one the four soldiers raised their hands, sending a mix of fire, earth, water, and lightning bolts to obliterate the enraged duo. However they were not going down without a fight.

Calm clarity descended over Lykos' mind, a burning desire to slay the soldiers guided by cold rationale. Grasping his magic in a way he had never managed to before he pushed his fury and magic out into the calm night air around them. Clouds began to form above them and the first rumbles and sparks of lightning bloomed violently into creation.

Grimm pushed his anger into the earth, forcing thick stone chains to spring out and begin to bind the soldiers. The spiked edges of the chains cut deeply into their skin and for the first time Lykos heard them scream in pain. Taking perverse pleasure in that fact, he directed his storm, larger and more violent than the one the criminal Drakken created during the Succession Trial, to strike out at them. Shards of hail and strikes of lightning repeatedly struck the four soldiers, burning and tearing into them while Grimm's chains prevented their escape. Finally after several blinding flashes of light Lykos let his grip over the storm fade.

Dropping to his knee Lykos gasped painfully as his strength fled him. Grimm fared little better, the magical chains he had created successfully halting the soldiers advance but Lykos had missed the stout wall he had created to halt their initial attack. Grimm too panted heavily as the mist cleared slowly.

On the ground were four charred skeletons, even the metal of their weapons and armor were melted by the intense energy caused by Lykos' lightning strikes. A small wind blew through them and the skeletons crumbled into dust, leaving behind stone shackles artfully suspended in air. But beyond them lay two earthen mounds.

"He did not steal my trick," Lykos stated angrily in denial. As he rose to his feet the two earthen mounds broke down, showering two crouching figures in mud and dirt. The only consolation was that both Giles and Viktor were red from exertion at holding back his storm.

"He did." Grimm glared hatefully at Viktor. "Heir Kolos is mine."

"That's fine, I have unfinished business with House Dumas."

"Lord Talal are you done throwing your temper tantrum?" Viktor mocked.

"Viktor you unimportant brat, cease your pathetic chatter. The men are talking." Viktor muttered obscenities as Lykos turned to Giles. "You know the punishment for traitors Giles."

Giles shifted uncomfortably before firming his stance. "Meaningless. So much has been lost following you, I refuse to allow House Dumas end in your war."

"Then die knowing that when this night is spoken of in the coming years, not one person will know the true name of the Traitor's House. Grimm, make it slow."

No further words were spoken as the four men rushed towards one another. Swords swished through the night, cutting through air on a whispers edge only to clash against one another in a calamity of thunder. Lykos squared off against Giles, Grimm against Viktor, and all four men fought for their lives knowing that their opponent wanted them dead.

No further magic was used. Just skill, trickery, and strength. Lykos and Grimm fought in unison, tired as they were they covered each others flanks with practiced ease. Giles and Viktor rapidly found themselves losing ground as the battle went on, taking on scratches and stabs from steel left unhindered on its deadly path. The victors of the battle were clear, it was only a matter of time.

Time that passed. Lykos thrust his sword through Giles' leg, causing the larger man to cry out in pain. It would be his undoing as Lykos grabbed his foes sword and unceremoniously stabbed it through his heart. Withdrawing both swords he paid no more attention to the demise of the Traitor's House.

Both Grimm and Viktor panted heavily although neither showed signs of slowing, knowing to do so would mean their certain doom. Lykos moved to aid his friend and slashed at Heir Kolos. Under their combined assault Viktor found himself disarmed and kicked to the ground. The battered heir looked up at Lykos and Grimm with fear in his eyes.

"Please let me live."

"He's begging my friend."

"That he is Lykos."

"What a coward."

"Please have mercy!"

"No."

"Mercy!"

Viktor's screams tore through the night.

Chapter Fifty-Nine

Standing over Viktor's cooling corpse brought no satisfaction to Lykos, no happiness. Falka's still form was only footsteps away, drenched in blood, water, and earth, peace denied to her even in death with the terrible wound through her chest. Lykos stroked her hair affectionately before turning to the somber Grimm.

"You need to take her body to her family."

"Yes we should."

"No. You should." Grimm gave him a blank look so he explained further, "we set out this night to buy time for our allies to escape this kingdom. That purpose still stands but I refuse to leave Falka here to be picked over by Tainted or desecrated by the Citadel. So you'll take her body to her family."

Grimm opened his mouth to protest but closed it, looking at Lykos evenly. "I can't talk you out of this can I?"

"He killed Shawna Grimm."

"Then make him pay Lykos. I've already lost too many friends tonight to lose another."

Parting from Grimm had not been easy but it had been the right choice. Lykos knew he needed to kill Alithis, he needed to kill the man who took the first memory of family away from him. Lord Kolos could not be stopped from taking the kingdom, not at this point, so he would settle for ending the life of the man who murdered his family.

The streets of Naos were no better than Aspida, torn apart by the gray clad soldiers. Here and there were patrols of the silent soldiers, each led by a man or woman bearing the mark of the Citadel. The featureless helms and armor only enhanced the already pronounced emotionless state of the soldiers, in sharp contrast to their lively leaders. As much as Lykos dearly wished he could aid the screaming common folk as they were subjugated he could not stop an army of sorcerers single handily. So with each step, each scream, each bloodied corpse he stepped past, he hardened his heart.

Despite his hopes otherwise the entrance to the Citadel was heavily guarded, with even more gray clad soldiers than he had seen so far. He despaired at the thought of fighting his way through them and began to plan a way to access the Citadel in other ways. He could always surrender himself but there was no guarantee they would not simple execute him on the spot. Finding a barge making its way into the Citadel would be time consuming and if they were wise they'd check each ship anyways, well aware of such a weakness used to such great effect in their invasion. More and more wild ideas flew through his mind before the obvious answer made him slap himself in the face.

Creating a portal on the Citadel's wall in a dark corner, he stepped through it and found himself in a dark, unused storage room, the cost of magic more than manageable at this point in his training. Exiting it, he stopped in shock at the sight before him: the entire Citadel was celebrating.

Musicians played their instruments as they moved through the dancing crowds. Slaves, collared to the stone walls and streets, served food and drink. Dancers and flesh workers littered the crowd and much mirth was to be had by the intoxicated crowd. Lykos found the sight sickening.

Stealing an ornate mask that lay on the ground he moved through the crowds, refusing to take part in their festivities. Emporo merchants, Vrachos quartermasters, Prodotis' sailors all rubbed elbows with one another equally. He realized that these men and women had lived within the Citadel and thus escaped his crusade through the kingdom. These slave owners had profited the most from their fellow man's suffering and even now they partied, ignorant of the purge taking place throughout the kingdom.

Lykos left the crowds behind as he approached the Citadel Keep. Like the gates leading into the quarter it was heavily guarded and once again he created a portal to bypass the fortifications. Shaking his head in disgust, he vowed to find someway of halting magical transportation into and out of places. A difficult skill to master or not, far too many people had the ability and he would never sleep peacefully again.

The Citadel Keep was exactly how he pictured it yet not. As the first stronghold of Mycenae it was sturdy and he had expected the thick, strong walls with plenty of space for supplies to last for a siege. Yet he could see the rooms where training took place, where families would be raised while the Tainted beat uselessly against the walls. That these same spaces were full of resting soldiers, supplies, and plotting commanders felt wrong to him. It was the last observation that made him hide in the shadow's and listen closely.

"Reports from Aspida and Naos," a man Adelram's age spoke. "The quarters are under our complete control and the captured common folk are being directed to holding areas. We've made little head way in the Riverfront and Kremos due to their fortifications but they'll break as soon as we gain control of their gates. I've authorized a centurion to direct a legion from the Reliquary to assist."

"What about Latom and Pyrgos?" an equally old woman with cold eyes spoke. Her only other noteworthy feature was her wardrobe, thick furs that reminded Lykos strongly of Svellheim.

"The soldiers proved more than a little zealous in taking Latom. One of the levies was broken and apparently it has begun to flood with water."

"Guess it's not bottomless after all," a different man spoke. The woman silenced him with a glance.

"My soldiers follow orders to the letter. Perhaps your centurion's instructions were unclear?" The woman's hard tone made the other two men flinch. Lykos realized that this woman was responsible for the unknown gray clad soldiers and made sure to listen attentively from his hiding spot.

"Perhaps," the first man reluctantly allowed. "Regardless Pyrgos has conflicting reports. The Talal ancestral home was reportedly razed to the ground but there has been no confirmation from Commander Alithis as to the death of Lord Talal. Furthermore when he retreated here he left the soldiers without any new orders. They've been butchering the Pyrgos' common folk in accordance to their last actual order."

"The abilities of your leadership are *underwhelming*. Commander Alithis has yet to impress me, perhaps he should stay in his tower until we win this war no?"

"Perhaps Vinr Freya."

Wishing he could stay and learn more but knowing time was of the essence, Lykos merely took note of Vinr Freya's name and title before moving to find Alithis' tower. He had an assassin to kill.

Chapter Sixty

Finding Alithis' tower was not too difficult. While the Citadel Keep was ringed with many towers around its walls, only one rose from the actual keep itself. Sneaking his way through the building to its base was marginally more difficult but a liberal use of magic and skill meant he made his way into the heart of the most secure part of the kingdom with pitiful ease. Magic truly had no equal.

He climbed floor after floor, finding no occupants on any level. There were many luxurious rooms full of Tainted Silk wall coverings and Tainted Raptor rugs covering the stone floors. The wealth in each room was truly absurd and he was not surprised that Kopanos could purchase an army of slave mages. However in one room he found something truly surprising.

The magic crystals that Lykos spent years of his life mining were strewn about in crates, chests, and the floor. But even more shocking was the low shelf near the door that contained a variety of carved crystals, bearing house crests. Lykos moved down the line, reading them in his mind. Kolos, Ashanti, Leano, Falknor....

Over a dozen different houses were represented here and many of them he had never even heard of. But his eyes kept trailing back to House Falknor's missing awakening stone for that crystal could be no other. He reached out a hand to grasp it but hesitated before actually touching it.

Could he touch it? Once more his thoughts trailed to the few times he had touched the crystals. In the mines it had felt like fire burning through his body, tortuously so. In his home it had felt electrifying, energizing, but shocking. The few times he had used smaller crystals to replenish his strength had also felt electrifying but to a lesser degree overtime. The real question was, what separated those crystals from the awakening stones used by the noble houses?

Slowly he touched the Falknor awakening stone, the surface cool beneath his touch. The electrifying feeling of foreign magic, so often felt with other stones, gathered in his fingertips. Picking up the magical crystal entirely, he braced himself for pain or death yet neither happened. He still breathed.

Frowning in thought he considered the softly glowing crystal in his hand. Either he was related to House Falknor, a possibility considering how intermarried the noble families were, or everyone was wrong about the crystals. Securing it in a pouch, he could not decide which answer he preferred to be truth.

Resuming his ascent up the tower he found several more storerooms full of crystals, including one where disassembled volka rested on workbenches. Burning any plans in the room took but a moment however he did not delude himself to think that his enemy did not already know how to create more of the useful devices. But every little obstacle he put in his enemies path now would help him survive later he decided.

Finally he reached the top of the tower, finding no one in any of the rooms contained therein. Furious at this almost useless expense of time and energy, he walked to the ladder in the corner of the room, determined to see if any part of Mycenae still resisted from the rooftop. Climbing it he was surprised to find Alithis standing on the precipice, observing the party and destruction down below.

Quietly standing on the weather beaten stone, Lykos slowly approached, determined to end the life of the man who killed his mother. However before his hands could touch the dagger at his waist, Alithis spoke.

"Somehow I'm not surprised you made it here." Alithis' gaze never left the kingdom below. "Do you see how they dance and cheer, ignorant of the suffering just beyond their sight? Their hypocrisy is simply delicious."

"You're a horrible human being."

"Perhaps but at least I've always been honest unlike some people...."

"And what's that supposed to mean?"

"I've watched you Lykos, ever since we ran into each other at the Stultus' ball. I doubt you remember, you told me one of us would have to go change. Your humor always was lacking."

"Considering my position as Lord Talal someone else will have to fill the role of jester."

Alithis ignored the jibe and turned around, finally looking him in the eyes. "Ah yes, Lord Talal. Rather interesting how you popped into existence. How easily you claimed a title you have no right to even now."

"You're giving a valiant effort at becoming the jester Alithis."

"It is rather amusing, after all there is one Lord Talal on this roof tonight and it is not you." Alithis' maniacal grin glinted in the moonlight. "It is I."

His demented laughter was cut off by Lykos tackling him off the tower.

Chapter Sixty-One

Lykos had only one thought going through his mind when he tackled Alithis off the Citadel Keep's tower and it was thus: Alithis, whoever he was, was going to die. It was that thought that he clung to throughout the evening, ever since he watched him murder Shawna in cold blood. Listening as the man claim himself to be the true Lord Talal, a title Lykos often worried about claiming, only drove him to the edge, literally.

Alithis was surprised at his chosen avenue of attack and thus they fell for several heartbeats before he reacted. However while Lykos had experienced free fall before, and thus wasn't ignorant of how to survive a fall if reluctant due to his apprehension of heights, Alithis had no such experience and struggled for those precious moments. Lykos took full advantage of this time and swung a dagger, only just missing Alithis' neck due to his struggles. Instead Alithis took Lykos' fist in the jaw, causing the man to howl as he bit his own tongue. Kicking off of him, Lykos infused his body with magic moments before he crashed into the ground of the Citadel's courtyard.

With his joints creaking as he stood up, Lykos looked to his left, expecting to see Alithis' broken body laying on the floor. Instead the wet and furious man was slowly rising from a fountain, his clothes steaming as his magic began to burn in his hands. Other than the waterlogged appearance, he looked no worse for the wear.

Of course he would land safely, Lykos thought nastily, dodging a fireball that flashed through the air. It exploded against a stock of firewood which immediately began to blaze. Lykos countered, sending several quick lightning bolts to the pool of water surrounding Alithis' feet, shocking the man badly. However an instinctual blast of magic sent him flying through the air, crashing into the keep's brewery.

Alithis gave him no time to recover, thrusting out both hands and moving the earth, stone, and wood making up the building. Expending a great deal of magic, Alithis forced the building to collapse on top of him, burying him under debris. There were no sounds in the courtyard save the settling of broken stone and crackling of fire as Alithis panted heavily. He began to laugh in glee but quickly stopped as the stone shifted before him.

"You are one persistent son of a bitch!" Alithis grinned a bloody smile as Lykos dragged himself out of the wreckage. "I killed that senile old woman, dropped a building on you, and you still keep coming after me! Bravo!"

Lykos coughed up blood and dust as he pulled himself free. "If you really were Lord Talal you would know that "senile" old woman was your mother."

"Facts are facts thief," Alithis stated as he swaggered forward, drawing his sword, "and nothing changes the fact that she was crazy if she believed a common slave like you could ever be of noble blood."

Lykos rose to his feet and drew his own sword, the steel comforting in his grip. "The only one crazy here is you!" he roared striking at Alithis. The blow was blocked.

"Is it crazy? To watch your birthright abused by a mere slave? To watch that everything that which should be yours by birth be wasted in a frivolous war, a frivolous cause?" Each question Alithis roared as he attacked Lykos who was forced on the defensive. "I was taken from my mother when my fool of a father died that night and I was raised as a prisoner while this kingdom was given peace! My fool of a mother was given another child's bones while Lord Kolos made plans for the true heir, me!

"I was raised under his thumb, each failure was harshly punished but I was smarter than my father. I saw the value of working with Lord Kolos and not against him. I worked and trained and learned secrets of magic lost to the ages from my lord's own hands, a privilege few know. And now I am feared, obeyed! And I will take my birthright and no amount of slaves is going to stop me!"

And now Lykos knew the truth as his arms grew weak, his strength waned. He was never a Talal, never noble blood, just Lykos. His will power felt drained as the harsh truth reared its ugly head but one tiny flame refused to die in his mind: Shawna.

"I may not have been Shawna's blood but I am proud she called me her son." Lykos struck back at Alithis who was surprised by his sudden strength. "She took me into her home, treated me as family, and while I may have lied I did everything I could to make her happy and safe. You stole her life from me so I'll take yours in return!"

"Have at it brother." Alithis' ugly sneer was as wretched as his life and the two men swung their weapons at each other with lethal intent.

The courtyard had long since filled with smoke from the fire, obscuring their vision and alerting others that something might be wrong. Citadel soldiers led mercenaries into the yard and began to circle the two combatants in a ring of steel and flesh. One young soldier moved to assist Alithis and shot an arrow at Lykos. His horrific screams of pain as Alithis immolated him alive caused the remaining men and women to hold their positions as the two men fought to the death.

Lykos' vision began to blur, his will power and desire to see Alithis dead the only thing that kept him going. Alithis likewise was just as haggard as Lykos, struggling to lift his weapon to block his strikes. These two men, masters of steel and magic and form, struggled against an opponent their equal in a battle of revenge. Lykos knew that to end this stalemate, to kill Alithis, he needed to take a mortal blow.

So he let his guard slip, a sloppy feint to the side. Alithis did not disappoint, lunging forward with his sword and stabbing him through the shoulder. Lykos could not stop the scream of rage and pain from escaping his lips as his nerves were tormented with cold steel but he still had the presence of mind to swing his weapon back.

The once sharp metal smashed through Alithis armored chest, carving a wide swath through his chest and stomach. His eyes widened in surprise at the sudden and violent death. Slowly he released his blade, still impaled through Lykos' shoulder, falling backwards as his life fled him. Alithis, the unknown heir of House Talal, died.

Lykos fell to his knees as the pain began to blind him, dropping his dull sword to the ground. He was unaware of the soldiers surrounding him, unaware of Lord Kolos and his commanders watching his battle. Uncaring of the danger he was in he reached into his pouch with unsteady fingers to pull out the Falknor awakening stone. The electrifying pulse of magic no longer felt shocking or painful but comforting and for a moment Lykos marveled at the wonder that was magic. He gripped his hand tightly around the crystal and the magic within reacted without his direction.

He disappeared into a portal, one moment surrounded by his enemies on all sides, the next he crashed onto the stone terrace in the garden of his now smoldering home. Lykos gasped at the unexpected movement and pain, laying stunned on the ground as the Falknor awakening stone burned brightly in his hand before fading into granite, its magic spent.

I could just lay here, Lykos thought to himself as he gazed at the depleted stone, the Falknor crest carved on the surface the only remaining ornamentation. *The kingdom could fall, the world burn to ash, the mountains crumble to dust and I could just lay here and disappear into the sands of time. It would be so simple, so restful to merely close my eyes and go to sleep.*

To give up.

...

...

...

...

...

...

...

...

Never.

Printed in Great Britain
by Amazon